Eagles in the Storm

Also by Ben Kane

The Forgotten Legion
The Silver Eagle
The Road to Rome

Spartacus
Spartacus: The Gladiator
Spartacus: Rebellion

Hannibal
Hannibal: Enemy of Rome
Hannibal: Fields of Blood
Hannibal: Clouds of War

Eagles of Rome
Eagles at War
Hunting the Eagles

Eagles in the Storm

BEN KANE

preface

1 3 5 7 9 10 8 6 4 2

Preface Publishing
20 Vauxhall Bridge Road
London S W 1 V 2 S A

Preface is part of the Penguin Random House group of companies
whose addresses can be found at global.penguinrandomhouse.com.

First published by Preface Publishing in 2017

www.penguin.co.uk

A CIP catalogue record for this book is available from the British Library.

ISBN 9781848094024 (hardback)
ISBN 9781848094031 (trade paperback)

Map illustration on endpapers by Darren Bennett, D K B Creative

Typeset in 11.5/15 pt Fournier MT by
Jouve (UK), Milton Keynes
Printed and bound by Clays Ltd, St Ives plc

Penguin Random House is committed to a sustainable future for
our business, our readers and our planet. This book is made
from Forest Stewardship Council® certified paper.

For all Irish rugby players, past and present. You gave — and give — your all for the four proud provinces, and we love you for it. 2016 will go down as a momentous year in Irish rugby, thanks to the victories over New Zealand, Australia and South Africa.

The glory is tinged with sadness too, because of the untimely death at forty-two of Anthony Foley, former Shannon, Munster and Ireland player. This book is also dedicated to Anthony, a giant of the game, taken far too soon.

List of characters

卫卫卫

Romans/Allies

Lucius Cominius Tullus, a veteran centurion, formerly of the Eighteenth Legion, now of the Fifth.

Marcus Crassus Fenestela, Tullus' *optio*, or second-in-command.*

Germanicus Julius Caesar, step-grandson of Augustus, nephew of Tiberius, and imperial governor of Germania and Tres Galliae.*

Lucius Seius Tubero, a Roman noble, now a legionary legate and enemy of Tullus.*

Marcus Piso, one of Tullus' soldiers.

Metilius, another of Tullus' soldiers, and Piso's friend.

Calvus, another of Tullus' soldiers.

Dulcius and Rufus, more of Tullus' soldiers.

Bassius, *primus pilus* of the Fifth Legion.

Tiberius Claudius Nero, emperor and successor to Augustus.*

Lucius Stertinius, one of Germanicus' generals.*

Aulus Caecina Severus, military governor of Germania Inferior.*

Caius Silius, military governor of Germania Superior.*

Lucius Apronius, one of Germanicus' legates.*

Potitius, one of Tullus' centurions.

Flavus, Arminius' brother.*

Aemilius, *primus pilus* of the First Legion.*

Chariovalda, a chieftain of the Batavi, and ally of Rome.*

Caedicius, camp prefect, and Tullus' friend.*

Publius Quinctilius Varus, the dead governor of Germany who was tricked into leading his army into a terrible ambush in AD 9.*

Nero Claudius Drusus, Germanicus' father, and a general who led extensive campaigns into Germany.*

Gaius, a soldier who owes money to Piso.

Gnaeus Aelius Gallo, a soldier taken prisoner by the Marsi.

Arimnestos, a Greek army surgeon.

Germans/Others

Arminius, chieftain of the German Cherusci tribe, mastermind of the ambush on Varus' legions, and sworn enemy of Rome.*

Maelo, Arminius' trusted second-in-command.

Degmar, Marsi tribesman and former servant to Tullus.

Thusnelda, Arminius' wife.*

Mallovendus, a chieftain of the Marsi tribe.*

Horsa, a chieftain of the Angrivarii tribe.

Inguiomerus, Arminius' uncle and ally, and chieftain of a large faction of the Cherusci tribe.*

Gerulf, a chieftain of the Usipetes tribe.

Osbert, one of Arminius' warriors.

Gervas, a Usipetes warrior who allies himself with Arminius.

Tudrus, a Dolgubnii warrior.

Segestes, Thusnelda's father, ally of Rome, and chieftain of a faction of the Cherusci tribe.*

Adgandestrius, a chieftain of the Chatti tribe.*

Artio, orphan girl rescued by Tullus in *Eagles at War*.

Sirona, Gaulish woman and carer for Artio.

Macula, stray dog adopted by Piso.

Scylax, Artio's dog.

Prologue

Autumn, AD 15

ⴕⴕⴕ

Near the Roman fort of Vetera, on the German frontier

Autumn sunshine lanced from a break in the banked cloud above, flashing off the Fifth Legion's eagle. A sign from the gods, many would have said. Divine-sent or not, the beams drew everyone's gaze to the glittering golden eagle. Senior Centurion Lucius Cominius Tullus was mesmerised. He forgot the nip of the gusting west wind, and stared. Perched on crossed thunderbolts with garlanded wings raised behind, held aloft by the bareheaded *aquilifer*, the eagle radiated power. The physical embodiment of the legion's spirit and the sacrifices made by its soldiers, it demanded reverence, expected devotion.

I am your servant, thought Tullus. I follow you, always.

As ever, the eagle made no answer.

Patient, Tullus waited and watched. His answer came perhaps a dozen heartbeats later when the aquilifer shifted position. The sun's rays again bounced off the eagle, this time searing Tullus' eyes. Blinking, awestruck, he repeated his oft-made vow to serve the eagle unto death. Before he'd finished the silent oath, his heart wrenched. Loyal as he was, the Fifth's eagle wasn't the standard about which he dreamed, nor the one which dragged him night after night, sweat-soaked and with racing pulse, from sleep.

Tullus' soul would always belong to the eagle of the Eighteenth, his legion for a decade and a half. The legion had been annihilated with two others six years before by Arminius, a Cherusci chieftain and one-time ally of Rome. Although Tullus had survived the bloodbath, dragging with him a handful of his soldiers, the mental scars it had left pained him yet. He lived for revenge on Arminius, but stronger still was his desire to recover the Eighteenth's eagle. One of the three lost standards had just been recovered, fanning hot his heartfelt wish.

A man coughed behind him, dragging Tullus to the present, and the parade. At his back, arrayed cohort by cohort to his left and right, were the soldiers of the Fifth. At right angles to the Fifth and forming the second side of a square, were the men of the Twenty-First, Vetera's other legion. The square's third side was made up of the fort's auxiliaries, a mixture of skirmishers, infantry and cavalrymen. Only the sentries, those away on official duty and the patients in the hospital had been excused from the parade.

Everyone was ready and waiting. They were no longer eager, thought Tullus, studying his men's expressionless faces, but it was hard to blame them for that. The cold out here was ball-tightening. Cloaks had been banned, for Germanicus wanted his troops looking their best, gleaming armour and weapons on view. The parade's purpose was to celebrate the army's brutal campaign in Germania, which had ended a month before. As well as honouring senior officers whose actions had stood out, the governor Germanicus would recognise individual soldiers' bravery. Tullus wasn't fond of ceremony, but after the summer's heavy casualties, occasions such as this were a morale boost for the men.

Another vicious blast of wind whistled by, raising goose bumps on his arms and legs. The last thing I need is men coming down with a chill, he thought, giving a loud order allowing his soldiers to stamp their feet and move about on the spot. He did the same for thirty heartbeats, and after checking for signs of Germanicus – there were still none – Tullus took the opportunity to pace along the ranks and engage in a little banter with his men, and to see that the cohort's five other centurions were happy.

Life had not been kind afterwards to the soldiers who had survived the ambush laid by Arminius; the majority had been split up from their comrades when they'd been transferred to other units. Matters had been made worse for Tullus by Tubero, a malevolent tribune of whom he'd fallen foul. Stripped from the rank of senior centurion of the Eighteenth's Second Cohort, Tullus had been reduced to an ordinary centurion in the lowlier Seventh Cohort of the Fifth, his new legion. It had taken five years and recognition by Germanicus before Tullus had been promoted again to his current position, commanding the Seventh Cohort.

After the disaster, Tullus had also been shorn of most of the troops he'd saved. Caedicius, one of Tullus' few senior-ranking friends, had ensured that not all were moved into other units, and he gave thanks for that mercy every day. Foremost among his old soldiers was his wiry, ginger-haired *optio* Marcus Crassus Fenestela. Piso and Metilius were two others, brave and resourceful legionaries – Tullus acknowledged them both with a word before moving on.

The soldiers of his new century were much the same as any men he'd led, Tullus thought, studying their faces. There were a few outstanding individuals, and a central core of good men, with a larger number of average ones. As was inevitable, he had a handful of bad soldiers too: layabouts and malcontents. Ruled with an iron fist, they still played their part. As an entire unit, his men were formidable. They had served with distinction and not a little bravery in the just-ended punishing campaign. Tullus was proud of them, but admitted that on rare occasions. Scant praise worked best.

Trumpets called from the fort's ramparts, some quarter of a mile distant. 'Chins up, chests out. Shields straight and javelins planted,' he barked. 'Germanicus is coming!'

'Will he be giving us anything, sir?' called a voice from the rear ranks.

'A cash donative?' a second man was quick to add. 'Or some wine, maybe?'

Centurions often punished soldiers who spoke out of turn, but Tullus was cut from different cloth. It was cold, they'd been here for more than an hour – in his mind, these were reasonable questions. 'Don't be expecting money, brothers,' he answered, smiling at the responding groans. 'This century, this cohort, didn't do enough to warrant that. Wine isn't beyond the realms of possibility, though.' They rumbled low-throated approval, and grinned like fools when he told them there'd be wine in any case – from him. 'It will be a small gesture, brothers,' said Tullus, striding back to his position at the very right of the front rank. 'You did well this summer gone.'

Everyone's eyes were now on the track that led to the fort, and the approaching party of riders. Close behind the horsemen came a cohort of Praetorians, a unit of Germanicus' imperial bodyguards. When the first horsemen were two hundred paces out, the camp prefect made a pre-arranged gesture. Tullus and every senior centurion issued an order to their cohort's trumpeters. A welcoming fanfare shredded the autumnal air. Repeated several times, it died away with perfect precision as Germanicus reached the low platform set on the fourth side of the great square parade ground. The Praetorians took up positions on either side of the platform.

A collective sigh rose at the sight of their commander, whose regal appearance demanded respect, even a degree of fear. He was an impressive figure, Tullus had to admit. Tall, well built and with a commanding presence lessened not at all by distance, Germanicus' armour shone as if burnished by the gods themselves. A red sash around his middle marked him out as a general. He was also the governor of Tres Galliae and Germania. Cynics could have called him – in secret – a pretty-boy nobleman playing at soldiering, but Germanicus was far from this. Blessed with good leadership skills, courage, charisma, and a ruthless streak as wide as the River Rhenus, he made an excellent leader.

On a less formal occasion, the legionaries might have cheered Germanicus, but today a reverent silence reigned as he climbed the steps on to the platform and was greeted by his senior officers.

Tullus smiled as the camp prefect offered Germanicus a seat, and the general declined. He's about to address his troops, thought Tullus with stirring pride. What kind of leader does that sitting on his arse?

'Brave legionaries of the Fifth and Twenty-First Legions. Courageous auxiliaries of Rome,' cried Germanicus, his voice carried by the wind. 'Fine soldiers of the empire all, I greet you!'

'GER-MAN-I-CUS!' upwards of twelve thousand voices answered, Tullus' among them. 'GER-MAN-I-CUS!'

'We crossed the Rhenus in the spring, we and thousands of others,' declared Germanicus. 'Forty thousand imperial troops, of one mind. We marched into enemy territory to avenge our dead, the general Varus and his legions, cruelly murdered by Arminius and his treacherous henchmen. We marched to crush the tribes who still resist Rome's rule, and to kill Arminius. We marched to recover the three eagles lost to the enemy.' Germanicus stilled the soldiers' acclaim with a raised hand. 'To an extent, we succeeded. Several tribes were vanquished – the Marsi, the Chatti and the Bructeri. The retrieval of the Nineteenth Legion's eagle is a cause for great celebration.'

Riotous cheering broke out. Masterful at working a crowd, Germanicus again let the troops express their happiness.

Old bitterness gnawed at Tullus, for the job hadn't been finished. He could never rest until the Eighteenth's eagle had been brought home. Nor would he be satisfied until Arminius, the man responsible for its loss and the annihilation of Tullus' men, was dead. Blood for blood, he thought, imagining Arminius under his blade. The traitor – once an ally of Rome – had to pay for what he'd done.

'Despite our successes, and the good fortune that saw the safe return of our soldiers, much was left undone,' Germanicus said when the noise had abated. 'Another campaign beckons us next spring. I will again lead you over the river, to victory. Arminius and his ragtag band of followers will be overcome and slain, and the two remaining eagles found. Rome *will* emerge triumphant!' He raised his right fist high.

'RO-MA! VIC-TRIX!' bellowed a hundred voices among the Fifth's ranks.

The call was taken up with gusto. It echoed around the training ground and rose into the windy sky, a clamouring bank of sound that seemed to challenge the gods themselves. 'RO-MA! VIC-TRIX! RO-MA! VIC-TRIX!'

Germanicus watched with a satisfied expression, and Tullus thought, He's a smart one. His words are perfectly pitched. The soldiers' devotion to him will be increased by the presentation of awards for bravery followed by a large issue of wine. He'll be able to do no wrong for months.

The senior officers were first to be honoured. Caecina, the veteran commander of the troops on the lower Rhenus, who had led four legions out of a terrible ambush on the way home that summer, was presented with the full raiment of a triumphant general. Caecina's pleasure was clear as Germanicus bestowed on him the gold laurel wreath, ivory baton, embroidered tunic and purple toga. Apronius, one of the legion legates, was recognised in similar fashion. To Tullus' annoyance, Tubero – newly appointed legate of the Fifth – was rewarded with a gold coronet.

Although the soldiers had cheered for the more senior officers, their response was much louder for the next group who had distinguished themselves, the centurions and lower-ranked officers. Tullus watched with approval as upwards of a dozen men were called forward by Germanicus and rewarded with *phalerae* – gold or silver disc ornaments worn on a chest harness – or torques of the same precious metals. After the final man had been honoured, Germanicus paused.

An expectant hush fell. It was time for the most valiant legionaries and auxiliaries to be recognised, thought Tullus, glancing at his men's eager faces.

'Before I mention you brave soldiers of Rome,' announced Germanicus to excited shouting, 'I have one other officer to call on.' Again he stopped. This time, a complete silence descended, leaving the squalling wind as the only voice.

This award – separate from the awards granted to the centurions – was breaking from the usual protocol. Intrigued, Tullus listened with the rest.

'Senior Centurion Lucius Cominius Tullus, of the Seventh Cohort, Fifth Legion, present yourself!' Germanicus' shout boomed across the training ground.

Stunned, Tullus wondered if he had misheard. He could feel his soldiers' gaze boring into him, however, and could hear their delighted muttering.

Shit, he thought. I'm not imagining it. Half a dozen heartbeats pounded by. On the dais some two hundred paces away, Germanicus waited.

'Best get up there, sir,' hissed Piso to Tullus.

He snapped back to the present. Self-conscious and already worried that his delay would have offended Germanicus, he stepped forward. Stiff-backed, guts churning, Tullus marched towards the platform, the weight of thousands of men's eyes upon him.

At the regulation ten paces' distance, Tullus snapped to attention, fixing his stare on Germanicus' midriff. 'Senior Centurion Tullus, Seventh Cohort, Fifth Legion, sir!' he cried.

Standing on the platform emphasised the general's great height – he towered over Tullus. 'You took your time, senior centurion,' Germanicus said with a frown.

'I did, sir,' Tullus faltered. 'I was surprised to be summoned. My apologies.'

Germanicus' lips twitched. 'Apology accepted.'

He thinks it's funny, Tullus realised, unsure whether to be relieved or annoyed.

Germanicus' expression became formal again. 'Soldiers of Rome,' he shouted. 'Senior Centurion Tullus is a man known to many of you. A veteran officer, he has served the empire for more than three decades. Until six years ago, he was in the Eighteenth Legion. When disaster befell that unit and two others at the Saltus Teutoburgiensis, almost every soldier of Varus' command fell or was taken prisoner by the enemy. Not Tullus. Like a hero of old, he battled on for days, although it seemed as if the gods wished every Roman in that cursed place to die. Fewer than ten score men escaped the massacre, most of them in ones and twos. Tullus brought to safety fifteen. *Fifteen!* Legionaries whose honour was intact, who lived to fight another day!'

Fresh cheers rose.

More embarrassed than he had ever been, Tullus' hope that Germanicus was done came to nothing as the general drew a fresh breath.

'Senior Centurion Tullus and his men remained loyal through the difficult times after our divine father Augustus' death. He risked his life then to
save my person from danger.' A still uncomfortable subject, Germanicus
didn't mention the previous year's bloody rebellion further, but continued,
'In the campaign that has just ended, Tullus distinguished himself on more
than one occasion, in particular during the difficult battle on the Long
Bridges road. These acts were not the first occasions in which Tullus has
marked himself out as a leader, as a true son of Rome – the number of
phalerae on his harness are proof of this. His soldiers love him, and would
march with him into hell if he ordered it. He has the respect of his fellow
centurions, and the regard of the tribunes and legates of more than one
legion. I can think of no finer officer, no greater embodiment of *virtus*, than
the man before me now.' Germanicus extended his hands towards Tullus,
palms up in recognition.

A moment's pause, and then from across the training ground came a loud
cry of 'TUL-LUS! TUL-LUS!'

Tullus' heart wrenched. Those were *his* soldiers' voices – he would have
staked his life on it. To his astonishment, the refrain was taken up, first by
the Fifth's other legionaries, and then by those of the Twenty-First. Even the
auxiliaries joined in.

'TUL-LUS! TUL-LUS!'

'Tullus.' Germanicus' tone was commanding. Irresistible.

He lifted his head and met Germanicus' gaze. 'Sir?'

'If Rome had ten thousand men like you, it would conquer the entire
world.'

'Thank you, sir,' replied Tullus, fighting to keep his voice from
choking.

The cheering had died down, and Germanicus raised a hand for greater
quiet. 'In recognition of Tullus' valiant service to the empire, he is to be
promoted. Henceforth he will be known as Centurion Tullus of the Second
Century, First Cohort, Fifth Legion!'

'TUL-LUS! TUL-LUS!'

If it hadn't been for the troops' roars of approval, and the wind chilling his face, Tullus would have believed himself in a fantastic dream. This was a huge promotion. He gave Germanicus his best parade salute. 'You do me great honour, sir!'

'The honour is mine, Tullus.' Germanicus' tone was solemn. 'I will have need of you again in the spring. Arminius and his allies must be defeated – and your legion's eagle salvaged from the enemy.'

'I'll be ready, sir,' said Tullus, bursting with pride.

PART ONE

Winter, AD 15

Near the Roman fort of Vetera,
on the German frontier

Chapter I

▨▨▨

T ullus was wandering through the settlement near his camp, Vetera. Blue skies and sun aside, it was a bitter winter's day; the icy air stung as he breathed in. A thick layer of snow decorated every house's roof and the narrow alleys between; brown slush coated the paved streets. Every passer-by, whether civilian and military, wore a cloak. Even the stray dogs had a hunched, miserable look to them. In spite of the chill, Tullus' mood was good. He was off duty, and back in the fort; everything was as it should be with his men. There was more to it than that, he decided. Since returning from the eastern side of the Rhenus three months before, life had been easy, slow – mundane.

Boredom was a better state to exist in than living under threat of attack night and day, which was how he and his men had spent the summer's campaign. Tullus put from his mind the blood-drenched memories. Today he was going to relax, first with a soak and a massage in the settlement's new-built baths. Afterwards, he'd savour good food and drink in his favourite local inn, the Ox and Plough.

The thought of its proprietor Sirona brought a smile to Tullus' lined face. A feisty, warm-hearted Gaulish woman, she had a fine figure and a temper to match any centurion's. He'd been chasing her on and off for years, and always been rebuffed. Tullus had decided in the end that a man had to keep his pride. Sirona was a lost cause, despite the access granted to him thanks to her care of Artio, his surrogate daughter. Although Tullus' wooing had ceased, the passage of time had not seen the embers of his passion go cold.

When he'd come marching over the bridge from Germania, three months back, the Fates had smiled on him at last. Sirona's smile for him then would have lit a dark room. Thus encouraged, Tullus had been swift to renew his suit. The first mistake had been to start after he'd consumed a decent quantity of confidence-boosting wine, the second his attempt to kiss Sirona at the same time. He could still feel the ringing slap she'd delivered to his cheek. Ten days had passed before a humiliated Tullus was allowed to re-enter her inn, and another twenty until relations had been restored to something near their previous cordiality.

'More haste, less speed.' Kicking at an untouched clump of pristine snow, he decided that marching to war was easier than trying to understand women.

'Centurion,' cried a passing legionary, saluting, and Tullus forgot Sirona. Images of the awards ceremony a month before filled his mind. It continued to feel strange that Germanicus had seen fit to elevate him to the post of second-ranking centurion in the First Cohort, and yet there it was – it *had* happened. Years back, when Tullus had led the Second Cohort of the Eighteenth, such an advancement had seemed possible, but the ignominy of having survived Arminius' ambush had snuffed out his career opportunities. Germanicus had seen something in him, however, and his recent recognition had made Tullus more senior to every centurion in the legion apart from the *primus pilus*.

The parading legionaries' loud acclaim when Germanicus had finished speaking had deeply touched Tullus. Feeling awkward even at the memory, he glanced about. No one was looking of course, and he chuckled at himself. The smith over yonder was too busy hammering, and his apprentice watching, to pay heed to a passing soldier. The same applied to the cooper fitting iron rings to a new barrel, and the swearing carpenter whose saw had slipped, taking the skin off his knuckles. Other passers-by, cloaked and hooded, paid no heed either, keen as they were to reach their destinations.

Even the barefooted, skinny urchin sidling towards Tullus had his own purpose. 'Spare a coin, sir?' he pleaded.

Tullus' usual response would have been to stride by with a curse, but the boy's hollowed, chapped cheeks and twig-like limbs stirred his sympathy.

I'm getting old and sentimental, he thought, searching in his purse and plucking out not just a copper *as*, but a silver *denarius*. 'Get some hot food in you,' he ordered. Sunlight winked off the coins as they spun through the air. 'Buy yourself a cloak or a pair of shoes as well.'

Even as the urchin's face twisted with delight – 'A thousand blessings on you, sir!' – his eyes flickered to the left.

Tullus' gaze followed the boy's, and he swore under his breath. Lounging against a shopfront was another urchin. This one was well fed, three times the size of the starveling before him, and his smirk revealed that he'd seen what had gone on. The instant that Tullus had moved on, he would take the coins for his own. Twig Limbs would be powerless to resist.

Tullus' anger flared, and he strode forward, trapping the better-fed urchin against the shop wall with the head of his *vitis*, or vine stick.

A loud squawk. 'I haven't done nothing, sir!'

'But you would have, maggot. You were going to steal my money from him, weren't you?' demanded Tullus, jerking his head at Twig Limbs, who was watching with eyes the size of plates.

'No, I wasn't, sir! I—' The urchin's protest turned into an *oomph* of pain as Tullus' vitis drove partway into his belly.

'Don't lie to me.' Tullus' flinty gaze, used to making hardened soldiers recoil, bored into the urchin. He was quick to look down, and Tullus hissed in his ear, 'If anyone lays a finger on that boy, or takes his coins – that means you *and* your lowlife cronies – I will hunt you down, and by all the gods, you'll regret the day you were whelped. D'you understand?'

'Yes, sir.' The urchin's tone was two notes higher than it had been. 'I won't go near him, sir, on my mother's life.'

Tullus lowered his vitis, allowing his victim to scuttle away. The boy didn't dare to look back.

Tullus waited until he'd gone, and wasn't surprised that Twig Limbs was still standing there, hero worship filling his eyes. 'Gratitude, sir. He's a nasty one. He—'

Wishing to keep his distance, Tullus cut him off. 'Don't share that money with anyone.'

'I won't, sir, and if I can ever help . . .' Twig Limbs' voice died away as his confidence did. His shoulders slumped.

Knowing he meant well, Tullus gave him a clout on the shoulder and walked away. Urchins like Twig Limbs were as plentiful as the stars in the sky. He couldn't help them all, nor did he want to, and there was no point getting close to one, or he'd never have any peace. Like as not, his gesture meant that he would be descended upon every time he entered the settlement from now on, for Twig Limbs would surely blab about his unexpected windfall to his friends. Or perhaps he wouldn't, Tullus decided. The fewer people who knew, the more chance the boy would keep his money.

Thoughts of street urchins made Tullus feel his purse, checking that it hadn't been slit. A pleasing quantity of coins lay within – Germanicus' recognition had included a sizeable cash donative. Spurred by his recent near experiences with death, Tullus was in the mood to begin spending his reward – but on what, he wasn't sure. His armour and equipment was of fine quality, and not in need of replacement. His calf-length boots were only two years old, and worn though his metalled belt was, he was attached to it. His polished vitis was like an extension of his right arm, and would see him into grey-bearded dotage.

On impulse, he stopped by a jeweller's premises, not something he'd ever done, and there browsed the display. Most of the goods were simple, low-priced items: the bronze ram's head bracelets, phallus and tiny *gladius* amulets favoured by legionaries, and the polished stone necklaces worn by their women. Higher-priced trinkets had been placed further back, close to the keen-eyed shopkeeper; more were on display in the shop. Reluctant to enter – what did he know about jewellery? – Tullus leaned forward to study some pearl earrings, a carnelian bracelet and a selection of silver necklaces. Frustrated, for he had no idea what Sirona would like, and too proud to ask, he walked away.

'Sir?' called the proprietor, a round-shouldered old Gaul with a silver beard. 'Can I be of help, sir?'

Tullus turned, feeling as awkward as if he'd been caught thieving. 'I need a present, for a lady friend.'

'You'll find something delightful here, sir, I promise you! Won't you step inside?'

Tullus would have rather attacked a German shield wall, but he *did* want a present for Sirona, and there was less chance of being seen or recognised off the street. Almost able to hear his fellow centurions' jokes — 'Buying trinkets for your lover now, Tullus?' 'Sirona let you get your leg over at last, eh?' — he ducked his head to avoid the low lintel and went in.

The premises were larger than they looked from outside, a long room part filled with display cases and cabinets, with worktables manned by busy craftsmen at the back. 'I can't stay long,' he said, suspecting from the shop-keeper's smooth manner that he was practised at keeping customers on his premises until they bought something.

'Your time is precious, sir, I know that. You do me honour even to cross the threshold,' the jeweller said, and bowed.

Tullus raised an eyebrow. There was no mistaking that he was an officer — the cut of his clothing and armour would tell anyone that, but the old man had no reason to think that he was anything more than a veteran optio, or perhaps a low-ranking centurion. Nonetheless, thought Tullus, it paid to be cautious. If the jeweller had the slightest inkling of his rank, everything in the place would triple in price.

'Just so you know, my purse is light,' said Tullus. 'Payday isn't for another while yet.'

'There are beautiful pieces to suit every taste, sir,' replied the jeweller with impressive diplomacy. 'How much were you thinking of spending?'

This was his opening gambit, thought Tullus, but two could play at that game. 'Show me your wares first. You can tell me their prices as I look. Start with those bracelets.'

'Of course, sir.' The jeweller wasn't quite able to hide his disappointment.

I was right, Tullus decided. The rogue is out to fleece me. Sure enough, the cost of the bracelets – a fine variety made from silver, gold, agate, red coral and even amber – was exorbitant. It was no better with the earrings and necklaces. 'Stop,' he ordered as the jeweller moved on to a gold filigree diadem encrusted with tiny gemstones. 'What do you think I am, a legate?'

The jeweller's smile was sly. 'No, sir, a centurion, newly promoted to the First Cohort.'

'You recognise me?' demanded Tullus, surprised.

The jeweller looked scandalised. 'You're a famous man, sir! Everyone in the settlement knows you, and how you survived the ambush on Varus and his legions. You're a hero, sir.'

Tullus' cheeks were warm now, which he didn't like one bit. 'Don't believe everything you hear.'

'Germanicus saw fit to honour you, sir.'

Defeated by this, Tullus threw him a glare. 'I did what anyone would have.'

'As you say, sir.' In spite of his previous acquisitive manner, there was respect in the jeweller's voice. 'It goes without saying that a man of your stature would receive a good discount.' He reeled off the pieces which Tullus had lingered over, reducing their cost by a third or more.

Tullus chuckled, amused by the jeweller's performance and sure that he would still make a healthy profit. Trusting his gut instinct, Tullus studied again the items that had first caught his eye and settled on a simple yet elegant bracelet fashioned from four silver plaits. A short but intense spell of haggling saw him beat the old man down to half his original price without looking too unhappy. Tullus was also content, and bargaining any harder would take more of his time than he was prepared to give.

'Your lady friend will love this,' the jeweller pronounced, slipping the bracelet into a soft goatskin bag. 'Perhaps you can visit with her one day.'

Tullus grunted, yet unsure that his gift would even be accepted, let alone received well. This approach had to be better than trying to make physical advances, he thought. Didn't it?

There was a distinctive crack as two heads collided, and Tullus glanced outside. Two men travelling in opposite directions had walked into one another. Angry shouts and insults were hurled as both denied responsibility for the accident. Uncaring, for neither were soldiers, Tullus was about to pay the shopkeeper when he caught a glimpse of a familiar face. It was one he hadn't seen for months, and which he would not have expected to see on this side of the Rhenus. 'Degmar?' he cried. 'Is that you?'

The young Marsi warrior stared into the shop with an amazed expression. There was no question it was Degmar – Tullus would have recognised him anywhere – but rather than give any acknowledgement, he darted down an alleyway opposite.

'Here.' Tullus slapped down some coins, snatched up his bracelet and made for the door.

'Sir?' The jeweller's confused voice carried after Tullus as he shoved his way across the busy street. A carter who had to wrench on his oxen's traces to avoid striking Tullus cursed, then realised he was an army officer and somehow converted the oath into a strangled mutter.

Degmar was already a dark shadow, far down the alley, and Tullus swore to himself. The warrior had a head start and twenty years on him. There was not a chance that he'd catch up, let alone find Degmar in the maze of back streets. All the same, Tullus took a few steps into the alleyway. The stink of human waste, thick and cloying, brought him to an abrupt halt. He spat in frustration. Degmar was gone, and covering his boots in shit and piss would do nothing but annoy him further.

Gripping Sirona's present, he made for the Ox and Plough. His good mood remained, but it was tinged now with unease. What purpose had Degmar in Vetera, and why had he run?

Chapter II

Sirona was well pleased with her bracelet, which relieved and delighted Tullus in equal measure. Her manner towards him warmed by a considerable amount, and she had allowed him to peck her on the cheek before he left that evening. Cocky as a stripling youth after his first kiss, Tullus marched back to the camp, all thoughts of Degmar forgotten. The following morning, real life and his duties brought him down to earth, and he recalled the chance sighting of his former servant.

During spring the previous year, Tullus had helped to rescue Degmar's family prior to their village being destroyed by the legions. The dangerous mission had been a success, but Tullus and Degmar had parted on strained terms. He hadn't ever expected to see the Marsi warrior again – Degmar hated Rome and all it stood for – which made his presence in the settlement even odder. Keen for another opinion, Tullus decided to confide in Fenestela. The pair had served together for half their lives, and trusted each other inside and out.

Their adjoining quarters made frequent meetings easy. Orders from on high had to be passed on daily; problems that one or other had encountered with the quartermaster or senior officers often had to be discussed. The pair convened to share camp news and gossip; sometimes it was just for a bite to eat, or a cup of wine. 'We're like an old married couple,' Tullus was wont to mutter. Fenestela's sarcastic response was always, 'Without any fun under the blankets.'

Tullus went to Fenestela's door at the earliest opportunity the next morning, a short time after the men had been up. This initial period involved Fenestela hounding the soldiers from their beds with dire threats, and was followed by a hiatus for ablutions and the day's first meal. Fenestela often breakfasted with the other junior officers, while Tullus tended to eat on his own. If he's not alone now, thought Tullus, hammering on the door, I'll tell him on the threshold.

Fenestela smiled as he saw who his visitor was. 'Come in,' he said, stepping aside.

'You alone?'

'Aye,' said Fenestela, frowning. 'Why?'

Tullus strode in without answering, his eyes raking the room, but there was no one else present. Like him, Fenestela had simple tastes. A plain table with a gaming board atop it and four chairs filled the chamber's central area. The other items of furniture were a couple of wooden chests and a stand for Fenestela's armour. Tullus' bedroom was just as plain.

'D'you not believe me, *sir*?' Fenestela's tone was irritated. Long comradeship and mutual respect meant that he only ever used the term when others were about, or when he was annoyed with Tullus.

'I do.'

'What's going on then?'

'I saw Degmar yesterday.'

'Degmar?' Fenestela's face now registered shock. 'Where?'

'In the settlement.'

'Did you speak with him?'

'He took off like a scalded cat the instant he saw me.'

'How strange.' Despite the early hour, Fenestela poured a measure of wine into two cups and handed one to Tullus, who didn't refuse.

'He's up to no good,' said Fenestela. 'What else can explain such behaviour?'

'We need to talk to him.' Tullus was unhappy that his suspicions had been confirmed.

'Easier said than done,' said Fenestela, his customary scowl returning. 'He'll be lying low somewhere, or already headed over the river.'

'There's no point in going to the legate, or anyone else — a chance sighting of one tribesman is proof of nothing.' Tullus threw back the wine.

'Where were you when you saw him?'

Tullus hesitated, and then admitted, 'In a jeweller's.'

'A jeweller's?' It was galling how much surprise, amusement and sarcasm Fenestela could pack into two words.

'What of it?' snapped Tullus.

Fenestela's lips twitched. 'So you were in this jeweller's, and Degmar was on the street.'

'Aye. That's why he didn't see me straight away, and how he got a head start when I called out.'

'Sure it wasn't because you had to finish buying whatever it was you'd chosen for Sirona?' A tiny chortle escaped Fenestela.

'I'd paid for it already!' cried Tullus, angry to feel so embarrassed.

'*It?*' asked Fenestela, innocent-faced.

'A bracelet — as if it's any of your cursed business!' Tullus retorted. 'Have you heard all you want yet, or can we talk about Degmar?'

'Best return to serious matters. I can weasel more information about Sirona out of you later,' said Fenestela with a wink.

'If you ever find a woman — not that that's likely, you dog — know that I'll never let you hear the end of it,' threatened Tullus.

'I wouldn't expect anything less,' said Fenestela, laughing. 'Now, back to Degmar. As you said, there's no point going to anyone more senior.'

'Aye. As usual, it's us who must keep our eyes peeled and our ears pricked.' The situation was depressing, and familiar. Before the fateful ambush six years before, the general Varus had refused to listen to Tullus' suspicions about Arminius, and the subsequent massacre had seen three legions annihilated. More recently, Tullus' former cohort commander had rubbished his fears of mutiny among the local troops. Within days, four legions had risen up in rebellion.

'I'll have Piso and the old guard stay alert too.'

Tullus nodded, pleased. Piso and most of the men he'd saved during Arminius' ambush were in his new century. It had gone against army regulations for them to move with him, but Tullus had enough high-ranking people who were well disposed to him, or friends – Germanicus and the camp prefect Caedicius among them – to ask that it be done. Truth be told, Tullus wouldn't have wanted his new command without Fenestela and the rest also transferring units. By this point Piso, Metilius and their comrades were as dear to Tullus as family.

He waved away Fenestela's jug, which was hovering over his cup. 'Later. There's a day to get through first.'

'I suppose,' said Fenestela, sounding disappointed. 'Best not to be drunk on duty. Doesn't look good to the men.'

'We can have a drop later, and a talk about Degmar.'

Tullus' jovial tone belied his concerns, which had been multiplied by Fenestela's reaction.

A warrior and hunter, and someone who hated Rome and everything it stood for, Degmar wasn't in the settlement to trade. Tullus' fears crystallised. Degmar *was* here to do ill.

Despite Tullus' worries, nothing untoward happened. His men drilled and marched, and grumbled their way through unpopular tasks such as sentry duty, and felling and hauling trees for firewood. No one – not Tullus, Fenestela or the soldiers who'd been alerted – saw hide nor hair of Degmar in the settlement. The various inn- and brothel-keepers who had been slipped coins swore on their mothers' lives that they hadn't spotted him either. Even Twig Limbs, a willing recruit to Tullus' cause, found no sign of the warrior.

If he had been seeking anyone else, Tullus might have decided he had imagined the encounter, but Degmar was the spitting image of a legionary whom he'd had to abandon during a vicious ambush in Illyricum years before. The man's terrified face and the sound of his anguished cries were burned deep into Tullus' memory. It *had* to have been Degmar. Several more days passed without incident, however. There had been no upsets in the settlement, no attacks on soldiers. Patrols returning from the east bank had reported nothing out of the ordinary. Arminius had to be plotting away, it was true, but he was hundreds of miles away in Cherusci territory. Life was moving on.

On the sixth afternoon, with his duties completed, Tullus decided he'd had enough. There was no way of discovering Degmar's purpose and in the absence of further evidence, no leads to follow. Whatever the warrior had been up to, it was done, like as not. To help clear his mind of the matter, Tullus determined to visit the jeweller's for a second time. His potential embarrassment was now outweighed by his desire to work his way further into Sirona's affections. One of these days, she had to allow him into her bed, and despite Tullus' inexperience at courting, another trinket wouldn't harm his chances.

Before leaving for the settlement, he vacillated briefly over removing his mail. The old jeweller was no longer a factor, knowing Tullus' rank, but remaining as he was – a cloak couldn't quite hide his armour from the front – meant he ran a greater risk of being spotted entering or leaving the shop. In the end, Tullus' further evening duties swayed him. It was more practical not to shed the cumbersome mail.

Checking his purse was full, he made for the door, vine stick in hand. Sirona would love today's gift, he decided, which would be more expensive than the silver bracelet. The thought of her pleased reaction almost made him whistle, before he remembered that he was still within the fort, and that high-ranking centurions had to maintain a certain public air. Besides, he thought darkly, if Fenestela heard, he'd intuit Tullus' reason, and the jokes about Sirona would never end.

Tullus was pleased to make it to the settlement without recognising many soldiers. That didn't mean that *he* hadn't been seen of course – he was well known – but there wasn't anything to do about that. The weather was on his side at least. A cutting wind and heavy flurries of snow had driven people indoors and reduced visibility to less than twenty paces. Daylight was fading fast and even the main avenue, often jammed with pedestrians and wagons, was almost empty.

Tullus was unsurprised when Twig Limbs appeared before him, his feet encased in a pair of cheap leather sandals. Showing off his worn cloak – he'd got both for a low price, he told Tullus with great pride – he again offered his help should it ever be needed. Touched, Tullus slipped him a handful of low-denomination coins. With Twig Limbs' thanks ringing in his ears, he made for the jeweller's shop, which lay on a side street not far from the new forum and the bridge over the Rhenus. Not a soul – in particular, another soldier or officer – was to be seen as he reached it, which pleased Tullus.

The jeweller's smile grew broad as he entered. 'Terrible weather out there, sir.'

'It's not good,' agreed Tullus, taking off his helmet.

Now recognising Tullus, the jeweller's face lit up. 'You've come back, sir!'

'I have.' Tullus set his helmet on a table.

'May I assume that the lady was pleased with your gift, sir?'

'Aye,' said Tullus, already feeling uncomfortable.

'And you wish to buy her another, sir?'

'That's right.'

'Something . . .' The jeweller trailed his fingers along the counter before him, stopping at the bracelets. ' . . . like these, sir?'

'No. I want a necklace this time, or some earrings.' Tullus almost said, 'Or both,' but managed to bite his tongue. Better to keep the devious old goat guessing his intentions as long as possible.

'One of my craftsmen has just finished this piece,' the jeweller said, reaching behind him and lifting up a shimmering necklace of silver decorated with dozens of little garnets. 'It's quite beautiful, sir.'

Tullus was no judge of jewellery – Hades, he'd only been in this place once – but the necklace *was* stunning. The garnets would match Sirona's dark brown eyes too, he thought. 'How much?'

'To you, sir, only fifty *denarii*.'

Tullus pulled his hand back. '*Fifty?*'

'The garnets are of the finest quality, sir. A great deal of time and expertise went into its making.' He held out the piece again. 'See for yourself.'

'Fifty is too much,' protested Tullus.

'I'm sure we could come to an agreement.' The necklace moved until it was under Tullus' nose.

'It is lovely,' admitted Tullus, taking it from the jeweller's grasp.

The unmistakeable tramp of hobnails drew Tullus' attention to the street outside. He watched in some surprise as two Praetorian guardsmen marched past at pace. To his astonishment, they were followed by Germanicus himself. The governor was cloaked and hooded, but given away by his commanding profile and great height – and the protection he had. Another pair of guardsmen took up the rear, and then the party had passed the shop's narrow window. 'What's he doing?' Tullus muttered to himself.

The jeweller's ears were long. 'It's not the first time I have seen the governor, sir. He visits the wine merchant a short distance down the street – the best for a hundred miles in any direction, or so the owner swears. Germanicus must like the stock there – he tends to come by once a month at least.'

Tullus chuckled. The notion that Germanicus went in person to taste wine would never have occurred to him. The governor had dozens of servants, flunkeys and staff officers – why not send one of them, or have samples brought to his quarters in the fort? Tullus had answered the question before he'd finished thinking it. Germanicus' workload had to be staggering, his responsibilities onerous. A secret visit now and again to a wine merchant was an escape, a slice of normal life denied to a man in his position. Good luck to him, thought Tullus. Still amused, he returned his attention to the necklace. 'It's a beautiful piece, but fifty denarii is too expensive.'

'What price *would* suit you, sir?' the jeweller asked, his eyes narrowing.

'Twenty.' The figure was insulting, but Tullus wanted to see his reaction.

'I couldn't sell it for that, sir!' The jeweller's hands reached out as if to take it back before, a little embarrassed, he smoothed them down by his sides. 'There's the cost of the silver and garnets, and paying the craftsman to consider – that price would leave me with no profit at all. I have to make a living, sir.'

'Of course you do. Twenty-five.'

'Forty-five is as low as I could go, sir, and that's being generous.' The old man's expression was pained.

'Thirty.'

'Forty-two, sir.'

'Thirty-two.'

'You're robbing me, sir! Forty.'

'Thirty-four, and that's my final offer.'

'No, sir.'

Tullus handed back the necklace to a startled Silver Beard. 'My thanks,' he said and made for the door. He had gone perhaps three-quarters of the distance when the jeweller cracked.

'Sir!'

Tullus turned, feigning surprise. 'Yes?'

'Will you take it for thirty-eight, sir?'

'Thirty-four, and I'll pay you right now.'

'You're merciless, sir.' He let out a loud sigh. 'Very well.'

Tullus hid his satisfaction. The jeweller put on a good act, but he wasn't dissatisfied with the price either. Tullus reached for his purse.

A loud sneeze outside followed by an angry rebuke from a second person attracted his attention again. Feet crunched in the snow. The sounds were too soft to be military hobnails, and they were being made by men moving with care. Tullus' suspicions were roused, and he moved further into the shop, making it harder to be seen should anyone glance inside. 'Down!' he hissed at the jeweller.

'Sir?' came the confused reply.

'Get down, below the counter. Do as I say!' ordered Tullus in a quieter version of his parade-ground voice.

Looking worried, the jeweller obeyed.

Deep in shadow, Tullus looked through the shop's window. Outside snow continued to fall hard, almost blotting out the shop opposite, which had shut its doors. The ready spears in the hands of the nine cloaked figures who came creeping past were plain enough, however. Bearded, some with plaited hair, and wilder-looking than the local tribespeople, they were German warriors, or he was no judge. Spying Degmar at the rear was proof of their identity – and their malign purpose.

The realisation of Degmar's intention in the settlement hit Tullus like a lightning bolt. He had been scouting out the wine merchant's premises, and the warriors – Marsi, surely – were here to assassinate Germanicus. They must have waited days for the governor to visit. Their presence implied the existence of an informant in the shop. Worry about that later, Tullus told himself. Think. Think, or Germanicus will be dead.

'Have you a spear?' he hissed at the jeweller.

'A spear, sir?'

'A group of armed men has just gone by,' explained Tullus with growing impatience. 'Unless I'm a fool, they're about to murder Germanicus. I haven't got time to go for help, and I can't stand by and do nothing. Now, have you got a cursed spear or not?'

'I – A spear. No, sir.' The jeweller's voice was apologetic. 'Would a knife serve?'

'I've got one of my own,' snarled Tullus. 'A broom then. You must have one of those.'

Sensing his urgency at last, the old man hurried to the back of the shop, returning with a well-used twig broom. Snatching it, Tullus stood on its end and with a mighty wrench turned it into a staff. 'Go to the main street. Find a soldier – any soldier – and say that Centurion Tullus of the First Cohort, Fifth Legion, commands them to the wine merchant's premises. Give them directions. Tell them if they love Germanicus their general, they are to come with all speed.'

The jeweller quailed before Tullus' fury. 'What if I cannot find any soldiers, sir? What if no one listens to me?'

Tullus seized his arm. 'This is a military fucking settlement! There'll be legionaries in the restaurants, the inns, the shops. Shout if you have to – I don't care as long as you get help. D'you understand me?'

'Y-you're hurting me, sir,' said the jeweller, wincing.

'If you don't do as I say, I'll do a lot fucking worse!'

The threat brought the jeweller to his senses. 'Find soldiers. Centurion Tullus' orders. Go to the wine merchant's. Save Germanicus.'

'That's it.' Tullus released his hold. 'Go. Go!'

'But my stock, sir, my jewellery – it will be stolen.'

'Don't you have craftsmen in the back? Family?'

'Only my wife, sir. The workers have gone home.'

'Tell her to close the shop then, fool. Move!' Tullus gave him a shove. He himself could wait no longer and tiptoed to the door, broom clutched in his hands. A furtive glance down the street through the driving snow told him nothing – anything beyond ten paces was invisible. 'How far is the wine merchant's?' he called over his shoulder.

'Twenty-five paces or so, sir,' came the answer. 'On the same side as my premises.'

Deciding his helmet would give him away as he closed on the enemy, Tullus left it behind. He shed his cloak and eased out on to the street, his heart pounding as hard and fast as a smith's hammer. What he was doing was insane – by the time he arrived, Germanicus' bodyguards might well be dead. One middle-aged centurion with a broom and a sword could no more take on nine young warriors than a man could stop the sun from rising in the east.

Yet Tullus could not stand by, not if he wanted to hold his head up in public again. Germanicus was his commander, and a prominent member of the imperial family. More important, he had trusted in Tullus when few others would, and had since raised his career from the abyss. I owe you my life, Germanicus, he thought, stealing after the warriors.

If dying was the price of repaying his debt, so be it.

Chapter III

A hundred miles east of Vetera, Arminius and his second-in-command Maelo were stamping through the snow in a Marsi settlement, their destination the chieftain's longhouse. Dusk blanketed the village; it was diluted but a little by the golden aura of their torches. The pair had arrived with a score of warriors an hour before, just as the sun was setting. It wasn't far from their home to these lands – the Cherusci and Marsi tribes' territory adjoined – but the harsh conditions had made the journey a longer one than usual.

'D'you think they'll all be here?' asked Maelo. Of medium build, with long brown hair and a typical beard, he could have passed for any warrior in a dozen tribes. Nonetheless, he was a skilled, dangerous fighter, and brave as a cornered bear. His sword had slain more men than Arminius' own, which was saying something. 'It's a good deal further to the Usipetes' lands than it is from ours,' he declared. 'No man likes to travel far from his hearth at this time of year.'

'Winter is a season for feasting and fornicating,' said Arminius, repeating the old expression. A large-framed man in the prime of life with striking looks and intense grey eyes, he had black hair and a jutting beard of the same colour. With his bearskin cloak, richly made clothing, silver-decorated baldric and fine *spatha*, or long Roman cavalry sword, he looked every part the chieftain. 'But they'll have come. My reasons for calling the gathering are sound. Germanicus *will* cross the river again in the spring. His army will be as big as it was this year, or larger. If we are not to be ground down piecemeal, tribe by tribe, we must lay well-made plans.'

Maelo nodded; this was an oft-discussed subject. 'Have you spoken to Inguiomerus yet?'

'As soon as we got here.' Arminius' uncle had reached the settlement a day before. Despite his weariness after their own journey, Arminius had wasted no time in meeting him. Inguiomerus led another part of the Cherusci tribe, and although his warriors had joined Arminius' forces during the previous summer, he had engineered the disastrous attack on a Roman camp at the campaign's end. Arminius had argued long and hard against that assault, but Inguiomerus' opinion had prevailed. In the resulting catastrophe, thousands of warriors had died. Soon after, Inguiomerus had acknowledged that his nephew should lead their warriors in the future. This meeting, called by Arminius, was the first since the tribes had returned to their settlements, bloodied and bowed. If things were to go well, it was vital that Inguiomerus' position had not changed.

'And?' demanded Maelo.

'My uncle is still of a mind to follow me,' said Arminius. 'He swore it was so, and I believed him.'

Maelo's face split into a craggy grin. 'That is heartening news. Counting his warriors and ours will give us eight thousand spears. Add the Marsi, and we'll have ten, perhaps eleven thousand to call on.'

'That doesn't mean the other tribes will follow us,' warned Arminius. 'Or obey me, even if they do. Remember last summer—'

Maelo laid a hand on Arminius' shoulder. 'Stop.'

Most men with the audacity to act so would have died, but Maelo was Arminius' most loyal follower, and one of his oldest friends – his only friend, if truth be told. Nonetheless he pinned Maelo with a baleful stare. 'Say your piece.'

'I recall as well as you how the chieftains acted. Refusing to listen to you. Always arguing, and half of them wanting to be the leader at any one time. Frustrating though it is, such is our people's way. They might also have followed Inguiomerus' lead at the end, but it wasn't to attack our tribe, or to kill you – they were fighting Rome, all of them! They hate the empire as much as you—'

'As much as I?' Arminius' laugh was bitter. 'How many of them have lost a wife and child? How many of them have had their family taken prisoner by the Romans?'

'Plenty have lost a wife, a babe, or worse, slain in the settlements destroyed by the legions.'

Arminius wasn't listening. 'I'll never see Thusnelda again, never see my child grow up. Curse Germanicus for a clever bastard!' It had been the Roman general's idea to abduct his pregnant wife the previous spring.

Maelo's grip tightened. 'Their loss grieves me every day, Arminius, and I know that my pain is as nothing beside yours. Let sorrow and rage guide you, however, and we *will* fail. The chieftains need a steady leader, a single-minded man with clear purpose.'

Arminius sucked in a lungful of cold air and stared at the glittering stars above. Somewhere in Italy, Thusnelda could be holding our baby and looking at the same sky, he thought. Bleak as the knowledge was, it calmed him. They were not dead. Stay well, my love, he thought. Guard my child. I shall see you both again one day.

He exhaled and then smiled; it was not a pleasant expression. 'I shall bury my wound deep, and the chieftains will listen to my counsel. They will follow me.' He held up a hand, forestalling Maelo's next comment. 'Fear not. I will act as their fellow chieftain, not their leader or king. I shall be the first among equals.'

'The gods be thanked. Your wits have not deserted you, Arminius, nor your silver tongue,' said Maelo, his teeth flashing in the torchlight.

Arminius' eyes met Maelo's. 'Thank you.'

'Ho! Is that Arminius I see?' asked a familiar voice from the darkness. 'That must be Maelo with him.'

'Here we are. Show yourself,' called Arminius.

Snow crunched as the speaker drew nearer. He wasn't carrying a torch, so it wasn't until the light cast by Arminius' and Maelo's torches reached his face that his identity was revealed. Stocky, with plaited hair and a square-edged chin, he led the Angrivarii tribe. Often in agreement with

Arminius, he was brave, resourceful and shrewder than most. 'Well met,' said Horsa, holding out a meaty paw.

'Well met,' said Arminius, giving his hand a firm shake; Maelo stepped up and did the same. 'How was your journey?' asked Arminius. Horsa's tribe lived almost a hundred miles to the north.

'Long. Cold. Unpleasant. My arse still hurts from sitting on a horse, but I'm here.' Horsa's laugh was hearty. 'Mallovendus' lackeys promise me that there are six piglets roasting in his hall, and three times that number of barrels of good beer. Why aren't you already partaking?' He indicated the longhouse, which lay a short distance down the path.

Arminius wasn't about to share what they'd been talking about. 'We heard you lumbering along behind us, louder than a charging bull, and stopped to see who it was,' he jibed.

'Watch your mouth,' said Horsa, chuckling. If he noticed the neat deflection, he didn't say. 'No point standing outside, eh? Our balls will freeze solid.'

Reaching the longhouse first, Maelo flung wide the door. A blast of warm, fuggy air washed out, carrying with it smells – some appetising, some less so – and the noise of a great crowd. Music was playing within, and shouted conversations being held. Children were shrieking and laughing; an unhappy baby added its wail to the clamour; and from the animals' section of the building cattle were making gentle lowing sounds.

As was traditional, the family's living and sleeping area occupied one end of the longhouse; their livestock were penned at the other, alongside stacks of hay and stores of wheat and barley. Torches blazed from brackets on the walls, and huge fires in the cooking area belched out waves of heat and the delicious aroma of roasting pork. Throngs of men, women and children were packed into the central open space, in the middle of which was a long, oak-hewn table. A hole had been cut in its centre, propping up one of the gold eagles taken from Varus' legions. Majestic and awe-inspiring, it was a powerful symbol of what the tribes had done to Rome.

It was shrewd to place the eagle in open sight, thought Arminius in approval. No better proof, no greater example of our success exists.

Every seat around the table was taken by chieftains and the bravest warriors, and at its head sat Mallovendus, leader not just of the settlement but of the largest faction of the Marsi tribe. An ox of a man with coarse features and a mane of red hair, he was in the midst of an arm wrestle with one of his followers, a brute almost his size.

Arminius made straight for Mallovendus. They didn't always see eye to eye, but the Marsi chieftain was a stalwart enemy of Rome, and his warriors were valiant, stubborn fighters. Whether it was because of the eagle Arminius had gifted them or not, Germanicus had attacked the Marsi in great strength the previous autumn, killing thousands and laying numerous settlements to waste. The tribe had fought further battles with the Romans since, and lost. Burning for revenge, Mallovendus had agreed to hold the meeting, making Arminius sure that his men would stand with him come the spring. The Marsi weren't enough, though, even when added to Arminius' and Inguiomerus' warriors' strength. To crush Germanicus' enormous host, Arminius would need every spear for two hundred miles or more.

'Mallovendus!' he shouted.

The Marsi chieftain's head turned. In the same instant, he spun back with a curse, but it was too late. With an exultant cry, his opponent slammed Mallovendus' arm to the table top. 'Two wins to one,' he said, holding out his other hand.

'I was distracted,' Mallovendus protested.

'My money,' demanded the warrior.

Arminius watched as Mallovendus paid up with good grace. He had his health toasted by the delighted warrior, who then swaggered back to his friends. His place was taken at once by another man, and Mallovendus threw a half-apologetic, half-amused glance at Arminius. 'Give me a moment,' he yelled.

Arminius took up a stance beside one of the beer barrels with Maelo and Horsa. Cups in hand, they watched Mallovendus wrestling his new opponent.

'I wonder if his loss was deliberate,' muttered Arminius as Mallovendus wrenched the warrior's arm to the table.

Maelo smirked. 'As a way to keep his followers loyal?'

'It wouldn't be the first time a man had done such a thing,' said Horsa.

Arminius nodded. In every tribe up and down the land, warriors obeyed their leaders out of respect, not because of any gods-given right. Using subterfuge – such as letting a man win at arm-wrestling – was just another trick of the trade.

Mallovendus won the second contest with ease, and his opponent cursed him to heaven and hell. This was nothing unusual – Mallovendus gave back as good as he got, before clouting the warrior around the head and telling him to train harder if he ever wanted to beat his chieftain. Sheepish-faced, the warrior returned to his comrades, who rained good-natured abuse on him.

The scene epitomised the differences between his people and the Romans, thought Arminius. No legionary would dare to challenge his commanding officer to such a contest, let alone defeat him as the first warrior had done, and then claim his winnings in an aggressive tone. Given the order, however, every legionary would march to the ends of the earth, endure harsh conditions and fight any foe, day after day and month after month. The Romans were fearsome, relentless enemies, united in purpose and, as Germanicus' campaigns were proving, fond of revenge.

Arminius' fellow tribespeople were brave as wild boar and resilient fighters, but they were hot-headed and lacked the Romans' discipline. Nor did they appreciate being told what to do, even when it made sense. The situation was what it was, Arminius reflected grimly. There wasn't a thing to be done about it, other than to make the best of it, as he had done six years before.

Turning to Arminius, Mallovendus raised his cup.

'Greetings!' Arminius cried in a voice designed to carry. 'I thank you for inviting me to your home.'

'Welcome!' Mallovendus got to his feet. 'Maelo's with you, I see, and Horsa, the finest leader the Angrivarii have had these twenty years and more. Welcome, all of you.' Jerking his thumb at the warriors to either side of him, he bellowed, 'Make room! No guest of mine shall stand by my table.'

The four shook hands with one another, and then, prompted by their host, took their seats, Arminius in the most honoured place to Mallovendus' right, and Horsa to his left. Inguiomerus, a striking-looking man, was sitting on Arminius' right. Maelo took the space on Inguiomerus' other side, showing the others present their unity.'

Servants were quick to place slopping beakers of beer in front of the new arrivals. Prompted by Mallovendus, the chieftains toasted one another's health, and drank; wished victory for their warriors, and death to Germanicus and his soldiers, and drank again; asked the gods to lend their support, as they had in previous years with storms and heavy rain, and drank once more; remembered the glorious dead who had fallen fighting the Romans, and threw down a fourth cup.

That done, Mallovendus let out an enormous belch and slapped a palm on the table. 'Donar's beard, but it's good to see you, Arminius. You too,' he said to Horsa. 'You must both be ravenous. I know I am. Anyone else hungry?' Grinning at the loud cries of assent, Mallovendus cast around for a servant. 'Bring food! One of those piglets must be ready!'

Arminius noted that Horsa was already deep in conversation with the chieftain to his left, a cadaverous-faced man who led part of the Usipetes tribe. Arminius didn't like Gerulf. He was always first to counter Arminius' opinion, and first to propose alternative plans, often involving considerable risk to everyone involved. He never seemed to understand Arminius' vision: to end Rome's influence over the tribal lands forever through a second massive military defeat.

'—journey?'

Arminius' gaze returned to Mallovendus. 'Eh?'

'How was your journey?'

'As you'd expect. Long and tiring.'

'You didn't hear me the first time. Pissed already?'

'Of course not.'

'Good. I thought you might be going soft.' Mallovendus refilled Arminius' cup. 'Get that down you.'

Arminius made a pretence of swigging deep, but he only took a mouthful. It was fine beer, strong and earthy-tasting, but slaking his thirst this early would not be wise. There would be food and more drink and singing before the talking began. He wouldn't get to say his piece for hours, and there was too much at stake to risk being drunk when that time came.

'The priests are predicting that this winter will be the harshest for many a year,' said Mallovendus. He clouted Arminius on the back, spilling his beer. 'Mayhap you'll have to stay awhile!'

Gods, I hope not, thought Arminius. Difficult though travel was, this was the month he had set aside to journey the land, winning chieftains to his cause. His forces needed to be ready the moment spring arrived. 'I'd have plenty of time to practise my arm-wrestling skills,' he replied, pulling a smile. 'Your beer is excellent too.'

'You'd not be short of a bed companion,' said Mallovendus with a sly jerk of his head at a full-breasted, comely woman who was clearing cups from the table. 'She's had her eye on you since you came in – had you noticed?'

'I hadn't,' said Arminius, surprised to feel pleased. He hadn't lain with a woman since Thusnelda's abduction – hadn't wanted to, truth be told. His groin stirred, forcing him to acknowledge that the body's needs were different to the mind's. 'Who is she?'

'The widow of a good warrior who fell last summer. She's a strong character – knows what she wants, and doesn't ask for anything in return. I'd plough her myself, but' – Mallovendus indicated his wife, a plump woman with a pleasant face – '*her* eyes are keener than an eagle's. She'd know what I was up to before I'd even spilled my seed. Not only would she box my ears – I would never hear the end of it.'

'You've strayed from home before?'

Mallovendus leered. 'What man hasn't?'

'I haven't,' said Arminius in truth.

Mallovendus studied his face in surprise. 'How long were you with Thusnelda?'

'Two years.'

'You were still star-struck then. Spend ten summers with the same woman, or twelve, and throw in a brood of children, and your eye will begin to wander. It's the way of the world.'

'Maybe so,' said Arminius, staring at the table top.

Mallovendus poured him more beer. 'A terrible thing, losing your wife like that.'

'Aye.' Arminius damped down his grief, kept his tone neutral. 'But I'm not alone in having suffered. Your people's woes in the summer were grievous, and not a person in this room can have escaped without the loss of someone dear to them.'

'You speak true,' said Mallovendus, his expression dark.

'Discussing war on Rome is the only reason I am here,' Arminius declared, before throwing a look at the attractive widow. 'That's not to say I wouldn't welcome other activities once the talking is done.'

'You're a man after my own heart. First we'll eat and drink, then we will talk. Once we've hammered out the details, you can do some private hammering of your own,' said Mallovendus with a wink. They both laughed, and Arminius' gaze wandered again to the widow, who gave him a bold glance that appeared to promise much. 'See?' urged Mallovendus. 'Your luck's in tonight.' Pounding Arminius on the back, he went to drain his bladder.

Arminius' good humour faded as his eyes met those of Gerulf, whose nasal voice carried over the clamour. 'Worked out how you're going to lord it over us yet, Arminius?'

'That's not what I am here for,' said Arminius in a courteous tone. 'We are here to plan our war with Rome.'

'So you say,' scoffed Gerulf. 'But a man cannot change his character, no matter how much he tries. I know you, Arminius. You have wanted to rule the tribes from the start, and ever it will be so.'

'That's not true,' lied Arminius, and praying that Horsa, who was listening, paid no heed.

'Is it not?' Gerulf's tone was mocking.

'No,' protested Arminius, hating the Usipetes chieftain for seeing through him with such ease. While his primary aim was to defeat the Romans, he did also dream of kingship over the tribes. 'I am here because of Germanicus. He is a dangerous enemy with a vast army. If we do not unite to fight him, we will all be enslaved sooner or later.'

With a sardonic, knowing smile, Gerulf fell to talking with Horsa once more.

Arminius studied the depths of his cup, fresh worries scourging him.

Was his alliance doomed to fail before it had even been assembled?

Chapter IV

◰◰◰

Particles of stinging snow whipped into Tullus' face, making him squint. The cold was savage — already his armour was icy to the touch, the skin of his arms and lower legs numb — but he didn't have far to go, and he'd fight better without the hindrance of his cloak.

He kept careful count of his steps. Eight, and he still couldn't discern the entrance to the wine merchant's. A dozen, and Tullus made out the dark shape of a doorway, and a shape within it — his gut told him this was the warriors' sentry. There would only be one, he decided, because the tribesmen needed every advantage possible to overcome Germanicus' well-trained bodyguards. Gripping the staff as if he were a hobbling grey-beard and hoping that his armour would be concealed by the failing light and the snow, Tullus shuffled forward another three steps, then four, five, six.

'Be on your way!' cried the sentry in bad Latin.

Gods, it was Degmar, thought Tullus, whipping up the staff with both hands and darting forward with all his speed.

Degmar brought up his spear too slowly to prevent Tullus' staff taking him across the throat. The blade shot past Tullus' left ear with a nasty whoosh of air and then Degmar was pressed back against the wall, struggling to breathe. Wild-eyed, shocked to see Tullus, he struggled like a madman, soon dropping his spear in order to wrestle with the staff. Tullus pressed in with grim intent, aware that he had one chance. If Degmar broke free, he'd raise the alarm. Even if Tullus succeeded, time was of the essence.

Germanicus could already be dead. 'I thought you a better man than this, Degmar,' he hissed. 'Murdering a man while he buys wine?'

Degmar's lips writhed, and his purple tongue protruded a little further, but he couldn't answer.

Who am I to hurl insults? wondered Tullus. We attacked his village at dawn, the morning after a great feast. His people – the women and children in particular – didn't stand a chance. Incapable of looking at Degmar any longer, but compelled to continue what he was doing, Tullus found a hidden reserve of strength. He pushed harder and, after a few heartbeats, the warrior's eyes glazed, and then rolled upwards. His entire body went limp.

No matter how evil Degmar's intent, Tullus did not want to kill the Marsi warrior. Worried that he had done so, Tullus let him down easily. He felt an odd relief when a forefinger on Degmar's bruised neck revealed a strong pulse.

The fighting had begun – from inside came the sound of raised voices, the ring of weapons and cries of pain. A prayer to Fortuna that he wasn't too late slipped from Tullus' lips. What he'd have given to have Fenestela at his side – Piso and Metilius too. They're not here, Tullus told himself angrily. You are alone and outnumbered, and Germanicus needs you. Stay focused.

The first casualty was lying behind the counter in the shop, which fronted the business. A young, bearded man in rough-spun tunic and trousers, he lay on his back, a startled expression still on his face and a deep wound in his throat. Blood was pooling around him, saturating his clothes and filling the cracks between the floor tiles.

Poor bastard, thought Tullus, treading with light footsteps towards the half-open door, which led, he presumed, to storerooms and the merchant's living quarters. He peered around the frame. Amphorae lined the chamber's walls, laid on their sides in special frames, and protected with beds of straw. Others stood upright: small, medium, large and vast-sized ones. A table with two chairs sat in the room's centre, several jugs and a dozen beakers on it the evidence of a wine tasting. Oil lamps hanging from bronze stands provided plenty of light. The only occupants were four sprawled bodies – the merchant, Tullus opined, given his paunch and fine clothes, and also two Praetorians and a warrior.

Seven to three, he thought. Terrible odds.

He stole towards the door in the far wall, broom still in hand. It was no weapon, but its length meant he might be able to take down another warrior before the inevitable blade work. Plentiful crimson droplets on the floor told him that at least one man was wounded. Let it be a warrior, Tullus asked, wondering with increasing dread if he'd come too late. Entering a passageway, he counted seven doorways, three to either side, with the last at the end. Another corpse, that of a warrior, was curled up ten paces in. Seeing no blood trail beyond him, Tullus deduced that he had been the bleeder. Six to three now – still poor odds, he thought. The noise of fighting, now much louder, appeared to be coming from the far end of the passage. The nearest two doors to Tullus were shut and, trusting that there was no one behind them, he hurried down the corridor. More closed doors – the next two – left him with a choice of three. All were open, and he could not yet discern if any were occupied.

'Degmar! Get Degmar!' someone shouted in German from the chamber at the passage's end. The sound of approaching footsteps followed.

Tullus broke into a soft-footed run. It was probable that all the warriors were together – he had to hope so. To maintain the element of surprise, he *had* to get past the open doors and reach the final doorway first. Youth wasn't on his side, and he prayed that he was closer than whoever was coming to fetch Degmar. Ten steps, then fifteen and a score, and Tullus was alongside the part-open door, standing on the hinge side. Fast and quiet as he could, he balanced the staff against the wall and slid his sword free.

'GET DEGMAR!'

'I'm going, I'm going,' grumbled another voice just on the other side of the planking.

Holding his breath, Tullus raised his blade to shoulder height, its point forward.

Hinges creaked, the door opened wide, and a stocky, yellow-haired warrior emerged into the corridor. Sensing someone at the edge of his vision, he turned. Tullus' sword rammed in and out of his throat, and he died. Tullus grabbed the man by his shirt and lowered him to the floor even as he slid off the sharp steel. Blood gouted all over the bottom of Tullus' mail and tunic, and his legs. Five to three, he thought. No – five to four, including me. His pleasure at the narrowing of the odds was brief. His numbers were theoretical, and it was likely that more of Germanicus' bodyguards were dead.

The truth of that revealed itself as Tullus sneaked a look into the next chamber. A Praetorian was stretched out nearby, multiple stab wounds to the neck and groin his cause of expiry. Five to three again, calculated Tullus with fresh concern. The dim-lit storeroom was filled with stacked amphorae. Maker's marks had been etched or stamped into their necks – the nearest ones to Tullus were from a part of Iberia famous for its smooth-tasting reds. Play this right, and he might survive to drink some again one day. Don't be a fool, he thought. Like as not, he'd soon be bleeding out over the tiles, like the Praetorian.

No one was visible in the chamber's gloomy central passage. Blade met blade a short distance away; Germanicus barked an order. A man cried out in pain, and another shouted in triumph. Tullus' sense of urgency soared. Broom in one hand, scarlet-tipped sword in the other, he entered the room. Narrow 'corridors' had been left on either side to allow access to amphorae piled further in. Each one was a ready-made defensible position where a pair of men could stand abreast, fighting a maximum of two enemies. Hope flared in Tullus' heart as he glanced to either side, seeking Germanicus and his assailants.

Tullus found them in the third corridor. Two warriors with their backs to him were attacking Germanicus and a Praetorian. A few paces nearer Tullus, a third warrior was propped, pale-faced, against an amphora. A sword cut to the meat of his right thigh had taken him out of the battle. Tullus didn't have time to worry where the fourth and fifth men were, or if the injured tribesman saw him. There was blood on Germanicus' face, and the Praetorian was wounded. Laying his staff against an amphora, for it would be no use now, Tullus tiptoed towards the mêlée.

He was halfway down the corridor when the hurt warrior's head turned, and two-thirds down it when the man bellowed an alarm. His cry came to an abrupt halt as Tullus' sword slid between his ribs. One of his companions glanced around at the commotion, and died in the same moment, as Germanicus took *his* chance. The second was a smarter individual, and his Praetorian opponent had also been distracted, allowing the warrior to stab him in the groin, between the strips of his leather skirt. Even as the Praetorian went down screaming, the warrior spun his weapon one-handed and thrust it at Germanicus. The blade screeched off the general's breastplate, gouging a deep line in the polished bronze.

Germanicus' sword had caught in his last opponent's flesh and he was struggling to free it as the warrior drew back for another strike. Tullus darted forward and plunged his blade deep into the warrior's back. A cry of agony rent the air and Tullus raised his boot to the man's arse, shoving him away, on to his knees. A precise stab to the back of the neck and it was over.

'Tullus? How in the all the gods' names?' Germanicus let out an incredulous, wild laugh. Sweat ran down his face, mixing with the blood, which was from a flesh wound to one cheek. He didn't appear to be otherwise hurt. 'Were you trailing me?'

'No, sir.' Tullus was still panting with effort. 'I was in . . .' Managing to swallow the words 'a jeweller's', he continued, '. . . a shop on the same street, and I saw you pass by. Moments later, the warriors came past. It was clear that they were after you. I followed, but only then.'

'We might have managed,' said Germanicus, indicating the prone, bleeding figure of his last Praetorian behind him, 'but I am doubtful. Once again, my decision to ignore your presence at Tiberius' triumph seems well placed.'

Three years before, Tullus and Fenestela had broken the imperial ban on survivors of Arminius' ambush travelling to Rome. Spotted and interrogated by Germanicus, their lives had been forfeit. Yet the general had seen something in Tullus, and been merciful. 'I came in here because of what happened that day, sir,' said Tullus.

'I'm glad you did,' replied Germanicus with feeling. 'Now, where do you think the other two whoresons have got to?'

Clay ground off clay, a loud, grating sound close by.

Confused, Germanicus turned. Tullus also spun, staring with suspicion at the amphorae to their right. Before he'd quite realised what was happening, one began to topple; it was followed by a second and a third. Fear flared in his belly. Any one vessel had the weight and power to crush a man's spine; more could kill. Dropping his left shoulder and wrapping his arm around a startled Germanicus, Tullus drove them towards the prone Praetorian and the room's side wall. With a mighty crash, three amphorae fell into the corridor, pushed over by the remaining warriors. There was a moment's shocked silence as the two parties stared at each other through the gap, and then one warrior made to hurl his spear at Germanicus.

Again Tullus manhandled the general, dragging him to the floor and the protection granted by the amphorae that were still standing. Air moved as the spear shot by; sparks flew as it struck a vessel to their rear and fell to the tiles, its energy spent. Tullus was about to reach for it when footsteps shuffled in the other corridor, and he stopped dead, his heart thumping. Would the warriors clamber over to attack, or try and knock over more of the massive amphorae? The latter choice was safer, and therefore more probable, he decided, but two could play at that game. He placed his lips against Germanicus' ear, and miming pushing, whispered, 'Help me, sir.'

Germanicus gave him a grim nod of assent, and together they stood. Tullus laid down his sword. Close up against the rows of vessels, they could not be seen by the warriors, who appeared to have stopped moving. Their purpose became clear as the amphora nearest Tullus wobbled a little. 'This one, sir,' he hissed, planting his hands on it and bracing himself. Germanicus stepped in alongside and did the same.

'On my count, sir,' said Tullus, urgency throbbing in his voice. 'One, two, three!'

They shoved in unison, fear giving them extra strength. There was no counter-thrust, Tullus thought afterwards, which meant that they must have acted a heartbeat before their enemies. Grinding off the vessels to either side, the amphora leaned and then fell away from them, taking another one with it. They struck the floor with a crash like thunder. Dust rose, and an agonised screaming began, similar to a rabbit caught in a snare.

'We got one, sir.' Tullus was grinning as he picked up the spear cast at them a moment before. A quick glance into the gap between the corridors revealed a frightened, bearded face. Even at close range Tullus was no spearman, so he yelled, 'Come on, you dog!'

The last of the warrior's resolve crumbled, and he was gone, his boots slapping off the floor.

Germanicus let out a long sigh, but Tullus didn't let down his guard. It would be stupid to die because he had miscounted their foes. 'Stay there if you would, sir,' he muttered. Germanicus began to protest, and Tullus said, in a tone that brooked no argument, 'They might not all be gone, sir.' Exchanging the spear for his sword, he leaned into the space left by the fallen amphorae. A warrior – the screaming-rabbit one – stared wide-eyed up at him from underneath the vessel pinning him to the floor.

He was going nowhere, thought Tullus. With luck, he'd last long enough to be interrogated. Returning his attention to the corridor, Tullus paced towards the central passage nice and slow, his blade ready. An odd excitement filled him now – fear was yet part of it, but there was a joy thrumming in his veins too, the mad joy that comes upon a man when he has stared death in the eyes close up, and lived to tell the tale.

You're in a good mood today, Fortuna, you old bitch, he thought. Most would have considered him insane to bait a goddess so – Tullus often called her filthy names in his head, and sometimes aloud – but he found it amusing. Truth be told, he wasn't sure if she was even real – not once in his life had he seen incontrovertible proof that she was anything other than a concept, a way to explain life's random nature. The same principle applied to all the deities, if he thought on it, but calling into question their existence was also not something that Tullus was prepared to do, even in his mind. Some of them must be up there in the clouds, he decided. Fortuna, Mars and Jupiter at the least. How else could I have made it through so many fucking battles?

He reached the central passage and peered to either side. Relief swamped him to see no one living. An open door off to his left, at the building's rear, seemed to signify that the last warrior had made his escape. With such a head start, he wouldn't be caught, but that wasn't the end of the world. Germanicus was unharmed, and there was a prisoner to interrogate. Two, Tullus realised with a pang. Degmar was lying outside. What had the poor fool been thinking to be part of such a madcap mission? The answer was simple, Tullus decided. Degmar's wife and babe were dead, and his family furious with him for 'collaborating' with the Romans. Life back with his tribe would not have been the idyll he'd imagined during his captivity.

'Drop your blade!'

Tullus' head turned in surprise. Two legionaries with drawn swords had entered from the doorway that led to the shop. Their flushed faces and unsteady gait told him where the pair had been before the jeweller had found them. Despite their drunkenness, their arrival meant the fight was over. Tullus threw back his head and laughed. 'I'm no German warrior!'

'Filth!' shouted one, advancing with his comrade at his side. 'Threaten our general, would you?'

'Look again,' barked Tullus in his parade-ground voice.

The first soldier blinked; his companion recognised Tullus, and his face paled. 'It's Tullus,' he said in a drunken stage whisper, adding with grave ponderousness, 'the hero of the Saltus T-T-Teutoburgiensis.' He attempted to come to attention and, swaying to and fro, he saluted.

The first soldier tried to copy his mate, but was so pissed that he had to brace himself against an amphora. Giving up on standing straight, he also saluted.

'Sincere apologies, sir,' said the second legionary, who appeared a little more sober. 'We came as fast as we could, me and my comrade. The merchant – the old man with a silver beard – told us to come with all haste, that Germanicus' life was in danger. More men are coming, I think, sir, but we got here first. No point waiting for reinforcements, I said. Germanicus needs us. So in we came. And here we are, sir,' he finished, looking self-conscious and more than a little woebegone. Threatening a senior officer – when drunk or not – merited severe punishment.

'You did well,' said Tullus, hiding his smile.

The pair gave each other an uncertain look. 'Sir?' asked the first.

'You were the quickest men here, and ready to risk your lives for your general. Germanicus is safe, in part thanks to you. Give me your names and units, and I'll see that you're rewarded.'

The two exchanged another glance, astonishment mixed with sheer delight. 'Thank you, sir!' they chorused.

Tullus took their names and centuries – he was pleased to find that they were both from the Fifth, his legion – and ordered them to go and tie up Degmar. Their blank expressions didn't surprise Tullus that much. He sighed and said, 'Let me guess. There *is* no warrior lying outside.'

'I'm drunk, but I'm not blind, sir,' said the soberer legionary. 'The first person we saw was the dead shop attendant, behind the counter.'

'He has the right of it, sir. There was no one outside,' added his companion. 'On our lives.'

'The whoreson escaped,' muttered Tullus. Degmar's life was forfeit for being part of the assassination attempt, and yet a small part of Tullus was relieved that he'd got away. Degmar deserved to die for what he had done, but not through torture, the probable fate of the man trapped by the amphora.

Ordering the two legionaries to search for any warriors who might yet be skulking in the shadows, Tullus went to find Germanicus.

To his amusement, the general had broken the seal on one of the toppled amphorae and was supping wine from his upturned helmet. 'Nothing like a brush with death to whet a man's thirst,' Germanicus said. 'Care for a drop?'

'Thank you, sir.' Unease niggled at Tullus even as he drank.

The River Rhenus, assumed by all to provide protection from attack, could no longer be relied on.

The tribes were as dangerous as ever – perhaps more so than before.

Chapter V

ⱤⱤⱤ

S everal hours passed in enjoyable fashion. The roasted piglets laid on
by Mallovendus were succulent and delicious, and Arminius would
have continued eating if his bulging stomach had allowed it. Demand
for the beer was high, yet it continued to flow in abundance and, in direct
consequence, the mood in the longhouse grew riotous. As men grew drunker,
it was inevitable that brawls should erupt. A sulky peace was restored after
Mallovendus threatened to castrate the next warrior to pick a fight.

There was storytelling, music and dancing – Arminius had even taken to
the floor once with the widow, cheered on by Mallovendus and the other
chieftains. The celebrations quietened a little as men fell asleep or staggered
back to their own houses. With the tables cleared, the children put to bed
and the women gathered in a gaggle by one of the fires, the time had come
for the chieftains to talk. Mallovendus had again gone to answer a call of
nature, but on his return, the council would begin.

Arminius was pissed. Not badly so, but his determination to abstain had
faltered in the face of Gerulf's barbed comments, and the pointed glances
he had aimed at Arminius throughout the evening. He had managed not to
react, but his thirst had become overwhelming, and he'd ignored Maelo's
attempts to make him slow down. It didn't matter, Arminius decided, full of
newfound confidence. A dozen cups of beer couldn't prevent him from
saying what needed to be said. His words would fall like seeds on fertile
ground. The chieftains – more than a score of them, from eight different
tribes – would not have travelled here in the depths of winter if they didn't

want to fight Rome, under his command. Gerulf would not stop him, and if he tried, Arminius would put him in his place.

'Happy with yourself?' Maelo's disapproving voice was in his ear.

Arminius twisted his head, furious. 'I am.'

'You shouldn't be. You're drunk. You also look as if you've swallowed a mouthful of sour milk.' Maelo's gaze flickered to their left, to Gerulf, and back again. 'It's him has you like this, isn't it? The prick has been staring at you all night.'

'You are sharp-eyed,' admitted Arminius with a rueful smile. 'It's an attempt to anger me before we begin talking, and it's worked, curse him.'

'You're not the only one who's drunk,' warned Maelo. 'Tempers are quick to rise when men have bellies full of beer. Gerulf will keep needling you. He'll tell them that you want to be the first emperor of the tribes or some such. Take his bait, and you risk losing everything.'

The idea made Arminius' rage bubble up, red hot, and he clenched his fists under the table. 'Why can't he see? United, we can defeat the Romans, but each tribe alone will be crushed beneath the Roman heel. It's no simple task either – Germanicus' army is far too big for that. *I* am the best candidate for leader. I am the one with years of experience of the enemy war machine. The ambush six years ago was my idea. Three legions were annihilated, and Varus committed suicide – because of me. *I* did all of it – not Mallovendus, Inguiomerus, Gerulf or any of the other fools at this table.'

'Listen to me, Arminius of the Cherusci,' said Maelo, taking his wrist in a grip of steel.

'I—'

'Shut your mouth,' hissed Maelo, cutting him off.

Shocked – even Maelo never spoke like this to him – Arminius obeyed.

'If the noise wasn't deafening, and everyone wasn't drunk, you would have just destroyed your alliance. It's rash to speak of fools when they're sitting all around.' Maelo's face was right in Arminius' now. 'Do I have to take you outside and shove your head in the snow for you to see sense? These men are here of their own volition, not because they are beholden to you. They too wish to destroy Germanicus' legions, and see our lands free of Rome's sway forever. Coax them with the right words, and they'll follow you like oxen after a bucket of grain. Insult them, act like their superior, and they'll leave without promising you a thing. Overnight, your army will shrink to just our faction of the Cherusci.'

'Inguiomerus—' began Arminius.

Maelo let out a *phhhh* of contempt. 'Blood relation or no, he won't throw his lot in with you if none of the others will. He's arrogant, but he isn't stupid.' Maelo's voice was boiling with fury now. 'Alone, we *will* be crushed by Germanicus, so you have to smile at Gerulf's jibes and turn his words against him. Make him the one whom the others doubt. Can you do that, Arminius?'

Shocked into clear-headedness, but also embarrassed, Arminius lashed out. 'What will you do if I fail? Will you leave me too?'

Maelo gave him a withering look. 'I have been your sworn man for more years than I can remember. My place is by your side until the end, wherever and whenever that may be. That said, I would rather my death be glorious than stupid. Our warriors are the best fighters in the land, but they cannot beat the Romans on their own. Think on that ere you speak to the chieftains.' He sat back, breathing hard.

Arminius digested Maelo's advice in silence while around them the merriment continued. Dice games were being played by those still sober enough to count; others were holding contests to see who could down the most beer. Some men were trying to stand on their heads and drain a cup at the same time. Much hilarity ensued as attempt after attempt failed. Different groups of warriors were competing against one another in singing the sonorous tribal war chant known to the Romans as the *barritus*. Out of tune, but as loud as during a battle, their voices rose to the rafters in a tremendous, deep-throated wave of sound.

'Well?' demanded Maelo.

Arminius scowled. He wanted to smash in every one of Maelo's pointed brown teeth. To do so would be the act of a fool, however. It was probable he would fail – Maelo was soberer than he – but it would also look bad, and damage his chances of winning over the chieftains. Worst of all, he admitted to himself, Maelo was correct. About everything. Curse my pride, Arminius thought, the familiar bitterness flowing through his veins. It ever threatens to be my downfall. His gaze met Maelo's again. 'You're right.'

The deep line marking Maelo's brow eased; there was even a hint of a smile. 'You couldn't bear the thought of being face down in a pile of snow – that was what made you see sense, wasn't it?'

'Piss off, you dog.' Arminius elbowed Maelo – hard. 'As if you could drag me outside and do that.'

'I can do it and more,' Maelo mock threatened, throwing an arm around Arminius' shoulders and pretending to heave him to his feet.

'I leave you two for a moment and you're grappling like beardless boys!' boomed Mallovendus. 'Who's got the upper hand?'

'I do,' replied Arminius and Maelo in unison, grinning.

'Fighting words, both!' said Mallovendus, amused. 'While I'd like to see such a contest some time, more pressing matters must come first.'

'Aye.' Arminius stepped away from Maelo and smoothed down his rumpled tunic. 'I'm ready.'

'I shall speak first. You'll be next, and we'll be able to see how the chieftains like what you have to say.' Mallovendus gestured to the nearest servants to fill every cup, and when that was done, he pounded a fist on the table. Heads turned. A few faces were guarded, or hostile, chief among them Gerulf, but most were open and expectant.

Stay calm. Get the better of Gerulf, Arminius told himself, and they'll join me. He shot a look at Gerulf, who smirked. Arminius' stomach began to churn, and his palms to sweat. He was relieved when Mallovendus began to talk, and even more so as his feelings were made plain. After welcoming the chieftains to his home, he laid out a vivid and horrific picture of what had befallen so many Marsi settlements during the summer. He placed all the blame at Germanicus' and Tiberius' feet.

To wait more than five years before taking revenge for the tribes' ambush on Varus was, Mallovendus said, the mark of ruthless, vengeful enemies. Men whose blood ran ice cold. How else was it possible, he shouted, for their cursed legionaries to kill every living thing they found?

The chieftains, including Gerulf, bellowed their anger, and Arminius' hopes of success rose.

'Men, women, children. The old, the sick. Even the infants in their cots were slain,' Mallovendus cried, spittle flying from his lips. 'The livestock didn't escape either, oh no! The whoresons killed every beast they could find, from the hunting dogs and horses, the oxen and sheep, right down to the last hen. What kind of enemy does this not just to one tribe, but to them all? We cannot let these atrocities go unanswered. Rome must pay – in blood!'

A thunderous roar went up. Arminius pictured Thusnelda, and their child, whom he had never held. You will pay, Germanicus, he thought, the rage thrumming through him. One way or another.

'Not content to wait until the spring,' Mallovendus revealed, 'I sent a group of my bravest warriors to Vetera of recent days, their task to assassinate Germanicus.'

Stunned, Arminius stared at Mallovendus, who winked at him as if to say, 'Didn't expect that, did you?' Maelo *was* right, thought Arminius again. To underestimate the chieftains was both foolish and dangerous.

'The attack failed, but that will not stop us,' Mallovendus announced. 'We will meet their legions when they cross the river, and wipe them out!'

'KILL!' yelled Horsa, battering the table. 'KILL!'

The cry was taken up by everyone in the longhouse. Even the women, and the children who were still awake, joined in. Arminius mimed the word, but he was studying the chieftains' faces. Most were on his side, he decided. It was up to him to win over the rest.

Mallovendus let the uproar continue for the space of thirty heartbeats before he raised his hands for calm. 'We are of one mind, and that is good. But brave hearts and ready spears cannot defeat Rome's legions on their own. We know how to defeat them, for we have done it before!' Mallovendus pointed a thick finger at chieftain after chieftain, until he had indicated most of those present, and every man who had helped Arminius to wipe out Varus' army. 'Through cunning and guile, stealth and bravery, we slaughtered three legions, and took their eagles. We sacrificed their senior officers to the thunder god Donar, and nailed the legionaries' heads to trees so that no one could mistake what had happened there.'

Again the chieftains voiced their loud approval.

'You have come to share counsel, and we will hear your words by the evening's end. Next, though, I wish Arminius of the Cherusci to speak. He is known to all of you, and needs no introduction, for it was he who banded us together before. He whose idea it was to lead Varus' legions off the paved roads, and into our well-laid trap. I am your host, but it is thanks to one man that we are here.' Showing real respect, Mallovendus dipped his head towards Arminius.

Pleased by the plentiful growls and mutters of agreement, Arminius stood. 'I thank you, Mallovendus, for your fine hospitality and heart-stirring words, and for your plan to slay Germanicus. I'm grateful to every one of you for travelling far from your homes to gather with us tonight.' He paused, and was gratified by the silence which followed. Gerulf's expression was disapproving, but Arminius didn't falter. This was his moment; he had been preparing for it for months.

Taking a deep breath, he began.

The chieftains listened, stony-faced, as he told them of Rome's plans to subjugate every tribe from the Rhenus to the Albis and beyond. They shouted abuse at the notion of imperial taxes for one and all, and cheered when he told them again, blow by blow, how they had helped to massacre Varus and his army. Arminius spoke of the summer's indecisive campaign as an opportunity missed, and he was careful to blame no one individual for their final, failed attack which had seen so many warriors slain. Now, he urged, the passion throbbing in his voice, was the time to unite once more. To stand together against the monster that was Rome.

Almost every face was captivated. Almost every chieftain was sitting forward on the edge of his seat. The time was ripe, Arminius decided. 'Shall we crush the legions again?' he asked.

'YES!' they bellowed.

'Shall we remove the legionaries' hobnailed sandals from our people's necks, and the emperor's thieving fingers from our purses?'

'YES!'

'Will our people live free forever more?'

'YESSSS!' Baying like wolves, the chieftains rose to their feet. Carried away by the moment, one Chatti chief jumped up on the table and grabbed the eagle, brandishing it aloft to the loud acclaim of his fellows.

I've done it, thought Arminius in triumph, even as he shook a fist in the air with the rest. They will fight with me. He threw a look at Gerulf, and was delighted when the man didn't meet his eye. Do your worst, thought Arminius. I am the better orator by far.

The clamour took an age to die down, but that was good. His hardest task was done; what remained, the time-consuming matter of organising their campaign, would be easy in comparison.

'The finest speech I've heard in years,' Mallovendus declared, pouring them both a large measure of beer. He clinked his cup against Arminius'. 'To victory, and Germanicus' death.'

Arminius repeated his words, and drank.

'That was well done,' said Maelo in his ear.

'No need to shove my head in the snow then?' countered Arminius.

'I'll let you off this time.'

Grinning, they saluted one another and finished their beer.

The noise began to settle as the hoarse-throated chieftains took their seats and replenished their drinks. Many a cup was raised in Arminius' direction; the questions about what they should do to counter the Romans also began to fall.

'You'll be answered soon,' said Arminius with calm authority. 'First, I would know how many spears each tribe can bring to our army.'

'*You* would know? At last your cloak falls away to reveal your true colours,' crowed Gerulf.

'What in Donar's name are you talking about?' demanded Arminius.

'All you want from us is our warriors and their spears,' accused Gerulf. 'If you could take them without us, you'd be a happy man, isn't that right?'

My life would be much easier for it, Arminius admitted to himself. Out loud, he said, 'It would be impossible for me to succeed alone. Your leadership, your bravery and your initiative are vital. They are what will help us to win this war.'

'Us?' jibed Gerulf. 'Don't you mean "me"?'

'Speak more plainly,' snapped Arminius, realising it had been short-sighted to think that Gerulf would give in without a struggle.

'You make a good case for fighting the Romans, I'll give you that. What's not so clear is why *you* should lead this enterprise,' said Gerulf. He paused, then added, 'Or are you planning for one of us to be in charge?'

Wrong-footed, Arminius faltered. 'I hadn't thought about it.'

'Come now. Do you expect us to believe that?' mocked Gerulf.

'My tribe brings the greatest number of warriors to the fight,' said Arminius, trying to regain control. 'When you add my uncle's men, the Cherusci will make up almost half the army, like as not.' He glanced at Inguiomerus, praying for his backing, and was pleased by his uncle's considered nod. 'Inguiomerus takes my counsel, and I had thought as the leader of the largest grouping, I—'

'There you have it,' cried Gerulf, interrupting. 'From his own mouth you heard it!'

Arminius' temper flared. 'Have you taken leave of your senses?'

'Far from it, Arminius,' replied Gerulf with a sly look. Letting his eyes wander from chieftain to chieftain, he sneered, 'Was there ever to be a debate about who commands us in this venture, in which many of us might lose our lives, or were we going to follow him like sheep? What gives this silver-tongued weasel the right to lead us? Have I forgotten a vote-casting, in which we elected him to take charge?'

'There has been no vote,' said a jowly-jawed Tencteri chieftain with clear resentment.

'Aye,' muttered a few discontented voices.

'Why ever not?' demanded Gerulf. 'Who's to say that you' – here he pointed at Mallovendus – 'or you' – and now he indicated Horsa – 'couldn't do just as good a job?'

'I could lead the army,' declared the Tencteri chieftain.

'And I!' cried several others.

'I too could do it,' said Gerulf, puffing out his chest. 'Let us put it to a vote. That will be the fairest way.'

Donar take him, thought Arminius with rising fury. The whole thing's going to hell now. Half a dozen of the fools will challenge my right to command. If my luck holds, I'll come out on top, but the bad atmosphere created will divide the alliance. Everyone who stood but didn't win will feel wronged. Images of chieftains arguing over battle tactics, or worse still, leaving with their warriors at a pivotal moment, filled his mind. I cannot let that happen. I will not, Arminius decided, even if I have to gamble everything. Standing, he beat his cup on the table.

A surprised silence fell.

'Vote if you wish. Pick your leader,' Arminius declared. 'You are your own masters, but I have no wish to quarrel with you, like children. Nor does my uncle. Our warriors will stay under our command.' A quick look was enough to see that Inguiomerus remained of a mind with him, and Arminius took heart. His tactic might yet work.

Chaos erupted. Angry shouts filled the air. 'Come now, Arminius,' roared Mallovendus, purple-faced. 'You must stand with us!'

'Will you let us fight the Romans on our own?' Gerulf's voice was furious.

'I will not be part of this madness, no, but you may act as you will. Choose a man to lead you. Fight, or sue for peace. Maybe even abandon your tribal lands as some have done and travel east, beyond Rome's reach.' Arminius cast around, staring at each chieftain. 'Voting for a leader might seem fairer, but it will *not* give you the man who can crush the Romans once and for all.'

No one spoke for one heartbeat, two, and, desperate to keep the initiative, Arminius leaped to the attack again. He jabbed a forefinger at Gerulf. 'Can you devise and execute a plan that will defeat eighty thousand Roman soldiers?'

Gerulf's mouth opened, but no sound came out.

'I thought not!' shouted Arminius. 'We'd follow *you* to a glorious death.' He rounded on Mallovendus. 'Are you the man to command our warriors, the man who'll defeat Germanicus' host?'

'I would do my best,' replied Mallovendus, bristling.

'Your *best*? That's not good enough, and never will be,' derided Arminius. 'Against that many Romans we need more than someone's best! We deserve a man with a plan that will work. A plan that will see Germanicus' army wiped from the face of the earth, or as near as. Who of you will take that weighty burden on his shoulders?'

'Not I,' admitted Horsa with a shake of his head. 'You can be an arrogant whoreson, Arminius, but you are a natural leader, and a fine tactician. You think it can be done?'

'I *know* it,' cried Arminius, encouraged by Horsa's reluctant approval. 'If we deliver such a crushing blow, I swear to you that the empire will leave us in peace – forever.'

The chieftains began talking among themselves. Sitting down, Arminius left them to it. 'Fine words, well said,' Inguiomerus mouthed from his seat.

'A risky strategy,' whispered Maelo, but his eyes were shining. 'They'll have to follow you now – you've given them no option. Even the most bull-headed among them knows the only decent general here is you.' He jerked his head to the side. 'Gerulf won't forgive you in a hurry, though.'

Arminius glanced sidelong at Gerulf, whose frowning, pinched expression couldn't have been missed by a blind man. Thwarted, he's going to be even more of a ball ache from now on, Arminius realised, coming to a sudden, drastic decision. Leaning close to Maelo, he said, 'Next time the dog goes for a leak, follow him. Kill him outside.'

Maelo's arched eyebrows were his only comment.

'It has to look accidental.'

'Leave it to me.'

Satisfied, Arminius sat back. Gerulf would soon be removed from the equation, but an election to choose a war leader remained a distinct possibility.

Arminius twitched with impatience as they conferred. With a show of nonchalance, he picked up a pair of discarded dice. To his surprise, he kept rolling fives and sixes.

After a time, Mallovendus was the one to put him out of his misery. 'We have come to a decision,' he announced.

Arminius' stomach knotted itself, and he set down the dice. 'I see.'

'The victory you described – you will lead us to it?' Mallovendus' voice was gruff.

'I will,' swore Arminius with utter conviction. 'I have done it before – most of you have witnessed the proof of that with your own eyes. With your help, and your warriors, I will do it again, but we have to be united! Are you with me?'

'Aye,' growled Mallovendus. 'We are.'

'You'll let me decide when and where to fight?'

'We will,' said Mallovendus in a grudging tone.

'Aye,' said Horsa, the set of his jaw evidence that he wasn't entirely happy. The others' 'Ayes' were also muted, but all the chieftains met Arminius' eyes – except Gerulf.

'My warriors will fight,' he announced, 'but if I don't like your plan, Arminius, I will take them back to our settlements.'

'Very well,' snapped Arminius. 'But do not expect to be given much in the way of responsibility come the spring.' Clambering on to the table, he snatched up the eagle and turned in a circle so that all might witness its glittering majesty at close quarters. 'Together, we will vanquish Rome's legions. Together, we will capture not just three of these, but half a dozen!'

The chieftains cheered then, loud and lusty, and Arminius gave fervent thanks to Donar. Most of the time, it was impossible to tell if the thunder god had any interest in the affairs of men, but on occasions like this, when Arminius had fought against the odds and emerged victorious, it felt as if he had divine approval.

Shoving his chair back, Gerulf muttered something under his breath as he made for the door. Few noticed him leave bar Arminius and his second-in-command; Maelo waited a dozen heartbeats before he too slipped away.

'Tell us your plan,' invited Mallovendus, pouring more beer for Arminius.

'Wait.' Arminius threw back the contents of his cup and held it out for a refill. 'It's thirsty work persuading you bastards to fight.'

The belly laughs and embarrassed looks that broke out following this risky comment filled Arminius with a dark delight. Gerulf had almost sunk his efforts, but *he* had triumphed in the end. The chieftains would follow his lead, to victory, and Gerulf's voice would never trouble him again.

The night had been a good one, Arminius thought. Catching the widow's eye, he smiled. It wasn't over yet.

Chapter VI

Months had passed, and in the Roman camp of Vetera, the bitter weather was becoming a distant memory. Spring was here at last, bringing with it more pleasant temperatures. Birds trilled their joy from the new-leafed trees and buds bloomed on every plant. It was late afternoon, but bright sunlight continued to stream through the windblown breaks in the cloud. A short distance downhill from the massive fort, legionary Marcus Piso was wandering the riverbank.

A tall, gangling man with spiky black hair, he had been in Tullus' original century in the Eighteenth, and a newish recruit at the time their legion had been wiped out. Piso was a wiser, tougher man now, and devoted to Tullus. Beside him strode Metilius, his friend and comrade, and another of Tullus' old soldiers. They were off duty and on the hunt for some fish. Neither felt the urge to throw a line in the water, but there were enough legionaries doing so for trade or purchase to be possible. The rich variety of fish in the Rhenus ensured that catching them was a popular off-duty pastime. Some enterprising individuals also netted water birds – duck, crane, snipe and, in the winter, goose. Beaver meat was available on occasion too, although it was expensive.

Fish wasn't Piso's favourite food – that was lamb – but it was more appetising than wheat porridge, which was all that was on offer today in the barrack room he shared with Metilius and four others. Theirs wasn't a full-strength eight-man *contubernium*, or tent group, but last summer's brutal campaign ensured their situation was far from unique. Piso had let slip his opinion of the evening's proposed menu during their training some hours before, and the nominated cook for the day, a jovial, red-cheeked soldier called Dulcius, had not been impressed. 'Boring, is it?' he'd growled. 'You cook then, or provide something tastier!'

And so it was that Piso found himself strolling the water's edge with Metilius. He'd pay for whatever fish they decided upon, and Dulcius would do the rest upon their return. It was a good trade-off, thought Piso with a glance at Metilius. 'Nice to be outside the walls and *not* in the settlement, eh?'

'Aye. Even I can grow tired of taverns and inns, inns and taverns,' replied Metilius. 'Whorehouses now – they're a different matter. I'd visit one of those every day, if I could but afford it.'

Piso chuckled. He too patronised the settlement's brothels, but not with the same frequency as Metilius, whose slight build, innocuous expression and dimpled cheeks gave the lie to his massive sexual appetite. 'You'd have more money to spend if you were good at dice. I've offered to teach you before—'

Metilius cut him off. 'I've no head for gaming or wagers – you know me when it comes to gauging the odds.'

Piso shrugged. 'If you change your mind, just ask.'

'That'll never happen,' said Metilius, giving him a nudge.

Piso shoved back, glad of Metilius' presence. His previous best friend had been Vitellius, another of Tullus' old soldiers, but he had been slain in the previous year's campaign. It had been a stupid, unnecessary way to die, brooded Piso, just as that of another good comrade, Saxa, had been unfortunate. Since their deaths, the bond between him and Metilius and the rest of their tent group had strengthened further. It would soon be tested, for the massive army gathering outside the camp's northern wall was almost ready to cross the river.

'Ho, brother,' called Piso, addressing a balding soldier with a full wicker basket by his side. 'You've been busy.'

Baldy didn't take his eyes off his fishing line. 'An *as* for the tench and carp, and the same for the catfish. The bream are bigger – they're two *asses* each. The big bastard of a pike will cost you a *sestertius*. He took an age to haul in.'

Using the hazel twig he'd brought to carry his purchases, Piso poked through Baldy's catch. 'What do you fancy?' he asked Metilius.

'I'm not cooking, so I don't care,' said Metilius in a cheerful tone. 'Not the catfish, though. They taste like mud.'

'Bottom-dwellers are all the same,' agreed Piso. He eyed Baldy. 'How much for six tench?'

'Six asses,' came the tart reply.

'I'm buying half a dozen,' protested Piso. 'Four asses.'

'Five.'

'Four.'

'Go on then.' For the first time, Baldy looked at them. He watched as Piso threaded his stick through the gills of six tench; then he held out a hand. What passed for a smile crossed his face as Piso's coins clinked into his palm. 'Gratitude.'

'You here much?' asked Piso.

'If the weather's like this, and I'm not on duty, aye. It's a fine place to while away a few hours, not least because we're about to spend months on the far bank, in danger of our fucking lives.' Baldy swept an arm from left to right, encompassing the green, tree-bound islands in midstream, the plentiful birdlife and the fast-flowing water. 'Beautiful, eh?'

'I suppose.' Piso cast a dour look at the far bank. 'D'you see many tribesmen?'

'On occasion, when the river patrols aren't about. The bolder ones come out in boats, pretending to fish, but their weasel eyes are always on us and the fort. They know we're coming for them.' There was a metallic noise as Baldy slapped the grass beside him, where his sword lay. 'Me and the other regulars, we always have these with us. Just in case, you know.'

'A wise move,' said Piso. It was unusual for off-duty soldiers to carry more than a dagger, but he couldn't argue with Baldy's reasoning. And yet things had been quiet since the assassination attempt on Germanicus during the winter, he thought. 'Should we do the same, Metilius?'

'I'm soon going to have to hump my cursed gladius everywhere, night and day,' Metilius grumbled. 'I'm not about to carry it when I'm off duty as well.'

'Aye.' Baldy was being over-cautious, Piso told himself. 'Come on. Let's see how the ships are coming along, and then we'll head back.'

Bidding farewell to Baldy, they continued their walk towards the new quay that lay beneath the fort. There was a jetty outside the settlement, but the huge numbers of vessels required for this year's campaign had meant a second structure had been built close to the camp. Scores upon scores of troop transports had been constructed there over the winter months, and work continued building more. Rumour had it that Germanicus had ordered almost a thousand in total. Piso prayed – often – that his unit wasn't among those selected to travel to Germania by sea. His stomach did a neat roll at the memory of the unpleasant voyage he and his comrades had endured the previous year.

Deciding that his luck would hold, and he'd be commanded to march into enemy territory, he studied the nearest ships, which were moored in rows, jutting out into the current. A carved wooden bird's head arched over the prow of each, and an open-fronted cabin for the captain was positioned at the back. Long, graceful and sleek, they had a single bank of oars, fifteen to twenty a side, one steering oar and a central sail. One to two centuries could fit aboard, depending on their length.

'They look seaworthy enough,' said Piso, trying to sound confident. 'But if Fortuna's kind to us, we won't ever have to try them out.'

'I'm with you, brother,' said Metilius, spitting. 'Give me solid ground under my feet any day.'

'Sea or land, victory will be ours – Germanicus will ensure that,' said Piso, and Metilius rumbled in agreement. They weren't alone in thinking this – since their return from Germania the previous autumn, morale had been high.

Their hobs clattered off the wooden planks, adding to the clamour. Sail-makers sat cross-legged on the dock, barking orders at their helpers as they made adjustments to great squares of hemp. Sawdust lay in deep piles around the carpenters, who were fashioning rowing benches for unfinished craft. Master shipbuilders, brought in from far and wide, strode about deep in conversation, followed by serious-faced clerks with writing tablets and styli. Soldiers and their officers clambered off vessels that had just come in from patrols. None of the men appeared to be nauseous, thought Piso, before remembering with disgust that the Rhenus was always calmer than the open sea.

At the far end of the quay was the shipbuilding area proper. Things here were quieter, for the day's work had already ceased. Wooden frames held upturned hulls in various stages of construction from almost skeletons to the completed article. Tree trunks lay in stacks; beside them stood the tables where they were cut and planed into suitable lengths. The harsh tang of pine resin filled the air – Piso spied pots sitting near the craft that had been painted with it that day.

'Seen enough?' asked Metilius. 'Let's go back – my belly's grumbling.'

A devilment took Piso. It was a lovely evening, and Baldy was right – the riverbank was beautiful. 'Dulcius and the rest can wait,' he said.

'Eh?'

'There's sawdust and wood shavings everywhere. We'll light a fire and cook our tench, stay out here while it's bright. The others can eat their porridge and get annoyed. They will have their fish when we return.'

A grin cracked Metilius' face. 'A fine idea. I should have brought a skin of wine, and some bread.'

'That will do for next time,' said Piso. 'Maybe the rest will come then too. We could even catch our own dinner.'

The matter settled, they set about gathering fuel.

Belly full, content, Piso stretched his feet towards the dying fire. It was dark now – hours had gone past – and Metilius was dozing beside him. The sky had cleared, and countless stars glittered in the vast blackness overhead. The murmur of the water as it sped by, the skitter of an animal in the rushes — an otter, perhaps — and the occasional bird call were the only sounds. Piso could have been by the mighty River Padus in Italy, where he'd grown up. At this hour, his widowed mother would soon be going to bed. His two younger brothers, both grown now, might still be at home, or they could have married and be living nearby.

Piso felt a pang of nostalgia. He hadn't seen or heard from his family for several years, and he determined to include a letter with the next cash payment he sent to his mother. His reading and writing was laboured, but he could pen a few lines. He might receive a reply written on his mother's behalf by the local scribe within the year, if he was lucky. Like most ordinary soldiers, Piso used migrant traders to carry his letters, men who acted as unofficial messengers for a fee. More reliable were veterans who'd taken their discharge and were returning to Italy, but finding one of those was easier said than done.

Metilius began to snore, and Piso smiled. He was a little drowsy himself, but the fire had burned right down, and his shoulders and back were feeling the cold. It wasn't yet warm enough to stay outside all night, at least without blankets. Still, it had been an enjoyable evening. About to poke Metilius with his sandal, an unexpected sound made him freeze. *Splash.*

Splash. There it was again — the gentle sound of oars dipping in and out of the water. A sudden sweat prickled Piso's brow, and he stared into the darkness. There were no naval craft on the river at this hour — he'd wager a month's pay on it. Night patrols were dangerous, and therefore only under-taken in times of dire necessity.

On instinct, he extinguished the fire with a few gentle stamps. Leaning over Metilius, Piso covered his mouth and hissed, 'Wake up, brother — nice and quiet!'

Metilius' eyes opened at once and filled with alarm, but he didn't make a sound.

Piso took away his hand. 'There's someone out there in a boat.'

67

'Tribesmen?' whispered Metilius.

'At this hour, who else would it be?'

'We must have sentries about, surely?'

'I can't see any near us,' replied Piso, peering. 'The finished craft are guarded right enough, but who'd think to place a watch on piles of planking?'

'And here we are with only our daggers.' Metilius scowled. 'Baldy would have something to say, eh?'

'Shhhh.' The splashing had stopped, but now Piso could hear men stepping out of their boat and into the shallows. He pointed towards the construction area, which was to their left. 'They're coming ashore, over there.'

'Between us and the rest of the ships, and the sentries,' whispered Metilius with dismay. 'We're cut off and outnumbered. Best thing to do is lie low. They'll never know we were here.'

'And let them get away with whatever they're about to do?' retorted Piso in a furious hiss. 'Take out your dagger, and follow me.'

'What are you going to do?'

'Get closer, see how many of them there are, and raise the alarm.'

'This wasn't what I planned for the evening,' grumbled Metilius, but he trailed after Piso all the same.

He left the remaining tench behind. It was wasteful, and Dulcius and the others would complain, but that was preferable to being lumbered with them in a dangerous situation. Grateful that they hadn't had any wine, Piso padded towards the mass of dark outlines that were the half-built vessels. He reached the first hulk without having seen anyone and, pausing, conferred with Metilius.

'It'll be safer to stay on the fort side of the ships,' muttered Piso. 'Stray too near the water, and we risk being trapped. Go the other way, and we can run towards the fort if needs be.'

Metilius grimaced. 'I don't like it. Two of us against gods know how many?'

'I don't fucking like it either, but it's our duty to do something. D'you think Tullus would hold back?'

'Course not, but he's a proper hero.'

'And you're one of his brave men.' Piso clapped Metilius on the arm, hoping that his own growing nerves weren't showing. 'We move fast,' he hissed. 'Keep close. Stay low. If we get separated, don't wait for me. Make your own way to the dock, and raise the alarm.'

'Aye.' Metilius' voice was unhappy but resolute.

Reassured, Piso crept to the ship's prow. Pinpricks of light marked the sentries' fires, some quarter of a mile away by the new dock. Looming above all was the fort, with its thousands of soldiers. Those men might as well be in Rome, thought Piso, fighting fear. Their best hope was that there weren't too many interlopers for the nearest guards to deal with. For long moments, he studied the darkness to the right – where he'd heard the splashing – and was frustrated to see only half-constructed ships. Piso began to wonder if he'd imagined the sound of a boat.

'What's that?' Metilius hissed in his ear. 'Listen.'

At first, Piso could discern nothing, but then . . . men's voices, not far away, and to the right. His guts lurched, but he gritted his teeth. 'Come on.'

Like two thieves, they stole towards the sounds, which were rising from behind the second hull. Inspiration took Piso and, getting down on to his knees, he crawled under the upturned ship. Metilius scrambled in after him. Thus protected, they were able to see the craft's other side, up to knee height. Piso's heart thudded – he could count at least ten pairs of legs. They were clad in trousers, which confirmed their identity as tribesmen, and their intent as malign. Worse still, he heard muttering in German. When he concentrated, it became discernible. 'Stay your hand,' ordered a voice. 'We're to light the ships at the same time. That way, more will burn before the Romans react.'

How Piso wished at that moment that he had his entire contubernium with him. Even with their daggers, they could have taken down half a dozen of the warriors from this position, and then finished the rest. The wisdom of his idea was soon called into question as more sets of legs came into sight. Dry-mouthed now, Piso pointed; Metilius gave him a grim nod back.

At least two boats had landed, if not more. It was time to get away and raise the alarm, before they were seen or heard. Piso jerked a thumb at the direction they'd come and, looking relieved, Metilius mouthed 'Aye'.

What they hadn't anticipated was for a warrior to have broken away from his comrades in order to empty his bladder. On his hands and knees as he emerged, Piso was horrified to see the man not three paces away, decorating the next hull along with an arc of urine. His spear was leaning against the ship's timbers. Although Piso, and Metilius behind him, were moving quietly, the warrior still heard them.

He turned, prick in hand, the stream of his piss curving with him, and his jaw dropped. Frantic, Piso stood, pulled out his dagger and threw himself forward. Warm droplets showered his legs, but there was no time to feel disgust, only fear. His initial blow, ill aimed, struck the warrior in the belly. A roar of agony tore the night air, and the man staggered. Wits gathered, Piso moved behind him and, with expert precision, drew his head back and cut his throat. Blood sprayed over the hull, washing away the urine, and Piso let the warrior drop. 'If you want to live, run,' he hissed at Metilius, who was gaping at him like a fool. 'Towards the dock. Go!'

Daggers in hand, they sprinted away from the river and the night raiders. Cries of alarm were rising behind them; Piso could make out pounding feet too. Let them go around the ship's stern, he prayed, not the prow. Please.

Their luck was in. No warriors were visible as they came out from between the inverted boats and turned sharp right towards the dock. Thanks to several watch fires, they could see the sentries. Angry shouts went up as their flight was heard, which spurred Piso and Metilius to greater efforts. They covered a hundred paces without encountering the enemy, and Piso shot a glance over his shoulder. A curse escaped his lips. Rather than give pursuit, the warriors had returned to their original purpose. Flames were licking from two hulls and, outlined by the light, Piso could make out figures setting torches to more.

'Hurry,' he urged.

'I'm no runner,' wheezed Metilius, but he managed to keep up with Piso as he belted on.

The sentries saw them coming, thanks to the burning ships behind them. 'Halt! Halt!' challenged a not-altogether-steady voice.

'We're legionaries like you,' roared Piso.

The sentry didn't hear, or his fear got the better of him. A javelin came hurtling through the air, driving between Piso and Metilius.

Piso screeched to a halt, aware that the man's companions might do the same. He cupped his hands to his mouth. 'WE'RE ROMAN, LIKE YOU! LET US APPROACH.'

'You're Roman?' came the confused reply.

'Yes, yes,' cried Piso, walking forward with Metilius.

'What's the password then?'

'I don't fucking know!' cried Piso with rising frustration.

'You could be German then – stay where you are!'

Piso had had enough. 'How many filthy Germans speak Latin like me, cocksucker? D'you see those flames back there? That's burning boats. A raiding party has landed, and we've come to tell your officer, so he can do something. Unless you want to be the imbecile responsible for half of Germanicus' fleet being destroyed, I suggest you let us past!'

A moment's hesitation, and then the sentry growled, 'All right, but walk nice and slow – and keep your hands in the air.'

Sharing a furious glance, the pair did as they'd been told.

They were met by four nervous-looking legionaries, three of whom held levelled javelins. The last, the man who'd thrown his, had his sword out and ready. By the look of his smooth cheeks, he hadn't been in the army long. 'Names and units,' he demanded.

'Marcus Piso and Caius Metilius, Second Century, First Cohort of the Fifth,' snarled Piso. 'We used to be in the Eighteenth. Know that we were fighting through the Saltus Teutoburgiensis while you were still sucking your mother's tit, and men like us don't need maggots like *you* screwing us over.'

The last of the sentry's confidence dissipated. 'I was just doing my job,' he said, looking to his companions for support, but they were studying Piso and Metilius with new respect.

'Consider yourself lucky that you're shit at throwing javelins,' retorted Piso. 'Now, unless you *want* more ships to burn, take us to your officer!'

The poor light couldn't conceal the rising stain on the soldier's cheeks. 'This way,' he muttered.

To Piso's relief, the optio in charge of the sentries acted the instant he and Metilius had explained what was going on. By happy chance, a patrol vessel had just returned late, and the centurion in charge was more than happy to add his legionaries to the twenty men gathered by the optio. Without armour and proper weapons, Piso and Metilius could not participate, but they watched as the force marched at the double towards the now bright-lit scene. 'Come on, you boys in blue!' roared the centurion.

Faced with a hundred battle-ready legionaries, the warriors fled to their boats. A short but vicious fight followed, which Piso could not see, but when the legionaries returned, a few men short, it transpired that they had managed to hole one of the attackers' craft so that it sank close to shore. A handful of tribesmen had got away, but most of their number were dead. Twelve hulls had been burned but, as the centurion told a grinning Piso and Metilius, there would have been far more if they hadn't raised the alarm. 'Good work, boys,' he said, clapping them both on the arm. 'Who's your centurion?'

'Centurion Tullus, Second Century, First Cohort, Fifth Legion, sir,' answered Piso with pride.

'I know Tullus,' said the centurion, nodding. 'A fine officer. Speaks well of his men too.' Embarrassed, Piso and Metilius shuffled to and fro, and the centurion laughed. 'You're to be commended for your actions. I'll see that Tullus hears of it.'

'Thank you, sir,' echoed the pair.

'Back to the fort with you,' ordered the centurion. 'A few cups of wine are in order, I would think. Your mates will want to hear what you've been up to.'

Saluting, the two friends began tracing their way to the east gate. After a distance, Piso remembered the fish. 'Dulcius and the rest won't be too happy when we return empty-handed.'

'Screw 'em,' declared Metilius with an evil smile. 'We're the ones with the exciting news. They can share their wine with us just to hear it.'

'Aye,' said Piso. 'Lucky we were there, eh?'

'Luckier still that you heard them. I'd have slept through the whole thing.'

'Arminius was behind it too, like as not,' said Piso. 'If he was, his reach has grown long indeed, to persuade the local tribes to attempt this.'

'Arminius might not be responsible. The Usipetes and the Marsi hate Rome as much as any tribe. Remember the attack on Germanicus?'

'True enough.' Piso's mind filled with dark thoughts of Degmar – Tullus had told them about his involvement in the assassination attempt. Whether Degmar had been here or not, the attack meant that the local peoples had lost none of their desire to fight Rome. Piso's earlier certainty of victory in the spring now seemed a trifle over-confident.

If only it were possible to offer a prayer to the eagle, he thought wistfully.

Chapter VII

⌘⌘⌘

P iso was trudging along one of the fort's main avenues with his five tent mates. It was early evening a day later, and their duties were done. His excitement, which had been bubbling up since the idea of paying their respects to the legion's eagle had been discussed, waned as the headquarters came into sight. It wasn't usual for ordinary legionaries to visit the shrine – in fact, Piso had never heard of it – but none of them could recall a specific regulation that prohibited the practice. In the comfort of their barrack room, bellies full of wine, his plan had seemed excellent, a way to venerate their legion's standard and ask for its help in the battles to come. With a little luck, it might ensure a safe return from the looming campaign. Now, with a steady rain soaking through their tunics, and the obstacle of the headquarters' sentries drawing close, it seemed drink-fuelled stupidity of the finest kind. Piso searched Metilius' face, seeing his own uncertainty mirrored. Unwilling to be the first to express apprehension, he kept walking.

A hundred paces from the imposing main entrance, Metilius cracked. 'Is this wise?'

His comment freed the logjam.

'We won't get over the threshold,' declared Dulcius.

'Even if we do, an officer will soon challenge us,' said Calvus, a gangling farmer and the newest addition to their contubernium. A genial, talkative type, he would tell anyone who listened how he'd only joined the legions out of desperation after cattle plague had wiped out his entire herd.

The two others rumbled their agreement.

Piso's courage rallied. 'We have to try! The Fifth is providing the sentries for the next three days, remember? Come on.' He strode off, praying that his attempt to shame them would work. Ten paces, and he was still alone. Sweat began to bead on his forehead. Twelve. Fifteen.

'Stupid prick,' said Metilius, catching up.

'You're no better,' Piso shot back, grinning. They had all joined him.

'If we get punishment duty because of this, you're buying the wine,' said Calvus. Being a new recruit with little money didn't stop him being generous with his wine.

'Agreed,' said Piso. 'It'll be cheap, mind. Decent stuff would be wasted on you savages.'

Their good-natured banter died away as the entrance drew near. Four sentries, stiff-backed, alert, were on guard outside the large double doors. Piso's first thought had been to slip inside as a wagon rolled in, but the sentries were standing on both sides of the threshold. 'Any ideas?' he asked of no one in particular.

'Tell them the truth?' suggested Calvus. A barrage of abuse rained down, and he scowled.

'They'll smell the wine on our breaths, and tell us to piss off,' said Piso.

Other suggestions were aired, but none were feasible. Piso's certainty ebbed further.

'There's Tubero,' said Metilius.

The sight of their legate striding towards the headquarters from the opposite direction made everyone take a sudden interest in the ground. Bad-tempered, arrogant and a vicious disciplinarian, Tubero was hated by one and all. Anyone who had been in the Eighteenth had extra reason to wish him ill. Years before, Tubero had deliberately ordered Tullus and some of his men into a situation that by rights should have seen them killed.

'Best leave it,' said Metilius. 'If Tubero recognises any of us, we'll be on latrine duties for a year.'

Piso smiled as the rest voiced reluctant agreement. 'No, Tubero gives us the perfect excuse,' he said.

'You must have drunk more wine than I thought.' Metilius jerked a thumb in the direction of their barracks. 'Let's go back.'

Piso shook his head. 'We wait a few moments, until the prick's got to wherever he's going, and then we tell the sentries the entire contubernium is on a punishment detail. We are to be made an example of, and we have to attend him in his office.'

'You don't know what Tubero's doing. He could be meeting another officer,' countered Dulcius.

Piso smirked. 'The sentries don't know that.'

'This is getting out of hand,' said Metilius, looking worried. 'If Tubero finds out that we lied to get into the headquarters . . .'

'He won't. Fortuna's with us – I can feel it!' Piso studied his friends' faces. Dulcius and a second man seemed with him, but Metilius and the rest appeared unconvinced. 'You want to pray to the eagle, don't you?' Piso challenged.

'Aye,' replied Calvus.

'This will be your only chance,' said Piso, adopting Tullus' parade-ground voice.

'Fuck it.' To Piso's surprise and pleasure, Calvus moved to stand beside him.

Metilius rolled his eyes. 'You'd better be right about Fortuna, Piso.'

Piso marched confidently towards the entrance, praying he was.

To his surprise and delight, the sentries accepted his story. One was even sympathetic. 'Tubero's in a foul humour, brother. Gods grant his mood improves before you find him.'

Muttering his thanks, Piso ushered his comrades inside. Three paces inside the large courtyard, and the foolhardiness of what he'd done sank in. The beating heart of the fort, the headquarters was full of senior officers talking together, or moving between the many offices. There were plenty of clerks and scribes too, but their soft hands and spotless tunics only made Piso and his companions appear more out of place. Ordinary legionaries were visible, but not many. A pair were sweeping the colonnaded walkway that lined three sides of the square, and another four staggered along behind a quartermaster, carrying a metal-bound chest. That was it when it came to the rank and file, and here they were, thought Piso in horror, half a dozen pissed soldiers with no real purpose.

'Don't stop.' Metilius gave him a discreet shove in the back. 'If you stand and gawp, someone will notice. Look purposeful, and we're less likely to be stopped.'

Metilius was right, Piso decided, but he still felt like a criminal caught in the act. Head low, avoiding men's gaze, he walked towards the great hall which faced the entrance. They skirted round a group of tribunes without being noticed. Various clerks gave them suspicious looks, but none issued a challenge. Everyone else has a reason to be here, Piso realised. He glanced around, eyes keen. If Tubero appeared, they had to take evasive action. His heart thumped as one of the legionaries sweeping the walkway spotted them, but rather than issue a challenge, the soldier shook his head as if to say 'Madmen'. Trying to remain calm, Piso looked away.

Metilius drew close. 'What are you going to say to the sentries outside the hall? And the ones outside the shrine?' he whispered.

Now Piso wished the ground would open and swallow him up. Winning over the men at the entrance had been lucky, but expecting Fortuna's help in getting past more sets of guards verged on the insane. 'I don't know yet,' he hissed.

'Better think of something fucking fast.' Metilius fell back a pace, leaving Piso at the head of their little group.

Dry-mouthed, his stomach in knots, Piso kept going out of stubbornness. It was all he had left.

To his astonishment, Fortuna's good mood continued. One of the two sentries by the massive gates to the main hall didn't just know Piso — he owed him a decent sum. An inveterate gambler, the soldier had run out of coin during a recent long night spent at dice. Against his better judgement, Piso had given him credit. He couldn't have been more glad at this moment.

'Gaius,' he said, lifting a hand. 'We're going to the shrine to pay our respects.'

Gaius was none too happy at this announcement. His gaze moved to his companion, then returned to Piso. 'Who gave you permission?'

'Let us through, and I'll forget the coin due to me,' said Piso in a low tone. 'Refuse, and I'll break your fucking legs next time we meet.'

Gaius' mouth worked. 'It's all right. They've been sent here by their centurion,' he said to his comrade. Throwing Piso a dark look, he stood aside, muttering, 'Be quick!'

Piso didn't need to be told twice. With a jerk of his head, he indicated that Metilius and the rest should follow.

Piso had been in the tile-floored hall on four-monthly paydays when the weather had been too severe to parade the soldiers outside, but a sense of awe still struck him as he entered. The massive rectangular chamber was dominated by a double set of great columns that ran off on either side. Imposing painted statues of the emperor's family filled the spaces between, and a mighty effigy of Tiberius, larger than any other, occupied the floor in front of the doors. The shrine lay through a doorway midway along the back wall, and beneath it was the strongroom containing the legions' monies. Surprised to have come this far, and needing to marshal his thoughts, Piso came to a halt before the likeness of Tiberius and bent his head, as if praying.

'What did you say?' demanded Metilius.

'Never you mind,' replied Piso, loath to reveal the simplicity of his success.

Metilius peered around the statue. 'Whatever it was won't work twice. The two sentries by the shrine look as if they're on the watch for Arminius himself.'

Piso joined him, and his brief enjoyment vanished. The stern-faced guards seemed just the types to challenge six dishevelled soldiers. He and his companions couldn't linger where they were without causing suspicion either – they had to act. Piso could almost hear Fortuna starting to cackle.

'Piso!' Dulcius' voice.

Bile washed the back of Piso's throat as he spied Tubero entering the hall behind them. Three staff officers followed. By force of will, Piso continued to pretend he was praying to the emperor. Relief filled him as Tubero entered an office to the left, but the mountainous problem facing them remained. Should they risk trying to enter the shrine, or skulk from the hall like beaten hounds? The second pathetic image stiffened Piso's resolve. He faced his comrades. 'It's so close. We can't leave now!'

The resounding silence that followed enraged Piso. 'Yellow-livers!' he hissed. 'Are you with me?'

At last: reluctant nods, and mutters of 'Aye'.

'Follow me.' Taking a deep breath, Piso rounded the statue of Tiberius and aimed straight for the sentries.

'State your business.' The challenge was issued at once.

'Well met, brother,' said Piso in his friendliest tone. He indicated his comrades. 'We're soldiers of the Fifth, like you. Many of us were also in the Eighteenth, under Varus. You'll know our centurion, Tullus.' Piso took heart from the sentries' nods. 'We'd like to pay our respects to the eagle.'

The older of the two sentries stuck out his jaw. 'This is most irregular.'

Piso pulled a broad – and what he hoped was winning – smile. 'Yet here we are.'

The sentry didn't look amused. 'None of you are officers.'

'The eagle is as dear to us, the soldiers, as it is to any officer. Or dearer,' added Piso, hoping to find solidarity with the sentry.

The sentry's stern expression eased. 'Maybe so, but I've never heard tell of ordinary footsloggers just sauntering into the shrine. You must have seen the number of top-rankers around, brother. If me and my mate get caught having let you in, we'd be fucked. Properly fucked. My advice is, get out of here before someone notices, or you'll be for the same.'

Piso's heart sank. He glanced at Metilius, whose shoulders went up and down in defeat. The others' dejected expressions said the same thing. To overpower the sentries would be madness, and result in the most brutal punishment.

'Tubero's over there,' said the sentry. 'If you want to avoid him, skirt to the left of Tiberius' statue.'

The taste of disappointment was bitter in Piso's mouth. How typical of Fortuna to let him get this far, he thought, only to fall on his face at the last obstacle. 'We tried,' he said to Metilius. 'That's better than nothing.'

'I suppose.' Metilius sighed.

They turned to go, but to Piso's horror, Tubero was walking in their direction. He didn't seem aware of their presence, but that would soon change. Whether he recognised them or not would be immaterial: the man was such a disciplinarian that they'd be punished just for being in the hall.

'Come on,' whispered Piso, making for the other side of Tiberius' statue. 'Quick!'

Five rushed paces, and Piso collided with Tullus. Mortified, he jerked to a halt, uncomfortably aware of his wine-filled breath. 'Apologies, sir.'

Tullus raised an eyebrow. 'Piso.'

'Sir.' Piso stared at the tiled floor.

'What in Hades are you doing here with your entire contubernium?'

Piso met Tullus' gaze and decided that lying would be a *very* bad idea. 'We came to see the eagle, sir.'

Tullus frowned. 'You see it on parade.'

'We wanted to pray in the shrine, sir. To tell the eagle we'll fight to our last drop of blood for it. That the enemy will never lay their hands on it.' Self-conscious, sure that Tullus would have them digging latrines for the whole summer, Piso looked down again. 'I also wanted to remember our old eagle. That's all, sir.' To his surprise, Tullus began to chuckle.

'Those are good reasons to visit the shrine, and you're fine soldiers. Come with me,' ordered Tullus.

The sentries dared not question an officer of Tullus' rank, and not twenty heartbeats later, an awestruck Piso and his comrades found themselves entering the shrine, Tullus at their backs. No one said a word. By unspoken consent, the soldiers placed their feet down with care, to stop their hobnails clashing on the floor. Light cast by dozens of oil lamps glittered off the gold and silver on display. This wasn't just the home of two legions' eagles. The standard of every unit, infantry and cavalry, rested here too. Piso's gaze fell first on familiar images of the emperor, human hands, discs, crescents, laurel wreaths and spear tips, but like a moth drawn to the flame, his gaze returned to the eagles.

Set apart from the other, less important standards, the iconic gold birds rested in special wooden stands that kept them upright. Identical in appearance, each could be differentiated from the other by the numerals etched into the rectangular, square-sectioned plinth upon which they sat. Piso and his comrades moved reverentially towards the eagle marked 'V'.

A pulse thrummed at the base of Piso's throat. The standard had been marched past him before, but he'd never stood so close, never had the opportunity to study it in all its glory. Crouched on thunderbolts, raised wings encircled by a garland, it was as good a representation of an eagle as he had ever seen, and the embodiment of aloof majesty. Its fierce, arrogant eyes bored into Piso, filling him with wonder and respect.

Who are you? it seemed to ask.

I am a soldier of the Fifth Legion, Piso answered in his head.

Why are you here?

To show my respect, Piso replied.

Will you follow me, even unto death?

It will be my honour.

There was no answer, but Piso's pride stirred. He had laid his soul bare to the eagle, and offered the truth. There could be no repeat of what had happened in the forest seven years before; if needed, he *would* die for the eagle. So would his tent mates.

Piso bowed and stepped back from the eagle. One by one, his comrades did the same. When they had completed their obeisance, Tullus nodded in approval. 'Done?' he asked in a low voice.

'Yes, sir.' Piso's admiration for Tullus spilled over. 'I can't begin to thank you, sir. Getting us in here – well, we're forever in your debt. Gratitude, sir.'

His friends rushed to agree. 'Aye, sir.' 'Thank you, sir.'

Tullus' fierce, eager eyes moved over their faces. 'In my mind, every soldier deserves the right to pray before the eagle.' A brief smile creased his features. 'Now, best get back to barracks, eh?'

'What about Tubero, sir?' Piso's belly gave an unhappy twist. 'If he sees us—'

'You leave Tubero to me.' Tullus' tone was granite hard. 'Clear?'

'Yes, sir!' Piso was so happy he could have wept.

Chapter VIII

⌘⌘⌘

Some ten days later, Tullus was sitting astride his horse on the parade ground outside the fort of Vetera, with his century and the rest of the First Cohort arrayed before him. The legion's most senior centurion and his direct superior, Bassius, the gaunt-complexioned primus pilus, was riding up and down inspecting the legionaries. The Fifth's nine other cohorts were there too, the Second beside the First, and behind them, in twos, the rest.

Further to Tullus' right were the soldiers of the Twenty-First Legion. Four other legions were present; so too were a score of auxiliary cohorts. The massive space, seldom filled, was jammed tight with troops. It was a stirring sight, and marked the opening of the year's campaign. Other army groups had already left – the legate Silius had led a strong force to crush the Chatti, while most of the cavalry and a number of legionary cohorts had sailed out on to the German Ocean, their task to land at the mouth of the River Amisia and strike southward, as Tullus and his men had done the previous year. The soldiers on parade would form Germanicus' main army, and be led by him in person. Their first task was to relieve the siege of Aliso, one of Rome's few remaining forts east of the Rhenus, which had been besieged by enemy tribesmen of recent days.

Lines of lambswool clouds covered the early-morning sky from end to end, moved along by a faint wind. Tullus was content. Conditions seemed set to follow those of the previous few days, with no rain. Cooler, settled weather would make the requisite twenty miles' march less arduous for his laden-down legionaries. There was no doubt that in the coming months they would endure hot temperatures and lack of water as well as fierce battles with the tribes led by Arminius. If his men were to be granted an easy start to their journey, thought Tullus, so much the better.

There had been no sign of Germanicus, but it wasn't usual protocol for an army commander to appear on such a day. He had addressed the legions five days before, telling them of the glorious victories they would win this spring and summer, and they'd cheered him to the heavens. Today, he wouldn't leave until the vanguard and a good portion of the immense column had set out. Like as not, Tullus decided, Germanicus was enjoying the last few hours he would spend with his wife and children until the autumn.

Sirona sprang to mind, unbidden, and Tullus had to hide a smile. Just two nights prior, his dedicated courtship had paid off in royal style when she had asked him to stay with her rather than return to his quarters in the fort. His long wait had been worthwhile, he thought, allowing the smile to emerge. Gods, but it would have been good to see her again today, and Artio. Such a benefit was beyond anyone except the likes of a legate, however – army duties took priority over everything. Besides, Tullus doubted whether Sirona would have permitted a formal farewell. After their night together, she had ushered him from the inn before the sleeping Artio awoke, allowing him only a few kisses as they parted.

For the second time in his life – the first had been the previous year, and because of the same people – Tullus felt a pang of regret to be going to war. Artio and now Sirona were as dear to him as family – they *are* my family, curse it, he thought. Leaving them was difficult, and growing more so. Even Twig Limbs had wormed his way into Tullus' affections. Once, he would have laughed at the idea of retiring, of leaving the legions in which he had spent most of his life, but now the notion of setting up house with Sirona and Artio, and using his savings to try his hand at business, appealed.

He shoved all notions of civilian life from his mind. I will think of Sirona and Artio each night before sleep, he told himself, but the rest of the time things will be as they always have. My men will come first until the day we come marching back over the bridge, gods willing with the tribes defeated, Arminius dead and my legion's eagle recovered.

Tullus eyed the Fifth's eagle, borne by the *aquilifer*. This standard-bearer, easy to spot with his lion-skin headdress and scale armour, had the sacred and important job of carrying the eagle. On a day such as this, he would march at the front of the legion, in the ranks of the First Cohort. Because the Fifth Legion had been chosen to form the vanguard today, the aquilifer would lead the entire army to war. Even Tullus, who'd had problems identifying with the Fifth because of what had happened to his old legion, felt his pride stirring to see the eagle there, proud and imperious. It's ready for the honour of leading us, he thought. It's ready for the fight. As I and my soldiers are. As every man present is.

Trumpets blared from the fort's walls, and Tullus let out a long breath. The wait was over. Germanicus had given the order for the army to set out. The signal was echoed by the Fifth's trumpeters, and in turn by the other legions' musicians. Auxiliary cohorts sometimes had their own tribal instruments, and the scouts who would march out first – a mixture of skirmishers, cavalry and light infantry – were no different. A terrible racket rose from their ranks – drums, horns and out-of-tune singing – as they tramped and rode towards the settlement and its bridge.

'They sound like a thousand cats being murdered at once,' observed Bassius, riding at Tullus' side. A thin man in late middle age with short grey hair, he bore a savage scar that had left his mouth lopsided. Tough, fearless and an excellent leader, he was esteemed by everyone, not least Tullus. 'Maybe even two thousand cats,' the primus pilus mused.

'The higher figure, I'd say, sir,' opined Tullus, wincing.

'They're good fighters, though, and there are no Arminius-like figures among them.' Bassius gave the signal and the First Cohort began to march forward, following the scouts. He nudged his horse and took up a position alongside the first ranks.

Tullus rode on Bassius' left; he could join his own century when they were done talking. 'It helps that their womenfolk and families live on this side of the river, sir,' he said in a cynical tone. The auxiliaries serving in this area tended to come from Gaul and Germania, and the majority had settled close to the Roman forts along the Rhenus.

'Aye, that makes a difference. Few men will turn traitor if their loved ones sleep by a Roman fort – in the lions' den, as it were,' said Bassius. 'But some auxiliaries with families living elsewhere have remained loyal since Arminius' ambush. Most of the Chauci, the Frisii, even some Cherusci. What do you think of them?'

'After the Saltus Teutoburgiensis it took me years to trust any auxiliaries, sir. It was Flavus, Arminius' brother, who won me over in the end.'

'Flavus is a good man. Loyal to the empire, and so are his warriors. You spent time with him during the raid that freed Segestes and took Thusnelda prisoner, I believe.'

'Aye, sir. We had time to talk. Flavus told me how he felt about Arminius. There's never been any love lost between the two of them – they're like cat and dog.'

'Families are ever thus – fighting, disagreeing or falling out,' said Bassius, shaking his head. 'The bonds that hold us soldiers together are more reliable. Forged by sweat, blood and sacrifice, they're stronger than steel. So it has been, and it will always be, eh?'

'Aye, sir,' replied Tullus, eyeing his men with pride, and not a little love.

'Once a soldier, always a soldier. Me, I intend to die in my armour.'

'You'll never retire, sir?'

'Why would I? I love my men, and my legion. I have no wife, no children, and what brothers and sisters of mine survive dwell in Italy. I haven't seen them for two decades and more. The Fifth is my family, and has been these many years.' Bassius threw Tullus an enquiring look. 'I would have thought the same of you.'

'You'd have been right, sir, until Arminius wiped out the Eighteenth. Life changed then. I can still imagine myself in harness to the bitter end, but there's more of me these days that would like to settle down near Vetera. I might even get married.'

Bassius arched an eyebrow. 'There *is* something to the rumours then. Would the woman in question be the proprietor of the Ox and Plough?'

'Does everybody in the cursed legion know my business?' cried Tullus in frustration.

'Every centurion does, that's certain,' replied Bassius with a chuckle. 'I'm glad for you, Tullus. Sirona's a good woman.'

'She is that, sir,' said Tullus, pleased by Bassius' regard. 'But there's a war to win before I see her again.'

'Arminius to kill.'

'Two eagles to hunt down.'

'Achieve those objectives, and I'll sacrifice a bull to Mars,' said Bassius with feeling.

'So will I, sir,' swore Tullus, 'and maybe one to Fortuna as well.'

'I gave up offering that unreliable old witch anything years ago. She been good to you?'

'Once or twice, sir.' Despite his cynicism, Tullus had prayed to Fortuna during the muddy bloodbath that had been Arminius' ambush. Several times during the living nightmare, Tullus' luck had held against all possible odds, making him wonder ever since if the goddess of luck had been smiling down on him.

Whether she might do so again was – as ever – unclear.

Chapter IX

◨◨◨

Someone coughed, the harsh noise breaking the silence. Tullus, who had been peering eastward, whirled in fury on his soldiers, hidden with him among the trees a short distance from the gravelled road to Aliso. 'Quiet!' he ordered in an angry hiss. 'The next man to make a fucking sound will rue the day he was born.'

A day and a half had passed since the army had left Vetera, and the fort of Aliso was about a mile away. Returning auxiliary scouts had revealed that it was under attack from several thousand tribesmen. Although Germanicus' forces outnumbered the attackers many times, the general was wary of a trap. The column had therefore halted some way further to the west, and a strong patrol sent to assess the situation.

Tullus had been put in command of the two centuries of legionaries, fifty Chauci warriors and three *turmae* of cavalry. A dozen bemused trumpeters, poached from other centuries with the permission of their officers, were mixed among the infantry. They had marched for about three miles under a cloudy sky before his caution – and an upcoming large area of open ground – had had them move off the road and into the trees on either side.

Tullus had been studying the spruce, beech and sessile oaks on the far side of the exposed, boggy terrain for some time. 'I can't see anything,' he said in German to the lead scout, a surly Chauci warrior with fetid breath. 'Can you?'

'I see nothing. As I said, no one there.'

The warrior's flippant answer irritated Tullus, although by now he was used to the Germans' disregard for authority. 'How can you be sure?'

'We went through there yesterday. No one watching then, so no one watching now.'

'That makes no sense,' muttered Tullus. 'The warriors besieging Aliso must know that Germanicus' army is coming.'

'They know.' A smirk. 'Is game of bravery.'

'Eh?'

'Warriors from three tribes are attacking Aliso. Each wants to show the others that they are the bravest.'

'So the tribe who puts out sentries are cowards?'

The Chauci warrior laughed. 'Aye.'

'That's fucking stupid,' Tullus declared with contempt. 'And an easy fucking way for an enemy to creep up on you unawares.'

The warrior shrugged his indifference to Tullus' opinion. 'Is the tribal way,' he said. 'Courage more important than anything.'

'If Arminius were here, there'd be sentries on the road.'

'Arminius.' The warrior hawked and spat, and mumbled something else.

'What's that?'

The warrior met Tullus' gaze with a hard one of his own. 'Arminius too much like a Roman. He has lost his tribal heart.'

This revelation from a supposed ally was unwelcome. 'You serve Rome, and follow Germanicus' orders. You fight with us.'

'Aye.'

'But your heart remains tribal.'

'Of course,' said the warrior, giving Tullus a scornful look.

Defeated by the man's logic, and wondering about his loyalty, Tullus returned to more pressing matters, such as his patrol. To reach Aliso, they had to cross the open ground one way or another. Even if the scout was wrong, he decided, it was improbable that more than a few warriors were keeping watch, because their only job would be to carry word to their fellows. He might as well lead his entire patrol onward. Mind made up, Tullus gave the order.

Two-thirds of his cavalry rode at the front, interspersed with the Chauci scouts. Tullus, his century and the trumpeters marched next – he had left his horse with the column – and were followed by the other century. This, the third in his cohort, was commanded by a good-natured centurion named Potitius. At the rear came the final *turma*.

'Keep a sharp eye out, brothers,' Tullus commanded as they began. 'If you see anything, let me know at once. I'd rather a false alarm over a deer or a wildfowl than to see German spears flying at us.'

The proximity of Aliso and the possibility of ambush wasn't lost on his men. An uncomfortable silence reigned as they covered the quarter-mile of marshy ground, which was dotted with heather, bog rosemary and goat-weed. Long-stalked water avens nodded here and there. A solitary crane perched by the side of a murky pool, its black eyes studying the horses and soldiers as they passed. The clouds, dark grey and heavy now with mois-ture, felt as if they were pressing down from above. Pattering rain began to fall, and Tullus' spirits dipped despite himself.

The scene bore a close resemblance to Arminius' ambush, and to the battles they had fought with his tribesmen the previous year. Coincidence, Tullus told himself. It's coincidence and nothing more. Half the terrain for three hundred miles consists of mud, bog and water. When it rains, which it does most of the year, one part of this godsforsaken wasteland looks the same as anywhere else. The scout said that there were no sentries, and there'll be none. Tullus managed to quell his unease, but the moments it took to reach the trees dragged by. With each step, he expected volleys of spears to come humming in, or to hear a rousing rendition of the fearsome barritus.

His suspicions were misplaced. Other than the chattering of an aggrieved blackbird, nothing happened. Tullus sent the Chauci warriors ranging off to seek for signs of the enemy. He kept the rest of the patrol on the road, waiting, until they had returned.

That too was a fraught time, but Tullus paced among his men, issuing advice. 'There's nothing worse than an untied lace on a sandal when you're in the thick of it,' he said for the ten-thousandth time in his career. 'Laces, belt, chinstrap, armour strapping – check them all, or do it for your comrade. Loosen your sword in the scabbard. Make sure your mail is sitting right. If you need a piss, have it now.'

As always, the last instruction persuaded a number of soldiers to empty their bladders, prompting the usual jibes and insults. Tullus watched with some amusement. Such wisecracks were good for morale, and helped keep the men's minds from the battle they could soon be fighting.

The Chauci scouts came loping back a short time later. 'No warriors anywhere close,' the warrior with fetid breath announced in an I-told-you-so voice. 'What now?'

'We make for Aliso through the trees,' said Tullus. 'Which side of the road provides better cover?'

He conferred with his fellows. 'Left side.'

'We go that way then. Dismount and follow us,' Tullus ordered the cavalry. 'You'll wait for us in the first glade.' Commanding Potitius to dog his footsteps with his soldiers, he nodded at the warrior. 'Take us to the fort.'

The nerve-racking walk, about three-quarters of a mile, was made with care, but more than two hundred men could not move through the woods in complete silence. Twigs cracked as soldiers trod on them, and curses were muttered as shins collided with fallen timber. Now and again, javelins knocked against shield rims. The man with the cough spluttered once or twice. Tullus, at the front with the Chauci warriors, fretted about the noise they were making. At regular intervals, he halted the entire patrol to listen for cries of alarm or running feet as frightened warriors fled back to their camp.

He heard nothing, and so they went closer and closer, until sounds from Aliso could be discerned. Shouted voices – at this distance, it was impossible to tell if they were Roman or German – held conversations with one another. Horses whinnied. Men sang. There was no indication of battle, which set Tullus to thinking. According to the scouts, the fort showed no signs of falling. The attackers might be organising an assault, but Tullus decided it more probable that the warriors were getting on with day-to-day tasks in their encampment. That increased his patrol's risk of being discovered. Warriors would be using the woods to empty their bowels, go hunting, even to lie with their women.

It was as if Fortuna, filthy-tempered, had been listening to Tullus' thoughts, and cackled to herself. Not ten heartbeats later, half a dozen warriors ambled out of the trees in front of Tullus. Carrying spears but no shields, it was obvious that they were in search of something for the pot. Their easy banter came to an abrupt halt as they froze, shock writ large on their faces.

'All men, shields ready! First three ranks, move to my left. Fourth, fifth and sixth ranks, to my right. The rest form up behind them in turn. DO IT NOW!' Tullus took several steps towards the enemy. 'Ready to die, you whoresons?' he roared in German. The Chauci scouts began hurling abuse in their own tongue.

The startled warriors, Usipetes from their trouser patterns, turned to flee. Only one had the presence of mind to lob his spear at Tullus. It was a good throw, penetrating the middle of his shield and protruding a couple of fingers' breadth on the other side. With a curse, Tullus tossed the useless thing at the warriors and ordered one to be handed to him from behind. In the time that took, the warriors had broken and run. Chauci spears hummed after them.

'We go now, back to the army,' said the warrior with bad breath, jerking his head the way they'd come. 'Too many warriors for us to fight.'

'You think they'll pursue us?' asked Tullus, picturing a repetition of the horrors he'd endured with his soldiers during Arminius' ambush.

Another shrug. 'Maybe, maybe not. We go now, more chance to get away.'

The warrior's apparent indifference was masking fear, Tullus was sure of it. Remembering the terror on the faces of the hunting party, he said, 'They have no sentries out. For all those warriors know, we could be the vanguard of Germanicus' entire fucking army.' Ordering his men to follow him, he stole towards the fort.

The Chauci scouts obeyed, but with poor grace.

Tullus soon came to the tree line. The scene that greeted him could have been painted by a now beaming, good-willed Fortuna. The warriors who'd chanced upon the patrol were in full flight. Several hundred paces away, the fort stood, strong and robust – Tullus could even see sentries pacing on the ramparts. Earthworks had been built to surround it, but they were incomplete and of varying quality.

Closer to the trees, a chaotic arrangement of tents ran in every direction, as far as the eye could see. Trails of smoke rose from scores of fires. Warriors lazed about in small groups, sharpening spear blades, cooking or talking with their friends. Larger numbers of their fellows were watching wrestling matches or mock combats. Grazing horses filled the grassy areas; there were also a number of sheep.

Of sentries there was no sign, anywhere. The contrast with a Roman encampment near an enemy position was stark. All that was missing, thought Tullus in bemusement, were women and children. Two heartbeats later, he spotted several women washing clothes in timber buckets. At their feet, a couple of toddlers were crawling about.

He glanced again at the hunting party, who were still running and shouting. Heads were beginning to turn, but no one had realised what the warriors had seen. Tullus sensed a golden opportunity. A risky one, true, but he was ready to seize it. German tribesmen were as brave as any enemies he'd come across, but they could also be as flighty as livestock caught in a sudden thunderstorm. He sprinted back towards his patrol.

'Potitius!' Tullus bellowed. 'Send two men to fetch the cavalry. When they arrive, they're to attack to the left and right of our positions. Tell them to listen for the trumpets sounding the recall.'

'Get the cavalry. Attack to left and right. Listen for the trumpets. Yes, sir,' replied Potitius. 'What are we to do?'

'Charge!' yelled Tullus. 'The Germans are at sixes and sevens, and those pricks who saw us can't know we're only a patrol. We could be Germanicus' army, come to slaughter them. We ARE Germanicus' army!' Seeing his men's surprise, Tullus explained, pacing to and fro in front of them. 'Attack their camp now, and they'll panic – I *know* it.'

Piso's face lit up. 'This is why you brought the trumpeters, sir!'

'Aye, Piso, that's right,' said Tullus with an evil smile. When he and a motley group of soldiers had fled from Aliso in the aftermath of Varus' army's massacre, the pursuing tribesmen had been scared off with a ruse similar to what Tullus planned now. 'Sound the advance with enough vigour, and the savages will be convinced Germanicus' eight legions have arrived. Trumpeters, get up here! Potitius, bring your men along the side of my century. Quick!'

While Tullus waited for Potitius' soldiers, he had the grinning trumpeters ready themselves. 'You will move forward with me to the tree line. Then I want the charge sounded, loud as you can. Understand?'

'How long for, sir?' asked one.

'Until I tell you to stop. I want every warrior in that camp to shit his breeches. Think you can do that?'

'Aye, sir,' they answered, their eyes glinting.

Tullus gave them a satisfied nod. Potitius was ready too. 'Follow alongside our column,' Tullus ordered. Beckoning to his own men and the trumpeters, he tramped towards the fort. Let your good mood continue, Fortuna, he asked. I'll make it worth your while.

At the edge of the trees, Tullus grinned. The hunting-party warriors had reached their encampment and were shouting and making wild gesticulations in the Romans' direction, but word had not spread far. Tribesmen close by continued to cook, to talk with one another by their fires. His plan could yet work. He turned to the trumpeters. 'Blow, as if your lives depended on it.'

Tan-tara-tara. Tan-tara-tara. The notes rang out, sharp and clear. Again and again they sounded, and Tullus watched the enemy camp with bated breath. Scores of surprised and fearful faces were regarding the tree line. The hapless warriors who had seen him and his men redoubled their efforts to warn their fellows.

Tan-tara-tara. Tan-tara-tara.

By the tenth rendition, Tullus could feel the earth trembling. His cavalry was close. Perfect timing, he thought. 'Forward,' he ordered. 'Potitius, take up a position to my left. Spread your men out one rank deep – we want the enemy to think there are thousands of us. We advance at the walk. Trumpeters, keep sounding.'

Tan-tara-tara. Tan-tara-tara. Tan-tara-tara. Tan-tara-tara.

They emerged into the open to utter chaos. Shouts – frightened and angry – filled the air. Not a single warrior was ready to face them. All Tullus could see were men and a few women running to the east. Tents and possessions abandoned, they were fleeing for their lives. Those with horses were scrambling on to their backs and joining the deluge. Even the sheep had begun to move away from the woods.

'FORWARD!' Tullus shouted. 'FOR ROME!'

'FOR ROME!' yelled his and Potitius' men.

They had covered perhaps fifty paces when Tullus' cavalry plunged out of the trees. Roaring their own war cries, they split up to form a small wing on either side of his troops. Fresh wails of dismay rose from the tribal camp, and Tullus grinned, scenting victory. His combined infantry and cavalry presented a fearsome proposition to a disorganised force, and expecting Germanicus' army within the day, the tribesmen could have no idea how vulnerable they were.

Within fifty heartbeats, his gamble had paid off. Every warrior was in full flight to the east and south. Any chance that they might rally vanished as the fort gates opened to disgorge a strong force of legionaries and several turmae of cavalry. Alert to what was happening – and possibly thinking that the legions had arrived – Aliso's commander was lending his support. Tullus' heart sang, and loud cheering broke out among his men.

They had earned the right to shout, but he was under no illusions. The victory had been nothing more than a successful ruse – a clever one, it was true – but a ruse nonetheless. In ordinary circumstances, the tribesmen were fearsome fighters, and scared of no one. They would be back with thousands of their fellows, at a time and place of their choosing. Legionaries would die then, that was certain.

If Germanicus wasn't careful, Arminius would recreate his terrible ambush for a second time.

Chapter X

It was a clammy spring morning. Heavy rain had fallen on the tribal camp the previous day and during the night. Paths had become quagmires and lighting fires was nigh on impossible. The clouds were clearing little by little, but drops of water yet fell from the sodden trees, some finding their way with unerring accuracy on to the back of Arminius' neck. He was trudging between his warriors' tents, doing his best to lift their despondent mood.

He too was damp, tired after a poor night's sleep, and hungry. It was hard not to fall into a foul temper, not least because of the pressing matters on his mind. The year's campaign had not been under way for long – Germanicus' host had crossed the Rhenus less than a month before, and thus far everything had gone the Romans' way. The Usipetes besieging the fort of Aliso would never have withstood an onslaught by Germanicus' legions, but to be caught with their cocks in their hands like a drunkard pissing on his neighbour's vegetables had been stupid. The Usipetes should have known the enemy was nearby, and retreated in good time to the surrounding forests, from where skirmishing actions against the invaders could have been waged. Instead they had fled headlong to join with his warriors. One small consolation, Arminius supposed, was that they had suffered negligible casualties.

The Usipetes were not alone in their misfortune. Disobeying Arminius' orders to link up with his army in secret, thereby keeping the Romans unaware, the Angrivarii tribe had risen in rebellion some ten days before.

Germanicus' instantaneous reaction had seen a strong, fast-moving force of cavalry and skirmishers dispatched to the Angrivarii territory. News since had been scant. Even if the fighting was going against the Romans, which was less likely than Arminius wished, the tribe would be bogged down for some time and therefore unable to add to his numbers.

'Ho, Osbert!' Arminius stopped by the tent of one of his best warriors. Thickset, massive-chested, and fond of fighting and drinking, Osbert looked to have been indulging in too much of the latter. His eyes were bloodshot and flecks of food matter, perhaps even vomit, decorated his bushy beard.

'A big night last night?' asked Arminius.

'Aye,' croaked Osbert with a rueful rub of his head. 'There was light in the sky when we called an end to it.'

Osbert's tent mates – three of his friends – were in no better shape. With a resigned sigh, Arminius left them to it. Good numbers of others were in a similar state as he made his way through the disorganisation that was his tribe's section of the camp. He would have preferred his warriors not to indulge so, but nothing would be gained by calling them to task. As Gerulf had always been quick to point out, Arminius was not their master. To be fair, it was hard to blame his men for their behaviour.

The Roman army was more than thirty miles away as the bird flew, fifty as the warrior ran. Battle would not be joined today or the next, even if Arminius decided to fight. While he and Germanicus played cat and mouse, as they had done for days, those men who weren't scouting or harassing the enemy – the vast majority of Arminius' forces – had to sit on their hands. When it was dry, they could hunt, train, and practise the various battle drills taught them by Arminius and Maelo. When it rained, however, there was little to do but huddle in their tents, gamble and drink.

'Arminius! Where is Arminius?' The voice belonged to a warrior who'd come running from the direction of the Marsi tents, which lay a short distance away.

'I'm here,' replied Arminius, raising a hand. He waited for the warrior to draw near, hoping that his urgency didn't signify a surprise attack by

Germanicus. 'Greetings,' he said as the warrior, a lean-framed man with a wispy moustache, reached him. 'You bring news?'

'One of our patrols has returned. They clashed with the enemy two evenings ago as it was growing dark. The fight went well, and they took a number of prisoners – Chatti auxiliaries for the most part, but one is a Roman officer.'

'These are good tidings.' Arminius felt his ill humour lifting.

'Mallovendus said you would want to be there when they're questioned,' added the warrior.

'Mallovendus was right. Take me to him.' He grilled the messenger as they walked but learned little, for the prisoners had only just arrived. Even so, Arminius' excitement grew with each step. There was no certainty that he would learn anything of worth, but thanks to the Romans' bitter determination to defend their comrades, prisoners were rare.

Reaching the Marsi area of the camp, they spied a crowd of warriors gathered in a circle. Every neck was craned. Men stood on tiptoe and leaned on their comrades to see. The protests at Arminius' shoving through their midst died away as he was recognised. Emerging into the centre, Arminius found Mallovendus and a dozen tired-looking warriors ranged around the bound prisoners, who were kneeling by a large, sputtering fire. Eight in number, all were tribesmen but the last. Helmetless but dressed in a mail shirt, he wore a typical Roman metalled belt. His lack of phalerae or torques reduced the chance of him being a centurion, thought Arminius, fighting disappointment.

'You arrived quicker than a crow to a corpse!' boomed Mallovendus.

'My thanks for sending word,' said Arminius, nodding his recognition to the warrior who'd guided him. 'Have you found out anything?'

'They've been softened up a little, but I haven't bothered asking any questions yet.' Mallovendus' smile was all teeth.

Arminius stalked towards the prisoners. 'These men are Chatti?'

'Aye,' replied Mallovendus.

'Chatti warriors helped to steal my wife. Chatti warriors deprived me of ever seeing my child. Could any of you whoresons have been in my settlement that day, I wonder?' grated Arminius, his flinty gaze wandering over each of the seven. In the middle of the line, a skinny man's eyes made an involuntary flicker to the right. Arminius honed in on the movement with lightning speed. 'Donar has answered my prayers,' he cried, jabbing a finger in the faces of the three warriors the man could have been looking at. 'One or more of you was there, or your friend *thinks* you were.' He regarded the thin prisoner. 'Who was it?'

'I don't know what you're talking about,' protested Skinny.

'Wrong answer,' replied Arminius, kicking him in the solar plexus. He dropped face first to the ground and lay, groaning.

Arminius breathed, setting aside his rage and his inclination to start torturing the three warriors. His desire for vengeance on those who had abducted Thusnelda was unimportant at this juncture. Discovering something of Germanicus' plans was vital. Moving towards the Roman, Arminius caught Mallovendus' watchful eyes on him, and knew he'd made the right decision. Appearances had to be kept up, and his revenge could wait. 'Name. Rank. Cohort. Legion,' he barked in Latin at the officer, a fine-featured young man with a long, straight nose.

'You speak our tongue,' said the officer. Surprise twisted his face. Understanding dawned next; it was followed by fear. 'You are Arminius,' he muttered.

'How observant,' replied Arminius in a dry tone. 'Your name. Rank. Cohort. Legion.'

'Gnaeus Aelius Gallus, optio, Third Century, Ninth Cohort, Twenty-First Legion.'

Arminius could taste disappointment in his throat, cloying and bitter. A junior officer from a low-ranking cohort would know next to nothing of Germanicus' intentions, and still less of Thusnelda, far away in Italy. Arminius studied him through jaundiced eyes. Could Gallus be lying about his rank?

Gallus was in his mid-twenties, and therefore young to be a centurion. His armour was rusted in places, not unusual when an army was in the field, but also not something that Arminius imagined centurions in the more senior cohorts would tolerate. If Gallus served in a higher-ranked cohort, he was a poor example, Arminius decided, concluding he was telling the truth. There was little chance of extracting useful intelligence from him, nor could he save the poor fool from being tortured and killed – not that Arminius wanted to anyway.

I've got to ask, he thought. 'What does Germanicus plan next?'

'You're going to kill me whatever I say.' Gallus' voice was resigned.

'I'll be busy with the warriors,' confided Arminius. 'But my friends here will kill you, yes. It will be slow and rather painful, I would think.'

Gallus looked as if he might be sick. 'If I tell you what I know, can you give me a quick end?'

'I can,' Arminius declared.

Gallus stared, trying to gauge if Arminius was lying or not. After a moment, he gave a little shrug. 'Rumour has it that the army is to make for the *tropaeum* erected by Germanicus' father, Drusus.'

'Tropaeum?' Arminius could not recall the word's meaning.

'It's an altar of sorts, made from helmets, shields, spears, armour and so on. Drusus' tropaeum was built out of spoil taken from the Marcomanni. I'm not sure of its exact location, but it lies to the north or northeast. It marks the furthest point a Roman army has ever journeyed into Germania,' Gallus added with a hint of pride.

'Ah, that. I know where it is,' said Arminius, his good humour returning. He glanced at Mallovendus, who didn't speak any Latin. 'It seems that Germanicus is to march to the altar constructed by his father more than twenty years ago. You know the one on the west bank of the River Albis, in Dolgubnii territory?'

'Aye. It's in the middle of nowhere, and was torn down years ago by the locals.' Mallovendus shook his head in disbelief. 'What help will visiting a pile of rusting metal offer his campaign?'

'Perhaps he wishes to achieve the same glories as his father. Asking the gods for their blessing there would be a powerful gesture,' said Arminius.

'Whatever his reason, the journey will take his legions almost a hundred miles further to the east. More tribes will want to join us because of this, not least the Dolgubnii – they will be unhappy to have their lands invaded. I'd wager the Semnones will also be feeling nervous – and there will be opportunities for us to fight the Romans. If we can manoeuvre Germanicus to one of the rivers, say the Alara or the Amisia, and place our forces on one side while his are on the other, that would be a fine thing, would it not?'

'Attack his soldiers as they cross, you mean?' Mallovendus' smile was brief. 'Germanicus is no fool. He'll see through our ruse.'

Arminius made a dismissive gesture. 'One way or another, we'll bring the dog to bay. When it happens, we'll overwhelm his soldiers as we did before.' He enveloped one fist with the fingers of his other hand. 'There will be no escape.'

'I like the sound of that,' said Mallovendus, leering. 'D'you wish to question the Roman further?'

'I see no need – he's a low-ranker.'

'You're more interested in interrogating those,' stated Mallovendus, indicating the three warriors Arminius had singled out.

'I am. With your permission?'

'Do what you like to them. If they were part of the raiding party who took my wife, I'd, well . . .' Mallovendus' expression grew murderous. 'My men will be happy with the others, and the Roman.'

'Excellent.' Arminius drew his dagger as he walked away from Gallus. The trio of warriors quailed; one started asking for mercy before Arminius had even reached him. Arminius didn't utter a word. Grim-faced, he grabbed the pleader's head with one hand and pulled him close. Babbling shrieks left the struggling warrior's mouth as Arminius probed and sliced with his blade. There was a brief spurt of blood, a deeper sound of pain and the pleader's eyeball dropped to the ground before him. His two companions stared in horror.

'That's just the start,' said Arminius in a pleasant tone, still with a firm grip of his moaning victim. 'Now, tell me. Did any of you take part in the raid that saw my wife Thusnelda taken prisoner, and her maggot of a father, Segestes, freed?'

The pair gaped at him, and Arminius let the tip of his dagger rest just below his victim's second eye. 'Well?' he asked.

'Arminius!' cried Gallus, interrupting.

He twisted his head. Gallus had been pinned down, a warrior holding each of his limbs. A fifth was pulling down Gallus' undergarment, the knife laid alongside clear indication of the warrior's purpose. Arminius sneered. 'What?'

'You said I could have a swift death!' Raw terror oozed from Gallus' voice.

'I lied,' snarled Arminius, turning his back.

'Noooo!' wailed Gallus, his protest becoming a high-pitched scream as the knife-wielding warrior set to work.

Arminius felt no sympathy. Gallus deserved an agonising death, as did every Roman who crossed the Rhenus with fire and sword. Germanicus and his legions, so brutal in their treatment of the tribes, would learn this lesson – the hard way.

Before that, Arminius had the opportunity to revenge himself on some of those who had stolen away his wife. This was a scenario he had never imagined possible. He would savour it. Prolong it. Enjoy it.

Chapter XI

❧❧❧

Low cloud covered the landscape; an intermittent drizzle fell, as usual. Swarms of tiny flies hung in the humid air, biting any exposed areas of flesh. Piso and his comrades were tramping along behind the First Cohort of the Fifth. Piso's feet hurt, in particular his left. A new blister, maybe two, had formed on its ball – he was sure of it. Another to add to the many he already had, Piso thought with grim resignation. He was loath to break from the security of the ranks to inspect it. Better to endure the pain and see to it later, in camp.

He wasn't sure what to feel worst about: the blisters, new and old; his aching back and shoulders; or the numerous raw patches of skin where his new plate armour tended to rub. His plethora of insect bites and damp clothing were minor complaints in comparison. Piso's comrades were in the same boat, more or less, which was some consolation. It meant saying nothing was the best policy. Anyone who grumbled was shouted down and made the butt of his comrades' jokes until something else took their fancy, and that, he knew, could take time.

Today the Fifth was in the body of the miles-long column, a safer place than the vanguard, for which he was grateful. Whichever unit had to lead the army suffered frequent, stinging attacks by the enemy. Even if a man wasn't injured or killed in the short but brutal clashes, it wore him down. If only the cursed enemy would fight, thought Piso for the hundredth time. But Arminius was too shrewd for that, too fox-like in his cunning. Battle wouldn't be joined until he was good and ready, Tullus said, until his warriors had chewed more of the legionaries' morale away.

Superstition prevented Piso from uttering it out loud, but their situation bore an uncomfortable resemblance to the ambush on Varus' legions, and the attacks on Caecina's army the year before. The latter assaults had failed, but the former had resulted in one of the worst defeats suffered by Rome for generations. Not since the disastrous campaigns by first Crassus and then Marcus Antonius into Parthia had so many legions been lost, Metilius liked to grumble. Piso was a gambling man, and the current odds were not something to place money on, let alone risk his life for. Not that he or his friends had much choice in the matter, he brooded. Germanicus' mind was made up, and his army must follow.

The legions were marching north, or perhaps a little northeast, their target some long-forgotten monument Piso had never heard of. 'Where in Hades are we going again?' he asked.

Tullus heard, as he so often did. Materialising by Piso's right shoulder with disconcerting speed, he matched his pace. 'Drusus' tropaeum. A monument erected after his magnificent victory over the Marcomanni. Twenty-five years ago, it was set up. You were still crawling about in the dirt then, I'd wager.' He threw Piso a piercing look.

'I was two, sir,' muttered Piso, hating the immediate baby noises made by his comrades.

'In that case, your mother was still wiping snot from your nose and shit from your arse, while I was there, with Drusus,' Tullus revealed. 'I was an optio then, and Fenestela an ordinary legionary. We fought the Marcomanni several times. Plenty of our brothers died, gods rest them, but we hammered seven shades of shit out of the tribesmen. The tropaeum may be old – indeed the entire structure might have been knocked down years ago by the savages – but it's a sacred monument still. If Germanicus wants us to find it and restore it to its former glory, then that's what we'll do. With smiles on our faces. Understand?'

'Aye, sir,' said Piso, wishing he'd kept his mouth shut. 'I'm glad to be marching towards it.'

'The right answer!' declared Tullus. With what passed for his smile – a grimace in anyone else's book – he marched off.

Fresh jeers and insults fell around Piso; well used to it, he gave back as good as he got. 'As if any of you want to be searching for it,' he snarled once Tullus was out of earshot.

Metilius let out an evil snicker. 'Course we don't, but we weren't caught complaining about it.'

'And you were.' Dulcius pointed out the obvious, as was his wont.

Piso wasn't done yet. 'A pile of rusting spears and rotten shields is the most we'll find – if we're lucky.'

'Better to have an objective than not,' said Metilius. 'And Germanicus might find a place to do battle with Arminius on the way.'

Metilius was right, Piso decided. Deep in enemy territory, their supply lines lengthening by the day, they needed purpose. In the enemy's absence, Drusus' tropaeum would do.

That evening, Piso and his comrades were sitting around their fire, blankets draped over their shoulders and bare feet shoved close to the embers. Spring it might be, but the nights were yet cold and damp. Stomachs full of flat bread baked over the flames and the roasted quarter-lamb that Metilius had procured – 'liberated', in his words, which meant he'd pilfered the meat from some unfortunates in another cohort – they were passing around a leather wine bag owned by Piso.

'One mouthful at a time, you dog,' Piso barked at Dulcius, who was sucking from the skin like a babe at the breast. 'My wine, my rules. Give it here!'

Dulcius made to hand it back, but with clear reluctance.

'My turn,' snarled Piso, slapping away Metilius' grasping fingers. He took a long swallow, doing his best to ignore the vinegary taste, and passed it with a warning look to Metilius. 'One mouthful!'

Metilius made a face when he'd swigged from the skin. 'Not an expensive vintage, is it?'

'Don't like it, don't drink it,' Piso retorted, grabbing it back. 'You could always provide your own.'

'His is just there,' said Dulcius, pointing.

'See how he drinks my wine rather than his own,' cried Piso.

'That's because he buys even cheaper piss than you,' declared Rufus, one of the other soldiers in their contubernium, with triumph.

Hoots of laughter broke out, and Metilius scowled. 'So none of you want any? That's fine.'

'We didn't say that,' said Piso, reaching behind Metilius and snatching up the bag of wine. Ignoring Metilius' protests, he took a long swig before handing it to the man on his other side. 'You can have it back when it's empty,' Piso said to Metilius.

'Bastards.' Knowing better than to pursue his skin, Metilius made loud objections about each man's consumption as his wine moved around the fire. No one paid a bit of notice – each of them had had the same happen countless times before, whether with a piece of cheese, a cut of meat or a leather bag of sour, cheap wine.

'Good to see everyone in fine spirits,' boomed Tullus, appearing from the shadows, still in his armour and vitis in hand. He signalled them back down as they leaped up, saluting. 'Rest easy, brothers.'

The six subsided, happy to see their centurion, but a little uneasy, a little self-conscious in his presence.

'Aren't you going to offer me a drink?' demanded Tullus, his eyes on the skins.

'Of course, sir. Sorry, sir,' spluttered Dulcius, standing up and passing Piso's skin over. 'Here you are.'

Placing the opening to his lips, Tullus raised the bag high. He was quick to lower it. 'That's vile,' he said, making a face. 'This all you can afford, Dulcius?'

'Not mine, sir. It belongs to Piso.'

'And I thought you were a man of taste, Piso,' said Tullus, stoppering the skin and hurling it at him. 'Did you purchase some of Verrucosus' slops?' He was referring to the owner of the dirtiest, most run-down tavern in Vetera.

'No, sir. This is a young vintage, that's all, sir,' said Piso with a wink. 'Try Metilius' wine – it's even worse.'

Everyone watched, Metilius with some trepidation, as Tullus took a pull from the second skin. He screwed up his face. 'Bacchus' sweaty balls, Metilius, that's fucking disgusting!'

'You swallowed it, sir,' countered Metilius as his comrades' shrieks of amusement rained down. 'It can't be that bad.'

'Only a fool spits out free wine when he's far from the nearest tavern,' replied Tullus, taking another mouthful. His gaze roved around the fire, assessing, gauging. 'Had enough to eat tonight?'

'Aye, sir,' Piso and his comrades rumbled. No mention was made of the lamb, by mutual unspoken consent. For the most part, Tullus could be relied on to turn a blind eye to such pilferage, but it didn't do to test him.

Tullus sat down opposite Piso. 'You ready for the march tomorrow? Prepared to fight?'

Their 'Ayes' were louder this time, as they knew Tullus wanted them to be.

'These past days have been frustrating, I know, but we'll bring Arminius to bay,' Tullus announced with cold certainty. 'The day we do, Germanicus will lead us to a great victory. Fortuna's with us this time, and Mars – I know it in my bones. We'll be there, in the thick of the fighting, brothers, to make sure those whoreson Germans meet the fate they deserve.'

Piso and the rest gave him an enthusiastic response. 'Roma Victrix!' 'Mars Ultor!' 'Germanicus!'

'With Arminius defeated, those of us who were in the Eighteenth will regain our honour, and perhaps the eagle that was taken from us.' Tullus stared into the flames, his expression brooding.

Piso's heart leaped. 'Has there been any news of it, sir?'

Tullus' frown deepened. 'No.'

An awkward silence fell. Unsure what to say – who knew if the eagles that had belonged to the Seventeenth and Eighteenth Legions would ever return home? – Piso could see his disquiet mirrored in his comrades' faces.

The wine skins began to move around the fire again as they took the only solace available. When one reached Tullus, he drank deepest of all, passing on the bag without looking at the next man, his eyes fixed on the burning logs.

Piso watched him sidelong, a new worry gnawing his guts. Like everyone who'd been in Tullus' old command, he knew that his centurion had suffered a grievous internal wound during Arminius' savage ambush. Never before had Piso seen it so plain: Tullus was a tortured man. He would not rest – could not, Piso corrected himself – until his old legion's eagle had been salvaged. While he shared Tullus' conviction that Arminius and his allies would be defeated, Piso felt a deal less certain about the hunt for the lost standards. Iconic items, magnetic symbols of power even to non-Romans, they would be treasured and kept safe by the tribes who held them – all the more so because of the recovery of the Nineteenth's eagle the previous year.

Tullus was the bedrock of his men's existence, the foundation upon which they relied. Piso wasn't alone in regarding him with a reverential awe. Never before had Piso stopped to consider that his centurion might have human frailties, yet the stark evidence of this faced him over the fire, not six paces away. Tullus' eyes were haunted, his shoulders threatening to stoop. Piso didn't like it.

Dangers posed by the Germans aside, Piso thought, what did the future hold for Tullus? Not much, if the Eighteenth's eagle wasn't found. Dear as Sirona and Artio were to Tullus, they weren't capable of healing his deepest injury.

'We'll find it, sir,' Piso blurted.

Tullus looked up. 'Eh?'

'We *will* get back our eagle, sir, on my life. Me and my brothers, we'll do anything it takes, won't we?' Sharp as needles, Piso's eyes roved over his comrades.

'Course we will, sir,' Metilius was quick to add. The others muttered their support. 'The eagle will be ours again, sir.' 'Aye, sir.' 'No doubt about it, sir.'

'The whole cohort feels the same way, sir,' Piso continued, even though he wasn't sure of that. Spreading the word about how important it was for Tullus would be his new mission, he swore to himself. If Tullus heard it from enough mouths, perhaps it would help.

A brief, weary smile marked Tullus' face. 'You're good boys. An officer couldn't ask for better soldiers.' Grimacing, he got to his feet, waving a dismissive hand as they also made to stand. 'Don't stay up all night. We've got another long march tomorrow.' He tramped off into the darkness, not in the direction of the next contubernium along, but towards his own tent, making Piso's concern for him resurge.

Chapter XII

By all the gods, there it is,' said Tullus, pointing with his vitis. 'Do
you see? That's manmade, or I'm no judge.'

Fenestela, come from his position to confer, peered at the low
hummock that stood some hundred paces in front of them, its lower slopes
decorated with trees. 'Diana's left tit, I think you're right.'

'I usually am,' replied Tullus, his tone sarcastic.

Ten days had passed since his conversation with Piso and his comrades.
While half the army provided a protective screen, several legions including
the Fifth – and Tullus and his men – were combing a range of low hills close
to the River Albis. More than 250 miles east of the Rhenus, a hundred from
the cold and hostile German Sea, the windswept site had the feel of the
world's end. Guided here by Flavus, Arminius' brother, who knew the area
because of its proximity to his own Cherusci tribe's homeland, the legions
had been searching for Drusus' tropaeum for two days without success.

'Screw you, *sir*,' Fenestela said under his breath.

Tullus chuckled, not the slightest put out. 'Who'd have thought we
would return to this spot – if I'm right, of course. The last time you and
I were here . . .' He paused, reliving the vicious battle he and his men
had waged as part of Drusus' army, a generation before. The Marcomanni had
been like every German tribe: courageous, tough enemies, warriors unafraid
to die even when it had become clear their cause was hopeless.

'A hard fight, it was.' Fenestela's expression was sombre. 'We lost more
than a dozen from the century.'

'That sounds right.' A sigh escaped Tullus. So many men had died under his command over the previous twenty-something years that he had long since forgotten most of their faces. Try as he might, he couldn't rid himself of the nagging guilt that he should have saved more, impossible task though that would have been. The unwelcome emotion lurked in the dark recesses of his soul, emerging when his spirits were low, or when he stood in a place such as this.

Tullus' skin crawled. He could almost see shadowy figures at the edge of his vision, wraiths from his past come to life. With a fierce blink, he forced them to disappear. The only figures in sight were his legionaries of the Fifth, standing in a long line and motionless because he had stopped. They were good men, he thought. Fine soldiers. He would keep them alive whatever the cost.

Fenestela indicated the hummock. 'Best go and see if your old eyes were right or not, eh?'

'There's nothing wrong with my eyesight, curse you,' growled Tullus, swiping at Fenestela with his vitis, but his optio was already gone, returning to the century's rear.

Grumbling to himself, Tullus gave the order to advance.

An hour later, Tullus was atop the mound, waiting for Germanicus. His hunch had been correct. At the top of the hummock, he had found an oak trunk, now cast down, but still decorated with a mail shirt. The entire area was scattered with spear heads and shield bosses. Helmets and swords weren't as plentiful – few Germanic warriors could afford such expensive equipment, so they would have been taken as booty. Mail was scarce for the same reason. Leaving the enemy slain at a tropaeum wasn't uncommon, but the local tribes appeared to have buried these corpses at the same time as they had torn down Drusus' altar and the weaponry that had decorated it.

Tullus' soldiers and the rest of the cohort were content: finding the tropaeum had ended their sweaty, laborious search. With Bassius in command, three centuries stood guard in a semicircle, facing east and south, while the rest had settled down to wait for their commander. They weren't allowed to sit, but Tullus and the other centurions had permitted them to down their shields and to rest their javelins against the trees. Sacred site or no, the legionaries relished the opportunity for a rest. Food and wine had been broken out. Banter and easy conversation flowed. Games of dice and *latrunculi* were being played. Jokes and filthy stories filled the air, but in low voices. Overgrown, despoiled, this was still a sacred place.

Peeeeep! Peeeeep!

Tullus had been waiting for this signal – Bassius had agreed with his suggestion for Fenestela to wait a couple of hundred paces away, on Germanicus' likely approach route. Two blasts of his whistle meant their general was coming. 'Germanicus is here! Pick your shields and javelins up, you lazy bastards. Form up by the century,' Tullus shouted.

Mention of the hallowed name had men scrambling for their weapons and equipment. Tullus paced up and down, scowling and barking at the individuals who weren't moving fast enough. Watched by their centurions, the two other centuries hurried to do the same. By the time the noise of hooves was audible, the hummock was ringed by an almost complete circle of legionaries facing inward. A gap had been left through which Germanicus and his escort could ride. Straight-backed, javelins planted and with their shields resting on the ground before them, the soldiers made an impressive sight.

Tullus remained beside the largest pile of evidence, the oak trunk that had stood here, and a dozen or more shield bosses, their once polished surfaces rusty and tarnished.

Germanicus' entrance was everything Tullus had come to expect. In full general's attire, he rode a fine grey stallion wearing magnificent decorated harness. Although the army had been on the march for days, Germanicus' armour gleamed as if new, and the scarlet crest on his helmet looked fresh-dyed. Head to toe the army's commander, thought Tullus. Following Germanicus was his usual retinue of staff officers, servants and Praetorians. Slowing his mount, he walked it towards Tullus, who came to attention. 'General!' he cried, saluting.

Germanicus' stern expression eased. 'Centurion Tullus. We meet again.'

'Yes, sir!'

Germanicus' gaze was already focused on the bosses and great trunk at Tullus' feet. Slipping from his horse's back, he handed the reins to Tullus – not a demeaning gesture, but one of recognition – and said, 'You think this is the site of my father's tropaeum?'

'I wasn't sure at first, sir. I thought that the weapons here might have been left for another reason, but then we found the oak trunk and I saw the view.' Tullus pointed east. Between the beeches and spruces perched on the mound's eastern side, the wide sinuous band that was the Albis was visible, some half mile away. 'A man doesn't forget a sight like that.'

Germanicus stared at Tullus in surprise. 'I didn't know you were here.'

You never asked, thought Tullus. 'It was my honour to serve Drusus, sir.'

'Did you ever have occasion to speak with him?' There was a longing note to Germanicus' voice.

'No, sir. I was but an optio then – there was no reason for us to meet. I saw him often of course, and I fought close to his position once. He was a great leader.'

'So they say.' Germanicus' expression grew sorrowful. 'My memories of him are few. The strongest I have are of his funeral.'

'He was taken from us too soon, sir. Every soldier in the army grieved at his passing. The tumulus in Mogontiacum is proof of that.' Tullus had vivid memories of a visit to the town many years before when he'd watched the local troops racing around Drusus' monument.

'My uncle Tiberius says that he planned to go further east with his army. Do you remember aught of that?'

'There was talk of it, sir. The weather was good; there would have been time to construct a bridge using boats.'

'It never happened. Do you know why?'

Tullus studied Germanicus and wondered if *he* knew. 'The rumours were that Drusus dreamed of a huge Suebian woman, sir, an evil spirit. She told him he was destined not to see the lands on the far bank of the Albis.'

Tullus hesitated, not wishing to repeat the ghoul's final words. Spread by a loose-lipped priest in whom Drusus had confided, they had travelled through the army like a forest fire.

'She warned him that his life was soon to end,' grated Germanicus. 'Is that not so?'

'Aye, sir, I think so.' Tullus looked down, his mind full of bad memories. Ordered by Drusus to strike camp the moment the tropaeum had been finished, the army had set out for the Rhenus, hundreds of miles distant. Their journey, through hostile territory, had been unpleasant from the start. Wolves had trailed after the legions, and howled in the darkness outside their fortifications. Shooting stars had blazed overhead night after night. A pair of young boys had been seen riding through the tent lines one evening, although children were banned from entering the camp. On more than one occasion, women's wails – as if parted from their babes – had risen from the ramshackle tents of the army's followers, but when patrols were sent to investigate, no one could be found who would admit to making the cries. 'It was a troubling march, sir,' said Tullus, 'and it got worse when your father was thrown from his mount.'

Germanicus made the sign against evil.

It was uncommon for men to die from a simple fall, yet that had been Drusus' fate, thought Tullus. Perhaps he *had* been visited by an evil spirit.

'Whatever my father's destiny, I have had visions only of victory,' Germanicus declared, staring at the far bank of the Albis. 'It would be pleasing to take my legions further east this summer, but that is not my purpose. Arminius and his warriors have yet to be crushed. We will linger here long enough to see the tropaeum rebuilt and consecrated once more, but then our hunt will continue.'

'A good plan, sir.' Tullus was pleased by Germanicus' calm attitude regarding his father's end, and by the planned ceremony at the tropaeum, which would allow him to honour not just Drusus, but Tullus' own soldiers who'd fallen during Arminius' ambush.

'The men will enjoy the gladiator fights,' Germanicus declared.

'Funeral games, sir?'

'My brother and I held them in memory of our father some years ago, but this is a more fitting place than Rome – they will take place here, where his campaigning came to an end. The gods will look well on such sacrifices.' There was a wild glint in Germanicus' eyes. 'How many prisoners have we taken?'

'I'm not sure of the exact figures, sir. One, two thousand?' Tullus felt no sympathy for these German tribesmen. They all had Roman blood on their hands.

'Spartacus once had four hundred captives fight until just one was left living. The survivor – a senior centurion – had to carry the news of his army's defeat to Rome. I'll not be bettered by a slave,' Germanicus continued, striding to and fro as if delivering a speech to the Senate. 'Five hundred warriors will take part. Their deaths will honour my father's shade, and win divine assistance in defeating Arminius.'

Tullus was impressed. He had forgotten how ruthless Germanicus could be. 'The final warrior will bear word to Arminius, sir?'

'Aye.' Germanicus' tone was granite hard. 'Unless he is a complete coward, Arminius *will* fight then.'

Chapter XIII

਼਼਼

'Germanicus did *what*?' roared Arminius. It was mid-morning, and he was knee-deep in a river close to his camp, bare-chested – interrupted in the middle of his ablutions. Maelo had arrived at the head of a group of warriors, bringing with him a man who'd been sent, it seemed, by Germanicus himself.

'He paired off five hundred warriors, and forced them to fight to the death,' repeated Maelo, his tone grim. 'The two hundred and fifty left had to do the same thing, and so it went on. This man is the only one left.'

Arminius peered at the figure standing a dozen paces behind Maelo, waiting to be summoned. A big man, he stood with bowed shoulders and matted hair covering his face. Tears and cuts marked most parts of his tunic and trousers, offering glimpses of multiple wounds. It was a wonder he was able to walk, thought Arminius, a dark fury thrumming through him. 'What's his name?'

'Tudrus. He's Dolgubnii.'

This man would be no relation to the warrior who had been one of Arminius' most trusted followers, but his name rekindled bad memories of the older Tudrus' death at the Romans' hands. Rage filled him too at Germanicus' savagery. Arminius waded in grim silence to the pebbled shore. Drying himself with his old tunic and throwing on a clean one, he beckoned to Tudrus.

Every step the warrior took made him wince. Blood oozed from a long gash under his ribcage, and serous fluid oozed from others. His nose looked broken, and the tissue under his swollen right eye had turned a nasty blue-purple colour. 'Arminius,' he croaked. His eyes rose for a heartbeat before dropping again to regard his mud-encrusted feet.

'Only a fool would say well met, but you are welcome nonetheless,' said Arminius in his most charismatic voice. 'You are Tudrus of the Dolgubnii, I'm told.'

'I am.'

'You must need a drink. Food. To have your wounds tended.'

'Forty miles I've walked to find you. I'll take some water.'

'You bring word from Germanicus?' How he wished the Roman general was before him instead. He'd have torn the bastard limb from limb.

'Aye.' Nothing could disguise the sorrow in Tudrus' single-word answer.

Arminius filled his skin from the river and handed it over. Tudrus drank like a man who'd crossed a desert without finding a single waterhole. Nodding his thanks, he sat with a grunt of pain.

Arminius lowered himself down beside Tudrus and waited.

'The Dolgubnii don't have enough strength to fight Germanicus – who does? – but we did our best, picking off smaller patrols and attacking foraging parties while our women and children fled over the Albis to safety. About ten days ago the band I was with took on a Roman scouting party that was larger than it seemed. Most of my friends were slaughtered. A blow to the head knocked me out, or I would have been slain too. Better I *had* died.' Bitterness oozed from Tudrus' voice.

'But you lived,' said Arminius, eager to hear every detail.

'Aye. I was taken as a slave, I and the other poor bastards made captive by the Romans. Tethered together like animals' – Tudrus rubbed at his neck, which was still marked by rope burns – 'we were marched in files at the army's rear, swallowing its dust and treading in mule shit with every pace. Anyone who tried to escape was killed. Dying like that was pointless, stupid, so I bided my time. It's a long way back to the Rhenus, I told myself. An opportunity would arise.' He made an angry gesture. 'Things changed when we reached the Albis. It seems Germanicus was overcome with emotion to stand where his father had, a quarter of a century ago. Nothing would satisfy the whoreson but to hold funeral games in celebration.'

'That's when the five hundred warriors were chosen,' said Arminius, picturing the scene.

'It was. The Romans have several thousand prisoners now – plenty to choose from. Centurions inspected us, picking out the biggest and strongest. There was no wasting time: we were led straight to the foot of the mound where Drusus' altar had been. Legionaries had formed a great square with their shields; fifty of us were forced into it first. Germanicus ordered us to choose opponents and kill one another, or be crucified. When his command was translated, some warriors refused. They were nailed to crosses at once. The rest of us agreed, like cowards, and weapons were thrown in to us. Armed, a group of men charged Germanicus – they too were brought down, with javelins and arrows. Those who remained were given a final chance to obey, before we too were slain.' Tudrus sighed.

Gods, but Germanicus was cunning, thought Arminius. 'So you fought?'

'Aye. The winners of each bout were allowed to rest for a short time, and then we went at it again. We continued until only I was standing.' Tudrus' voice was muted, his gaze fixed on the ground between his bent knees. 'I was tied up close to Germanicus then, and the next fifty were brought in and made to do the same. After them came the third set of men, and so on. The whole process took hours, and near the end there were ten of us left. We fought one another until there were five. Five left from five hundred.' Tudrus' voice died away.

Arminius and Maelo had been riveted by the horrific story, their eyes fixed on Tudrus, but now their gaze met, each mirroring the same burning rage.

'Germanicus had an officer toss a coin to decide which man would sit by while the other two pairs fought each other,' Tudrus continued. 'They did the same when there were three. You could say I was lucky – I "won" both times the throw was made, so I got to rest twice while the other poor bastards had no respite at all. The last warrior I had to fight was so tired he could barely hold a sword.' Tudrus let out a short, unpleasant laugh. 'At least his end was quick.'

'You had no choice,' said Arminius.

Tudrus' tortured eyes regarded him. 'Every man has a choice.'

'They would have crucified you if you hadn't fought.'

'That's right. I could have chosen to die right at the start, but I didn't. Instead I slew eight warriors. Eight of my own kind. What kind of man does that make me?' asked Tudrus, his voice cracking.

'A survivor,' said Arminius, thinking, I would have done the same.

'This for being a survivor,' said Tudrus, making an obscene gesture.

The uncomfortable silence that fell was broken by Arminius. 'Did Germanicus say aught to you?'

'He said that his legions are ready, whenever you and the mongrels who follow at your heel can muster the courage to fight.'

Blood pounded in Arminius' ears. Aware that men were watching, he breathed deeply and asked, 'What of Germanicus' movements now?'

'I heard talk of marching west to rejoin the troops that had been tasked with crushing the Angrivarii,' said Tudrus.

The nugget of information made sense, Arminius decided. His calm returned as he pondered the best course of action. *He* was Germanicus' target, so the legions stood nothing to gain from crossing the River Albis and waging war in the east. To the north lay the ocean, to the northwest Roman allies. Heading south would take his enemies even deeper into tribal territory – an endeavour too risky even for Germanicus and his vast army. West or southwest were the only directions that made sense. 'So our game of cat and mouse continues. Good. Time is on our side, not Germanicus'.'

'He's trying to provoke you into battle,' said Maelo, entering the conversation.

'He is, and he'll fail. Sooner or later, we will catch his legions in the right place, and then we will fight.' Standing, Arminius clasped Tudrus' shoulder. 'You did well. I thank you. Let my healers tend your wounds. Then you can rest, and take food and drink.'

Tudrus didn't appear to have heard. 'Will you consult with the gods before breaking camp?'

Arminius wasn't a devout worshipper, but Donar had lent his aid in the victory over Varus, he was sure of that. It also looked good to follow tradition. 'Aye, quite likely. Why?'

Tudrus got to his feet. He stood a good hand and a half taller than Arminius, and despite his wounds was still a fine physical specimen. 'I will give myself to the god. To Donar. My life for your success in battle.'

Shocked, Arminius said, 'You're exhausted. You—'

Tudrus cut him off. 'My wife died two years hence, not long after our babe was taken by a fever. All my battle brothers are dead, or slaves. I have no reason to live, Arminius. I will hang from the tree. I will offer my flesh for Donar's ravens to feast upon. Let my sacrifice appease the thunder god.'

Arminius' eyes moved to Maelo, who shrugged his shoulders as if to say, 'Why not?' Looking again at Tudrus, Arminius asked, 'You're sure?'

'I've never been more certain. If you don't permit this, I'll hang myself anyway. There's nothing left for me in this world.' Tudrus' tone was drained.

It would be a powerful offering, thought Arminius. According to custom, those who went willingly to their deaths were sure to catch the gods' attention. Sitting in the heavens on his lightning-bound throne, with thunderclouds roiling around him, Donar would smile at Tudrus' death, and lend his support to Arminius for a second, momentous battle.

'Well?' demanded Tudrus, his bloodshot eyes boring into Arminius.

Arminius' conscience pricked him then: Tudrus' ordeal had unbalanced him. He needed rest, and nursing. Given those, he would return to his senses, and wish to live. Arminius considered this for little more than a heartbeat. 'Yours is a noble offer. I will talk to the priests.'

A rictus – it may have been an attempt to smile – twisted Tudrus' face. 'Make your words persuasive, Arminius of the Cherusci. Donar is watching.'

Arminius nodded, feeling a trickle of sweat run down his back.

* * *

Evening was falling over the land, and in the depths of the forest close to the tribal camp, a murky twilight already reigned. An odd, unseasonal chill hung in the clammy air. Bird calls and animal sounds were commonplace elsewhere in the wood, but not here. Arminius and Maelo were waiting at the edge of a muddy clearing; among the trees to either side – decorated with horned cattle skulls and a number of human ones – stood every chieftain in his alliance. Eager to witness the rite but awed by the eerie atmosphere, no one spoke. More nervous than he would have expected, Arminius kept his expression stony.

The open space was dominated by a hewn stone altar covered in spider-like runes. The throat-slashed corpses of two legionaries sprawled to one side of the great rock slab. Their deaths and the reading of their bucket-collected blood had formed the ceremony's opening act. Next had come the ritual bending and twisting of swords and spears, the hammering flat of vast silver cauldrons; these offerings would be tossed into a sacred lake at the first opportunity.

Flanked by half a dozen acolytes, an old, red-robed priest was intoning prayers to Donar. Alone and naked before them, his body covered in wounds, stood Tudrus. Ropes bound his arms behind his back – he could not have been more vulnerable, and yet the proud set of his shoulders and his firm chin told those watching that he was ready to meet his end.

The straggle-haired priest, a wizened, bent-shouldered figure who looked to have been spawned in an earlier, darker time, ceased his chant. An instant tension developed, and Arminius felt his pulse quicken.

Placing a claw-like hand on Tudrus' arm, the priest rasped, 'Are you a freeborn man?'

'Aye,' replied Tudrus in a loud, confident voice.

'Your name?'

'Tudrus, of the Dolgubnii tribe.'

'And you are come to the god of your own free will?'

'I am, if Donar will accept me.'

A cold smile marked the priest's lined face. 'That depends on the manner of your death, Tudrus of the Dolgubnii. If but a single sound leaves your lips before you leave this life, Donar will be displeased. Your soul will be denied entry to the warriors' hall, condemning you to roam the underworld forever.'

A slight stiffening of Tudrus' shoulders. 'I understand.'

Arminius didn't care if Tudrus' soul was cursed for all eternity – what mattered was winning Donar's favour. Steel your courage, Tudrus, he thought. Stay strong, or your sacrifice will not serve me.

The priest jerked his head, and an acolyte led Tudrus towards the branch of a great beech that hung inwards and into the clearing, some twenty paces from Arminius. A rope already hung from the bough, one end tied in a running loop. Reaching it, Tudrus faced Arminius and gave him a tiny dip of his chin, which said, 'I do this for you.'

Arminius' acknowledgement was a grave nod. Again his conscience reared its head, but he stamped it down. Donar, accept this man's death, he prayed. Grant me victory over Germanicus in return.

Tudrus bent his head and allowed the acolyte to place the rope around his neck and tighten it. The acolyte's companions, who had followed, took up the loose end with him and drew it taut. Tudrus braced himself.

'Are you ready to meet the god, Tudrus?' The priest's voice carried from the altar.

'Aye,' came the firm reply.

The priest issued an order, and the acolytes heaved as one. Tudrus' body jerked a handspan from the leafy floor. His face contorted with pain, and his body jerked from side to side, but he made no sound. The acolytes' next tug, even more powerful, saw his feet rise to the height of a ten-year-old boy. Face purple, veins bulging from his forehead, Tudrus thrashed to and fro in his agonies, but not a single whimper left his engorged lips. Protruding from their sockets, his bloodshot eyes stayed focused on Arminius, or so it seemed to the Cherusci chieftain.

Disquieted but compelled, Arminius held Tudrus' tortured gaze. Appearing to show respect, he did it because of his burning desire that Tudrus' end should be soundless, and acceptable to the god.

Most men hanged like this died fast, but the Dolgubnii warrior was made of stronger stuff. Arminius had counted seven times fifty, and still Tudrus writhed on the rope. Arminius felt sick. Tudrus' agony was so great that in the end he would *have* to make some kind of noise.

But he didn't.

As Arminius' count neared five hundred, Tudrus stopped moving at last. His muscled legs went slack. Urine began to dribble from his shrunken member; the smell of shit laced the air. It was impossible to tell from his mottled, twisted features if the peace he had longed for was his.

Arminius' eyes shot to the old priest. 'Well?' he wanted to shout, but a rare superstition prevented him.

With the support of an acolyte, the priest shuffled to stand alongside Tudrus' gently swaying corpse. He prodded its thigh and, like every man watching, Arminius tensed.

'The warrior died well,' wheezed the priest. 'Donar is pleased!'

Relief flooded through Arminius. Victory would be his.

PART TWO

Summer, AD 16

Deep in Germania

Chapter XIV

◫◫◫

A fternoon was passing, and the sun beat down on Germania from a clear sky. The high temperature, welcomed at first after the cool spring, was on the verge of being unpleasant. Swarms of tiny, biting flies hung around the head of Piso and a group of his comrades as they stood calf-deep in the Visurgis, enjoying the caress of the swift-flowing river. Following Tullus' orders, they were filling skins with water. Six days had passed since the funeral games, and Germanicus' army was more than a hundred miles from Drusus' tropaeum. It had crossed the Visurgis earlier that day, and halted on flat ground half a mile from the west bank. Four great encampments, which were still being completed, would provide enough space for the eight legions and auxiliaries; Germanicus had honoured the Fifth and the Twenty-First by placing them in the same camp as himself and his Praetorians.

Piso's cohort and four others had dug the defences the previous day, so they had the easier duty of keeping watch as the other half of the legion sweated over the construction of a deep ditch and a stout earthen rampart. This was an excellent development, because Piso and his comrades got to be here on the riverbank, slaking their thirst *and* cooling off. Although the scouts reported that Arminius and his forces were nearby, they were on the opposite side of the Visurgis. Attacking over the water this late in the day would be risky – half a cohort of auxiliary archers stood with Piso and his comrades, and the rest of Germanicus' army was only a short distance to their rear.

Out of the blue, someone splashed Piso from behind. 'Hey!' He spun to find a grinning Dulcius retreating at speed. Piso kicked out, sending up a shower of spray at his comrade. Dulcius slashed a hand over the river's surface in reply, raining water over Piso. The others took one look and joined in the horseplay. Chaos reigned for a time. The best moment came when Metilius dunked Dulcius on his arse, soaking him from head to foot.

Eventually, Piso put an end to it. 'Tullus or another officer will see,' he warned.

They returned to their task not a moment too soon.

'I saw you, you maggots!' roared Tullus, wading into the shallows alongside Piso and his companions. 'I ordered you to fill those water bags, not act like a gang of youths on a day out. Move it!'

We didn't do any harm, thought Piso resentfully, but he didn't dare say so. He held his skin under the surface and let it swell with water. Once stoppered, he threw its carry strap over his shoulder and unslung another empty bag. 'Tullus would do the same if he were an ordinary legionary,' he muttered to Metilius, his closest neighbour.

'What's that?' Tullus came striding over.

'Nothing, sir,' said Piso, wishing he'd kept quiet.

'Don't fucking "nothing" me, Piso!' Tullus' vitis struck the water with a mighty plash.

Knowing it could fall next on his back, Piso said, 'I was wondering when we might get to fight Arminius, sir.' He prayed Tullus would swallow the lie.

'Wonder all you like when you're sitting at your fire this evening,' thundered Tullus. 'Until then, stitch your lip and finish doing what I told you to do far too long ago! The same applies to the rest of you miserable dogs. Move!'

Every man set to with a will, while Tullus watched with a stony expression. Not until they had filled every skin to bulging point and marched back to the rest of the cohort, a short way back from the shoreline, did he relent. Turning his back on the men, he studied the far bank with grim intensity. Some hundred paces away, it was accessible through the shallow water — this was one of the four fords used by the army to cross the Visurgis.

'What's got into him?' whispered Piso, frowning. 'Arminius is miles away – the scouts said so.'

'He is jumpier than normal,' agreed Metilius. 'Maybe he knows something we don't – or senses it.'

'Aye, perhaps.' Unhappy, Piso shuffled back and forth. If Tullus was concerned, then he needed to be too. From that point on, he disregarded his comrades' muttered conversations, instead watching the other side of the river.

Nothing much happened for an hour, and most men had long since ceased paying attention to the track on the far bank. They ignored too the flitting kingfishers, and the regular plops as fish gulped down insects at the water's surface. Piso, on the other hand, had moved so little that his neck ached, and a knot had formed in the muscles under one shoulder blade. His gaze roved without pause, studying the path opposite, the trees, the bushes, the river. Nothing was going to stop his watch – Tullus' disquiet had seen to that. It was almost a relief when arcing sunlight from the setting sun illuminated, as if from nowhere, a group of horsemen on the track east.

'Enemy approaching!' Piso shouted.

An instant tension crackled the air. Men lifted their shields and javelins even before Tullus and Fenestela had given the order to do so.

'Sound the call for "enemy in sight"!' Tullus, gaze fixed on the riders, was striding back and forth in front of his men.

Soldiers in the other centuries had also seen the horsemen, and their musicians added their own clamour to that made by Tullus' trumpeter. By the time the party of perhaps fifty men had reached the water's edge, the centuries had formed up two wide, three deep, blocking the path on their side of the Visurgis. The auxiliary archers were positioned to either side, nocked shafts ready to shoot.

An odd and uneasy calm fell as the two forces watched each other.

'That's Arminius, or I'm a camp prefect,' hissed Piso, spying a fine-dressed, bearded figure on a chestnut stallion.

'Fortuna's saggy tits, you're right. What's he want?' demanded Metilius.

'Only the gods know,' said Piso, hoping Tullus would order them to charge over the river. Risky that might be, but Piso was ready. There – so close – was the evil bastard who'd engineered the deaths of many of his friends.

They watched, agog, as Arminius cupped a hand to his lips and called out in Latin, 'Ho, Romans! Is your general near?'

Bassius, the most senior officer present, stepped forward from his men. 'What savage is asking for him?' he shouted.

Arminius smiled, revealing his teeth. 'I had forgotten what boors you Romans could be. Savage you call me, but you are the ones who murder women and children!'

His companions' threats and insults carried over the water.

'I see you, Arminius, you treacherous dog,' yelled Tullus, joining Bassius. 'Come over and fight me! One to one, eh?'

Piso and Metilius exchanged an excited look. Despite Arminius' youth, Tullus would win such a contest – they were sure of it. Justice would be served.

'Centurion Tullus – what a pleasant surprise!' answered Arminius with a mocking half-bow. 'I am not here to seek a single combat, much as it would please me to end your life. I wish to speak with my brother Flavus. Is he here?'

'It's no business of yours whether he is or he isn't,' retorted Bassius.

'Why don't you piss off back to your camp?' demanded Tullus. 'While you're there, try to persuade the yellow-livered, spineless rabble who follow at your tail to fight us.'

'Have they lost their courage after we whipped your arses last year?' added Bassius. He glanced to either side. 'ARCHERS, READY!'

Arminius' face tensed, but he did not retreat. Nor did his nervous-faced companions. 'I come in peace,' he called.

'Loose,' hissed Piso. 'Go on, Bassius, give them the order. Kill the whoreson and the war will be over! There's not another chieftain like Arminius in all of Germania, Tullus says.'

Ten heartbeats passed, and no command fell from Bassius' lips.

'So you will not fetch my brother?' enquired Arminius.

'Tell him "No",' muttered Piso, but to his surprise, Bassius and Tullus bent their heads together in conferral.

After a short time, Bassius cried, 'We will ask Germanicus for an answer. You can wait for that?'

'It seems I have little choice,' came Arminius' stiff reply. 'As long as your archers can be trusted to stay their hands?'

'They will release whenever I tell them to,' answered Bassius.

This veiled threat made Arminius and his party uncertain enough to withdraw a safe distance from the bank. His move, made while muttering dire imprecations, was met with disdainful shouts and jeers from the assembled legionaries.

Piso watched in disgust as one of the messengers stationed by their position was sent to seek out their general. 'Why did they do that?' he asked of no one in particular.

'Germanicus is the commander – he has to be consulted on important matters, I suppose,' said Metilius, taking a pull from his water skin.

'He'll say the same thing as Tullus,' opined Piso. 'Piss off.'

Piso was wrong. The messenger returned not long after, bringing the surprising news that Germanicus had given his permission for Flavus to talk with his brother. Bassius relayed this to Arminius, who seemed pleased but suspicious. It wasn't surprising, thought Piso. The auxiliary archers were still in place, and during the wait, perhaps ordered by a mischievous Bassius, some had shot arrows over the river. The shafts had landed short of Arminius' position, but left no doubt that he was within range at the water's edge. Despite this danger, he had ridden down to the bank to talk with Bassius, almost daring the archers to loose again, it seemed to Piso.

'Where is Flavus?' demanded Arminius.

'He'll arrive soon,' answered Bassius. 'You could cross over and wait for him.'

'You must think I came down in the last shower,' said Arminius, chuckling. 'I will stay where I am, and your archers will withdraw while I talk to my brother. It would be too easy for an over-eager officer to order a volley. That might even be your intent, when I am distracted.'

Piso's hopes that Arminius would again be told to piss off were dashed once more. Sour-faced, Bassius sent a soldier to the cohort's rear. Almost at once, the sounds of tramping feet became audible as the archers marched off for a short distance. Arminius dismounted and remained where he was, watching the Romans with a cold, calculating expression.

Piso's muscles were still twitching with the desire to act. 'What are the odds we could rush him – take him by surprise?'

Metilius snorted. 'He'd be astride his mount before we got halfway across, and you know it. There's not a man alive who can outrun a horse.'

'Aye.' Disappointed and frustrated, Piso spat into the water. 'It's so tempting, though.'

'The archers were our best bet, and they're gone. It's time to see what the two brothers will say to each other.'

Cheered by the chance of witnessing this unusual encounter, Piso nodded.

The sun had dropped but a little further on the western horizon when Flavus cantered in on his horse from the direction of the camp. Piso knew him by sight – most men did. Blond-haired, stocky and with a commanding presence, Flavus was hard to miss. Lacking an eye – an old battle wound – he yet had the type of stare that most men avoided, and his status as auxiliary cohort commander and Arminius' brother made him unique in Germanicus' army. Dressed for the occasion in burnished mail and helmet, with his awards for valour prominent on his neck, chest and arms, he stopped to talk to Bassius – all the while acting as if his brother wasn't present.

'Arminius is furious,' said Piso to Metilius with glee. 'Look.'

Arminius' scowl, stiff-legged stance and folded arms spoke volumes, but he held his peace until Flavus had left his horse with one of Bassius' legionaries and come right to the river's edge.

'Greetings, brother. Are you well?' Arminius called.

'Well enough until I saw you,' Flavus answered. 'What do you want, traitor?'

'You call *me* traitor?' Arminius shouted. 'I am not the one who has forgotten his own people. Who wears with such smugness the badges, the petty trinkets given by Rome, that are nothing more than the marks of slavery. Here I stand, a proud, free man, and there you slouch, fat-bellied and soft-handed, nothing more than Germanicus' lapdog.'

'I have kept my word, unlike you, oathbreaker! If you have only come to insult me, I have but one thing to say: your fate approaches.' Flavus pointed at the sky. 'Donar's ravens are circling overhead, though you cannot see them yet.' He turned his back and strode away.

There was time for a few bold men to surge through the water and take down Arminius with javelins, thought Piso, again hoping that Bassius or Tullus would give the order. No command came, though – it seemed that Germanicus had decreed the brothers' meeting to be a form of truce. A golden chance was being wasted, Piso decided bitterly, and he was powerless to intervene.

Flavus was halfway to his horse when Arminius called out again. 'What of Thusnelda?' The contempt he'd shown Flavus had gone – his tone was almost plaintive.

Flavus glanced over his shoulder. What might have been regret, even sadness, passed over his face. 'She has been treated with respect, and dwells in a large house in Ravenna.'

'And my child?' The longing was palpable in Arminius' voice.

'You have a son,' said Flavus.

'A son,' Arminius muttered, bowing his head. 'I have a son.' He eyed Flavus again. 'What is his name?'

'Thumelicus. He thrives, and has already learned to crawl, I am told.'

'Will they ever be freed?'

'You know the answer to that as well as I do, brother,' replied Flavus with a scornful look. 'Disband your army and submit yourself to Germanicus' justice, and I promise to do what I can.'

'I may as well offer my neck to the executioner's blade,' cried Arminius, his eyes blazing with fury. 'Germanicus knows not the meaning of mercy! Ask the Marsi, the Chatti and the Angrivarii!'

His companions, who had ridden closer to listen to the conversation, set up an angry chorus. 'Kill Germanicus!' roared one in accented Latin. 'Death to Tiberius!'

Flavus lost his temper. 'Give me my horse,' he ordered, snatching the reins from the startled legionary. He leaped on to its back and urged it towards the water. 'Stay where you are, brother, and we can resolve this here and now.'

'Good enough,' screamed Arminius, pulling his mount closer. 'I used to beat you every time we fought as boys! Nothing's changed.'

Piso's happy expectation of a brutal fight in the middle of the river was dashed as Bassius roared at Flavus to stay where he was. When he didn't appear to hear, Bassius sent Tullus loping over. With a sharp tap on Flavus' thigh, Tullus got his attention. Piso and the rest couldn't hear what was said, but Flavus wasn't happy, that was clear. He made an obscene gesture at Arminius, now astride his horse. 'Our quarrel will have to wait,' Flavus cried.

'Coward!' taunted Arminius.

'Traitor!' Flavus shot back.

'Go back to Germanicus and lick his feet, spineless worm!'

Flavus seemed about to respond, but whatever Tullus said silenced him. Without a backward glance at Arminius, who continued showering him with insults, he turned his mount and urged it towards the Roman camp.

'Fetch the archers,' Bassius bellowed, and one of his soldiers sprinted off in the same direction as Flavus. During the time it took for them to reappear, Arminius ceased his tirade of abuse. Rather than retreating to safety, he took counsel with his fellows close to the river's edge.

The legionaries didn't like this cocky manoeuvre. Angry muttering broke out, and a few men stepped out of rank, towards the water. They were shouted back into place by furious officers.

'He's a cunning bastard,' snarled Piso, still itching to charge Arminius.

'That he is,' said Tullus, who had somehow heard Piso again. 'And he's trying to get under our skins. Ignore the maggot. He'll move quick enough when the archers arrive.'

Tullus was right, and the legionaries got to hurl their own insults as Arminius and his companions rode away. Bassius ordered a volley the instant the archers were close to the bank, and hilarity broke out among the Roman troops as their rain of arrows turned the Germans' contemptuous, slow withdrawal into a panicked, headlong retreat.

'That'll teach 'em,' Metilius proclaimed.

Piso was less sure. Removing himself from bow range didn't mean Arminius was a coward – far from it. His confidence had been palpable from the other side of the river. Worry gnawed at Piso as the command to return to camp was given.

What was that devious trickster Arminius planning?

Chapter XV

◪◪◪

Tullus was ready, impatient, for battle. His soldiers, his cohort were ready. The legion was ready – so was the entire army. The meeting between Flavus and Arminius had taken place the previous day, and now scouts by the riverbank had brought word that Arminius' warriors were massing on the far side. Germanicus' response had been swift – his entire host was to deploy on their own side, ready to fight. Familiar though he was with the slow, methodical process, Tullus had chafed throughout, his desire for revenge on Arminius stoked by the previous day's confrontation.

At last the waiting was over, and four lengthy lines had formed up. Under the mid-morning sun, they faced eastward, over the river. The whinny of excited horses and officers' shouts had ceased; the thunder of hob-nailed sandals striking the earth died away. From over the Visurgis came the Germans' shouts and taunts, but on the Roman side an almost complete silence reigned. Tullus was used to this calm before the storm, but the tranquil atmosphere remained gut-clenching. Upwards of sixty thousand soldiers were waiting to fight Arminius' host. Men would die in vast numbers, and soon.

Other things preyed on Tullus' mind. Military procedure had seen the army's front taken up by the auxiliary infantry, on this occasion a mixture of Raeti, Vindelici and Gauls. Although the Fifth Legion was near the centre of the second line, he could see nothing but auxiliaries in front of him. Blind to what was unfolding, Tullus had to rely on whatever formal orders were sent the Fifth's way and the snippets of news he could wrest from passing messengers. His frustration mounted by the moment.

No less annoyed, Fenestela came stamping up from his position at the century's rear. 'Heard anything new?'

'Not since the last time, no.'

Fenestela cursed. After a moment, he said, 'Arminius is going to wait for us to cross the river, isn't he? The woods on either side of his army sound perfect for him to spring a trap.'

'That's why the cavalry has been ordered over first,' said Tullus.

Fenestela rubbed his beard, and didn't answer.

Horsemen could react faster than infantry, thought Tullus, but that didn't mean the tactic was free of risk. Aware of the high stakes, Germanicus had chosen high-ranking officers to lead the double-pronged attack: the legate Stertinius and Aemilius, the primus pilus of the First Legion. The Batavian cavalry would follow straight after these units, their task to hit Arminius' centre.

Mars, bring them success, Tullus prayed. Let us join them soon. Together we will crush Arminius' warriors.

'Have the cavalry gone yet?'

'We would have heard them,' said Tullus with an irritated shrug.

Trumpets rang out and the familiar rumble of hooves rose from first one side of their position, and then the other. Smiling, Fenestela observed, 'There they go.'

'Now we wait again,' grumbled Tullus.

'At least you've seen Arminius' disposition,' said Fenestela. 'Explain it to me again.' Once Tullus' unit had been in place, he had secured permission from Bassius to spy out the battlefield, but Fenestela had remained with the men.

Grateful for the distraction, Tullus described what he'd seen from the riverbank some two hours before. 'A large plain faces on to the river, bounded to left and right by beeches and oaks – as you know. Arminius' warriors all appear to be drawn up at the far end of the open ground, with more forest behind them.'

'He'll have men hidden in the trees on either side.'

'Aye. Stertinius and Aemilius best stay alert as they advance,' said Tullus, chewing a knuckle. The odds seemed to be in their favour, but with Arminius, anything was possible.

Massive cheers from the auxiliaries at the front marked the advance of the Batavi horsemen a short time later. In the distance, Arminius' warriors could be heard singing the barritus. Dim and unthreatening, it still conjured vivid and unpleasant memories to Tullus. Aware that the bizarre sound might affect his men's morale, he patrolled the front rank of his century. He'd acted in the nick of time. Whether it was the barritus or not, his men seemed nervous. 'You're good boys,' he told them. 'Stick with me, and you'll be fine.'

'When will we get to fight, sir?' asked Calvus.

'Too fucking soon,' muttered a soldier from the depths of the ranks.

The chuckles this elicited were uneasy.

Tullus held up a hand in warning, and his men quietened. 'It depends on what happens with the cavalry. If things go well, they will break up the enemy formation somewhat. That news will prompt Germanicus to order the auxiliaries forward. It could be that they will smash the German line – do our job for us, if you like.'

'Let's hope so,' added the hidden wit.

'Enough,' barked Tullus. It was pleasing that, several ranks in, harsh words were hissed in the culprit's ears. Raising his voice for the benefit of those other than the inexperienced Calvus, Tullus said, 'If the auxiliaries need a bit of help, we and the other three legions in this line will be sent in.'

Calvus gave him a determined nod. He was green but brave, thought Tullus. Fortuna grant that that was enough to keep him alive.

'Remember your training, all of you,' advised Tullus. 'Stay close to your comrades on either side. Throw your javelin well. When you close with the enemy, keep your shield high. Remember to use your boss – it's a weapon, not just something to polish for parades or to admire your face in. I've seen you preening, Antonius,' he said, indicating the soldier who fancied himself the best-looking in the century. Tullus let his laughing men insult Antonius for a time before he continued. 'Smash a warrior's nose with the boss, and he'll be hurting so much you can stick him with your blade. Even if he dodges out of the way, he will expose his neck, allowing you to prick him in the throat. It's easy.' He winked.

They grinned like wolves then, and the anxious atmosphere that had been present before was gone, as if carried away by the wind.

It soon returned as they waited. The air filled with a cacophony of noise. Horses galloped, men shouted. Horns blared. The German barritus grew louder. Screams rang out, weapons clashed. In front of Tullus, the auxiliaries were roaring encouragement at their mounted comrades. He took heart from that – the fight wasn't going badly, in this moment at least. Despite this, his nerves were as taut as a bowstring at full draw. To distract himself, Tullus spoke again to his men, telling them how the enemy would run once the legionaries were brought into play.

Cheering broke out a short time later as, accompanied by four Praetorian cohorts, Germanicus forded the river, his intent to find out first-hand what was going on. The auxiliary infantry, who would be ordered forward next, began chanting in their own languages and sounding their horns and battle trumpets.

Tullus' soldiers shifted from foot to foot, also eager to end the interminable wait. Every so often, he had them check their equipment. Already emptied bladders had to be drained again, but without the soldiers leaving their positions. Loud complaints rose from those within splashing distance. The worst offender was Calvus. Rather than piss himself, he projectile-vomited down the back of the legionary in front – Piso, who promptly gave him a black eye. Tullus affected not to notice the altercation. Piso's reaction was reasonable enough. Amused, Tullus listened as Calvus was told in no uncertain terms how he would clean Piso's armour that evening. 'You'll keep at it until it's shinier than the day it was made, you stupid shit. D'you hear me?'

'I'm sorry,' mumbled Calvus, puce with embarrassment.

'It's a little late for that,' snarled Piso. 'You sure there's no bread left in there, no last bits of porridge?'

Calvus gave a miserable shake of his head.

Piso turned his back, and fresh jokes rained down on the unfortunate Calvus. Tullus made a mental note to pretend that night that he could smell vomit on Piso, whether it was true or not.

Time dragged by. The din from across the river continued, yet it was impossible to discern who was winning or losing. The Germans were holding their ground against the cavalry, Tullus decided, because the auxiliaries still hadn't been ordered to cross. That wasn't good – the Roman horsemen should have gained the upper hand by now. In his experience, prolonged encounters weren't a strength of cavalry.

A deep-throated *Ahhhhh* of dismay rose from the auxiliaries. Things were *not* going according to plan, Tullus thought grimly. He could bear the tension no longer. Ordering Fenestela to take command, he made for the nearest gap between the auxiliary units. Less than halfway to their front ranks, his eyes drinking in the savage cavalry–infantry battle playing out on the other side of the river, Tullus heard the trumpeters with Germanicus sound the retreat.

'What happened, sir?' asked Piso as he returned to his position.

'Fuck knows,' replied Tullus. 'It's not good, though.'

Some hours later, versions of what had transpired were racing through the camp. Aware that at least half would be unfounded rumours, Tullus reserved his opinion until he had spoken to someone who'd been there. Lingering around the main gate, he chanced on an acquaintance, an optio known to one and all as Iron Fist. One of the best boxers Tullus had ever seen, he was still Vetera's champion at thirty-five years of age. According to Iron Fist, the initial two groups of cavalry had crossed the river without incident and aimed for the enemy flanks. Soon after, the Batavians had splashed through the water. Led by their charismatic, dashing leader Chariovalda, they had charged at Arminius' army, whereupon a small mounted force of the enemy, appearing to be caught in the open by his advance, had retreated in haste. Taken in, the Batavians had given pursuit, but it had been a trap.

'As they chased their quarry to the woods on one side of the plain, hundreds of warriors appeared. Out of nowhere it seemed, but the filth had been hiding among the trees,' said Iron Fist. 'It was a slaughter at first, sir, but you know the Batavians. They formed a circle and fought like wild beasts. Plenty of them died, but they took down good numbers of the enemy. Chariovalda fell along with many of his nobles, but the rest of his men held out until we drove off the enemy.'

'It's no surprise that Germanicus pulled everyone back,' said Tullus.

'He did the right thing, sir,' agreed Iron Fist. 'There was no room for the legions to get past the fighting and, like as not, there were more barbarians among the trees. But tomorrow's another day, eh? We'll not let the same thing happen to us twice.'

'Aye,' said Tullus, relieved that their losses had been light, and wondering what instructions would come from Germanicus.

None had arrived by the time night fell, which wasn't altogether surprising. Their general would be considering his tactics. Arminius was a clever, devious enemy. His army could have vanished by dawn, eager to find another spot for ambushing the legions. He might have had his warriors dig pits on the plain for the cavalry to ride into, or even attacked the Roman camps.

Although it was sensible to see what the morrow brought, Tullus' desire for revenge had been fanned white-hot by Arminius' proximity. A chance had been missed to kill him during the confrontation with his brother Flavus. The battle should have been fought today. Still irritable as the moon rose, Tullus settled himself on the section of fortifications delegated to his century. Double the usual number of sentries had been ordered; an archer also stood every fifty paces along the rampart. He stared out into the darkening gloom and wondered what Arminius was planning in his camp, less than two miles away.

Once Tullus might have asked permission to mount an assassination attempt on the Cheruscan leader, but he was an older, wiser man now. With

Arminius' exact whereabouts unknown, the mission would be doomed to fail. No, their best chance of slaying Arminius was in open battle.

'You think we'll fight tomorrow, sir?' Piso's shining armour – the result of Calvus' work – was visible fifteen paces away.

'That depends on Germanicus,' Tullus snapped, 'and I haven't been talking to him lately.'

'No, sir,' said Piso in a disappointed voice and set off on his allotted path, the short distance between him and the next sentry along.

Tullus' gaze returned to the ditch below the rampart, and beyond that the cleared terrain that ran east to the river. The trees which had been felled to prevent a secret approach by the enemy had been sawn up, serving as fuel for the soldiers' fires, or mounted as sharpened stakes on the fortifications' outer aspect. Tullus was grateful for the light cloud cover, which meant a bright moon and favourable conditions for spying the enemy. Strain his eyes as he might, however, nothing moved. An owl was calling in the distance, its lonely cry echoed by another even further off.

'Who's there?' There was an alarmed note to Piso's voice.

'What is it?' Tullus' gaze shot to the ground before the camp and back to Piso again.

'I saw something, sir, about two hundred paces out.'

Cursing his middle-aged eyes, Tullus peered again. This time, he saw the crouching figure of a man, edging his way towards the ditch. Tullus was about to order the general alarm sounded, but he couldn't see anyone with the newcomer. One warrior – warrior it had to be, for there were no Roman troops outside the walls – could do little harm, he decided, but it was best to be prepared anyway. 'Tell the archer near you to light an arrow,' he hissed at Piso. 'On my command, he's to shoot into the ditch and set the kindling on fire.' Large bundles of dry twigs and branches had been placed in the defensive trench. In the event of an attack, the Romans would have illumination to kill the enemy by.

Sparks flew beside Piso almost at once as the archer set to work with his flints.

Tullus searched again for the stooping figure, found him about a hundred paces out and cried in first German, then Latin, 'HALT!'

The man stopped. 'I . . . unarmed . . . I . . . come in peace,' he called out, his bad Latin proving he was no Roman.

'Stay where you are,' ordered Tullus.

Light flared close to Piso; the archer had lit the pitch coating the head of his arrow.

'Loose!' ordered Tullus.

Yellow-orange flame streaked from the rampart to the bottom of the ditch. Light flickered, guttered, and then burst into new life as the dry timber ignited. Tullus waited until the blaze had taken a good hold before he cried, 'Raise your hands! Walk forward, nice and slow, so that I can see you.'

The man obeyed. Despite his slow advance, Tullus had the nearest trumpeter stand to. He also commanded the archer to ready another shaft, and every sentry close enough to prepare his javelin. 'HALT!' he roared when the warrior was thirty paces out.

The interloper wasn't an impressive specimen. Of slight build, wearing a ragged tunic and trousers, he had a pinched, narrow face that spoke of a hard life. Arms in the air, he stood looking up at the ramparts with a resigned expression. 'I . . . wait,' he said in his accented Latin.

'Fucking right you wait,' growled Tullus, struggling to see beyond the fierce glow in the ditch. 'Can you spot anything – anything at all?' he asked Piso and the sentry on his other side.

After a short delay, the answers came back in the negative. Tullus couldn't make out anything threatening either, nor hear it. 'Walk towards me,' he ordered the warrior. 'Stop!' he shouted when the man was right by the burning wood.

Unarmed, the warrior posed no threat, Tullus decided. 'Stay alert. Keep watching for signs of the enemy,' he ordered Piso and the other sentries.

'What do you want?' Tullus demanded.

'I . . . Chatti. I wish . . . talk.'

'So you say! Your people will call you traitor just for standing here – why did you leave them?'

The warrior's bloodshot eyes flickered to and fro. 'I . . . fight with comrades. I . . . drink too much. I . . . ordered to return to settlement . . . by chieftain.'

Beware the spurned, Arminius, thought Tullus with some satisfaction. The Chatti warrior's dishevelled appearance and blotchy complexion gave some credence to his story. 'So you came here. Why?' Tullus demanded.

'I have information . . . about Arminius' . . . plans.'

Real excitement thrummed through Tullus. He cast a look at Piso. 'See anything?' Piso hadn't; nor had any of the sentries for a hundred paces in either direction. If Arminius was planning an attack, it was a fucking bad one, thought Tullus. Instructing the warrior to make for the nearest gate, he clattered down the ladder and went to meet him.

Chapter XVI

Pitch-soaked torches, their ends planted in the ground, lit up the entrance to Germanicus' vast tent. Stony-faced Praetorians were ranged around its entire perimeter, each man standing by another flaming brand. This was how things had been since the attempt on the general's life in Vetera the previous autumn. Tullus found it reassuring – Germanicus meant a lot to him. Not only had he resurrected Tullus' career, but he was an excellent leader. It was *he* who would see Arminius beaten, his army destroyed – and the Eighteenth's eagle recovered.

Tullus' respect for the emperor's nephew didn't extend to his bodyguards, however. Paid worlds more than the average legionary, often with little combat experience, the Praetorians tended to regard themselves as superior beings to the rank and file. This attitude endeared them little to ordinary soldiers. Tullus stalked up to the pair on duty either side of the tent's entrance. The Chatti warrior, whom he'd had searched, scuttled behind him. Piso and Metilius came after, hands ready on their sword hilts.

'Halt!' both sentries bellowed.

With a hard stare, Tullus obeyed.

'State your name, rank and business,' snapped one, a slab-jawed monster two hands taller than Tullus.

'Centurion Tullus, Second Century, First Cohort, Fifth Legion. I wish to speak with our commander.'

The tall Praetorian raised an eyebrow at his companion. 'He wants to see the governor, at this hour.' His cold gaze returned to Tullus. 'It's a little late, sir.'

There was so little emphasis on the last word that a red mist descended over Tullus. 'I'm aware of the hour. My news is important,' he snarled.

'We've got our orders, sir. The governor has retired for the night.' This was delivered with more than a suggestion of smugness.

'He needs to hear this man's news.' Tullus jerked a thumb at his captive.

The Praetorian's contemptuous gaze travelled up and down the warrior, then over Piso and Metilius, and finally returned to Tullus. 'News,' he said. 'From this creature, sir?'

'That's right,' replied Tullus, his anger bubbling.

'I don't think the governor would appreciate being woken because of this piece of filth, sir.'

Tullus had had enough. 'You, think? Don't make me laugh!'

The Praetorian's brows lowered in fury. 'I—'

'Shut your mouth, you jumped-up maggot!' Tullus used his full parade-ground volume. 'I've been a centurion longer than you've been wiping your own arse. I've fought twice as many battles as the times you have stood on parade, and I have killed more men than the number of times you've polished your fucking armour. Germanicus knows me, moreover, and this piece of filth is a deserter from Arminius' camp! I suggest you go and speak with the governor. NOW!'

The Praetorian floundered for words, and failed. His companion was also dumbstruck.

'Do you understand, you useless piece of shit?' thundered Tullus.

'Yes, sir.' With a 'What else can I do?' shrug of his massive shoulders at his shocked companion, he lumbered inside.

Tullus acted as if the second sentry wasn't even present while they waited. Both Piso and Metilius seemed mightily pleased – they would have loved seeing the Praetorian put in his place, thought Tullus with some amusement.

The Praetorian soon emerged with news that Tullus was to wait for a staff officer. Said official appeared within twenty heartbeats, still adjusting his baldric and metalled belt. In his early thirties, thin, with oiled hair, he gave Tullus a tight smile – in other circumstances, his response might well have been hostile – and asked, 'You are *the* Centurion Tullus?'

'I am, sir.' Tullus took huge satisfaction from the dismay blossoming on the Praetorian's face. Yes, I could end your career when I go inside, he thought. Stew on that, maggot.

The staff officer's supercilious expression eased a fraction. 'You have news for the governor?'

Tullus gestured at the Chatti warrior. 'This man has come from Arminius' camp, sir. I thought Germanicus would want to hear his news.'

The officer sniffed. 'As you say,' he observed. 'You and the savage come with me.'

He led Tullus and the wary-faced Chatti warrior through an antechamber, carpeted throughout. Painted statues of Mars, Juno and Minerva, the sacred triad, watched their passage. The smell of burned wick laced the air, which told Tullus that the dozens of lamps on the vast bronze lampstands had been extinguished not long before. In all probability Germanicus hadn't been asleep. Despite the urgency of Tullus' visit, that was a good thing.

Through several partitioned rooms they went, with one dedicated to Tiberius, the emperor, and another laid out as a *lararium*, the shrine found in every Roman household. The last was a large dining area, complete with three couches arrayed in the usual fashion around a low table. This is how the other half live, thought Tullus. Even on campaign, Germanicus dines as he would in his palace at Rome, while we soldiers eat sitting by our fires.

The officer halted before a final woollen partition, decorated in clever fashion like a mosaic floor. Two Praetorians, as stony-faced as their comrades outside, stood outside. The officer gave them a nod and let out a nervous cough. 'Sir?'

'Who is it?' demanded Germanicus from the other side of the partition.

'I have Centurion Tullus with me, sir, and a German tribesman he says carries important news.'

'Send in Tullus.'

'At once, sir.' The officer gestured at Tullus, and mouthed, 'Go.'

The Chatti warrior looked none too happy.

'They won't harm you.' Tullus lifted the partition.

The room beyond wasn't Germanicus' bedchamber, he was relieved to find, but another reception area. A painted bust of a severe-faced Tiberius, fleshy-jowled as he was in life, watched over all. Comfortable-looking couches lined the 'walls'. Documents, inkwells and iron styli covered the bronze-inlaid surface of an oak table with feet carved into lions' paws. A tired-looking Germanicus raised his head from the paperwork as Tullus entered. Dressed in a purple-bordered belted tunic, he retained a majesty, a presence which demanded respect.

'I might have known it would be you,' he said as Tullus saluted.

Never sure if Germanicus was joking or toying with him – often Tullus suspected it was both – he muttered, 'Sorry to disturb your rest, sir. I came only because it's serious.'

Germanicus' smile was broad. 'Tell me.'

Briefly Tullus explained the Chatti warrior's presence, then summoned him inside. Germanicus listened, one eyebrow raised.

'This is Germanicus, imperial governor of the military districts of Germania and nephew to the emperor Tiberius. He is one of the most important people in the empire,' hissed Tullus. 'Kneel!'

With poor grace, the warrior obeyed.

Exasperated – even this lowliest of Germans regarded himself equal to all – Tullus pushed the back of the warrior's head, forcing him to look at the floor. 'Do not move until given permission,' Tullus ordered.

'A poor-looking specimen,' observed Germanicus in a dry tone.

'He is that, sir,' agreed Tullus. 'But his story has a ring of truth. He gambles and fights, and was commanded by his chieftain to quit Arminius' camp and return to his settlement. Disgruntled, he came instead to us.'

'You,' barked Germanicus.

Prompted by Tullus' whispered 'Look at the governor', the Chatti warrior raised his eyes.

'Yes, sir?' he replied in Latin.

'Tell me what you know.'

Encouraged by Tullus' nod, the warrior began. It seemed that Arminius had chosen the site at which he would fight – or try to fight – the legions in the coming days. This very night, he and the chieftains allied to him had gathered in a local grove sacred to Donar, the thunder god, there to ask for divine blessing on their enterprise. 'There is more,' the warrior revealed. 'He also intends to attack your camp. Under cover of darkness if possible.'

Germanicus had listened in silence. Nervous, the warrior looked to Tullus, who motioned that he should wait.

'What are your thoughts, Tullus?' asked Germanicus.

Startled – what did his opinion count? – Tullus replied, 'Sir?'

'Is he telling the truth?'

Tullus felt the weight of the warrior's desperate gaze. If he answered in the negative, the warrior would meet a quick fate. That wasn't Tullus' concern – if the warrior was lying, he deserved to die. What mattered was giving Germanicus good advice. Ten heartbeats pattered by.

'I think he is, sir,' said Tullus. 'If the man's putting on a show, it's a good one.'

'That was also my conclusion,' said Germanicus, nodding. 'Suppose he's acting, however – suppose he has been sent by Arminius. What then?'

'It seems to me that you have several options, sir. You don't have to fight on Arminius' chosen ground – there's time yet to catch him somewhere else. We can be ready for the night assault – under Caecina, a similar attack was routed, with massive enemy casualties. And if this man is telling the truth as we think, then you've got Arminius' measure.'

A second silence fell, which Tullus did not break. He'd said his piece – the rest was up to Germanicus. Aware that his fate hung in the balance, the warrior fixed his gaze on the floor once more.

'I'm told the men are . . . disquieted by today's events,' said Germanicus out of the blue. 'Would you agree?'

'I can only speak for my soldiers, sir,' said Tullus, 'but they are a little out of sorts. It's nothing to worry about – not like last autumn. They will fight tomorrow, if that's what you want.'

'Good.' Germanicus rose to his feet, and gave the warrior a measured nod. 'I believe you, to a point. You will be kept in the camp under guard, until the truth of your story is made clear. If things come to pass as you've told me, you will be well rewarded. If not—'

'A thousand thanks, sir,' cried the warrior. 'I did not lie – you'll see.'

Summoning a Praetorian, Germanicus had him escorted away.

Expecting to be dismissed as well, Tullus was surprised when Germanicus said, 'Come with me.'

'Sir?'

'I am going out into the camp.'

Tullus felt the first stirrings of alarm. 'Now, sir?'

'I want to gauge the men's mood, in particular the auxiliaries. See if their morale really has been affected by today's disaster. It *was* a disaster,' Germanicus repeated as Tullus registered surprise. 'Chariovalda was a fool, and too many men died because of him. He had express instructions to charge the main body of Arminius' army, and to disregard feints or attacks by other enemy groups. It was a simple trap – a child could have seen through it – but he was taken in nonetheless. Idiot.'

Silence was the prudent option, decided Tullus.

After a moment, Germanicus chuckled. 'I'd wager you would have followed your orders to the letter.' He waved a dismissive hand as Tullus opened his mouth. 'You don't need to answer. If you had led the attack, we'd be celebrating victory, like as not. So you'll accompany me?'

'I'd be honoured, sir. Use my cloak,' said Tullus, unfastening his cloak pin. 'It's grimy enough to belong to an ordinary soldier.'

'You need to go unrecognised as well.'

'Two of my men are outside, sir. I'll take one of their cloaks.'

'I'll send for it.' Germanicus lowered his voice. 'We're going to leave by the back of the tent, you see.'

'Your guards, sir—'

'What about them?' There was a childish glee in Germanicus' eyes. 'I won't be in any danger. You'll be with me.'

'Aye, sir,' said Tullus in a tone more confident than he felt.

If anything happened to Germanicus, the blame would be laid at his feet.

Chapter XVII

A rminius edged his boots closer to the fire and pulled his cloak a little tighter. It was late – approaching midnight, he thought. An occasional nicker from a horse, low murmuring from a few tents and owl calls from the trees around were the only sounds. The air was chilly, and dead calm. Each cloud of his exhaled breath rose straight to the clear sky above. A bright white-yellow moon reigned supreme there, reducing the stars to pinpoints. He had been sitting with Maelo for hours, talking over the day's fighting.

Both men felt frustrated that an opportunity had been lost. If the rest of the enemy cavalry had fallen for Arminius' ploy, the legions would have swarmed over the river to their assistance and been struck from both sides by thousands of warriors hiding in the trees. It would have been a slaughter. Instead Germanicus' level-headedness and his soldiers' discipline had seen the Roman casualties confined to the Batavi and a few riders slain during their extrication.

'It's not all bad,' said Arminius. 'Germanicus had to retreat over the Visurgis a deal faster than he'd have wanted to. Quite the undignified exit for a general, I think – and his troops will have seen him scrambling to safety. It will have affected their morale.'

'A pity about the Chatti whoreson then, eh?' muttered Maelo. 'If his story is believed, Germanicus will know about our planned attack.'

Arminius nodded. Word had not long reached them from one of the Chatti chieftains about a drunkard who'd been banished for making trouble.

Instead of returning to his settlement, he had crept off in the direction of the Roman camp. Challenged by the patrol that had seen him, he had vanished into the darkness.

'With any luck, the fool will have fallen and broken his neck,' said Maelo, slurping from his wine skin.

'Wiser to assume that he's talking to Germanicus this very moment.'

'So we'll call off the assault?' A good part of the evening had been spent spreading Arminius' orders. More than two-thirds of his forces would be ready to strike the Roman camps before sunrise, with the rest prepared to ambush the enemy if they broke and fled.

'No. We need to strike while the iron's hot – the chieftains are keen to fight, and so are their warriors.' Arminius felt Maelo's eyes on him at once. 'Last year's disaster won't be repeated, don't worry. I'll send scouts to spy out the land first. If there's even the slightest hint that the Romans know of our plan, the whole thing will be abandoned.'

Maelo grunted, satisfied. 'Idistaviso looks a decent site for the battle, if it comes to that.'

'It lacks the river, but will suffice, Donar willing,' said Arminius, rubbing a thoughtful finger over his lips. Even if their attack on the enemy camp was successful, Germanicus' army's size and the defences would prevent a complete victory. If Germanicus took the bait, the battle proper would take place at Idistaviso, a plain just a few miles away. It was bounded on either side and to the rear by trees; Arminius intended to place his warriors at its eastern edge, occupying both the flat ground and the higher terrain behind. Germanicus' troops would be exposed for more than a quarter of a mile as they marched to reach his forces, a time they could be subjected to harassing attacks from both left and right. This small benefit wasn't anything like the advantages of seven years before, worried Arminius, but he couldn't prevaricate all summer. Despite their keenness to fight, the chieftains were growing restless.

'What do you make of our chances? Even odds? Two to one for – two to one against?' Maelo's voice was matter of fact.

'Not two to one for, sad to say.' Arminius let out a bitter laugh. 'More like evens, if Donar aids us.'

'Did Tudrus' sacrifice mean aught, I wonder?' muttered Maelo.

'Who knows?' replied Arminius, feeling uncomfortable and concerned that Donar might have perceived his callous motive for Tudrus' sacrifice. 'The gods do as they wish.'

'Ever has it been so. We're in their hands.'

'There is *one* more thing we can do,' said Arminius, spying a figure heading in their direction.

'Who's this?' hissed Maelo, reaching for his sword.

'Rest easy. It's a Usipetes warrior whom I fell into conversation with earlier. He speaks fluent Latin.'

Startled, Maelo spat out a mouthful of wine. 'Eh?'

'Before our ambush on Varus, his mother had paid for him to be tutored in Vetera, reasoning that a warrior with Latin would have a greater chance of rising through the ranks of the auxiliaries.'

'Can he be trusted?'

'The boy is from a good family, and he's loyal, according to several of his chieftains.'

'What are you up to, Arminius?'

Arminius didn't answer. As their visitor drew near, he called out, 'Well met, Gervas.'

Gervas stepped into the firelight, blinking. A pale-faced, spindle-limbed youth of perhaps twenty summers, he wore a dark brown tunic and the patterned trousers common to his tribe. 'Arminius.' He dipped his chin at Maelo, who gave a tiny nod by way of response.

Arminius gestured to the blanket partway round the fire. 'I've been waiting for you.'

Gervas' face was anxious as he sat. 'Am I late?'

'Not at all. This is the perfect time for your mission.'

'Care to explain?' demanded Maelo.

'Tell him, Gervas,' ordered Arminius.

'Many Roman soldiers will be discontented after today's battle. Wouldn't it be good to unsettle them even more?' Gervas' face split into a shy grin. 'With Arminius' blessing, I'm going to ride to the Roman camps and speak with the sentries. I'll offer wives, money and land to every legionary and auxiliary who joins our cause.'

'There are more than sixty thousand Roman troops on the other side of the river,' challenged Maelo. 'Will you talk to them all?'

Gervas looked abashed.

'Maelo is ever the counterweight,' said Arminius. 'Continue.'

'Some of my friends speak a little Latin,' said Gervas. 'They'll do the same job in different places around the enemy camps.'

Maelo let out a *phhhh* of contempt.

'Have some faith,' said Arminius. 'The ruse might not win over many legionaries, but the auxiliaries *must* be unhappy this night. They'll have watched the Batavi being slaughtered, remember.'

'It's worth a try, I suppose, but setting one of their camps on fire would work better,' said Maelo.

'That can't be done,' retorted Arminius, irritated. 'We do what we can against the monster that is Rome, and sowing unrest in their ranks is a useful tool.'

'Good enough.' Maelo got up and wandered towards the nearest trees. 'Nature calls.'

Arminius eyed Gervas. 'We have nothing to lose by trying your plan. If even half a dozen auxiliaries desert, it will have been worth the effort. Report to me when you return, no matter the hour.'

'I will.' Rather than rise, Gervas remained sitting.

'Is there something else?' asked Arminius in surprise.

'Aye.' A nervous throat-clear. 'It's nothing, like as not, but it has been troubling me.'

'Speak,' commanded Arminius in his most winning tone.

'Do you recall the meeting organised by Mallovendus some months back – the one when the chieftains agreed to follow you?'

'Of course,' said Arminius. His success in the face of Gerulf's antagonism and a memorable coupling with the buxom widow meant that the night had been a fine one.

'A man dear to me died that evening – one of the tribe's chieftains. He was my father's cousin, Gerulf. After my parents were killed in a longhouse fire many years ago, he reared me as his own.'

It was news to Arminius that Gerulf had been Gervas' relation, but he acted nonchalant. 'I remember, yes. A sad matter. Fell drunk into a snowdrift when he was out for a piss – wasn't that what happened to him?'

'That's what men say.' Gervas' expression had hardened. 'Apart from one, that is.'

'Who might that be?' enquired Arminius in jocular tone.

'A greybeard, one of the oldest living in Mallovendus' settlement. Ninety summers and winters he'd lived, or so he said.'

'He *said*?'

'A chill took him a month ago.'

'What a pity,' lied Arminius. 'Did he still have his wits before he expired?' He could see Maelo – reappeared, but lingering in the background – ten paces behind Gervas. With the slightest dip of his chin, Arminius indicated that Maelo should remain where he was. 'At such a ripe age, most men's brains have turned to porridge.'

'He was growing forgetful, it's true,' admitted Gervas. 'But he seemed certain of one thing that night.' For the first time since he had spoken of Gerulf, his confidence seemed to waver. 'He was outside relieving himself. Wary of falling in the snow, he was leaning against the wall of his hut and in virtual darkness. A thin man came out of Mallovendus' longhouse, not twenty paces off, and stopped almost at once to piss.'

'Most of us did that a lot during the course of the evening. Mallovendus is a generous host – his beer never stopped flowing.' Arminius knew what Gervas was about to say. So did Maelo – he had his dagger out and ready. Arminius checked him with a warning glance. 'Let me guess. It was Gerulf he spotted?'

Gervas' frown deepened. '*I* think so, but what made you suggest that?'

Arminius gave a careless shrug. 'Because you brought him up.'

'The old man saw someone resembling Maelo come out of Mallovendus' longhouse and creep up behind the pissing man. Wrapping a hand over his mouth, the attacker bundled him off between the houses.' Gervas glared at Arminius, and looked about for Maelo, who moved, catlike, further into the shadows.

'You think Gerulf was abducted and murdered?' Arminius asked with false solicitude.

'That's what it looked like, aye.'

'It could have been someone having a joke with a friend, surely? Warriors are always playing stupid pranks on one another, play fighting, wrestling and so on.'

'I don't think so. The greybeard was frightened but he lingered, you see, peering from his almost closed door. Not long after, he saw the figure return to Mallovendus' longhouse. Light from within fell on the man's face as he entered.' Gervas' voice shook a little as he said, 'It was Maelo, he swore.'

'I doubt that greybeard could have identified his own son at ten paces, let alone someone he didn't know at a much greater distance,' demurred Arminius, using all his charisma. 'It must have been hard enough to make his way from bed to door and back without falling over.'

'The next day he watched Maelo talking to Mallovendus. He was sure who he'd seen.' There was a stubborn note to Gervas' voice.

'Why would Maelo kill Gerulf?'

'You can answer that.' Gervas did not look at Arminius as he spoke.

'Come now,' said Arminius, hiding his fury. 'It's true that Gerulf wasn't fond of me and Maelo, but for one of us to stoop to murder? That is too much.' He fixed wide, persuasive eyes on Gervas.

'The greybeard was sure it was Maelo who killed him!'

Arminius pulled a winning smile. 'Even if it was Maelo whom he saw the second time, what of it? At one stage during the evening Maelo went back to the house we had been quartered in to fetch a skin of good wine. I wanted to share it with Mallovendus. Perhaps the greybeard, rest his soul, spied Maelo as he got back.'

After a moment Gervas' gaze dropped. 'Aye, I expect you're right.'

'Gerulf was a good man – his loss must grieve you still,' said Arminius, thinking, I'm well rid of the prick. Now, let this stripling youth believe me, or Maelo will have to lay him in the mud too.

'It does,' muttered Gervas.

Arminius let a dozen heartbeats patter by before urging, 'Best leave now. Your mission will take at least two hours, and the moon has passed its zenith. You don't want to be anywhere near the Romans' encampments come the dawn.'

Maelo chose this point to come strolling back, a rueful look on his face. 'My bowels are in a bad state, I can tell you. What did I miss?'

'Just the final details of what I'll say to the Romans,' said Gervas, giving Arminius a pleading look that asked him to remain silent.

'Donar guide you,' said Arminius as Gervas crept away.

'He believed you?' whispered Maelo.

'Most of him did, but some doubt remained.'

'I'd best keep an ear to the ground then. There'll be trouble if he starts pouring his theory into other men's ears.'

'We have more to worry about than him at this juncture,' said Arminius. He gave Maelo a knowing look. 'If it comes to it, he'll be no harder than Gerulf to get rid of.'

Chapter XVIII

◫◫◫

'Best keep the hood up, sir,' advised Tullus. Having exited the
tent without alerting any of the patrolling Praetorians, he and
Germanicus were making for the auxiliary lines. Nothing could be
done about the governor's great height, but if there was any chance of him
remaining anonymous, he *had* to conceal his face.

'I suppose there's no other way.' Germanicus' voice was unwilling.

'Afraid not, sir. Every man in the camp knows you.'

'True.' Germanicus complied at last.

Thanks to the late hour, the thoroughfares were almost empty, but
activity continued around many tents. The bright moon above lit the scene
brightly enough to make out every cohort's position, and each century's
tent lines. Keen to eavesdrop, Germanicus soon strayed close to one side of
the avenue.

'We could go to the auxiliaries' positions this way, sir,' Tullus suggested.
'You can listen to the chatter as we walk.'

'These soldiers are from the Twentieth, aren't they?'

Tullus cast a look at the nearest standard. 'Yes, sir.'

'They have little reason to love me.'

'Because of the mutiny, sir?'

'Aye.' Germanicus' eyes held no regret. 'There was no other way
to bring it to an end, whatever they may think. If the troublemakers
hadn't been dealt with, the trouble would have festered like an untended
wound.'

The bloody conclusion to the legionaries' uprising had seen hundreds of men, guilty and innocent, slain in the camps along the Rhenus. Tullus had played his part to restore peace to Vetera – and the bloody memories of that time sometimes played out in his dreams, the only occasion he had been forced to turn his blade on his own kind. Yet almost eighteen months later, he too could think of no fast and efficient alternative that would have suppressed the mutiny.

'You disagree with me?'

Startled, Tullus realised his silence had been taken for disapproval. He met Germanicus' stare with a firm one of his own. 'I don't, sir. It was a terrible few days, but men who have slain their officers and defied their general can't be left alive. A lot of water has gone under the bridge since then – the soldiers have spent months in Germania under your command, and beaten numerous tribes in battle. One of the eagles is back in our hands. The men respect these achievements. They'll follow you anywhere. Listen in, sir, and you'll see.'

Germanicus looked pleased.

Tullus was almost sure that he was right, but his nerves began to jangle as they wandered into the tent lines of the Twentieth's Fifth Cohort. First in their path were the tents belonging to the Fourth Century. They looked the same as every other unit's lines: at the near end, a large tent for the three junior officers and an even bigger one for the centurion; after that, ten tents, each one used by a contubernium of legionaries. Getting past the tents belonging to the centurion and other officers was the riskiest part – by dint of their rank, they tended to stare at passers-by more than ordinary soldiers. Their luck was in, however – the flaps of all the large tents were laced shut.

Outside the first legionaries' tent, a fire yet smouldered. Three blanketed shapes were lying around it, propped up on their elbows. None looked at Tullus and Germanicus.

'I'm telling you, Sextus, you've picked up something nasty from one of those whores you keep visiting.' This from the man closest to the tent.

'Feeling as if you're pissing tiny shards of pottery is not right,' added one of his companions. 'You've been complaining about that since before we left Vetera.'

Tullus glanced at the third man, whose unhappiness was plain. 'What am I supposed to do?' he protested.

'Go to the surgeon,' urged the first man.

'I'll be the laughing stock of the century,' said the afflicted soldier.

Tullus knew what would be said next, and had to contain his mirth as the second legionary growled, 'You already are, Sextus!'

'Are . . . complaints of that type common?' asked Germanicus once they were a safe distance away.

'Aye, sir. Men will be men, and the brothels are always busier before the start of a campaign. The risk of catching a disease rises accordingly.'

'I had no idea.' Germanicus sounded bemused rather than annoyed.

'No reason you should, sir. It's down to the likes of me and my junior officers – and the surgeons, of course – to deal with ailments and illnesses. That man will be able to fight tomorrow, never fear.'

'How can you be sure?'

Tullus let out a grim chuckle. 'There's not much a vine stick can't encourage a soldier to do, sir. A man's really got to be ill before a centurion lets him go to the hospital.'

They had passed two more tents by this stage, and at the next the occupants had retired for the night. The men of the fifth and sixth tents were gathered around a single fire, gambling and drinking wine. One spotted Tullus and Germanicus and cried, 'Ho, friends! Care to try your luck at dice?'

'My purse is empty,' grumbled Tullus as he'd heard his men do countless times. 'And my brother's.'

'Payday is always too far away, eh?' said the soldier, giving them a friendly wave and turning back to his companions.

'I wonder if Germanicus is playing dice with his staff officers,' said a legionary closer to the fire.

'If he is, he's using *aurei*,' cried another.

Germanicus had stiffened, and Tullus caught him by the elbow. 'Keep walking, sir,' he hissed. To his relief, the governor obeyed.

'He's not wasting his evening like us poor fools,' retorted the soldier who'd spoken to them. 'Germanicus will be tucked in his blankets already, getting his beauty sleep before the battle tomorrow.'

A rumble of approval went around the gathering, and the comments began to flow. 'Germanicus is a good general – and no airs or graces about him either, not like some.'

'He's steady too – when the Batavi got it in the neck today, he didn't panic.'

'If there's a fight tomorrow, we'll teach those savages a lesson they'll never forget,' declared one of the legionaries. 'Germanicus will be proud of us.'

'See, sir?' whispered Tullus. 'They hold you in high regard.'

A wide smile spread across the governor's face. 'It seems so.'

After an hour of wandering the camp, it had become clear that the sentiments of other soldiers were no different. Even the auxiliaries were keen to fight, burning for revenge on the warriors who had slain so many of their kindred. Returning to Germanicus' tent, word reached them of Latin-speaking German warriors who had ridden up to the walls, offering land, women and money to the sentries if they would change sides. Germanicus laughed as the messenger told him the sentries' answer: that they would take the warriors' wives and land for their own, but as spoils of war. Dismissing Tullus then, he made no indication of his intentions for the next day.

Tullus' curiosity had become overwhelming, and so, taking a deep breath, he asked, 'Are we to fight Arminius tomorrow, sir?'

'Orders will be issued at dawn.'

'Yes, sir,' said Tullus, fighting disappointment. With a crisp salute, he walked away.

He'd passed the two Praetorians and was halfway across the next room when Germanicus called out. 'Have a restful night, Tullus. See that your blade is sharp for the morning.'

Chapter XIX

◫◫◫

Arminius was seething. His temper had been foul since a dejected Gervas had returned in the middle of the night, his mission an abject failure. Dawn had seen Arminius' mood worsen steadily. It now took all of his effort to maintain a genial expression as he encouraged the warriors straggling back across the Visurgis. They had been hours too late, he brooded. As he'd emphasised to the chieftains the evening before, their best chance of success was to attack the Roman camps under cover of darkness. In the cold before dawn, most legionaries would be sound asleep, and the sentries dull with tiredness. Yet here they were, he thought with a furious glance at the sun's position high above, after midday.

His own Cherusci had been ready at the appointed time of course, but the other tribes had not appeared at the arranged spot outside their camp. Arminius ground his teeth. He had waited a while, allowing his allies the benefit of the doubt. Once he'd realised they weren't coming and sent men to investigate, upwards of an hour had been lost. Time had been wasted locating each of the chieftains' tents in the sprawling camp, and more still rousing them. The laggards had been wrapped in their blankets – sheepish-faced, one Bructeri chieftain had even admitted that he and others had spent the night drinking to their victory today. Small wonder that many of their warriors had done the same. It was good that Maelo had stepped in, thought Arminius, and prevented him from attacking the Bructeri imbecile. That reaction would have seen his alliance splinter this very day.

It had been pointless even to approach the Roman camps. Unless the sentries were blind and deaf, any chance of a surprise attack had gone, hours since. It scarcely mattered whether the banished Chatti drunkard had reached Germanicus or not. But the chieftains, embarrassed by their failure to meet at the appointed hour, had insisted on trying. Losing control, Arminius had lambasted them loud and long before the warriors departed. He breathed deep. The attack had been called off the instant the alarm had sounded in the enemy camps. There had been no casualties.

Had he just handed the advantage to Germanicus, however? The legionaries' loud cheering as his warriors withdrew had been audible here, by the river. The chieftains whom he'd lectured were avoiding his gaze or throwing resentful looks in his direction. Worry gnawed Arminius' guts, but he told himself that upwards of thirty-five thousand men had joined his cause over the previous month — it was a large enough figure to defeat Germanicus' legions and, despite the chieftains' surly attitude, the warriors' hatred of Rome would see them fight well.

Idistaviso was also well suited for his purpose. Not far from the location of the previous day's clash, the plain lay between the Visurgis and an undulating line of hills. Bounded to the east by a tree-covered slope, its breadth was varied to the west by the river's weaving course, and to the north and south by jutting spurs of high ground. The legions would not all fit into the confined space, which would reduce their numerical superiority by a large degree, and his warriors could be positioned to fall on the Romans from three sides.

Victory would be theirs, thought Arminius. Try as he might, however, he could not stifle the niggling concern that he was making the biggest mistake of his life.

The next two hours passed in a blur. Arminius rode hither and thither, conferring with the chieftains and telling them how the warriors were to be organised. Even with the Romans close at hand, and a prior agreement that they would obey his lead, this was no easy task. The chieftains questioned Arminius' tactics, and more than one had to be won over — again. Valuable time was wasted coaxing and wheedling. Harassed and furious, he took to galloping between the tribal groupings and soon wore out his mount. Maelo, ever prepared, was on hand, exchanging his horse for Arminius'. 'Go,' he said. 'Do what you have to. I'll be here, with our men.'

Arminius left his men, and set out to talk to Mallovendus again. The Marsi chieftain was central to his plans. His core of seasoned bodyguards included some of the finest warriors in Arminius' forces. The Marsi would stand in the army's centre with the Bructeri and the remnants of the Angrivarii, facing the brunt of the Roman assault. Right behind them, up the slope and sheltered amid the trees, Arminius' Cherusci were ready to add their strength when the time came.

He found Mallovendus standing a hundred paces in front of his men, a deliberate move that showed every man watching that he was scared of no one. To reinforce the point, the Marsi chieftain had set his body-guards to a spear-throwing competition, almost as if they were gathered for a feast day rather than a battle. Good-natured banter filled the air. Wagers were being made. All that was lacking was some wine and a piglet roasting on a spit, thought Arminius, amused despite his concerns. 'Who's winning?'

Turning from the display, Mallovendus grinned. 'It's an even match at the moment. A hundred and eighty paces this pair threw.' He pointed at two warriors. Like many, the heat had made both strip to the waist. One was fair-haired and of slender build, but with well-defined muscles; the other was a shaggy-haired giant, half again as large as Mallovendus. 'They're big rivals.'

Sour-faced, the giant was striding to and fro, declaring to the assembled throng how his next spear would fly so far that the fair-haired warrior might as well go home. His opponent's mild-mannered response, that he had a gold coin which said otherwise, made the assembled crowd cheer, but enraged the giant. Bunching his ham-like fists, he threw himself at the fair-haired man. Only the intervention of other bodyguards saved a fight from breaking out. Encouraged by the spontaneous aggression, warriors who were taking bets redoubled their efforts to part the spectators from their coin.

Tan-tara-tara. Tan-tara-tara. From the westward end of the plain, Roman trumpets signalled the legions' arrival.

Mallovendus stepped in at once. 'Enough, you fools!' he shouted. 'ENOUGH!'

Surly-faced, the two rivals stepped away from each other. The crowd of Marsi fell silent, and the tramp of hobnailed sandals reverberated in the muggy air. Trumpets sounded again. Hooves struck the earth. The shouts of Roman officers could now be heard. Arminius felt the atmosphere, until this juncture full of good humour and bravado, change. A score more heart-beats, and the morale of his entire army would plummet.

Mallovendus had noticed too, and to Arminius' relief, gave him a look as if to say, 'Speak.'

Arminius raised his voice. 'A fine contest. You are mighty warriors!'

Mallovendus' bodyguards liked that, rumbling in approval and giving each other pleased glances. Even the giant and the fair-haired warrior seemed appeased.

'It's time to put the competition from your minds. Soon there'll be legionaries aplenty for everyone's spears. Throw as these men can' – here Arminius indicated the two rivals – 'and hundreds of the enemy will fall before they even reach us. More still will have lost their shields, making them easy prey. Are you ready to do that? Ready to shed Roman blood?'

'YESSSSSS!'

Arminius raised his sword high. Sunlight flashed off the polished steel: his weapon would be seen by every warrior within eyeshot. Even if they couldn't hear his exact words, they would sense what was being said, and that was enough. 'KILL!' he roared. 'KILL!'

'KILL! KILL! KILL!' yelled the bodyguards. Veins bulging in his neck, Mallovendus was also shouting.

Arminius faced the front of his army, sword aloft. Every man's eyes were on him now – he sensed their expectant gaze. 'KILL! KILL! KILL!'

With a rumbling sound akin to thunder, his call was answered from three sides. Spears began to clatter off shields; that too was taken up by every warrior.

'KILL! KILL! KILL!' *Clash, clash, clash.* 'KILL! KILL! KILL!'

The hairs on Arminius' neck stood up. Donar was looking down with approval – the god's gaze weighed heavy on his shoulders.

Come then, Germanicus, thought Arminius. Come, and die.

Chapter XX

꒰꒱꒰

Germanicus' army had crossed the river a short time before, and was moving on to a plain bounded on both sides by trees. Idistaviso, it was called, Tullus told his soldiers. This was where Arminius and his warriors now waited — and where they would meet their end. They cheered him long and hard after that declaration. Despite the strength-sapping heat, a sense of expectation hung over the marching legionaries. Jokes were being made. Piso was refusing bets on a Roman victory — that was certain, he said — but was offering four to one that Arminius would be slain by the day's end.

Behind the auxiliary infantry for the second time in as many days, Tullus was chafing to get to the enemy. It made sense for non-Romans to enter the fray first, softening up the Germans while the more valuable legionaries waited, but he'd been waiting for this battle since Arminius' destruction of Varus' army, seven long years before. It was more than that, Tullus brooded — this confrontation was what he had *lived* for. Restless, sweating, he was unable to stay in position and paced up and down the gap between his century and the next as they advanced. 'Ready, brothers?' he asked, catching the gaze of each and every man. 'Ready to avenge your fallen comrades of the Seventeenth, Eighteenth and Nineteenth? Ready for blood?'

'Aye, sir.' 'Let me at 'em, sir!'

'A word, sir?' Fenestela appeared by Tullus' elbow.

Tullus stopped, letting the ranks tramp by. Gods, but he loved that repetitive sound. It filled the air, reverberated from the ground up into his feet, physical proof of the legions' might. 'What is it?'

'Leave them be. Keep talking the way you are, and you'll unsettle them.'

Tullus' anger flared, but he held his peace. Fenestela wasn't just his optio – he was his most trusted friend. 'Speak.'

'I was in the forest too, remember. This is what I've been waiting for, as much as you, Tullus. Your passions are running high – it's the heat, like as not. Settle down. Breathe. The men will play their part. They love you. They'll follow you anywhere. Anywhere.'

From the somewhat taciturn Fenestela, this was a long speech. Tullus watched the legionaries' faces as they passed him. They gave him resolute nods. Fierce smiles. Unblinking stares. Bare-toothed wolf leers. Tullus' heart swelled. 'They're good boys – all of them.'

'You've made them that way, Tullus. You. They're some of the finest legionaries in the whole fucking army – just as our comrades in the Eighteenth were. They'll do our fallen brothers proud today – have no fear of that.'

'Aye,' Tullus said, his voice thick. He gave Fenestela a grateful nod. 'You're right.'

'They'll need another talk before the fighting starts.'

'Don't try and tell me how to do my own job, you dog.' Tullus threw Fenestela a baleful glance.

'I was thinking the sun might have curdled your already addled brains, old man,' said Fenestela in an innocent voice.

'Piss off, optio,' ordered Tullus, without heat. 'Back to your position.'

'Yes, *sir*.'

They marched on, soon hearing for the first time the German barritus. Whether because of the fine conditions, or the distance from which it was coming, the deep-voiced chant had little impact on the legionaries. 'Trying to stiffen their backbones by singing, are they? The whoresons must be shitting themselves at the size of our army,' cried Metilius to widespread laughter.

A grim smile creased Tullus' face. The contrast from seven years before could not be more stark. In the pelting rain and limb-sucking mud of the forest, constant renditions of the barritus had eaten away at his legionaries' morale like rats at a store of grain. Eerie, sung by invisible enemies, it had been easy to think that evil spirits were to blame.

The barritus presaged the beginning of the battle. Even as the chanting grew louder, the auxiliary cohorts came to a sudden halt, causing Tullus – again unable to see what was going on to their front – to conclude that the front units must be close to the eastern end of the plain. The auxiliaries' leaders – their own chieftains – began shouting. Horns were sounded, drums beaten. The auxiliaries roared war cries in Gaulish, German and other tongues, and pounded their feet on the rock-hard ground. Weapons battered off shields.

The din went on for some time, which Tullus expected. Before any carnage began, men on both sides needed to go through the same ritual. To draw on their courage and dampen down their fear. To prepare themselves to meet enemies who would kill them. They had to be ready to protect their comrades and, if needs be, to die.

The barritus fell away to nothing. As if ordered to do so, the auxiliaries' clamour also came to a gradual end. So it begins, Tullus thought, palms damp with unwelcome sweat. Fortuna, be good to us today. I've given you enough rams and bulls over the years – and there'll be more if we win.

Among Tullus' soldiers, men cleared their throats. Spat. Muttered prayers. The auxiliaries were doing the same, but their ranks were solid. They too were ready for the fight.

A mighty cheer, coming from thousands of throats, went up beyond the auxiliaries' position.

'Here they come,' said Tullus, setting his jaw.

Time slowed from that point, forming a succession of crystal-sharp memories in Tullus' mind. The enemy's centre charged the auxiliaries – this was clear from the din, and also from messengers who ran back, warning that the legions should be ready. Savage fighting erupted as the tribesmen struck — the auxiliaries' formation wavered with the force of it, before they steadied themselves and shoved forward again. Trumpet calls to left and right sent the Roman cavalry galloping off to assail the German flanks. The legionary cohorts on either side were attacked by warriors storming out of the trees. Safe for now in the middle of the second line, the Fifth's soldiers had to listen to the shouts, screams, clash of weapons — and wait.

Tension gnawed at Tullus. The same strain was in his soldiers' faces. Someone had vomited — he could smell shit too, and piss. Sweating, rosy-cheeked, Calvus was repeating the same prayer, over and over. Even Fenestela, come to have a word, looked uneasy. 'It'll be us soon,' he said.

'I hope so,' muttered Tullus, hating the delay. It was nigh on impossible that he and Arminius would meet on the field, but Tullus asked that it happen anyway. He'd have given his entire life savings to lay Arminius in the mud. His own life too, if he hadn't had the extra task of trying to recover the Eighteenth's eagle. Killing Arminius would be sweet, but retrieving his legion's standard sweeter still.

In front of Tullus, the auxiliaries' lines swayed to and fro, and began to move forward. Ten steps they went, then another five, and twenty more. Cheering broke out in their ranks. Horns were blown. Amid the din, chieftains' voices, hoarse with effort, issued commands.

Tullus' men muttered among themselves. Two soldiers took a step forward. 'Back into line!' bellowed Tullus. 'Steady! Our turn will come soon, brothers — very soon. You know the drill. Check the laces on your sandals one more time. Get your comrade to look at the straps on your armour. Loosen your swords in their sheaths. Swallow a little water to wet your mouths.' He patrolled along the front rank, watching as they did his bidding. 'Good boys,' he said every few steps. 'That's it. When the fighting starts, stick with the man to your left and right. Look out for them, as they will for you. Remember your training. Shield high, sword ready. Punch and stab. Punch and stab.'

The auxiliaries in front of Tullus moved forward again, this time more than fifty steps. Elated cries rose from their ranks. Gaps appeared between the different units, opening up the battlefield. Tullus' excitement grew as the rest of the auxiliary line also began to advance. Still no order came from Germanicus. He was in the same line as Tullus' cohort, but in the middle. From his horse's back, he would have a good view of the unfolding battle – he'd give the order when the time was right.

This knowledge could not ease Tullus' eagerness, his overwhelming passion to reach the enemy. He stared at the sky. The sun was still high, but it had moved from its position overhead. It was an hour after midday, perhaps two. There was plenty of time to finish the Germans, Tullus decided.

His gaze dropped. The brightness above was blinding, three-quarters-closed eyes or not, but something – a movement above – attracted his attention, and he looked up again. His heart almost stopped in his chest. High, high in the sky, a great bird with characteristic finger-like wing tips and a fan-shaped tail was soaring east. An eagle. It was an *eagle*, thought Tullus in disbelief, and utter delight. No other bird had such a wingspan. Further movement caught his eye, and he let out an incredulous laugh. There were four of them. No, five, six – eight. Symbols of the legions, most regal of birds, they were flying for Germanicus' army, Tullus decided. More concrete proof of the gods' approval there could not be.

'Look!' he shouted in his best parade-ground voice, pointing upwards. 'FUCKING LOOK!'

Heads lifted. Men gasped. Arms were raised, prayers offered. 'It's a sign!' cried Piso. 'A sign from Jupiter!'

'See, brothers?' Tullus was beside himself with excitement. 'EIGHT eagles in flight, travelling over Arminius' army! They are the guardian spirits of every legion here today!'

'Roma!' shouted his men. 'Roma!'

More and more soldiers began to notice the majestic birds, and soon the cheer was rolling off in all directions. 'ROMA! ROMA!'

Germanicus must have seen the eagles too. He has to give the order *now*, thought Tullus.

Twenty feverish heartbeats later, the trumpets sounded the advance. It would be a chaotic affair: the legionaries would have to work their way between the auxiliary units, but it was worth the risk, thought Tullus. The din of battle had been drowned out by the continuing shouts of 'ROMA! ROMA!' It seemed every legionary in the army had joined in.

A rapid consultation with Bassius, and their tactics were set. The six centuries would file forward into the nearest 'tunnel' between groups of auxiliaries. Closer to the fighting, they would fan out one by one into wedge formations. 'Punch into the enemy lines like that, and we could break 'em at first pass,' declared Bassius, an evil light in his eyes.

'Aye, sir.' As centurion, Tullus' place was at the most dangerous point, the tip of the wedge. Instead of fear, he felt an odd exultation. This was no soaking-wet, mud-encrusted struggle for survival in the bog or the forest. This was a proper battle, when Rome's legions could fight at their best. This was what he'd been waiting for. He would seize the opportunity with both hands. 'My boys are ready.'

'May the gods give us victory.' Bassius gave Tullus a measured nod. 'I'll see you afterwards.'

'We'll share a cup of wine, sir.' Neither knew if the other would survive, but it was bad luck to wish anything but the best outcome.

Tullus waited until Bassius and his soldiers were going by. Lifting the whistle that hung round his neck, he blew three short blasts. Trained to recognise his commands, his men stilled. 'We follow the Roman birds, brothers!' shouted Tullus. 'Shall we have our vengeance on Arminius?'

They screamed their enthusiasm back at him.

'Shields up. Javelins ready. With me!' Hefting his shield, Tullus strode after Bassius' century.

Danger and death beckoned, yet Tullus hadn't felt this alive in years.

Chapter XXI

The sun beat down, its heat unforgiving, its light blinding. Piso's entire body was covered in sweat, his mouth drier than a month-old hunk of bread. His heart beat off his ribs as if he'd just run ten miles, and in his left fist, his shield had metamorphosed into pure lead. Any metal Piso was wearing: his helmet, armour, javelin head, was too hot to touch. He cared not a jot. He was near the point of the wedge, a position of huge honour.

Tullus was at the apex, with Piso and Metilius right behind him. Dulcius, Calvus and another tent mate comprised the third row, behind Piso and Metilius. Four men made up the next rank, five the next and so on: eleven rows of soldiers, shaped into an armoured triangle. A few paces separated each man from the next: room was needed to hurl javelins. That done, the legionaries would close up tighter than tight.

They'd just cleared the auxiliaries' ranks and seen the battlefield for the first time. A lull in the fighting reigned, an odd moment when by some unspoken consent enemies pulled back from each other, to rest, drink water and treat their injured. Piso stared. The area between the two armies was littered with bodies: most were German. Not fifty paces away stood Arminius' warriors, a long line, many rows deep, stretching off to either side. Despite being bloodied and reduced in number, there was no sign of their wanting to withdraw. Their formation was solid, and chieftains strode about, shouting, gesticulating and making obscene gestures at the Romans.

'They're carrying on like Tullus,' muttered Piso to Metilius. 'But not one is half the man he is.'

They both studied their centurion. Fierce concentration marked his face. His teeth were part bared, and his gaze was locked on the enemy, reminding Piso of a wolf watching a flock of sheep before it struck.

'Seven years he has waited for this. No wonder he's keen,' said Metilius, throwing a glance at Piso. 'I'm the same.'

'Aye,' growled Piso. 'And me.'

He could sense the same readiness in those behind him. Javelin butts thumped the ground in an uneven, repetitive rhythm. Hobnailed sandals stamped up and down. No one was foolish enough to step out of the wedge, but the men *wanted* to advance. They *wanted* to close with the enemy. Piso could feel it. Even Calvus seemed eager.

'The cohorts to my left are almost in place, Tullus.' Bassius' voice carried from his position at the point of a wedge to their left. 'You ready?'

'Yes, sir,' Tullus replied.

'The other centuries, and the cohort beyond – what about them?'

'A moment, sir.' With a shout, Tullus caught the attention of the Third Century's centurion, who passed on Bassius' query.

Waves of heat hammered down on Piso and the rest. He imagined stripping off his armour and jumping naked into the Visurgis, not a mile to their rear. Such pleasures would have to wait. Live through the slaughter first, Piso thought.

'They're ready, sir,' bellowed Tullus. 'On your command.'

'GO!' Pitched to carry, Bassius' voice was followed by a long blast on his whistle.

'ADVANCE!' Tullus pointed his sword straight at the enemy. 'Stay close, brothers!' he ordered, tramping forward.

'Here we go,' whispered Piso, tightening his grip on his javelin. 'At fucking last.'

Five paces they went. Ten. Seeing them, the nearest warriors tightened their formation. The legionaries were walking towards a wall of shields, with a fierce, angry face over every last one. German spears began flying, and Tullus barked a command. Everyone on the outside of the wedge ducked behind their shields; those within raised theirs over their heads. *Thunk. Thunk. Thunk.* The spears landed in flurries. Piso's shield wasn't hit, though; nor were those of Tullus and Metilius. No one cried out in pain that Piso heard.

'Men with damaged shields, rip the spears out!' yelled Tullus. 'There's time!'

Ten paces closer to the warriors, and Piso's heart felt too big for his chest. Thirty paces was good killing distance, and the enemy spears were raining down thick and fast. It was time to throw their javelins, surely.

Tullus took them even closer before he gave the order. 'Javelins ready! LOOSE!'

With the ease of long practice, Piso drew his right arm back. Picking a bull-necked warrior with a black beard, he took aim and threw. His javelin streaked the short distance in two heartbeats. Blood sprayed as the iron-tipped missile skewered the man's throat. 'I got him!' Piso's cry was lost in the crescendo of shouts and screams as his comrades' javelins landed. At such close range, even Calvus could not miss. The devastating volley punched holes in the German line, and Tullus was ready. Ordering close formation, he broke into a half-run. 'With me!' he roared.

Keeping pace, Piso blinked away the sweat stinging his eyes. Three steps, five, eight. The nearest warriors were screaming insults and raising their shields and spears – they were keen to fight.

'Jupiter, Greatest and Best. Jupiter, Greatest and Best.' Carrying from several ranks back, Calvus' high-pitched voice was infuriating, but there was no time to tell him to shut his mouth. Piso blocked his ears to the sound.

'With me, brothers!' roared Tullus.

They hit the German line with a massive crash, forcing their way into the warriors' midst.

Piso stepped over a body – the man he'd killed with his spear, perhaps – and now he had to clamber over a second, all the while keeping his eyes to the front, and staying close to Tullus. Cursing, for to stumble was to die, Piso smacked his shield into that of the first warrior to meet him. A youth of no more than eighteen, his eyes wide with fright, he pushed back at Piso as best he could. It was a one-sided contest; with his heavy armour and shield Piso outweighed him twice over.

Wood splintered as Piso's iron boss split the youth's willow shield; an oomph rose as the air left his lungs. Spear flailing in his right hand, he was driven backward, losing his footing. Down he went on to his back, and Piso stabbed him in the throat: in, out with the blade. Piso forgot the youth, quickly checking *he* was still near Tullus, and that Metilius and Dulcius were close by. That done, Piso met the charge of his next opponent, a yelling bare-chested warrior in green and brown woven trousers.

Bang! went their shields, and Woven Trousers thrust with his spear, straight at Piso's face. Air whistled and Piso fell into a crouch behind his shield, at the same time stabbing forward, blind, with his sword. Woven Trousers let out a mighty bellow. Confident now, Piso pushed hard with his blade, feeling it slide deeper into flesh. He stood. Woven Trousers had dropped his spear and shield; both his hands were wrapped around Piso's razor-sharp sword, half buried in his side. Piso pulled his right arm back, slicing Woven Trousers' fingers to ribbons, and, reversing the movement, stuck him again, higher up, under his ribcage. Woven Trousers' mouth gaped like a fish out of water, and he died.

'Help me, brother!' It was Dulcius' voice.

Piso's head twisted to the left. His comrade was engaged in a desperate fight with two warriors, both armed with spears. Focused on killing Dulcius, the closest, he did not even see Piso's simple sword thrust that ended his life.

'Manage the other, can you?' Piso cried.

'Aye!' shouted Dulcius.

Piso faced forward again; he watched Tullus smash a warrior so hard with his shield that he careered into the man behind him, and they both fell. With a snarl, Tullus advanced, stamping down with his hobnailed boots, once, twice, thrice. His crimson-coated blade rose and fell in a blur. Gurgling cries were cut short, and Tullus straightened. 'With me?' he roared over his shoulder.

'Aye, sir!' answered Piso and Metilius.

'ON!' There was a gap in front of Tullus; he moved forward several steps. 'You maggots!' he yelled at the nearest warriors. 'Ready to die?'

A trio of similar-looking warriors, cousins perhaps, glanced at each other. One said something and then they charged together, their clear target Tullus. Kill the centurion and the wedge would stop, thought Piso in alarm. 'Metilius!'

'Aye?'

'See the three whoresons?'

'I do, aye!'

Piso fitted himself tight against Tullus' left side, felt Metilius do the same on his right. Sensing their urgency, Dulcius shoved up against Piso's back; Calvus and their other comrade did the same behind him and Metilius.

The first warrior to close died with Metilius' blade in his left eye socket. Aqueous fluid spurted; the steel ran deeper, shearing bone and the softer brain matter beneath. Metilius cursed, trying to free his sword, and the other Germans arrived, hammering their spears at Tullus from two angles. Eager to retaliate, Tullus bent his knees a moment too late. A spear rammed into the brow of his helmet, snapping his head back.

Piso saw this from the corner of his eye. Cursing, he plunged his blade into the armpit of Cousin One, who'd struck the blow. A simple strike, it was lethal. Blood sheeted the ground as Piso's sword came out and Cousin One fell, thrashing like a hooked pike. Cousin Two now shoulder-charged a dazed Tullus and shoved him back a step. With a triumphant cry, Cousin Two raised his spear high and prepared to thrust down, over the top of Tullus' shield.

Piso didn't know why Metilius wasn't there to stop the blow falling. His own right arm wasn't long enough to reach Cousin Two. If Piso left the wedge, he might save Tullus, but he would leave a hole for the enemy to drive into. That was a disaster he didn't want to be responsible for – yet

Tullus would die otherwise. Riven with indecision, aware that he had to make up his mind *now*, Piso hesitated.

Cousin Two's face took on a startled expression; then it twisted into a rictus of agony. A high-pitched wail left his throat, and he slumped down, out of Piso's sight. 'Take that, you filth,' muttered Tullus, pulling free his blade, which he had somehow plunged into Cousin Two's thigh. 'And that,' Tullus said with a precise stab into Cousin Two's open mouth.

Piso could have cried with relief. Ashamed not to have saved Tullus, he said, 'My apologies, sir, I—'

'Later, Piso,' said Tullus in his parade-ground voice. 'FORWARD!'

Awed by Tullus' resilience, Piso knew it had been a close-run thing. He determined to stick to Tullus as tight as a flea to a dog's ball sack from that point on.

The wedge pressed on. Battered by the legionaries' unrelenting assault, the warriors began to edge backwards. Roman morale rose, and fresh war cries went up. The formation's pace picked up. At its front, Tullus was like a man possessed, hacking down any German to come within reach of his blade. Chests heaving with the effort, Piso and Metilius stayed at his shoulders, playing their part. Behind, their comrades punched and stabbed, stabbed and punched.

'Push!' cried Tullus. 'They're breaking!'

Baying like hunting hounds, his soldiers drove forward. Braver warriors, few in number now, died beneath their blades or fell screaming to the rutted earth. Fear twisting their faces, others turned to run. The slow were cut down, and the legionaries advanced another ten steps. More Germans were slain. Tullus killed a chieftain and, with clinical precision, beheaded him. With a mighty heave, he lobbed the severed head high into the air. Turning end over end, showering those below with blood, it dropped into the maelstrom. With startling swiftness, every German who'd seen lost the will to fight. Courage vanished, terror blossomed, and the warriors dropped their weapons and fled. Anyone who stumbled or fell was crushed underfoot. Tullus continued to move forward at a steady pace. 'Kill the injured and the fallen if you can, but keep walking!'

Piso was filled with the same mad, soaring joy that he'd felt on the Long Bridges the year before when Arminius' army had crumbled. At any moment, Tullus and the other centurions would unleash them on the fleeing enemy. Piso was startled, therefore, when a sharp *peeeeep* signalled the halt. Not expecting the order, Dulcius collided with him.

Other soldiers were also caught unawares, and Tullus twisted his head. 'HALT!'

The wedge ground to a stop. 'They're running, sir,' protested several voices.

'I can see that, you maggots,' Tullus barked. 'But Arminius will have fresh men in the trees. We're not walking into their embrace. Catch your breath. Dress your wounds. Have a drink – and stay in formation!' Craning his head to left and right, he assessed the situation.

Piso's bladder was twinging. How could it have filled again? he wondered, irritated. Ready for his comrades' jibes, he was relieved to hear other men's urine pattering off the ground as he did the necessary. All done, he eyed Metilius. 'You hurt?'

'A scratch on my sword arm.' Wincing, Metilius let Piso bandage him up.

'Dulcius, you all right?' called Piso.

'Aye. We all are in this row. There's a man injured just behind us, but he's not too bad.'

Shouted questions soon revealed that the century had suffered two men dead and six wounded. Tullus grinned when he was given the news. 'Light casualties – we did well. Bassius has halted,' he announced. 'So has the century to our right. We hold this line for the present.'

Piso studied their front afresh. Scores of fleeing warriors remained in sight, but their numbers were thinning fast. The majority had reached the shelter of the tree line, and therein Tullus had seen the danger. A dart of fear struck Piso as he too realised.

The German counter-attack began almost at once. Hundreds of chanting warriors came loping from between the beeches and spruces. This was no frantic charge – they took time to form a solid line. Sunlight flashed off their spears. A good number were wearing mail, which signified them as Arminius' best fighters. More and more emerged, until several thousand stood before the Roman wedges, a powerful rendition of the barritus resonating from their throats.

As the Germans began advancing, a grim-faced Metilius thumbed his phallus amulet. 'It's not over yet.'

Chapter XXII

B lack fury consumed Arminius as he watched the battle from his forces' left flank. The Marsi and his Cherusci warriors had done well at first, and even though the determined auxiliaries had shoved them back, the warriors had been more than ready to renew their assault. The unexpected appearance of a group of eagles over the forest could not have come at a worse time. There had been an unstoppable momentum to the legionaries' armoured wedges. Even if he'd been in the thick of it, Arminius wasn't sure their line could have held. Broken moments before, the terrified warriors were now running for their lives.

He cursed Donar for letting the mighty birds be seen, and also for not changing the weather. Why had the god not lashed the Romans with heavy wind and rain, and terrified them with his thunder and lightning, as he had seven years before? We are your followers, Donar, and this is your land, thought Arminius. Help us, not the invaders.

More warriors were being cut down in the centre. Those few still fighting were surrounded and slain. Trumpets sounded, and fresh cohorts emerged, moving forward towards the fray. Bitterness swelled in Arminius' chest, but he thrust the feeling away. The struggle was far from over. He could see hundreds of his mail-clad warriors, held in reserve until now, moving out into the sunlight. Tired from their advance, the legionaries in the wedges might not withstand an assault from these veteran fighters. Spying Maelo at the front, Arminius took heart. If anyone were to drive the Romans back, it would be his second-in-command.

Arminius had planned to be there, but moving about his army and dealing with his cursed chieftains had seen him caught on the left flank as the fighting started. Keen to do what he could, he had led two stinging attacks on the nearest section of the Roman line, comprised of auxiliary archers. Running in with raised shields, his warriors had reached the bowmen with minimal casualties, and caused chaos each time. Their lines remained ragged. One more charge and we'll break them, thought Arminius. Smash into the side of the troops beyond, and panic will set in. Victory could be ours.

It worried him that most of Germanicus' legions still hadn't been deployed, but this attack was as good a chance as they'd get this day. Arminius set to rallying the warriors with whom he found himself, a mixture of Angrivarii, Sugambri and Bructeri. Encouraged by their successes, they bellowed their enthusiasm for his rousing cries. Placing himself in their centre with a large group of mounted warriors, he gave the signal.

With a thundering of hooves, the horsemen charged the thinned ranks of the auxiliary archers, followed by the running warriors. Arrows shot up at once, but not in the disciplined volleys of before. That was as well, thought Arminius, his nerves twitching. Able to cover his own body with his shield, he had no way of protecting his mount. If it was struck by an arrow, he would be thrown, and trampled to death by the horses behind. Several of his companions were hit, but Arminius' luck held. Closing on the archers, he aimed for a gap in the front rank, between a scared-looking, thin-faced man and a veteran bowman who was loosing shafts with ruthless efficiency.

Thin Face quailed and dropped his bow as Arminius galloped in. Wrapped up with his shooting, the veteran didn't look up until the last moment. It was a fatal mistake. With one stroke, Arminius sliced through the veteran's bow shaft and took off the top of his head. A quick glance to his left – Thin Face was no danger – and Arminius' horse had taken him another five strides into the auxiliaries' midst. Wails rose from under its belly as someone was trodden on; Arminius paid no heed. Cracking down his shield rim on an archer to his left, he broke the man's arm. He looked right, and thrust his blade into a bowman who was about to send a shaft into him from an arm's length away.

Arminius drove on another fifteen paces, other riders close on each side. He slew another two of the enemy, and crippled another. Resistance from the confused, fearful archers crumbled further as the warriors on foot arrived, pouring into the space left by the horsemen. Unused to fighting their enemies at close quarters, most bowmen chose to run. Arminius and his companions slew them in scores, easier than spearing fish in a pool.

He began to rally his men: with so many fresh Roman troops on the field, it was rash to pursue the bowmen without reorganising first. Frustration filled Arminius to see the warriors who'd charged already plundering the dead. Precious time was lost restoring order. 'Move,' he shouted. 'We've got to chase the bastards quickly, or they will regroup – and Germanicus will send other troops against us.'

Surly-faced, the warriors assembled in a line. Arminius took heart. There had been few casualties, and these men were hungry for Roman blood. More of their brethren were appearing from the woods, drawn by the prospect of defeating the enemy. 'Ready?' he cried.

'AYE!' shouted the warriors.

Arminius had raised his arm, ready to give the order when a familiar sound reached his ears. *Tramp, tramp, tramp.*

No, he thought, *NO!* Raising himself up on his horse's back, he peered beyond the archers. The bright sunlight made it impossible to see far, but spotting clouds of rising dust was enough. The nearest Roman units – whether auxiliary or regular legion, Arminius couldn't tell – were coming. They had to be stopped. If one part of the tribal line was driven back, defeat beckoned.

'Reinforcements are coming,' he shouted. 'We advance on my command.'

'Lead on, Arminius,' shouted a familiar voice. 'The Usipetes are with you!'

Recognising Gervas for the first time that day, Arminius smiled. 'Are the Sugambri and Bructeri also ready?'

'AYE!' roared a thousand voices.

Stiff-armed, Arminius pointed towards the approaching Romans. Gods only knew where this attack would take them – he could only hope for success, and that Maelo was also triumphant. They would meet somewhere in the middle, and carve a victory even more glorious than his ambush in the forest.

Darts of pain radiated from Arminius' top lip, the shallow cut made by the dying blow of his last opponent. He also had a more serious injury, a slash on his right calf. Blood oozed down his leg and the wound pulsed with a life of its own. He blocked out the throbbing ache. Composed, driven by relentless purpose, he fought on. The other riders were with him, but the situation on either side of their little formation was slipping from his grasp.

How much time had passed since the auxiliary infantry had appeared to support the archers, Arminius wasn't sure. The hammer blow of their arrival had stopped his warriors' advance. The delay in reorganising his men had been fatal, allowing the two sides to meet on flat, open ground, negating any advantage his warriors might have had. To their credit, thought Arminius, they had brought the auxiliaries to a standstill – and even driven them back in a few places.

Their success had been short-lived, however.

Sour-faced, Arminius watched an auxiliary officer organise a small wedge of his men; moments later, they punched a hole in his warriors' line. Excited yells went up, and more auxiliaries poured into the gap. Arminius' warriors fought on with grim purpose, but the process had a slow, inevitable feel to it, like watching the sea creep in and destroy a child's sand fort. Curse it all, thought Arminius. We've lost, here at least.

The time to retreat had come. If he delayed any longer, the slaughter of his warriors would be total. Arminius hated Rome with every particle of his being, but he had a grudging admiration for the ruthless intensity with which its soldiers hunted down beaten enemies. Discipline, it was always their fucking discipline that won out. Arminius swung his gore-spattered sword arm around to the rear. 'Pull back!' he bellowed at the riders around him. 'With me! Fighting withdrawal!'

No one argued, and Arminius knew he had made the right decision. Gervas was among the dozen horsemen who stayed with him; together they made a series of sallies against the nearest auxiliaries, allowing their comrades and the warriors on foot to retreat some distance. Seeing what was going on, the auxiliaries redoubled their efforts, and Arminius lost five riders in one brutal charge, cut down, pulled to the ground or crushed beneath their hamstrung mounts.

No longer capable of holding back the enemy, he aimed his horse towards the tree line. Perhaps there they could make a stand. It was a futile wish, he thought with increasing bitterness. Only at Cannae, more than two centuries before, had retreating soldiers returned to the fray, and his men were not Hannibal's Gauls.

'Look out!' cried Gervas.

The noise of pounding hooves filled Arminius' ears. Confused, he glanced to his rear. Waves of auxiliary infantry there, but no horsemen.

'To the right!' Gervas screamed.

Arminius looked, and his heart sank. Scores of enemy cavalrymen, more auxiliaries, were riding hard in their direction from Germanicus' right flank. A clever move, Arminius thought. Many of the retreating warriors hadn't seen them yet. A few heartbeats later, it was clear that the Roman cavalry had judged the angle of their attack to perfection. They would strike the main body of warriors – and Arminius' riders – before they reached safety.

He sheathed his sword – no easy feat when riding – and, ignoring the pain, rubbed hard at the cut on his top lip with the palm of his hand. That done, he smeared his cheeks and forehead with blood. Better to escape unrecognised than to die here, for nothing, he thought, as the shame of his action lashed him. Tugging out his blade again, he felt the weight of someone's stare and, looking to his right, realised that Gervas had seen. Uncomfortable, Arminius turned his head away.

Short distance though it was to the trees, the ride took an age. Shouting fierce war cries, the auxiliary cavalry closed with Arminius' forces. Sunlight flashed off spear tips; screams rose after. What courage had remained to his warriors vanished, turning them into a panicked mob. Caught up in the confusion – men running hither and thither, injured warriors and corpses littering the ground – Arminius and his remaining companions slowed their horses. More than once, he had to kick away those begging for help, asking to climb up behind him. I will not die here like a fool, he thought. At last the path before them was clear, and Arminius' spirits lifted a fraction. He would live to fight another day.

In the same moment, a party of twenty Roman cavalrymen came galloping in from the right. Wheeling with impressive efficiency, they faced Arminius and his companions. Hooves, lots of them, hammered close behind. This was the advance party, Arminius decided, sent to delay his retreating warriors before the main body of horse arrived.

'We've got to charge,' he shouted to Gervas, the nearest. Twisting, he appraised the raggle-taggle band of horsemen and warriors with them. Every face was watching him. 'Charging is our only hope,' he repeated, thinking it was small hope indeed.

'I'm with you.' Gervas' jaw was set.

'And us,' said the three other riders. Behind them, the warriors' grim nods and rumbled agreement signified their willingness to try.

Black amusement mixed with Arminius' anger and despair. It was probable he would die within the next few moments. Perhaps this was his punishment for having shown Donar such disrespect. 'Ready?'

Without waiting for a response from Gervas or the others, he kneed his horse forward. Sword ready, shield held high, he covered perhaps a fifth of the distance to the enemy cavalrymen before they reacted. Challenge accepted, they rode towards him and his men. From the corner of his eye, he was aware of more horsemen arriving from the right – another unit of auxiliaries.

Close in, Arminius recognised the cavalrymen as Chauci. Although part of the tribe had fought with him before, many remained loyal allies of the empire. It was ironic that they rather than Roman legionaries would slay him. Death was the only fate Arminius would accept – he could think of nothing worse than being made captive. Not only would he be denied a joyous reunion with Thusnelda and his son; he would be displayed chained in a triumph, for the Roman public to abuse. No, death was preferable. Picking his target, a solidly built warrior with a swirling pattern-decorated shield, Arminius urged on his horse.

The tribesman drew back his spear arm. His nearest comrade, another experienced-looking warrior, had also seen him coming. It had been foolish to curse Donar, even to himself, thought Arminius. The god would always have the last laugh.

I'll take at least one with me, he decided, judging that the first man was the weaker target.

Ten paces out, the warrior somehow recognised him. 'Arminius?'

'Aye,' snarled Arminius, raising his sword.

With a sudden jerk of the reins, the warrior pulled his horse aside, leaving open the route to the trees. 'Go,' he ordered. 'Go!'

Arminius needed no second telling. With a quick, grateful nod, he obeyed.

Chapter XXIII

卍卍卍

O n the plain of Idistaviso, Tullus wiped his brow clear of sweat for perhaps the hundredth time since dawn. Lowering his arm, well tanned from the summer's campaign, he noted it had turned a deep shade of red. No man could stay in this furnace and not get scorched, he thought. The sunburn would hurt tomorrow; for now, he had a dry mouth, cracked lips and a throat hoarse from shouting orders.

The muscles of his arms trembled with fatigue; wielding his shield and sword was exhausting. Pulses of pain throbbed from his neck, shoulders and lower back, the spots most affected by the dead weight of his mail. The old crone who niggled at the old injury in his left calf was hard at work, probing with her sewing needle. These were small prices to pay, however, given the carnage of the past six and more hours. Victory was theirs. Pride filled Tullus that only four men of his century had fallen.

The sun was dropping in the sky, and the worst of the heat had been and gone. The battle proper had ended some time since. Two legions and the cavalry were still pursuing the enemy off to the east and south, and archers were having sport by the Visurgis, shooting warriors trying to hide high in the trees. The voices of legionaries and auxiliaries mixed as they wandered about, searching for loot. Hundreds of injured warriors were wailing their pain at the unforgiving blue sky. They'd be quiet soon enough, thought Tullus. The legionaries were in no mood for clemency.

His men had done well, holding their position as the Cherusci had swarmed down at them from the tree-covered slopes. Side by side with the other wedges, they had fought the tribesmen to a standstill, killing or wounding hundreds. The Cherusci had had some success – Bassius had been slain, and his wedge almost wiped out, but they hadn't managed to capitalise on it. Foot by bloody foot, the wedges had ground forward, keeping their shape, slaughtering the enemy and robbing them of their will to fight.

The centurions of fresh-arrived units had seen what was happening and formed their soldiers into the same deadly formations. Faced with a gigantic 'saw blade', the Cherusci had begun to retreat. At one stage Tullus was sure he'd seen Maelo, Arminius' second-in-command, trying to organise a counter-attack. He'd failed, and Tullus had been too far away to reach him. Maelo had disappeared in the chaos of the Cherusci with-drawal soon after. Tullus hoped that he was among the fallen, and Arminius too, but until both men's corpses were found and identified, he wouldn't believe it.

A passing unit of Chauci cavalry had reported that Arminius had led an attack on the auxiliary archers in the right flank. When his assault had failed, he'd fought his way free to the woods, the Chauci had reported. Tullus' demand for more information had been met with uncaring shrugs and the throwaway comment that 'Arminius was gone, and there was nothing more to be done'. Suspicious that there was more to this, Tullus had shouted after the Chauci that Germanicus would hear of it. There had been no response.

'Fucking savages. You can't trust half of them,' he muttered. His words weren't wholly true. The auxiliary cohorts, infantry and cavalry both, had acquitted themselves well. The bowmen had come off the worst, yet they had been saved by the Raeti, Vindelici and Gauls who'd stood in front of Tullus and his men the previous day. For all that the Chauci might have let Arminius escape, they had crushed the mass of retreating warriors on the right of the battlefield.

Roman legionaries could claim much of the glory too. It was they who had broken the enemy's centre and left flank, and who had driven most of the warriors from the field. It had been a good day – a day when pride had been restored to the empire's army, and in particular to those men who had seen their legions wiped out seven years before. If news were to come that Arminius had been slain and the Eighteenth's eagle found, Tullus decided, it would be the finest day of his life.

He knew better than to waste time wishing these ephemeral hopes true. Arminius had been thoroughly beaten. For today, that would do.

Germanicus had ordered the erection of a tropaeum to celebrate his victory, and would arrive before sunset to inspect it. Tullus strode amongst his men as they pillaged the dead for weapons to display on the altar, valuables for themselves – and, most importantly, skins of water. By the time the fighting had ended, every man's water carrier had long since been drained. Tullus had sent two *contubernia* to the river a while before, but they hadn't yet returned.

Noticing Piso by the body of a fine-dressed chieftain, Tullus called, 'Found much?'

Grinning, Piso proffered a thick silver torque. 'This, sir!'

'That'll keep you in wine for a while,' said Tullus with a wink. 'Watch Metilius doesn't sting you for more than his share, mind.'

'I heard that, sir,' said Metilius, walking towards the tropaeum, his arms full of swords. 'I have enough coin in my purse to pay for my own.'

'So you'll stand me a cup sometime?' asked Tullus.

'I'd be honoured, sir.'

'All of us would, sir,' declared Piso. 'You know that.'

Tullus let a smile cross his lips as his men – sweaty, covered in blood and dust – shouted their willingness to buy him drinks. 'Ah, you're good boys,' he said.

They cheered him then, loud and lusty despite their dry throats. 'TUL-LUS! TUL-LUS! TUL-LUS!' The men of other units threw curious looks – the shouts until this point had been for Roma, Germanicus and the emperor, Tiberius.

'Don't think you can get round me so easy, you maggots. There's work to be done yet!' Tullus' tone was a good deal gentler than usual, but he couldn't help it. I'm getting soft, he thought, his heart full as he watched his men bend their backs without another word from him.

More than an hour passed. A cooling breeze had arisen from the north, reducing the stifling heat. Tullus was supervising work on the almost finished tropaeum. Soldiers from different legions had shared the work from the start. Chosen by Tullus, a fine oak – the tree favoured by Jupiter – had been felled, and its branches and foliage cut away. From this had been fashioned a length of timber the height of two tall men and as thick around as Tullus' thigh. A strong branch had been trimmed to make the crosspiece and attached to the vertical section with rope.

Countless large stones had been hauled from a nearby slope covered in scree and piled into a great heap. Tullus had chosen the spot because it was where he had first seen the Cherusci turn and run. In truth, there would be many locations on the battlefield where men would say the enemy broke, but he was the officer organising the building of the tropaeum. He still wasn't sure how that had happened. Bassius' death had left Tullus as the ranking centurion of the Fifth, but officers of similar rank from other legions had also been present.

He suspected it had come about because of his ordeal with Varus. Once Tullus might have refused the job, but not today. It was fitting that he, a veteran of the Saltus Teutoburgiensis and contributor to this victory, should take primacy. It moved him that the legionaries of other units seemed to feel the same way – not long since, they had laid down their tools and let Tullus' men put the finishing touches to the tropaeum.

The large wooden cross had been dressed as if it were a person, with a fine mail shirt and iron helmet stripped from the corpse of a senior Angrivarii chieftain. Bloodstains caked the mail and the helm had a long, blade-shaped dent in the crown. Over the left 'shoulder', a baldric had been draped; from it hung a sword in a silver-bound scabbard. Two hexagonal shields, both splintered, had been affixed to the left 'arm'. Scores of helmets, swords and shields had been heaped at the mound's base. A hole at its top lay ready. Lines of rope trailed away from the vertical section.

Managing to look eager despite their exhaustion, Piso and his comrades stood ready to manoeuvre the structure aloft. Hundreds of legionaries and officers were on hand, eager to witness the first celebration of their triumph over Arminius' forces. Scores of tied-up prisoners, many injured, knelt nearby.

A clinking noise made Tullus turn his head. Fenestela, who had been absent for some time, was emerging from the throng, dragging lengths of chain. Four legionaries accompanied him, similarly encumbered. 'What in Hades is that?' demanded Tullus.

'Chains, sir,' replied Fenestela, ever droll. 'Lots of them.'

'I can see that,' rumbled Tullus, ignoring his men's stifled laughter. 'Care to explain?'

'I went scouting into the trees, sir, making sure all the enemy had fled,' said Fenestela. 'I found the chains about a quarter of a mile away, along with some food and water, supplies and so on.'

'You think the Germans brought them to use on *us*?'

'That's what it looks like, aye.'

'Arrogant fucking savages!' Tullus seized a length of the chain and raised it high. 'See this, brothers? This was for the Cherusci to bind us with, after they had defeated us!'

The eruption of angry shouts, whistles and catcalls that followed soon morphed into chants of 'TUL-LUS!' and 'GER-MAN-I-CUS!'

'And, with perfect timing, here he is,' said Tullus, hearing horsemen. 'Your general comes!' he roared.

'GER-MAN-I-CUS! GER-MAN-I-CUS! GER-MAN-I-CUS!' The cheering grew deafening.

The crowd nearest the Visurgis parted, allowing a party of riders to canter in. Germanicus led, and was followed by Caecina, Tubero and many of the army's senior commanders. Tullus and Fenestela both came to attention and saluted.

Almost as dirty as the soldiers, and as covered in sweat, Germanicus continued to look every part the general, every part the victorious leader.

'This triumph was Tiberius', Tullus, not mine,' he said, smiling to show that, despite his words, he was pleased by the recognition.

Far away in Rome, Tiberius didn't even know this battle had taken place yet. He hadn't ever had anything to do with Germanicus' army – everyone knew that. This was politics talking, but Tullus knew his place. 'As you say, sir.' He quietened the men with a gesture, and cried, 'TI-BER-I-US!'

Surprise bathed the nearest faces, then realisation sank in. 'TI-BER-I-US!' shouted the soldiers. 'TI-BER-I-US!'

Germanicus gave a tiny nod of approval and slipped from his horse's back. A servant took its reins. Beckoning to Tullus and Fenestela, the general paced to inspect the mound. Tullus took huge satisfaction from Tubero's angry expression – he hated this recognition of him by Germanicus. Fuck you, Tubero, thought Tullus. You arrogant whoreson.

Stooping here and there, Germanicus examined the weaponry and helmets. His gaze lingered on the bloodied mail shirt and battered helmet on the 'body'.

Tullus had been pleased with the tropaeum, but now a sudden nervousness took him. 'Perhaps we should have searched more of the battlefield,' he muttered to Fenestela. 'There could be finer trophies out there.'

'Nothing you can do now,' came Fenestela's unhelpful reply. He met Tullus' sidelong glare with an innocent expression.

'A fine display,' Germanicus commented at last. He acknowledged Piso and his companions, who grinned like fools.

Mightily relieved, Tullus glanced at Germanicus. 'Shall I give the order, sir?'

'Aye.'

'Haul it up, brothers!' cried Tullus.

Piso and his comrades set to with a will. Lifting the cross, they worked its base into the hole at the mound's top. Four men placed it on their shoulders so it was almost parallel with the ground, while Piso and Metilius moved to stand opposite them. Picking a rope each, the pair pulled on a count of three. Held from beneath by the four soldiers, who walked up the mound as Piso and Metilius heaved, the cross eased itself into the footings.

A huge cheer rose as it came upright. With eager hands, Piso and his companions moved rocks around the cross's base, support to keep it standing. That done, they undid the ropes and moved away.

Germanicus clicked his fingers, and a scribe hurried forward with a calf-skin parchment. An expectant silence fell as Germanicus unrolled it – even Tullus felt a rush of excitement.

'This altar has been built to celebrate today's famous victory, and is dedicated to the glory of the gods Mars, Jupiter and Augustus. In this place, the German tribes were beaten – slain in their thousands. The Cherusci. The Angrivarii, the Marsi and the Sugambri. The Usipetes, the Chatti. The Bructeri and the Dolgubnii – all vanquished by the army of Tiberius Caesar!' Germanicus looked around, catching the eye of man after man. 'You did this – all of you!'

'TI-BER-I-US! TI-BER-I-US! TI-BER-I-US!'

Germanicus listened to the soldiers' acclaim with a satisfied expression.

Tullus stole a look at the senior officers. Caecina and the rest seemed happy, but Tubero had a face that would have curdled milk. All the prick could see, thought Tullus, was him standing beside the governor. It was beyond Tubero to realise that Germanicus was recognising his soldiers' achievement, but also binding them to him even more.

The legionaries' yelling died away little by little. When silence had fallen, Germanicus spoke again. 'Our losses were light today, the gods be thanked. Fewer than a thousand of our soldiers fell, while the enemy lost more than seven times that number. A grievous cost to us was the death of Primus Pilus Bassius of the Fifth Legion. He was a fine officer, who served the empire for almost forty years. He will never be forgotten.' Germanicus bent his neck, showing his respect.

Every man copied him, even the commanding officers.

Tullus' grief, held back until now, welled forth. Rest in peace, Bassius, old friend, he thought. He had already decided to burn Bassius' body by the base of the tropaeum later that evening. Burial was out of the question. The local tribespeople who came to defile the altar would dig him up and mutilate his body. Instead Tullus and his men would watch the flames consume Bassius' body, as Romans had done of old. On their return to Vetera, he would have a fine tombstone on the road leading from the legion's fort – Tullus would see to that.

'With the army still at war, the Fifth Legion needs a new primus pilus.'

Tullus' heart jumped in his chest – Germanicus was looking straight at him.

'I can think of no better officer to fill the position than Centurion Lucius Cominius Tullus.'

Loud rumbles of agreement rose from the gathered soldiers. Tubero looked as if he'd swallowed a wasp.

More embarrassed than he'd ever been, Tullus fixed his gaze on the ground before Germanicus' feet.

'Approach, centurion!' ordered Germanicus.

Tullus stamped forward, conscious of the dust and caked blood covering every part of him. 'SIR!' he bellowed and came to attention.

Germanicus' gaze travelled over those watching, and then he said, 'By the power vested in me, I name you primus pilus of the glorious Fifth Legion.'

As the soldiers gave loud voice to their approval, Germanicus added, 'May you serve as well as Bassius.'

'I will do my best, sir!'

'I know you will,' said Germanicus with a smile.

'One request, sir.' Risky though it was, he had to strike while the iron was hot.

Germanicus raised an eyebrow. 'Yes?'

'I would ask to move some of my men into the First Century, sir. Soldiers who were in the Eighteenth.' Tullus licked dry lips.

'After what you rescued them from, it's not for me to separate you.' Real respect marked Germanicus' face. 'Take as many as you wish.'

'Thank you, sir.' Tears pricked Tullus' eyes. It was, he thought, only fitting that Piso, Metilius and the rest of his men from the Eighteenth would share this victory with him.

Chapter XXIV

𐊆𐊆𐊆

Piso and his comrades were sprawled outside their tent. It was far too warm to consider sleeping in the close confines of its muggy interior. It was also late – hours had passed since sunset, but they had not long returned from the battlefield. Conversation was dwindling fast. The black and white stray dog adopted by the contubernium, Macula, had given itself up to sleep, its paws already twitching in a dream.

The day had been memorable, thought Piso, enjoying the fuzzy feeling that came with drinking a lot of wine. Victory over the Germans had been exhilarating, and erecting the tropaeum's cross in front of Germanicus an unexpected bonus. Tullus' promotion to Bassius' post and their own elevation to the First Century had seemed to prove that Fortuna was in the best of moods.

Anxious that their fallen comrades would escape the attention of the local tribes, the legionaries had requested that all the bodies be burned. Tullus had agreed. Axes brought from the camp had allowed the felling of trees. The smell of burning flesh from the pyres had been awful, but Tullus had seen to it that wine was on hand. Proud of their hard-won victory, grieving for the fallen and lubricated by the wine, the carousing legionaries had stayed on the battlefield for some hours after sunset.

Metilius broke the drowsy silence. 'It was a fitting way to send them off, eh? Bassius would have approved.'

'Better to burn than be dug up by the savages, that's for sure,' Piso agreed, but he was brooding about Vitellius. After the battle of the Long

Bridges the previous year, they had buried him in an isolated spot, hoping this would be enough to save his grave from discovery.

'We couldn't have cremated 'Tellius,' muttered Metilius, reading Piso's mind. 'It was autumn, remember, and raining every day. Even if we'd got a fire lit, the smoke would have attracted every warrior for miles.'

Piso sighed. There hadn't been an alternative, but it still hurt that they had interred Vitellius' body miles from anywhere. Good soldiers like him shouldn't die, thought Piso. Bitterness coursed through his veins at the thought of a man like Tubero, who seemed set to sail through life without ever coming to harm. Arrogant and uncaring, he was disliked by every soldier in the legion. Worse still, his stupidity had almost got Tullus and twenty men killed once. Why couldn't Tubero have died? Piso wondered.

A sudden devilment took him. If he were somehow to trim the legate to size, Tullus — as long as he didn't know Piso had done it — would be pleased and amused. The prank wouldn't bring Vitellius back either, but it would make his shade smile. Piso's first idea was to cut most of the way through the legate's saddle girth, but that was too risky. Even if Tubero was only injured, no effort would be spared to find the culprit, and the punishment would be extreme. Something demeaning would work better, Piso decided with regret. Something humiliating.

Nothing feasible offered itself to his drink-befuddled brain, hard as he tried. Metilius was snoring beside him, and drowsiness soon stole up on Piso. He was almost asleep when a foul smell brought him back to reality. Realising that the dog Macula had farted, Piso grimaced and rolled over. An instant later, a broad smile split his face.

He knew just the way to get at Tubero.

'You want to do what?' hissed Metilius in disbelief.

Noticing that Tullus had heard, Piso ignored his friend. It was early morning, and the First, Third and Fifth Centuries were heading towards the Visurgis to fetch water for the entire cohort. Enormous numbers of German dead remained in the river after the battle, so Tullus was marching them upstream. 'We'll come to fresh water in the end,' he declared.

Piso waited until they'd found a suitable, unpolluted spot before speaking to Metilius again. 'Tubero needs to be taught a lesson,' he said as they filled the first of many water bags.

Metilius gave him a resigned look. 'So do most of his kind, but it's never going to happen. You might as well try and pull the sun from the sky. They do as they choose, Piso, and *we* do what we're told. That's the way it has always been, and the way it will remain.'

'This will work,' said Piso, grinning.

Metilius rolled his eyes. 'Don't tell me you've done something already . . .'

'Peace! I'm not stupid.' Piso checked to make sure no one was close, before whispering, 'Macula gave me an idea.' Smiling at Metilius' confused look, Piso muttered something in his ear.

'Have you taken leave of your senses?' Glances were thrown at them, and Metilius lowered his voice. 'How would you do it?'

Again Piso whispered.

'There are sentries!'

'Who walk around in circuits. As long as we time it right, we can get in and out without being seen.'

'*We?*'

'That's right.' Piso gave Metilius an evil smile. 'You're going to help me.'

The day – again, scorching hot – dragged by. Germanicus' scouts, a combination of cavalry and auxiliary infantry, went out in their hundreds, tasked with locating Arminius and his warriors. They returned through the afternoon, all reporting that the Cherusci chieftain and his forces were less than five miles away. Tullus, expert at wringing information from others, discovered from various scouts that the Germans were building a rampart of some kind. Pleased that there would be no immediate retaliation, Piso and his comrades gave little consideration to the news.

Left by Tullus to their own devices – 'Rest up. There'll be fighting tomorrow or the next day – mark my words' – Piso and his comrades lounged in the baking shade of their tent. He kept Macula close by him; the dog was vital to his plan. Idle gossip filled the air. Would Arminius face up to their army again, and when? Was it possible that the two legion standards still in enemy hands would be found this summer? Could the eight eagles seen the day before mean a Roman victory in the next clash with the Germans?

Twice during the afternoon Piso left Macula in the care of Metilius and strolled, as casually as if he were in the settlement at Vetera, towards the camp's centre. Tubero's vast tent was positioned with those of the legion's tribunes, a short distance from the headquarters. Under the pretence of offering odds on the chance of battle the next day, Piso spoke with the sentries on duty by the tribunes' tents. He didn't risk approaching the soldiers outside Tubero's – the fewer clues there were, the greater chance of his never being discovered. That was if he succeeded, Piso thought. The alert manner and erect carriage of the six soldiers guarding Tubero's quarters had driven home the danger of what he was going to attempt. Nonetheless, he pressed on with his snooping.

The sentries were due to be changed at sunset, Piso discovered, and the fresh men would remain on duty until dawn. This discovery shaped his plan: the best time to act was when the guards were tired. They *had* to try at sundown, therefore, when Tubero's duties would still have him in the camp's headquarters. To go in near sunrise risked the legate waking to find one of his own soldiers within his bedchamber. Piso didn't want to consider what the punishment for that infraction might be.

Their comrades knew nothing other than the pair were going 'on a mission'. Piso hoped that their ignorance would protect them in the event of being caught. Their tent mates' well-being, as Metilius darkly warned Piso, would be the least of their worries if that happened. 'We'll be fine,' Piso replied, praying that he was right.

Close to the time he and Metilius were about to leave, events took on an unexpected and dramatic turn. Piso was again following Macula around, and about to add another warm turd to the five lumps already concealed in a ragged piece of cloth.

'What's that you've got there?'

Tullus' voice made Piso start. He turned, putting on his best grimace. 'Picking dog shit up is a filthy job, sir, but it's better than standing in it.'

'It's worst at night, sir, in your bare feet,' added Metilius with perfect timing.

'Scylax shits wherever he pleases,' said Tullus in an understanding tone. Scylax was the name given to the pup he'd rescued with Artio. Now Artio's pet, Scylax lived at Sirona's inn. Every legionary in the cohort knew and loved the animal. 'It sticks to the hobnails something terrible, eh?'

'Yes, sir,' agreed Piso and Metilius.

With a nod, Tullus left them to it.

Piso let out a ragged breath.

'We can still change our minds,' hissed Metilius in his ear. 'There'd be no piss-taking. You and me are the only ones who know.'

Piso wavered for a moment, but then – picturing Tubero's smug face and the legate's anger towards Tullus and his dead comrade Vitellius – he stuck out his chin. 'Stay if you wish. I'm going.'

'Fuck you, Piso,' whispered Metilius. 'You can't do it alone.'

'Is that right?' Shedding his metalled belt in favour of a simple leather one that would not alert the sentries with the jangling from its 'skirt', Piso scooped up his parcel of turds. 'I'll be back later,' he announced to his other comrades.

Curious looks followed him, but Metilius did not.

Disappointment filled Piso as he walked fifty, then a hundred steps from their tent. Metilius was a tried and tested brother-in-arms – he should have accompanied Piso, even if he disagreed with him.

'You're a stupid bastard,' growled Metilius by his left elbow.

Piso spun, delighted. 'Are you coming?'

'You'd fuck it up on your own.'

Grinning like a madman, Piso travelled a dozen strides before harsh reality crashed home again. 'If Tubero's in his tent, we abort the plan.'

'Clearly.'

'We walk away if there's someone around the back of the tent.'

'If any of the sentries give us a suspicious look, we give up.'

The odds of success appeared so slim that Piso wavered again. 'Maybe—'

To his surprise, Metilius shoved him on. 'We're *doing* this. For Tullus and Vitellius.'

Piso rolled his tongue around a dry mouth. He was strolling along the back of Tubero's tent, the wrapped-up turds held against his body. To his left was a side wall of the large pavilion that formed the camp headquarters. Thirty paces off, Metilius was kneeling and affecting to lace a sandal by a corner of the large tent; in reality, he was keeping an eye out for sentries. By their calculations, Piso had a hundred heartbeats – now eighty-five – to get inside without being seen. Once there, he would have ample time to complete his task, as long as he kept count of his pulse and emerged when the sentries had passed by. Ample time, thought Piso sourly. This is fucking madness. Tubero wasn't there, but there was every chance of being discovered by a servant. Piso's nerve weakened – and strengthened. There could be no backing out now, he decided. The dice had been cast.

Before his courage failed him again, Piso took a look around. Seeing no one other than Metilius, he knelt, lifted the tent's bottom panel and peered inside. He'd chosen an antechamber, close to the dining area perhaps. There were tables covered with clean plates, glasses and cutlery. Twig brooms were stacked together. Ornate bronze lampstands with lions' feet stood in a line. There was no one within eyeshot, so he placed his package inside and rolled after it, letting the leather fall behind him.

He was already perspiring, but the tent's oppressive heat and the terror brought on because he was now committed brought fresh sweat to his brow. Calm down, he told himself, breathing deep. By his somewhat confused calculation, the sentry was due at any time. Twenty heartbeats later, a meas-ured tread and the shink of mail proved his theory to be correct. I'm inside, thought Piso. I may as well look around. Curiosity awakened, he crept towards the partition that divided this chamber from the next.

Also empty, but lit by flickering oil lamps, it was a dining room. Luxurious reclining couches were arrayed in the usual fashion. Tables and chairs finer than any Piso had seen offered simpler ways to sit and eat. Crouched low, package in his hand, he stole inside. There were two exits; from beyond one, he could hear voices. Panicked, he aimed for the other way out. Tugging back the partition a finger's breadth, he glanced into the next chamber. Hope flared in his breast. It appeared to be a sitting room, or area to relax in; there was a chance that it led to Tubero's sleeping quarters.

Piso had little option other than to try it. He tiptoed inside, around the cushion-covered armchairs and a painted statue of a graceful, half-nude Diana, to the partition in the far 'wall'. His luck continued to hold – there was no one in the next room either, but wooden storage chests suggested that he'd reached Tubero's private quarters. His hopes were confirmed as he lifted the lid of one and found fine tunics and undergarments within. With a flash of inspiration, he eased a stinking turd on to the clothing. This was so amusing that he did the same to the contents of a second chest, rolling the shit up in the folds of a pristine toga.

Full of new confidence, he made his way into another chamber, finding it with delight to be Tubero's bedroom. Dominated by a massive wooden bed, it had more furniture than Piso's parents' entire house, all of it beautiful and expensive. The gulf separating him from Tubero had never been more plain, and bitterness gnawed at Piso. Metilius was right. He and their comrades would live their entire lives at the bottom of the social ladder while Tubero and his kind lived in luxury at the top.

With furious purpose, Piso smeared three turds over Tubero's bed sheets, lifting the decorated coverlet back into place with great care. Piso saved his best idea until last. Hoping that Tubero entered first, not a servant, he arranged the last pieces of shit in a row across the threshold. Task accomplished, it was time to leave. Where the patrolling sentry was, Piso had no idea – he had long since forgotten his mental count of one hundred.

He made it to the dining room before Fortuna, cackling to herself, intervened. A servant, talking over his shoulder to a colleague, came into the chamber at the same time, but from the entrance opposite. Terrified, Piso dropped to his hands and knees and crawled under a table. He watched, breath held, as the servant walked around its edge, so close that Piso could have reached out and touched him.

'Get back in here – I need you!' cried a voice in what Piso presumed was the kitchen.

'Coming, coming,' grumbled the servant at the table. He sniffed. 'Has Tubero got a new dog?'

'Not seen one. Why?'

'It smells as if one's taken a shit in here.'

As the servant vanished whence he'd come, Piso stifled a laugh. If the smell was bad in this room, it would be multiple times worse in Tubero's bedchamber, and that was before the prick stepped in the turds in his doorway.

Once Piso had managed to slip unseen from Tubero's tent, he would have liked nothing more than to loiter nearby. To overhear the legate's reaction as he trod in Macula's shit or found his ruined sheets was worth a month's pay, a grinning Piso said to Metilius. 'Maybe two,' his friend had added, snorting with laughter. The risks were too great to linger, however. Their mere presence in the area as they had strolled about Tubero's tent could have put them in danger, and so they ambled back to their century's position, chortling as they imagined the legate's outraged response. Interrogated by their comrades, the pair gave in and told their tale, but not before swearing everyone to secrecy. Much hilarity ensued, and a bemused Macula was fussed over more than ever before.

That night, Piso slept like a baby. Awakened by the dawn trumpets, it took a moment to remember what they'd done. A chuckle escaped him.

Metilius opened his eyes. 'What?'

'I hope Tubero had some spare sheets,' whispered Piso.

They both dissolved into laughter.

'Out of your blankets, you maggots!' Fenestela's staff thwacked the leather over their heads. He stuck his head in the open flap and glared at them. 'What's so fucking funny?'

'Nothing, sir.' Piso scrambled out of the tent, followed by Metilius and the rest of their comrades.

'Don't lie to me, Piso. You were giggling like two children.' Fenestela jabbed him in the chest with the butt of his staff. 'What's the joke?'

Panicking, without a ready lie, Piso flailed about. 'Er, we—'

'We were talking about Calvus' visit to the whorehouse when we get back to Vetera, sir,' said Metilius, pitching his voice to be heard.

Calvus went bright red as a wave of comments flooded in about how he'd fail to rise to the job, finish before he had even got undressed, or catch the pox.

Fenestela's lips twitched; he gave Piso a suspicious look before striding off to wake the rest of the century.

'D'you want to be found out?' hissed Metilius.

'Of course not,' retorted Piso, embarrassed and angry.

'Have a lie on the tip of your tongue then.'

Not long after the morning meal, news swept the tent lines that Tubero was out for blood. Piso had known his prank risked severe punishment, but had shoved his concerns to the back of his mind. Now the real gravity of what might happen was rammed home. Nervous, he and Metilius could do nothing but keep their heads down, and hope that the legate's unpopularity meant that even if someone had an inkling of who'd been responsible, they would say nothing.

An official messenger arrived soon after. Once he'd gone, Tullus had the legionaries line up before their tents. 'It seems that a lowlife crept into our legate's tent yesterday evening and spread dog shit round his bedchamber,' he announced. 'It was in Tubero's bed, rolled up in his clothes – everywhere.'

With great effort, Piso held in his amusement. Tiny choking noises emanated from several comrades, but died away fast. To laugh now would bring down Tullus' wrath.

'Tubero is furious. Incandescent! Every centurion in the legion has been tasked with finding out if any of his men were responsible for this heinous crime.' Tullus' stony gaze bored into the eyes of each soldier he passed. 'Stand forward if you can shed light on the matter.'

No one moved a muscle, still less broke ranks to admit their guilt.

Piso was properly worried now. What a fool he'd been. His rash behaviour could yet see his neck under the executioner's blade.

Slow and careful, Tullus paced along the lines of men for a second time.

Piso's fear soared as he approached. By the time Tullus came abreast of him and Metilius, his heart was hammering like a captured bird's. Face blank, Piso kept his eyes focused in the middle distance. To his considerable relief, Tullus walked by without stopping.

'I'm proud that none of you were involved.' The tonking of Tullus' vitis off one of his greaves was an acute reminder of his power. 'Let's forget about the matter – there are more important things to deal with. Get yourselves ready. Germanicus is marching the army to meet Arminius. We leave within the hour.'

Excitement swept the legionaries. There was a rush to don sandals and shrug on *subarmales*. Men sorted through piles of equipment, finding their armour and swords. Not daring to discuss things with Metilius – that could be done later, when Tullus wasn't close – Piso busied himself preparing his gear.

'Have you seen Macula recently?'

Piso jumped. He hadn't heard Tullus arrive. 'Macula, sir?' Piso's stomach did a neat roll as he glanced about. 'No.'

'My servant's taken him to stay with a mule-driver in the wagon train,' said Tullus in a low voice. 'Best for those who have dogs *not* to have dogs for the moment, eh?'

He knows, thought Piso with increasing panic, he fucking *knows*. 'Yes, sir,' Piso said, miserable not to have foreseen that all such men could be questioned.

'Macula can come back when this has blown over.'

'If you say so, sir,' replied Piso, hedging his bets.

'It was dangerous as hell to do what you did, but well done.'

Still unsure if it was safe to admit his guilt, Piso put on an innocent face. 'Do what, sir?'

'Don't be coy, maggot! Sneaking into Tubero's tent with a bundle of Macula's turds. I couldn't have come up with a better plan myself.'

Piso's knees almost gave way. Tullus knew – he was pleased! – and he wasn't going to turn him over to Tubero.

But Tullus hadn't finished. He poked Piso in the chest, hard. 'Don't ever do something that stupid again.'

'No, sir,' muttered Piso, his momentary elation dissipating.

'You're too good a soldier for me to lose. So is Metilius.' Tullus leered. 'Oh yes, I know he was with you. The two of you are thick as thieves, and Fenestela heard you laughing this morning.'

Piso shuffled his feet, and hoped that whatever punishment Tullus had in mind wasn't too severe.

'I won't forget it.'

Piso's jaw dropped.

'What are you gaping at?' bellowed Tullus, every part the centurion again. 'Germanicus wants you ready for battle! Go on then, or you'll feel my vitis across your back.'

Piso hid his grin as he hurried to obey. They'd done it, and Tullus' reaction had made it worthwhile.

Chapter XXV

≡≡≡

D awn had brought with it another clear sky. On the eastern horizon, the sun wasn't yet visible, but the temperature had begun to rise. It would be another scorching day, like the two that had passed since the Roman victory at Idistaviso. Some miles to the east of the battleground, Arminius was sitting close to his tent on a stout fallen tree trunk. Left leg stretched out before him, he watched the healer remove the bandage encasing his calf.

Fear tickled Arminius' spine as the cloth wrapping, stiff with dried blood, was unwrapped little by little. He closed his eyes, no longer willing to look. The dressing had been on since the battle – he'd been too busy trying to keep his alliance together to have it seen to. He was convinced that Germanicus could yet be beaten this summer – all they needed was the right terrain. Against the odds, Maelo had found the perfect site, several miles away. Mightily encouraged, Arminius had used all of his considerable charisma on the chieftains. As a result, many thousands of warriors remained in the huge camp, keen for revenge on the Romans.

His leg throbbed with pain and, suddenly nervous, Arminius opened his eyes again. Would he pay a terrible price for delaying the healer's inspection? Although there was no smell and the pain had been bearable, the cut could still be festering. Over the years he had seen countless men sicken and die from smaller wounds than his. First they became inflamed. Purulent discharge and spreading redness up the limb followed. Next came fever, severe discomfort and gangrene.

Gods, Arminius prayed, don't let me die like that. Needle darts shot up his leg as the last of the bandage had to be tugged free. 'Well?' he demanded.

Instead of answering, the healer, an amiable Marsi old enough to be his father, placed the crusted strips of cloth to his nostrils and took a deep sniff.

Arminius presumed the worst. 'Has it gone bad?'

The healer glanced at Maelo, who was standing beside Arminius. 'Is he always so stiff-necked?'

'Aye, most of the time,' said Maelo with a chuckle.

Irritated, Arminius bent forward to study his wound, a shallow slash that ran down the side of his calf. Its edges were dark red, but the tissue further away was of normal colour. Sanguineous fluid oozed from the cut, yet he could see no pus. Relief filled him. 'It hasn't gone bad!'

'Not yet anyway,' came the healer's dry reply. He slapped away Arminius' fingers. 'Don't touch!'

Arminius reined in his temper. There were already too few healers to deal with the numbers of injured warriors, and this man was reputed to be the best of the lot.

The healer probed with his fingertips along the line of the cut. He smiled as Arminius hissed in pain. 'You can feel that. Good. How about here?' He was pressing on the tissue three fingers' breadth further away.

'It hurts, but not as much.'

'Here?' The healer had reached the back of Arminius' knee.

'Nothing.' He studied the healer's face. 'Which is good.'

'It's doing well, considering you haven't been off your feet except to sleep. I advised that you lie down when possible.'

'That's easier said than done when there's an army to marshal, and chieftains to meet with,' countered Arminius. 'How long will it take to heal?'

'Fully? A month. Ten days before it won't bleed if you use the limb too much.'

Arminius let out a sarcastic snort. 'I knew you'd say something along those lines. Germanicus won't wait, I'm afraid.'

Tutting, the healer ferreted in his basket. Opening a pot of pungent-smelling salve, he applied a fine layer to the cut. 'Do what you must, but understand that the more hours spent standing, the greater the chance of bleeding and poison setting in.'

'I'll be astride my horse.'

The healer gave him a contemptuous look. 'That's almost the same thing, and you know it. As for fighting, well . . .'

'I am grateful for your treatment, old man, but I can no more rest than I can fly like a bird. Germanicus' host is close at hand. Another battle looms, and I must be there to lead the tribes. If I am not—' Arminius stopped, unwilling to vocalise the growing worry in his heart, that his warriors, well beaten two days before, might not prevail when the armies met again. 'Treat the wound as best you may, and let the gods do the rest.'

Tutting some more, the healer applied a fresh bandage. 'That will last a day – if you rest. If you don't, these will come in useful.' He handed Maelo three rolls of cloth and a small pot of the salve. 'You know what to do?'

'I've dressed a few wounds, aye,' said Maelo.

The healer's knees clicked as he stood. 'My work's done then.'

'Let me pay you,' said Arminius, reaching for his purse.

'Beating Germanicus is all the reward I need.' Pain twisted the healer's face.

'You lost family last year?' asked Arminius. The Marsi tribe's suffering when the legions had entered their territory had been grievous.

'My wife. Thirty-two summers we'd been married.'

'My wife was also taken,' said Arminius, dark memories clawing at him. 'She's not dead, but I will never see her again.'

'I heard what the Romans did. It was a cruel thing.' The healer's eyes, damp with unshed tears, locked with those of Arminius. 'Promise that you will crush Germanicus and his legions.'

Moved, Arminius nodded. 'I will do everything in my power.'

'A man can ask for no more than that,' said the healer, hobbling away.

'He'd fight if he was able,' Arminius observed.

'Revenge is a powerful emotion,' said Maelo. 'It sustains you.'

Arminius could see Thusnelda's face close to his, her lips upturned to kiss. He blinked, blotting out the painful image, and was grateful for Maelo's squeeze of his shoulder.

'I can only imagine how hard it is for you. I'm lucky to have no wife, no children.'

'You must want a son,' said Arminius in an effort to lighten the mood. 'I can see a little Maelo charging about, creating havoc wherever he goes.'

'Maybe one day. Let's win the battle first, eh?'

'Aye.' Arminius drew lines in the dirt with a twig, sketching the lie of the land around their massive earthwork, nicknamed 'the Angrivarian wall' by his warriors thanks to its position on that tribe's land. Still under construction on the ground discovered by Maelo, it would be ready by the next day. With a river and bog on one side and a forest on the other, the defence would give his warriors a powerful advantage of height over the advancing Romans. 'We'll go over my plan first, then talk to the chieftains.'

Midday – sunny and baking hot – was upon them the next day before Germanicus' army had deployed. Made aware by his scouts of Arminius' forces' position, he had been unable to pass up the opportunity of battle, and another victory over the tribes. Arminius' scouts had brought news of the legions marching in their direction hours since. Safe and shaded in the trees that lined one side of the battleground, he had waited for the enemy's arrival and then the legions' preparation for combat. It was a lengthy but familiar process, one in which he had participated many times during his service to the empire.

First came the auxiliaries, a mixture of archers, slingers and infantry. Legions formed the next rank, four today, and with them Germanicus and his Praetorian cohorts. Another four legions comprised the third rank. Groups of cavalry guarded the flanks. It was a huge army, outnumbering Arminius' diminished forces by at least ten thousand men. That was not an issue, he convinced himself. Hemmed in by swampy ground and dense forest, their path blocked by the earthen rampart before them, the Romans would struggle to bring more than a third of their men to the fray.

Maelo padded to his side. 'Can we do it?'

'Ever the plain speaker,' said Arminius, his tone cynical.

Maelo shrugged. 'I see no point being any other way.'

'We can do it if everything goes to plan, aye.'

'Driving the enemy from the field is the best we can hope for. There's no chance of wiping out eight legions. If that was going to happen, we would have already succeeded.'

Arminius sucked on the harsh truth of Maelo's words. 'Perhaps, but give Germanicus a bloody nose today, and his campaign will end. His supply lines can't be stretched any further. When his forces split up, we can harry them all the way home. Sooner or later, Rome will realise that its legions will get the same reception every time they cross the Rhenus.'

'It'll be a close-run affair.' Maelo's gaze was fixed on the vast enemy host.

'Life isn't meant to be easy.' Arminius punched Maelo's arm.

An amused snort. 'I suppose not.'

'Remember your task?'

'Do you think me a dotard?' Maelo relented before Arminius' frown. 'I'm to stay here. My cavalry are to strike the enemy's flank as they advance towards your position at the earthwork. My warriors will form a second wave, to attack when I judge the time right.' Maelo cocked his head at Arminius. 'But the main brunt of the legions' assault will fall on your men.'

'Let them come. We'll be ready.' Despite the bluff tone, Arminius could not rid himself of doubt. He quelled it as best he could. The scene was set, and both armies were in place. Battle would soon commence. There was little to do but offer a final prayer to Donar, and to trust his warriors.

Throbs of pain rose from Arminius' wounded leg as he shuffled to the edge of the rampart. A sticky feeling in his boot told him the bleeding had started again. Energised by his warriors' efforts – the ground below was littered with Roman dead and wounded – he gave consideration to neither. The fighting had been going on for some time – an hour perhaps – and in that time the Romans had launched two massive attacks on the earthwork. Both had been thrown back in decisive fashion, and now the enemy had retreated a short distance to rest and regroup. Clouds of dust rose as fresh units marched forward into the front line. Riders galloped to and fro, carrying orders.

The warriors with Arminius, a combination of Angrivarii and his own Cherusci, were in ebullient spirits. Good numbers were using the lull as an opportunity to leap down from the rampart and strip the dead legionaries and auxiliaries of their mail shirts, water bags and valuables. Following his instructions, they were leaving the enemy wounded alive. Not even the Romans liked tramping over their own comrades, Arminius announced to a chorus of laughter.

'Retrieve any undamaged spears,' he shouted. 'Javelins and shields too. Spread the word.'

The nearest warriors grinned and waved acknowledgement.

Squinting into the bright light, Arminius gazed to his right, and the narrow space between the earthwork's end and the marshy ground. In the days prior to the battle, he had ordered the rampart be constructed well into the bog, but the warriors he'd chosen had given it up as a bad job. Harassed, trying to do a dozen things at once, Arminius had not found out until it was too late. The best he'd been able to do was to task Mallovendus and his best warriors with the weak point's defence.

It had not come as a surprise that a keen-eyed Roman had noticed the gap. Shrewd as a fox, Germanicus had sent four cohorts on a probing attack when the fighting had begun. Thanks to the prolonged hot spell, the bog had hardened, providing a solid surface to fight upon. A savage struggle ensued, and despite the warriors' best efforts, they had been driven back step by bloody step. Alerted to the situation by a messenger, Arminius had sent his half of his reserves to Mallovendus' aid. The five hundred Cherusci warriors had stopped the gap for a time, but even they had begun to struggle. If the rest of the Roman line hadn't been thrown back, Arminius brooded, the four cohorts would have swarmed around to threaten his right flank. As it was, they had had to withdraw, or face being isolated.

Once the battle recommenced, they would be back, sure as a slighted woman seeking revenge. Arminius wondered again if he should command from the weak spot, but it wasn't feasible. The most important place for him to be was here, in the centre. Mallovendus would do his best, and the extension of the rampart using stacked Roman corpses would be a brutal deterrent to the attacking legionaries.

Arminius' attention moved to his left flank, and the trees hiding Maelo and his forces. The dust clouds and distance between their positions meant that it had been hard to know what was going on during the fighting. The break in hostilities had revealed large numbers of slain: from the glints of sunlight off armour, Arminius judged the majority to be Roman. Maelo was playing his part, he thought with satisfaction. If matters continued in this vein, the battle was winnable.

He closed his eyes and prayed. My thanks for your help thus far, great Donar. Stay with us. A rumble of distant thunder suggested that the god was watching. Arminius took heart.

Officers' shouts carried from the enemy lines. Sandals tramped the earth. Dust rose, cohorts moved. Cavalry units began deploying on the Roman right flank.

'They're coming,' Arminius yelled at the warriors below the rampart. 'Get back up here!'

'There's time yet,' called back a burly warrior with swirling tattoos on his chest.

A brief buzzing sound, not unlike a swarm of angry bees, filled Arminius' ears. Again it came, and again. Puzzled, he stared at the Roman positions. Men dressed in simple tunics, no armour, were arranging themselves in front of the legions. More high-pitched buzzing sounds carried through the baking-hot air. Two heartbeats later, soft thuds off the earth below the earthwork announced the arrival of missiles. Realisation sank in, and Arminius roared, 'Slingers! Enemy slingers! Get back up here, NOW!'

The burly warrior was still smiling when a slingshot bullet struck him in the side of the head. A faint expression of surprise marked his face as he fell, dead before he landed.

It had been a lucky strike – the slingers were still finding their range – but the remaining warriors came scrambling up the rampart with alacrity. Arminius had everyone withdraw thirty paces. Soon a wall of mismatched hexagonal tribal shields and curved Roman ones had formed, facing forward and over-head. More buzzing sounds, and thunks as the bullets landed, followed. As the slingers settled into a rhythm, the volley became continuous, sounding like a violent hailstorm battering a barrack roof. Arminius was grateful for his shield; the burly warrior's death had been a fluke, but the hen's-egg-sized lead bullets were lethal. Thanks to the shield wall, however, there were few further casualties.

'Let them shoot to their hearts' content,' declared a heavy-boned youth. He glanced at Arminius. 'Is this the best the Romans can do?'

Arminius was staring through a gap in the shields. Behind the slingers, he could see legionaries manhandling large wooden frames forward. 'Those volleys were just the start,' he grated.

'The start?' asked the youth.

'The heavy artillery barrage comes next.'

The youth's grin vanished, and an unhappy silence fell.

From far off, Arminius heard the familiar sound of torsion arms being wound back. Never had he imagined being on the receiving end of the legions' deadly machines. If memory served him right, each legion had fifty-five bolt-throwers. Acid caught at the back of his throat. 'Prepare yourselves!' he cried.

Chapter XXVI

◰◰◰

Tullus was unhappy from the first moment he'd marched on to the swamp- and forest-bordered plain with his men. It was far too similar to the ground Arminius had ambushed Varus' legions on, and it was clear what tactics the Cherusci leader would try. This was a different day, Tullus told himself. A separate battle. Germanicus was a superior general to Varus, and his enormous army outnumbered the enemy forces, which had already lost thousands of men. This awareness settled Tullus' nerves, but he remained on edge.

More than an hour passed, and still Germanicus' army baked in the searing-hot sun. Two attacks had been launched on the enemy positions. The fighting hadn't gone the Romans' way; in truth, most of the auxiliaries and legionaries had come off worst. Trying to reach an enemy standing on the rampart Arminius' men had built – more than a man's height above them – was insanely difficult, and yet spirits remained buoyant. Germanicus had seen to it that everyone had heard about the four cohorts who had forged a path across the marshy ground on the far left of the earthworks. That weak spot would be exploited in the next attack, after the slingers and artillery had softened up the enemy. Germanicus had also ordered his Praetorian cohorts and four legions into combat. Once again Tullus was filled with a mad excitement. He and his men had not yet drawn their weapons, but that time was at hand – and Germanicus would lead the army in person.

'Today is our day. *Our* day! I can feel it in my bones,' he told his soldiers.

'How are we going to scale the enemy rampart, sir?' asked Calvus.

The question was in most men's minds, thought Tullus. He glanced at Piso. 'Remember that tree trunk in the forest?'

'Aye, sir.' Piso would never forget it. It had been on the third day, when the slaughter had been almost complete. Splattered with mud and blood, exhausted and close to giving up, he and his comrades had been following Tullus because . . . well, because he was Tullus and he would not let them rest. The end had seemed nigh when a massive beech had been toppled in front of them, blocking the track. Rousing chants of the barritus had come from every side as hundreds of warriors prepared to wipe them out – and then Tullus' mad instruction had come from nowhere. Somehow it had worked, getting them to the other side.

'Tell Calvus. Tell them all,' instructed Tullus with a fierce grin.

'We'll form a kind of testudo against the rampart,' said Piso, proud to be chosen. 'It's the height of a man, so two ranks should be enough, the first kneeling, the second crouching. The rest of us will run up the shields at the enemy. Simple.'

His comrades liked the sound of it. 'Clever,' said Calvus. 'Good old Tullus,' declared another. 'Me to be part of the testudo,' said a wag from the depths of the ranks. Men grinned; others chuckled.

'I've sent word to every cohort, and to the other legions,' shouted Tullus. 'We'll all be doing the same. The fucking savages won't know what hit them!'

Piso and his comrades cheered, and when the advance sounded not long after, they tramped towards the enemy positions with renewed purpose.

'The Praetorians are beside us, brothers,' Tullus muttered as he strode along the side of his century. 'Look at the arrogant pricks!'

Derogatory comments from his men filled the air. 'They're all shining armour and polished helmets – I doubt there's a veteran among them.' 'Ever used those swords in battle?' 'Overpaid, noses-in-the-air sons of whores!'

Knowing Tullus for a primus pilus, the glowering Praetorians didn't dare respond to the jibes until he'd moved out of earshot.

The slanging match with the Praetorians kept his soldiers occupied for most of the distance to the enemy rampart. A grim silence fell thereafter, for the final section had a plentiful covering of Roman dead and dying. It was a familiar scene, but desolating in its savagery. Pleas for help, requests for water and more plaintive cries filled Tullus' ears. Disturbed by his men's arrival, clouds of flies rose from gaping wounds, staring eyeballs and shining loops of bowel. Unerring in their ability to spot carrion, scores of buzzards hung overhead.

'Mother,' groaned an auxiliary with a spear through his belly. 'Mother.' A blank-faced legionary sat cradling his bloodied right arm, which was missing a hand. 'Hot sausages, four for an as,' he said. The slowing spurts of blood from the man's savage wound revealed he'd soon be dead. 'Hot sausages, four for an as. Hot sausages, four for an as.' The words rolled around in Tullus' head.

A hundred paces out, and the German warriors manning the top of the rampart were in full cry. *HUUUUMMMMMMMM! HUUUUM-MMMMMMM!* Spears hurled by the strongest flew high into the air and streaked down into the mass of advancing legionaries and Praetorians. Faint cries carried; none of the injured were close by. That would change fast, thought Tullus. 'Raise shields,' he bellowed. 'Keep moving, brothers!'

Sixty paces, and the enemy spears fell like rain. Thin-bladed and thick, leaf-shaped and almost triangular, they punched into the legionaries' shields. Every so often, one scythed through a gap. Shrieks and curses followed, but most were turned by the armour of the men beneath. Tullus remained calm. The Germans' barrage was already ending. There would be a respite at the rampart's foot, an opportunity for those with undamaged shields to hand them to the men at the front. Opportunity might present itself to tug out the spears.

Thirty paces out, and the enemy barrage had ceased. Naked berserkers prowled up and down, beating their chests and screaming insults at the Romans. One turned his back to the legionaries, crouching and parting his arse cheeks in the ultimate gesture of contempt. Roars of coarse laughter went up from his fellows. The barritus reached a new crescendo. *HUUU-UMMMMMMMM! HUUUUMMMMMMMMM!*

'Let them sing, brothers,' shouted Tullus. 'We don't fucking care, do we?'

'NOOOOOOOOOO!' the nearest men bellowed.

'Ready javelins. Aim high,' Tullus ordered. 'In your own time, loose!'

His sweating men cocked their right arms back and threw. More uneven than a training-ground effort, the volley damaged plenty of enemy shields. From the screams, some warriors had also been injured.

Slowing, Tullus repeated his previous commands. 'At the base of the rampart, the soldiers in the front rank will move forward. Work in fours. Two men from each group are to stand against the earthwork, shields over their heads. The next pair will kneel close behind, shields angled against those of the soldiers in front. Pass it on!'

'Aye, sir!' 'Yes, sir!' 'We're ready, sir!'

'The instant the "ramps" are ready, the men of the second rank are to charge up, in fours also. Once they're up, the third rank follows.'

Again his soldiers rumbled their understanding.

They tramped closer, keeping pace with the cohorts on either side. Fifteen steps separated them from the bottom of the enemy earthwork. The barritus continued to batter their ears, the berserkers to threaten their worst. Great waves of heat rose from the earth, carrying throat-clawing, fresh-corpse odours: blood, shit and piss. The sun beat down, burning exposed skin and heating helmets and armour until they were painful to the touch.

'That's it, brothers,' said Tullus. 'Almost there.'

Ten paces. Try as they might, the legionaries could not avoid walking on their fallen comrades; some were still alive, yet Tullus kept his gaze fixed on the enemy. His men were all that mattered right now.

More crazed than his fellows, a tall berserker leaped down to confront the legionaries. Stumbling as he landed, he was unable to stop Piso's neat sword thrust, made without breaking formation. In between the ribs went the blade, a few fingers' breadth, and out. The berserker fell on to his knees, as if praying, but a solid blow from Piso's shield sent him backward to lie staring, blank-eyed, up at his shocked companions. 'That for your stupidity.' Piso stamped down with a hobnailed sandal, and his comrades cheered.

'First rank, ready,' shouted Tullus. 'GO!' Shield raised against spears, he stood side on and watched. With pleasing efficiency, the dozen soldiers broke into fours. One pair from each quartet rushed to the rampart and lifted their shields high, while the third and fourth men knelt behind and did the same.

'Second rank, move!' Tullus longed to charge up the shield ramp at the screaming enemy, but he had to see the bulk of his century to the top of the earthwork first.

Metal clashed above his head. A man screamed. Another cursed, in German. *Thunk* went a shield boss as it hit something. 'ROMA!' bellowed a voice. 'Die, whoreson!' Air moved close to Tullus and, with a meaty sound, a body landed nearby. A second followed it. Hoping they weren't both Roman, he sent the third rank to the attack.

The instant that the twelve soldiers had gone, Tullus had the men forming the bridges move aside. Piso and Metilius were among them, faces purple from the effort of their toil. 'Ready?' asked Tullus.

'Aye, sir,' panted Metilius.

Tullus clouted him on the shoulder.

The new ramps were in place. Tullus beckoned to Piso, Metilius and the two others who would accompany him. Drawing his sword, he shouted, 'Fifth rank, ready!' Then, to the four men, 'With me!'

Tullus got a fresh glimpse of the top of the rampart as his hobs clattered off the first shield. The struggle was savage. Twenty-four soldiers had gone up, but a good deal fewer than that were standing. Another went down as he watched. Worried that he and his men might have bitten off more than they could chew, Tullus pounded on to the second shield, skidding a little on its domed surface, and on to the earthwork. There was no time to savour the solid earth beneath his feet, no chance to feel anything but gut-clenching fear. The soldier in front of him was making a terrible, high-pitched sound – he was dying.

Tullus got there in time to step into the space left by the soldier as he slumped to the ground, and to stick his opponent, a grey-bearded warrior, before *he* had a chance to tug free his spear. Greybeard went down, looking surprised, and Tullus lunged forward, stabbing the next German in the mouth. Teeth splintered, blood bubbled and, with a horrible gurgling noise, the warrior died. Wary of being isolated, Tullus stepped back and checked he had a legionary to either side.

Perhaps intimidated by the sight of two of his companions dropping so fast, the next warrior approached Tullus with care. Caution was his undoing. As his eyes shifted downward, checking that he didn't trip over a corpse, Tullus slammed into him with a mighty blow of his shield boss. The warrior stumbled backwards and Tullus felt men at *his* back – reinforcements. 'Small wedge!' he roared. With a soldier at each shoulder, Tullus moved forward. Apprehensive, the nearest warriors edged back, and he pushed on three steps. Screaming a war cry, a man with braided hair came at him, spear held overhead, ready to lunge.

Knees bent, head dropped so that only his eyes showed above his shield, Tullus rammed his sword into the warrior's belly before the spear thrust came. Not too far – he didn't want the blade to wedge in the backbone. A little twist to slice the guts and Tullus tugged it out. Bawling like a newborn, the man fell.

Tullus' eyes roved left to right and back. The nearest warriors were scared – he could see it in their faces. 'Bigger wedge!' he bellowed. 'FORWARD!' Trusting that men were at his back, he took another step.

A berserker was next to hurl himself at Tullus. He died spitting curses with Tullus' and Piso's blades in his chest. More warriors shuffled forward, brave in spite of Tullus' lethality, but he was like a man possessed. A tiny part of him imagined each foe to be Arminius, and all Tullus had lived for since the rain-sodden carnage in the forest was to lay the Cherusci chieftain in the mud. Never mind that Arminius was who knew where on the battlefield, each warrior was in some way part of him. Kill enough of the filth, Tullus reasoned dimly through his battle fury, and Arminius would be revealed.

In that sweltering, blurred-focus time, the gods seemed to furnish Tullus with energy. His customary aches – at the base of his spine, in his neck, in his left calf – vanished. Once more a twenty-year-old, his muscles were made of steel, his heart strong as an ox's. Every warrior in front of him died. Big, small, tall, short, young or old, it didn't matter – he killed them all. As each gasped his way to Hades and he saw they were not Arminius, Tullus pressed on, his blade imbued with a life of its own. A living extension of his untiring arm, the sharp steel thirsted for a home in enemy flesh; it longed to cleave faces and slash wide throats.

His vitality infected Piso and Metilius – the pair who had placed themselves at his shoulders – and they too fought like the Titans of legend. The ranks that came after were no different. With their centurion like this, every man could smell victory. Tullus pressed on, knowing that fear spread with the speed of a fire consuming a wooden tenement block.

Push the Germans hard enough, and they would crack.

Crack, and they would run.

Run, and the battle was won.

Chapter XXVII

◫◫◫

Tullus' relentless momentum – that, and the mad light in his and his men's eyes – soon had an effect. Warriors edged sideways, to fight different Romans, or backwards, beyond Tullus' blade's kiss. Ten steps, he went, and then another ten. The tribesmen's ranks were thinning – he could see open ground beyond. He did not know it, but Fenestela and others of his soldiers had formed their own wedges. Cutting deep into the German ranks, they were adding to the casualties, and to the crumbling of the warriors' resolve. Neither man was aware that to their right, Germanicus and his Praetorian cohorts were driving their own path into the enemy's midst.

Bursting into open space, Tullus thought that they had done it, that the Germans had had enough. He had reckoned without Maelo. From nowhere he came, it seemed, a hundred or more warriors at his back. It had been almost seven years since Tullus had clapped eyes on Arminius' second-in-command, but there was no mistaking him. To Tullus' immense frustration, the next wedge over took the brunt of the enemy attack. Scores of warriors broke away to assail Tullus' formation, but not Maelo.

'Part turn to the right. Steady!' Slow, careful, Tullus edged around, keeping himself at the point. His men came with him and when the warriors closed in, they met Tullus, bloody-handed, enraged, at its tip. The first German to near him fell, stabbed through the cheek. The next two were dispatched by Piso and Metilius. More warriors were on them even as the initial ones fell. Their mail, shields and helmets made them dangerous adversaries. Tired from their savage struggle thus far, Tullus and his men should have been driven back.

Should have been.

Tullus' muscles were now screaming with weariness. His spine ached as if he'd been hammering in a forge all day. Constant sweat stung his eyes, and his mouth was drier than the bottom of an old, empty wine barrel. Stab and punch, punch and stab – he traded blows with a warrior in a conical helmet. Younger than he, and fresh to the fight, the tribesman seemed the natural victor. He hadn't had a lifetime's experience of war, however, nor did he have Tullus' white-hot desire for vengeance.

'Arse-fucker!' snarled Tullus in German. 'Filthy arse-fucker!'

The warrior's face twisted with anger, and he drove forward, which was Tullus' exact ploy. *Thunk* went their shield bosses as they closed, each trying to reach around the other's shield with his sword. The blades caught and snagged in their mail shirts without penetrating. As the warrior drew back his arm for another attempt, Tullus shoved in with an almighty blow of his shield. He couldn't have judged his moment better – the warrior was driven back, delaying *his* thrust. Tullus stabbed him above the neckline of his mail, right in the base of the throat.

Hot ichor showered Tullus, and he laughed.

He was still laughing when he killed the next warrior, and the one after that. A fleeting pause followed as Tullus' next opponent hung back. From the corner of his eye he saw Metilius go down to a strike by a huge warrior with a hunting spear. Calvus stepped into his place, only to fall two heartbeats later. Another soldier – Tullus couldn't see who – moved up; with a wolf's snarl, the warrior leaped anew to the attack.

Grief-stricken for Metilius, Tullus stuck the German in the armpit as his spear went back, ready to thrust. Tullus was about to check on Metilius, but as the warrior fell Maelo somehow appeared in front of him.

Time stood still.

'Maelo,' croaked Tullus, fitting a world of hatred into one word.

'I thought it was you.' Maelo's spear strike was lightning fast.

Tullus jinked his head to the right; Maelo's blade hissed past, and then back. Tullus tried a fast one-two with his shield and sword, but Maelo danced out of reach. They gazed at each other with mutual loathing. 'Where's your mongrel leader?' demanded Tullus. 'Hiding in the trees? Why isn't he here, fighting?'

Maelo didn't answer. Cat-soft on his feet, he came closer. Stab! Stab! His spear licked forward, seeking a home in Tullus' face. Punch. Punch. Tullus battered with his shield. Stab. Metal screeched as his sword point connected with Maelo's armour. Tullus tried a headbutt, but Maelo saw the move coming and jerked out of the way. Next time he closed, he slid his shield down off Tullus' with a powerful drive. If Tullus hadn't known the move, he would have suffered several broken toes. As it was, the bottom rim of Maelo's shield caught the front of his left boot, trapping it. Lifting his shield a fraction, Maelo thrust with his blade.

It was risking a maiming injury, but Tullus had to take *his* chance. Without moving his leg, he reared up over his shield. Pain shredded his foot as Maelo's sword went in. With gritted teeth, Tullus stabbed with *his* blade. Pithed through the spine, Maelo went limp. As Tullus pulled back his arm, Maelo toppled slack-limbed to the dirt.

Tullus' ruse had come at a price. Streaks of pure agony were radiating from his foot. Worried, he shot a glance over his shield. His left boot was ruined, the leather sliced open at the toe. The wound beneath was obscured by welling blood.

'You all right, sir?' This from Piso.

'I'm fine, aye.' I have to be, thought Tullus. Around them, the fighting was dying down, but it continued to rage off to their right, where the Praetorians were. 'How's Metilius?'

'I'll live, sir,' croaked a voice before Piso could answer.

Tullus turned in delight. Ashen-faced, Metilius was sitting upright, left arm cradling his other. Tullus was so pleased that his own pain receded for a moment. 'I was sure you were dead!'

'If the blow had landed anywhere else, I would be, sir.' Metilius pointed to a small hole in his mail at the right shoulder. 'That brute was as strong as Hercules. He broke something, I'm sure.'

'Better that than being halfway to the underworld!' Tullus gave Metilius an approving nod.

'Calvus didn't fare so well, sir.' Glazed-eyed, Piso was standing over his comrade's gore-spattered corpse. The huge warrior's spear had left a massive, lipped wound in Calvus' throat. Flies blanketed the clotting blood, and his blank, staring eyes. His cracked lips gaped, as if he was trying to take a final breath.

'He wouldn't have known what hit him, the poor bastard,' said Tullus. Putting Calvus from his mind, he checked again for signs of the enemy – there were none living close by – and called for Fenestela. The optio appeared, looking as grimy and bloody as Tullus felt, but unharmed. The pair shared a brief look, full of relief. 'I want a head count. Make it quick. Send word to the other centurions to do the same,' said Tullus.

The losses in his century were bad, but not as severe as they could have been. Ten soldiers were dead, or soon would be. Five of the eleven injured wouldn't be fighting again before next spring, but once the remaining half dozen had had their wounds dressed, they were able to join their comrades standing before Tullus.

'Forty-six men ready for duty, sir,' said Fenestela, saluting. Noting Tullus' drawn expression, his gaze dropped. 'You're wounded.'

'A scratch.'

'Get your boot off. Let me see.'

'There's no time.' The lacing would take an age to undo, he thought, let alone retie after Fenestela had inspected Maelo's parting gift. 'I'll manage.'

'You're sure? It's still bleeding.'

'Only a little.' The blood loss wouldn't kill him, but the pain was reaching new heights. Tullus could no longer weight-bear on his left foot. To walk after the enemy would be difficult, never mind fight them.

'I should take a look,' said Fenestela, his voice concerned.

'Leave it!'

'Yes, *sir*.' Fenestela glowered.

Soon after Tullus had had the cohort's casualty report – fifty-three dead, four score injured – a messenger arrived from Germanicus' position. The enemy had been broken on the left, and the Twenty-First and auxiliaries were mopping up. Every other legion was to turn to the right and aim, two cohorts wide, for the trees that bordered the battlefield where Arminius and his best warriors had withdrawn. It wasn't a full retreat by any means – according to the messenger, many of the Praetorian cohorts were still involved in bitter fighting.

'There's a story to dine out on, brothers. *We* drove back the enemy before the pretty-boy Praetorians,' Tullus told his men as trumpet calls repeated the messenger's order. 'The glorious Fifth!'

His soldiers' shoulders went back. 'FIFTH! FIFTH! FIFTH!'

The men in other centuries heard Tullus' words, and took up the cry. It spread to other cohorts as they marched, increasing in volume until the sounds of fighting beyond their position were almost drowned out.

At the right of the front rank, Tullus somehow managed to walk at the normal speed, limping and cursing. He ignored the pain lancing up his leg, the spatters of blood left behind in each print of his left boot, and kept a silent count. A hundred paces were achievable. After that, he had to match that target with another hundred. Twice that wasn't impossible either, but by half a thousand, Tullus was fighting a losing struggle.

He had never been more relieved to hear the halt sounded. Sweat streaming down his face, he leaned both arms on his grounded shield. A puddle of blood soon formed around his left boot. Curse it, he thought.

'You all right, sir?' asked Piso.

'Aye,' retorted Tullus, but with less certainty than before. Loath to admit his weakness, there was no denying he would be a liability in the fighting to come. He didn't care about himself, but he wasn't sure he could bear the responsibility – through negligence – for the death of one of his men. 'Optio! Get up here,' he shouted.

Fenestela stomped up, his usual scowl in place. 'Here I am, *sir*.'

'Closer,' ordered Tullus. Never had he had to pass over command to Fenestela during a battle, and his pride was stinging. He was the primus pilus, for Jupiter's sake. Tullus lowered his voice. 'I can't go on.'

Fenestela's sour expression vanished. 'Your foot?'

'Still bleeding, and I can hardly walk. I'd die quicker than Calvus did when the fighting starts. That, or someone would die because of me.'

'It's not your fault,' said Fenestela.

'A fucking foot wound!'

'You might lose the leg yet,' Fenestela shot back. 'Better to withdraw now, before you do more damage.'

Fenestela was right, thought Tullus. 'Take charge of the century. The centurion of the Second Century will assume command of the cohort. Send him word.'

'And you?'

'I'll limp back, out of the way. There'll be a surgeon somewhere away from the fighting.'

'You're taking half a dozen men as escort.'

The fierce light in Fenestela's eyes caused Tullus' protest to die in his throat. 'Very well.' Miserable, he watched Fenestela call Piso over, and mutter in his ear. Piso shot a look at him, and Tullus glowered back.

'Message for the primus pilus!' shouted a voice.

Tullus spied the Praetorian fifty paces off, loping along the front of the Fifth's position as he searched. 'Here!' Tullus shouted.

The Praetorian was in his mid-twenties, thin-faced with deep-set, thoughtful eyes. Bloodstains marked his sword arm, evidence that he'd been at the fighting's heart. He gave Tullus a crisp salute. 'Orders from Germanicus, sir.'

'Speak.' I wonder what Germanicus will make of my having to leave the field, thought Tullus, shame lashing him.

'Fresh legions are advancing from the third line, sir. The Fifth and the Twenty-First are to withdraw. The battle will go on until sunset, the governor says, and the day's camps need building. The Fifth and the Twenty-First are to make a start.'

Tullus threw back his head and laughed. 'Optio – Piso doesn't need to go anywhere.'

Fenestela intuited the reason, and grinned. 'Very good, sir.'

The messenger looked on in confusion. 'What shall I report, sir?'

'Tell the governor that the Fifth will be honoured to help build the camps.'

As the messenger returned whence he'd come, Tullus glanced at the heavens. Thank you, Fortuna, he thought. I needed this one.

Chapter XXVIII

🗝🗝🗝

rminius was deep among the beech and spruce trees, about halfway along the length of his warriors' battle line – he hoped. It was impossible to be sure. Everything was confusion, and had been since the morale-wrecking barrages by the Roman artillery. Not that many men had been slain by the bolts and stones, or the infernal, whizzing slingshot bullets, but the fear and disorder they had sown had been widespread. It was hard to blame his warriors for their apprehension, Arminius decided. What man's spirits wouldn't be affected by skull-crushing stones hurtling in from afar?

They had rallied well enough once the artillery had ceased shooting, and the omens for holding the rampart had looked good. Thousands of battle-ready warriors standing on an earthwork a man's height above the Romans. Hundreds more reinforcements sent to the boggy ground, including nigh on fifty berserkers. What Arminius hadn't counted on was the legionaries' renewed vigour. Heartened by seeing their enemies cower beneath the artillery barrage, and encouraged by Germanicus' presence, they had attacked with bloody-minded purpose. A spectator couldn't have guessed that they had lost many hundreds of men in their two previous failed assaults.

It would have been wiser to remain there, brooded Arminius, and let my cursed leg bleed. If I'd stayed, we might have held them. For a time, his warriors had done just that, battering back the legionaries as they scrabbled desperately to climb up. Beginning to think that all would be well, Arminius had made his first mistake. Concerned that his men in the forest weren't attacking the Roman flank as they'd been told, and having had no reply despite sending two messengers, he had taken it upon himself to go and remedy the situation.

Raging, he punched one hand into the other. I should have known. Without his magnetism, his leadership, there had been an inevitability to the legionaries winning a foothold on the rampart. Since the dawn of time, soldiers had fought harder if their commander was close by.

His second mistake had been not to leave Maelo in overall control of the forces in his absence. Arminius had suggested it of course, but the chieftains' protests had been vociferous. Their biggest grievance had been that Maelo didn't lead a tribe. Why should he tell them what to do? Frustrated, in severe pain with his leg, Arminius had argued, wheedled and lost his temper. He would have got his way in the end, but the chieftains' surliness meant that their warriors would not have fought well. Exasperated by their hard-headedness, a furious Arminius had left the situation as it was, and ridden to the forest.

He hadn't been back since, because his hands had been full arranging the defence of the tree line. Needless to say, much of that time had been taken up negotiating with obstinate chieftains who didn't want to listen to good counsel. Weakened by his wound, suffering from the extreme heat, it had taken an age to settle matters to Arminius' satisfaction. It felt as if Donar was laughing at him then, for the situation in the centre had deteriorated. Despite the dazzling sunshine – hard to look out at from the shady trees – and clouds of dust enveloping the battlefield, it had been clear that the Romans had forced their way on to the earthwork. Worse still, they were holding the position, which meant legionaries were swarming up from the plain. Arminius could have wept. It was as if every cursed Roman sprang from the same father's loins. They were brave as lions. Disciplined and pig-headed. The bastards just would not give up.

Mind spinning, Arminius had been wavering – he cursed just to think of himself, in pain, indecisive – and thinking about returning to the rampart when word had come from Maelo. Germanicus' Praetorian cohorts were atop the earthwork, but they weren't alone. Soldiers from other legions had fought their way up too. 'Maelo's about to attack with his last reserves,' the messenger had panted. 'He'll do his best, he said, but things are tough.'

Arminius had made light of the news before his warriors, but inside, his worries flared into bright new life. He knew Maelo well. In someone else's words, the message could have meant that the battle's outcome hung in the balance, but in Maelo's it felt like a final farewell. Claws of grief ripped at Arminius still. His friend was as good as dead.

Arminius couldn't let grief consume him. The battle was still there for the taking, and it was time to see what was going on. He kneed his horse forward, towards the tree line. Warriors moved out of his way. Grim-faced, they gave him silent recognition. A nod here. A chin dipped, a head inclined there. There was no cheering. No threats about how they'd butcher the Romans. Even the few remaining berserkers were quiet. Deep in thought, worried, Arminius didn't make any acknowledgement.

'You promised us victory,' shouted a voice. 'From here it doesn't look much like it's going to happen.'

'Nor from where I'm standing,' said a sour-faced warrior close to Arminius. 'Germanicus has eight legions out there, and it's only taken three or four to seize the rampart. There are, what, ten thousand of us in the forest? We might defeat one or two legions, but eight?'

Arminius lost all control. 'If your fucking chieftains had obeyed my orders here *and* on the rampart,' he shouted, 'I would have been where I was needed – over there. You lot would have hit the Romans' flank as we beat them back from our position. If you'd done that, you stupid bastards, maybe you wouldn't be staring death in the face!'

The sour-faced warrior's jaw dropped.

Arminius gave him a contemptuous look, and his gaze raked the other shocked faces. 'It's the truth I speak.' He clicked his tongue and aimed his horse for the tree line again. The hair on his neck prickled – he could feel hundreds of pairs of eyes on him, could taste the warriors' resentment. He'd ridden perhaps a quarter of the distance before the first cry went up.

'You're no better than us, Arminius of the Cherusci!'

Stiff-backed, Arminius pretended he hadn't heard, but more followed in its wake.

'D'you think you're king of the tribes, you dog?' 'Arrogant bastard!' 'Thusnelda must have been glad to see the back of you!'

Arminius' vision blurred, and he spun his mount in a tight circle. 'Who said that? WHO SAID THAT?' he screamed, driving forward, using his horse's bulk to force a way.

Already the warriors' anger was muted. Few would meet Arminius' gaze, and those that did seemed embarrassed, even ashamed. Some muttered things like, 'Thusnelda was a good woman.' 'It was a terrible thing, taking her like that.' Arminius paid them no heed. Nostrils white with fury, heart pounding, he twisted his head from side to side, demanding, 'Who spoke? Who insulted me? Show yourself, you yellow-livered filth!'

At this, a broad-shouldered warrior moved into Arminius' path. Bructeri from his trouser patterns, his bare chest glistened with sweat. A battered, hexagonal shield dangled from his left fist. Red stains marked his spear blade. Hard-faced, he glared at Arminius. 'I said it.'

'It was you?'

'Aye.' The bare-chested warrior planted his feet a little wider. 'Me.'

'You motherless get. You filthy, sheep-fucking animal.'

The warrior opened his mouth to issue an angry retort. He never saw Arminius' sword slice through the air. Didn't feel it cut until the blade had taken off the top of his head, and by then it was too late. Brain matter and blood showered. He dropped, lips still trying to talk. The shorn section of his skull, complete with hair, landed ten paces away. The corpse fell to one side, scattering the nearest men.

'Anyone else care to slur my wife?' Arminius sawed on the reins, bringing his horse around in a full circle.

No one answered.

'Good.' Leaning over, he spat on the warrior's body. 'If I had time, I'd cut off his prick as well, but there's a battle to fight. That is, if any of you still have the stomach for it.' He glared around him; no one would meet his gaze.

'Will you fight – or will you run, like whipped curs?' he shouted. 'If you're going to flee, best do it now.'

A semblance of calm returned to Arminius in the following silence, and the magnitude of what he'd done sank in. I went too far. Much too far, he thought. I could have lost them. He eased his stern expression, tried to look encouraging.

Another ten heartbeats pattered by.

'I won't run.' Gervas' voice was loud. 'The Romans have slain too many of my people. I'd never be able to hold my head up again if I fled.'

'I'll stay,' said two of his companions.

'And I,' cried an unseen man off to Arminius' left.

Like an abrupt change in the direction of the wind, the warriors' attention veered from Arminius to matters at hand. There was no loud chanting as he would have wished, but plenty of men clattered spears off their shields.

Arminius' relief was brief.

His warriors would fight, but could they prevail?

Chapter XXIX

꙰꙰꙰

lose to the defensive ditch of the still-in-construction camp, Tullus was sitting, grim-faced. The sun's rays continued to hammer down, their heat merciless. Flies buzzed around his bloodied boot, returning no matter how many times he swatted them away. Perhaps an hour had passed since Germanicus' order had come through. Rumours from the battlefield had it that Arminius' warriors were being beaten back. It was satisfying news, but it increased Tullus' frustration at not being there.

The wounded surrounded him. Groans and muttered curses mingled with medical orderlies' voices. Dozens of the specially trained soldiers were treating casualties laid in rows on the hard ground, placed there by more orderlies who, job done, raced back to the battle for more. Half the able-bodied legionaries were digging the ditch while the rest stood guard, forming a screen between the camp and the battlefield. Strong parties ferried skins of water from the River Visurgis.

Tullus didn't care to be seen on his arse, but a surgeon had been found to examine his foot, and a hospital tent hadn't yet been set up. The ground it had to be. Greek, as his kind so often were, the dark-skinned surgeon was thin, almost bald and harassed-looking. The tip of his tongue protruded from between his lips as he unlaced Tullus' boot. 'Tell me if the pain is too much, sir,' he said.

'It hurts like a bastard no matter what you do,' replied Tullus with a grimace.

'I have some poppy juice—'

'Get on with it.'

The surgeon shrugged. 'I'll have to cut the boot off, sir,' he said not long after.

'Do what you must. It's ruined anyway.' A new pair of boots mattered not – it was what the surgeon might find that concerned Tullus. Unless Fortuna was in a foul humour, he wouldn't die of the injury, but it was more than possible that his career was at an end. A soldier who couldn't march – even a primus pilus – was no use to anyone.

Despite his worries, Tullus hadn't bothered looking for a surgeon until they reached the already chosen spot for the camp. Fenestela's protests had fallen on deaf ears. 'There are men in greater need of attention than me,' Tullus had growled, putting an end to the conversation. Not long since, the wagons that had ferried the soldiers' tents here had been organised to bring the casualties from the battlefield, and already a steady stream was coming and going. According to the most recently arrived mule-handlers, the fighting continued to be brutal, but the Germans were retreating. Victory seemed certain, Tullus decided, although he didn't say it out loud.

'Hades!' Waves of sweet agony powered up his left leg.

'My apologies, sir. There was a clot between your foot and the boot. I had to pull them apart.' The surgeon washed his hands in the bronze bowl by his side, and then used a drying cloth passed to him by a medical orderly.

'It's started bleeding again,' said Tullus.

'That can't be helped, sir. It will clean the wound.'

Tullus peered down, but with the surgeon bent over his lower leg, there was little to be seen, so he leaned back on his hands and cast an irritable eye around him. 'You there!' he shouted.

Visible only from the waist up, several soldiers in the nearby ditch glanced around.

'You!' Tullus shouted, pointing at a jug-eared man he recognised from the Third Century of his own cohort. 'I see you, shirker! Put more energy into swinging that pickaxe or I'll break the thing over your head. The rest of you, get back to work!'

Every soldier took a sudden interest in the bottom of the ditch, and the rhythmic thumping as their pickaxes sank into the soil picked up speed.

The surgeon sighed, drawing Tullus' attention back to his foot. 'Well? How bad is it?' Tullus demanded.

'I've seen worse, sir.' The surgeon probed with his fingers, making Tullus hiss with discomfort.

'Aye? So have I! What damage is there?' Tullus wanted to ask if he'd always be lame, but a rare fear stilled his tongue.

'Toes four and five are unscathed, sir. Your big toe and the third one are lacerated from whatever blade went through your boot. A couple of stitches will see them right.' The surgeon held something up towards Tullus. 'The second toe has been part amputated.'

Tullus realised with disgust that the bloodied morsel of flesh being proffered by the surgeon was the tip of his toe. 'Rot in Hades, Maelo,' he muttered.

A blank look from the surgeon.

'Maelo was the warrior who did this to me.'

The surgeon's eyebrows arched. 'You knew him, sir?'

'He was Arminius' second-in-command. I met him before he turned traitor.'

'He's dead, I take it, sir?'

'Aye. Taking that wound was how I got the better of him.' Tullus bent forward to examine the damage. His nostrils filled with the ripe cheesy smell of unwashed foot mixed with the coppery tang of blood. It wasn't a pretty sight. Black-red clots and trailing smears coated his foot from the midpoint of his arch to his toes. Other than the second toe being half its original length, it was hard to make out much. Tullus' unhappiness didn't ease. 'It looks nasty.'

'The bleeding seems to have slowed, sir, which is good. You'll disobey my advice to stay off your feet, I know' – here the surgeon's face became resigned – 'so once I've finished, I'll apply a pressure bandage, which should do the trick. It will need changing daily for a few days, to check that there's no sign of sepsis.'

A tickle of dread caressed Tullus' spine. Fortuna, don't let infection set in, he asked. Anything but gangrene. 'What will the lasting damage be? I'm an old-fashioned centurion, see. Oftentimes, I march with my men.'

'You'll limp a little for the rest of your life, sir. You might also need a wrap of leather around the stump of the toe, but I see no reason why you shouldn't be able to march once it has healed.'

Tullus could have kissed the surgeon. 'Thank you,' he muttered. 'Thank you.'

'I'm just doing my job, sir.'

'Aye, well.' Tullus coughed. 'My manner before – excuse it, won't you? I was worried. The army's everything to me. If I had to leave because of a fucking toe . . .' Embarrassed by his outburst, surprised at himself, Tullus' voice died away.

'I understand.'

Tullus met the surgeon's gaze with difficulty, but saw only compassion. He nodded.

Swift and sure, the surgeon cleaned the area with vinegar, stitched Tullus' cut toes and bandaged the foot. 'There. I'm done. If you'll excuse me, sir? I'm needed elsewhere.'

'Of course.'

With his orderly trailing after, the surgeon headed towards the wounded men.

'Surgeon!' called Tullus.

He turned. 'Yes, sir?'

'What's your name?'

'Arimnestos.'

'Thank you, Arimnestos.'

Looking pleased, the surgeon raised a hand and walked on.

Left alone, with his men toiling under Fenestela's watchful eye, Tullus was soon at a loss. Unwilling just to sit there, he picked up the ruins of his left boot. There was no chance of wearing it – Arimnestos had sliced the upper almost completely away from the sole – so he had Piso strip a pair of sandals from one of the dead soldiers. The left one wasn't a perfect fit, but it did the job. His injured foot wasn't enclosed and, more important, he could walk. Pulses of pain rose from his toe the instant he put weight on the leg. Cautious, he moved about nice and easy, ten paces this way, ten that, until he was happy the bleeding hadn't started again. It felt as if a smith had used his biggest hammer on his foot, but he didn't care. He was mobile once more.

Chapter XXX

෴

Overhead, the sky was darkening. Light from the setting sun turned the ribbons of high cloud pink, red and every shade in between. Hundreds of swallows dipped and dived, feeding off insects, their high-pitched skirrs a reminder that high summer was here. Piso could have stared at the birds forever, but sleep threatened to take him long before that happened. He was sprawled by his tent, bone-tired. Exhausted. Fighting in the brutal heat had been strength-sapping, but helping to construct one of the army's camps afterward had drained the last of his energy. Even the grief he felt for Calvus was dull.

Afternoon had been passing before the last Germans had retreated. Many of the Roman troops had now returned, but columns continued to straggle in from the battlefield. The soldiers looked spent. Reports were that men were dropping not just from exhaustion and sun fever, but thirst.

Still dry-mouthed himself, Piso leaned up on an elbow and gulped a mouthful from his leather skin. Another trip to the Visurgis would be in order at dawn – he'd get permission from Tullus to take a dozen men. Piso had every intention of a sly dip in the river when the chance came – washing off today's blood, dust and grime would feel wonderful.

The delicious aroma of baking bread made his belly growl. He sat up.

It was Metilius' turn to cook, but his bruised collar bone had reduced him to temporary one-handedness. Sent back to his comrades by the surgeon – 'I'm in better shape than most of the poor cocksuckers in the hospital,' he'd declared – Metilius was making the most of being an invalid. 'Come on, Dulcius,' he needled. 'Those breads are starting to scorch.'

'Aye, Metilius is right,' said Piso, happy to stir up mischief.

Dulcius, more red-cheeked than ever thanks to the sun and the fire he was tending, scowled. 'Here!' he cried, proffering some long iron tongs to Metilius. 'Nothing wrong with your left hand, is there?'

'They're burning!' cried Metilius, pointing rather than accepting the tongs.

With a hair-whitening curse, Dulcius picked up one of the unleavened flatbreads that decorated the large flat stones ringing the fire. A staple on campaign, they were cooked by continuous rotation towards the heat, a task which required great vigilance and not a little patience. 'Catch!' Dulcius flung the bread, forcing Metilius to duck or be struck in the head. It landed on the ground behind him.

'It's covered in dust. And burned,' Metilius complained, but everyone was too busy laughing to hear.

'As if you've never done the same,' said Piso when the amusement had died down.

Flatbread on his knee, brushing off dirt, Metilius glowered.

'Piso.' Dulcius tossed another bread into the air.

Piso grabbed it with both hands. Piping hot, charred in places and half-cooked in others, it tasted better than many proper meals he'd had. 'Anyone got any wine?'

'I have,' replied Metilius, his tone sour.

'Get it out then,' demanded Piso.

'Aye, I'm parched.' This from Dulcius.

Metilius handed his skin over with poor grace. He paced after it as it went around the fire. As Dulcius reached out, Metilius snatched the skin away. 'You're not having any, you prick, until I have another flatbread. That one there – the best one.'

A sullen Dulcius handed over a fine, well-cooked bread. Metilius, who had thought to place his wine behind him, took it with a smirk. 'There you go,' he said, nudging the skin with his sandal. 'One swallow, mind.'

Sly, Dulcius produced unseen his own clay beaker and, as Metilius tucked into the flatbread, poured himself a hearty measure. 'Gratitude, brother,' he said, planting the now sagging skin by Metilius' feet.

Metilius realised at once what had happened. 'You filth!' With his good hand full of bread, he could only lunge at Dulcius' cup. Dulcius, laughing, spun out of the way, but placed an inadvertent sandal in the fire. Sparks flew, wood cracked and he leaped out of harm's way with a shocked roar.

Piso, Metilius and the rest collapsed with laughter. Dulcius stamped about, pride hurt more than anything, taking furious slurps of his wine.

'I'd pay good money to see this on the stage,' said Piso, wiping tears from his eyes. 'You two should pair up when you leave the army. I can see the notices now: "Metilius and Dulcius – clowns, acrobats and general fools. Three performances daily."'

Both Metilius and Dulcius told him what he could do with his suggestion, and a grinning Piso shrugged. 'You won't be much good at anything else – I'd give it serious thought.'

'Who won't be good at what?' boomed Tullus, limping up to their fire.

Piso explained, delighted inside to see Tullus hale and relatively unscathed. There wasn't a man in the century or cohort who hadn't been worried about his injury, thought Piso. 'It's fine to see you on your feet, sir,' he said.

'Takes more than a flesh wound to stop me.' Tullus' gaze roved over them. 'It's always the same. How long do I have to stand here before you offer me a drink? Don't think I haven't noticed that skin you're holding, Metilius.'

A cup was hurriedly produced, filled and handed over. Tullus nodded his thanks and waited until every man had stood up, beaker or cup in hand. He raised his arm. 'A toast. To Calvus. To the rest of our dead comrades, far too many of whom left this life today. They will not be forgotten.'

'To Calvus,' said Piso. Although he'd been careful not to get over-friendly with the gangling farmer, his death hurt nonetheless. 'To dead comrades.'

They all drained their cups. Sombre-faced, they glanced at one another. No words were necessary, thought Piso. He and his comrades were alive. That was more important than the day's victory.

'The trumpets will soon sound.' Tullus let out an evil chuckle as they tensed. 'It's nothing to worry about. Germanicus is to address the troops – this camp first. We're to assemble on the *intervallum*.' This large space between the inner aspect of the camp walls and the first tents served as protection from enemy missiles; it was also a place to gather.

Relieved, Piso asked, 'What's it about, sir?'

'You know as much as I do.' Tullus winked. 'Never fear, it won't be to do with Macula.'

'No, sir.' Piso flushed, wondering if Tullus knew he'd been to see the dog the day before. The mule-handler selected by Tullus was looking after Macula well, but it would be some time before it was safe enough to bring the animal back to the century. Tubero was not one to forget.

Sweaty despite having shed their armour, they belted on their swords and formed up with the rest of the men. In the nearby tent lines, the entire cohort was also getting ready. Led by Tullus and Fenestela, they marched out at an easy pace. More interested in cooking and eating or just resting, soldiers from other units paid them little heed. The avenues were quiet; most of the traffic consisted of messengers or those unfortunates with official duties.

Piso's hunch that Tullus was taking them to the intervallum early to get a good spot proved correct. He led them towards a section of the rampart close to the main gate. Torches flamed from the top of the defences; a large fire close to the wall lit the scene with an orange glare. A century of Praetorians was already in place. Perhaps two hundred other soldiers were waiting – other men with swift-thinking officers, thought Piso. Tullus stopped near the blaze, right below the walkway that ran along the top of the defences. He gave a nod to the nearest Praetorian officer, an optio in a battered helmet that was missing its crest.

The optio saluted. 'Primus pilus.'

'A tough fight today,' said Tullus. 'I heard your lot did well.'

'We did all right, sir,' replied the optio.

Ten heartbeats went by, and it became clear that the optio had no intention of mentioning Tullus' soldiers, who had been first on to the enemy rampart.

Tullus' face grew dark at this deliberate slight. In the end, he took a quick look over his shoulder. 'You're good boys. Better than *any* other troops,' he said.

Fucking Praetorians, Piso mouthed to Metilius, who in turn made a discreet obscene gesture at the optio.

Not long after, trumpets summoned the two legions in the camp to the intervallum. Time passed. Darkness was spreading across the cloudless sky; stars were appearing. Only the western horizon remained bright. Despite their central position, it didn't take long for Piso and his companions to grow bored. Incensed by the Praetorian optio's disrespect, confident since his prank on Tubero, Piso had a devilish idea. 'Sir?'

Tullus raised an eyebrow. 'Aye?'

'Permission to go for a piss, sir?'

'Make it quick.'

'I will, sir.' Ignoring Metilius' whispered question about what he was really doing, Piso sidled off, as if towards the latrines.

Piso's mission took longer than expected. When he returned, night had fallen and both legions were in place. There had been no cheering, which was something – Germanicus had not yet arrived, so he'd made it in time. Tullus would be unhappy with the length of his absence, but that would be it. Careful to avoid officers' eyes, Piso hurried between the files of men, using the firelight to guide him towards his century.

'Where in Hades have you been?' hissed Metilius as Piso wormed his way into their midst.

'You must have the shits.' Dulcius smirked. 'Glad I wasn't anywhere near.'

Their sotto voce questions and comments continued. Tickled first by their curiosity and then by their annoyance, Piso didn't answer.

Even in the sixth rank, it didn't take Tullus long to spot him. 'What took you so long?' he barked.

'Sorry, sir. Diarrhoea, sir.' The sniggers from his comrades started at once. He'd never hear the end of it, thought Piso, but no other excuse would serve.

Frowning, Tullus seemed about to say more, but was prevented by Germanicus' arrival. Spontaneous, loud cheering erupted. Thousands of hobnailed sandals pounded the earth. The Praetorians came to attention. Light bounced off Germanicus' armour as he bounded up to the walkway atop the rampart. Tall, regal, impressive, he faced the massed soldiers.

'GER-MAN-I-CUS!' The cheering redoubled.

The contrast between the governor and the filthy, blood-spattered legionaries could not have been more stark, or inspiring. Burnished bronze inlaid with silver. Crimson feathers. Red silk sash. Polished leather. Everything about Germanicus oozed power, wealth and status. Quiet fell, but rather than speak straightaway, he let the soldiers' expectations rise.

What a general, thought Piso with fierce pride. Our general!

'Soldiers of Rome!' Germanicus' voice was pitched to carry. 'Today's battle was long and hard-fought.'

Heads nodded. Men clapped comrades on the shoulder, growling in agreement.

'Despite the heat, the conditions and the enemy's determination, you prevailed. You are true sons of Rome! I salute you for your valour. Your resilience. Your devotion!' Germanicus extended his arms, palms uppermost.

Piso roared with the rest, long and hard, stopping only when his voice cracked.

Calm, composed, Germanicus waited until the clamour had ebbed away. 'Many of your brothers fell today, but their sacrifice will always be remembered!' Again the troops roared their appreciation. Germanicus continued, 'Come the dawn, work parties will be sent to find each and every body, whether they be legionary or auxiliary. The funeral pyres will be seen for miles, a warning to the savages that we yet remain in their territory. Upon our return to the Rhenus, every fallen soldier shall have a gravestone built — at my expense. Monies will be paid to those with families. Those soldiers whose wounds necessitate military discharge shall not go without either. Nor shall you brave men – come the next payday, every last one of you will receive a donative of seventy-five denarii.'

Cheering broke out as the delighted legionaries voiced their gratitude.

Germanicus next announced that the summer campaign was over, precipitating more celebration. When wagons arrived to distribute his own stores of wine, the troops went wild. Few noticed as the governor descended the steps and rode away, preceded by his Praetorians.

'Three months' pay and a skinful of the governor's wine – not fucking bad for one battle,' opined Metilius.

'It's worth a toast of this,' said Piso, ducking down and taking a long slurp from the wine skin he'd just plucked from hiding. Helped by the dim light, no one had noticed his 'paunch' – in reality, the leather bag sitting under his tunic at belly level, held in place by his belts. 'Here.' He thrust the skin at Metilius.

'It wasn't the shits had you gone so long – you were thieving this!'

Piso's shrug was nonchalant.

Metilius wiped his lips and handed the skin to a beaming Dulcius. 'Where did you get it? Not Tubero's quarters?'

'Even I'm not stupid enough to risk that again. It was from—' Piso was silenced by a sharp jab in the ribs from Metilius.

It was too late. Tullus – where in all the gods' names had he come from? – wondered a panicking Piso – had already snatched the wine skin from Dulcius. 'You didn't visit the latrines, Piso.' Tullus' tone was menacing. 'Where did you pilfer this?'

'It's mine, sir. I went back to get it – I thought a toast to Germanicus would be appropriate. You know, after he led us to victory today.' Piso's voice died away.

Tullus shoved his way in to stand right before Piso. 'D'you think I was born fucking yesterday?'

'No, sir.' Piso's mouth had gone bone dry. On either side, his comrades stood stiff as posts. Theft from another soldier was a serious offence, and they all knew it. Since deep antiquity, the punishment had been being beaten to death by one's tent mates. Nowadays, miscreants tended to be whipped and have their pay withheld – but that didn't mean the death sentence wasn't possible.

Tullus stuck his face into Piso's. 'Tell me, please, that you didn't take it from anyone in the Fifth.'

'Of course not, sir.'

'Don't "Of course not" me, maggot!' Tullus jabbed Piso in the chest with a forefinger once, twice. 'Where. Did. You. Get. It?'

'In a Praetorian tent, sir.'

It was unheard of for their centurion to be lost for words. Amazed, Piso watched Tullus' mouth open and close. And open again.

'I see,' said Tullus at last. 'I see.'

Piso's fears surged. This was it. His last memories would be of fists and hobnails punching and stamping him into oblivion.

To his astonishment, Tullus lifted the skin high. 'If it's from those cocksuckers, I'd best taste it.'

Piso's eyes shot to Metilius as Tullus drank. What does this mean? he tried to say, without words. Metilius' 'I don't know' shrug was no help at all.

'Not bad. It's better than the piss you lot drink, that's for sure,' said Tullus, smacking his lips.

'Er, yes, sir.' Terrified, Piso still had no idea what would happen.

Tullus took another pull. Everyone watched sidelong. Agog, nervous.

Thwack! The bag hit Piso in the chest. He grabbed it out of instinct.

'Dispose of the bag when it's empty. A long way from our tent lines.' Tullus was already several steps away. 'The first night in the Ox and Plough, you're buying. All night.'

'Yes, sir!' There could be no denying it, thought Piso, grinning. Their centurion was the finest in the entire bloody army.

Chapter XXXI

A faint light in the eastern sky heralded sunrise, but darkness reigned still over the land. The air was cool, refreshing – a world apart from the soaring temperatures. Patches of mist blanketed areas of open ground. Dew glistened on grass hummocks; it dripped from nodding water avens. Trees loomed tall and threatening out of the gloom. Graceful, cautious, deer grazed in twos and threes, their heads lifting at regular intervals to check for danger.

Arminius was riding back towards the battlefield with Gervas and a dozen warriors. Arminius' companions were wary, reacting to the slightest sound, but he, driven by intense grief and overwhelming anger, looked neither right nor left.

He had had no rest. By the previous day's end, the battle lost, he'd been so exhausted he could barely speak. Merciful sleep had not come to him. The fall of darkness had made no difference, nor the rising of the moon. Furious, frustrated, burning with the desire for revenge, he had watched it trace a slow, gradual path across the sky. He had lain awake as the owls screeched from the forest and injured warriors' moans had filled the cool air. Tortured by the chances that had been missed, worried by his army's huge losses, and in great pain with his wound, he had tossed and turned on his sweat-soaked blanket all night.

Gritty-eyed and drawn-faced now, his gaze roved over the ground before him, searching for movement, any sign of the enemy. Every so often, he would glance back at his lagging escorts. 'Keep up, you whoresons!' he snarled.

Ashamed, they closed the gap, but didn't speak.

It's bad luck to return to a battlefield where you have been beaten, thought Arminius. Dangerous too. Already the eastern horizon was tinged red. Germanicus might not have left any soldiers here, but they would return once it was light, sure as night followed day. Rather than act as a deterrent, the danger spurred Arminius on. Maelo was lying, stiff and cold, somewhere on the rampart. He could not be left there, carrion for the wild beasts, a feast for ravens and kites. Nothing mattered to Arminius at this moment but retrieving his friend's corpse. Most faithful servant, loyal-hearted and courageous, Maelo deserved a warrior's burial.

It was more than the rest of the slain would get, thought Arminius as the first whiff of putrefaction hit his nostrils. The bodies appeared soon after, and with them came the flies. Clouds of blue- and greenbottles, types he had never seen before, rose out of his way, circled, and settled to feed again. His stomach turned to think of the ripening meat's smell by nightfall.

The fighting had taken place some distance away, so these men had fled, only to die from their wounds before reaching safety. Perhaps they had been slain by the pursuing legionaries. It mattered not either way. Slack-limbed, open-mouthed, blood-spattered, they lay staring at the lightening sky, or face down in the grass, or half-submerged in muddy pools. None would ever stir again. Some were on their own, others with companions, lying together in death's cold embrace. Arrows feathered the bodies of men around the base of a tree. Arminius' mouth tightened – this was proof that some warriors had been used as sport by enemy archers. Roman filth, he thought.

The numbers of slain increased fast, and soon Arminius had to pick a meandering path between the sprawled bodies. Unhappy with the overpowering smell of death, shit and rotting flesh, his horse balked now and again. Ruthless, Arminius whipped it on. Unable to help the fallen and certain because of their location that none were Maelo, he himself paid the dead no heed.

Loud grunting drew Arminius' attention. His belly roiled again as he spied through the trees a group of wild boar – sows, piglets and males – feeding on corpses. He spat, but made no attempt to drive the creatures off – they would only return when he'd gone. His determination to find Maelo's body hardened. There would be no flesh rent by teeth for his friend, no eyeballs punctured by beak. No mutilations by vengeful legionaries. No swarm of fly-laid eggs, no resulting maggot infestation. No rotting away to bare bones. No long, gradual decay to dust under a cold sky.

Maelo would rot, be eaten by worms, but he would do so deep in the earth, after fitting words had been said. Dressed in fine clothes, with weapons and armour of the best quality, he would go to the next world as a man of his bravery and stature deserved. We'll toast you long into the night, until the stars dim in the dawn sky, thought Arminius, claws of grief tearing at him. You will never be forgotten – the brother I should have had.

Again his mount jinked. Cursing, Arminius raised his whip, only to notice that they had reached the rampart's edge. Sorry for his harsh treatment, he patted his horse's neck. It snorted, still disquieted by the carnage. Aware that their position was exposed, Arminius spent a few moments studying the plain beyond. Reassured to see no sign of the enemy, he concentrated on the nearer ground.

The first hundred paces outward from the base of the rampart were coated with Roman dead – as many legionaries and auxiliaries as there were warriors along the top. Thereafter, he noted with growing sourness, they thinned out. Two hundred paces off, there were few indeed and further out, none. It was brutal proof of the difference in casualties between the sides.

He set aside his anger. Maelo had to be found, and soon. Dismounting, Arminius handed the reins to one of his companions, and directed the others to do the same. 'We'll spread out – two lines, ten paces between each of us.' He pointed. 'Half of you go that way, half come with me.'

During Arminius' time with the legions, he'd fought many battles, but the massacre he had orchestrated in the forest had been the largest conflict by far, and until now the only one he'd visited afterwards. Although he was accustomed to bodies, and to the indignity of death, this place was hard to stomach. In the forest, nine out of every ten corpses had been Roman. Here it was the other way around. A toxic mixture of anger and sorrow swelled in his chest, making it hard to breathe the fetid air. You did this, his conscience screamed. You are responsible for this slaughter. This charnel house.

Arminius refused to let the idea take root. It would have happened anyway. Germanicus was always going to cross the river this summer. Even if I'd been dead, thought Arminius, the whoreson would have come seeking revenge on the tribes, each of which would have been ground down, piecemeal. If the chieftains had listened to me, had done what I told them from the start, we could have won here. It wouldn't have been on the same scale as seven years ago: Germanicus' army was too large. But we could have butchered enough of them to stop their campaign dead. Bloodied, battered, they would have retreated to the Rhenus, ripe pickings for the tribes every step of the way.

Arminius' mind spun in tighter circles, envisaging different tactics or ground he could have chosen for the battle. None would have worked, he concluded, not with the numbers of warriors he had and the thick-headed chieftains who led them. It all boiled down to one indigestible truth. Avoiding a fight here would have been the wisest choice. The rest of the summer could have been spent targeting and wiping out groups of Roman scouts and smaller patrols.

Yet a more conservative approach would have seen his alliance splinter into its constituent tribes, Arminius decided. Hot-blooded, courageous, his people could not have let the enemy pillage their lands unanswered. On their own, they would have met the legions face-to-face, and lost. So the battles of the previous few days *had* been necessary. If only his orders had been followed, their outcomes might have been different.

The defeat threatened serious personal consequences for Arminius. Rather than teach the chieftains obedience or a willingness to listen, the bloodbath seemed likely to break up his loose coalition. Defeated men were quick to point the finger, to forget that they had disregarded his commands in the first place. Fools, thought Arminius. They cannot, or will not, see the battle for what it was: a failure to obey.

'What's that?' Gervas was pacing to his left.

Arminius realised he'd been talking aloud. 'Nothing,' he muttered.

It was curious how Gervas, a warrior of another tribe, sought out his company. And yet it wasn't, Arminius reflected – the youth had lost Gerulf, who had been his principal influence. The other Usipetes chieftains were brave, but a disorganised crowd. Not one stood out, like Mallovendus of the Marsi. Or himself, Arminius, who led the tribes. It was natural for Gervas to be attracted by his leadership, his charisma. Cultivate the lad a little, and he might develop into a useful right-hand man. Arminius' heart squeezed with guilt. Here he was, thinking like this and Maelo wasn't even a day dead.

'Look!'

Arminius' head twisted. The warrior closest to the rampart's edge had spoken. 'What is it?' demanded Arminius.

'Over there. At the far end of the plain.'

Arminius focused his gaze on the distant ground, from where Germanicus' cursed legions had come the day before. Telltale dust clouds were rising from the direction of the Visurgis. Arminius cursed. It would be Roman troops. 'They're come to collect their dead, curse them.'

'We'd best go.' This was from one of the oldest warriors, a salt-and-pepper bearded type whom Arminius had known from boyhood. Several men voiced agreement. Gervas, he noted, wasn't one of them.

'We haven't found Maelo yet,' said Arminius, glaring.

'Linger here and the only thing we'll find is death,' said the old warrior, meeting Arminius' stare with a hard one of his own.

'Have you lost your balls? They're more than half a mile off,' cried Arminius. He cupped a hand to his mouth so the other group could hear. 'We have time yet. Keep searching!'

Cowed by his fury, the warriors obeyed, even the old warrior, although he was grumbling under his breath.

You turned your face away yesterday, Donar, thought Arminius. This is but a small thing. Let me find the body of my friend.

Perhaps twenty heartbeats later, he thought his prayer had been answered. Arminius chanced on a corpse that from behind resembled Maelo in more ways than one. Brown-haired, medium-framed. Under a mail shirt, a fine tunic. Thick woven trousers in dark green and brown. Nervous, Arminius rolled the man over. Instant disappointment filled him. Despite the sword cut to the face, the clotted blood everywhere, the mud in the mouth, it wasn't his friend. Rest in peace, thought Arminius, letting the body flop back on to its front.

Three more dead warriors he examined, then five. Eight. He refused to look towards the plain and the approaching Romans. Fuck them, thought Arminius. Let the filth come. I'll kill them all. He knew his words for fantasy, but his grief had given birth to a mad stubbornness.

'The Romans have seen us. I'll not stay and die for nothing. Coming?' the old warrior asked his fellows. All but Gervas voiced agreement.

Arminius' fury burst its banks. 'Stay where you are!' he screamed. 'I did not give you leave to go!'

'This for your permission.' The old warrior made an obscene gesture. 'Last time I looked, you were a chieftain of the Cherusci – not a king or a Roman centurion; and I was a free man – not a slave, or a fucking legionary.' He set off towards the horses at a good pace. The others followed. The second group soon noticed, and joined them. So too did the warrior holding the mounts, calling with an apologetic shout that he'd tethered Arminius' and Gervas' horses to prevent them chasing after the rest.

'Stupid, bull-necked, headstrong bastards,' Arminius shouted, the veins bulging in his neck. 'Like every cursed warrior under the sun, they know best. What they should do is listen, and obey!' Wrapped up in his fury, he didn't catch the odd expression that flitted over Gervas' face. Muttering under his breath, Arminius resumed his search of the dead.

'Maelo would not want this – he would not wish you to throw away your life,' said Gervas.

'What would you know?' snapped Arminius, thinking: Not so long ago, Maelo came close to cutting your throat and burying your corpse in the forest. 'Go – go! There's no need for you to die.'

'I'm staying.'

'Suit yourself.' Arminius' shrug was fatalistic. Death would be a welcome release for him at least. His army had been battered into submission and thousands of his men were dead. What was left of his forces would fall apart in the coming days. Like whipped mongrels, the warriors would skulk back to their settlements, hoping that the Romans would leave them in peace.

During the long, dark winter to come, snug in their longhouses and with nothing to do but drink and talk, the survivors would brood, and begin to apportion blame. Arminius couldn't imagine the chieftains agreeing to follow his leadership again, not after this. It was hard to see how even his uncle Inguiomerus would place his warriors under Arminius' command once more, and when Germanicus' legions crossed the river the following spring, as surely they would, resistance would be fractured. Guaranteed to fail.

With a chance of seeing his wife and child, Arminius would have had reason to look to the future, but they were captives in far-off Italy: as good as dead to him. Being slain now would end his suffering. Meeting Maelo on the far side, he'd have good company during his long wait for Thusnelda.

'Look!'

Arminius turned and gasped. Gervas was standing over Maelo's blood-soaked body. Arminius' heart wrenched to see his friend so waxen. Grey. Dead. 'You found him,' he said stupidly.

'Get the horses,' said Gervas.

Arminius stared at Maelo, dazed with grief.

'Fetch the horses. Now!'

Stumbling like a drunk, Arminius obeyed. At the edge of his vision, he saw the Roman riders rein in. Heard the officer shout in Latin, 'Wait! It could be a trap.'

Unhindered, Arminius brought the horses to Gervas and together they manhandled Maelo's leaden corpse on to the withers of one. Looking back as they rode away, Arminius smiled. Donar's shield was protecting them. Why else would fifty Roman cavalrymen refrain from chasing two weary Germans?

Maelo would be buried in a fitting way after all.

PART THREE

Summer, AD 16

Deep in Germania

Chapter XXXII

꙳꙳꙳

It was late. After another roasting-hot day, a calm, warm night beckoned. Thousands of stars dotted the huge expanse of the sky. In the legion camp where Tullus and his men were billeted, peace reigned. Sentries paced the ramparts, but most men had retired. Not Tullus. Restless, his shortened toe aching, he'd come to stand atop the defences and be alone with his thoughts. Eyes attuned to the darkness and ears pricked, he stared into the distance, wondering if Arminius had the balls to launch a surprise attack. Nothing broke the calm, however. All was as it should be. Owls called from the forest. Water pattered over stones in the nearby river. Undergrowth rustled as small, nocturnal creatures went about their business.

Almost a month had passed since the legions had crushed Arminius' warriors at the massive earthen rampart – the Angrivarian wall, many of the prisoners called it. A lot had happened in that time, and much as they might have wished it, thought Tullus, his men were not home yet. Nor were they out of danger. More than a hundred miles separated them from the River Rhenus, and safety. Arminius' alliance had been broken, but that didn't mean every tribe had bent the knee to Rome. Far from it.

'The brave, stubborn bastards,' muttered Tullus to himself. 'People should know when they're beaten.'

'Would you? Would I?' Creaking sounds announced Fenestela scaling the nearest ladder. 'We'd fight on to the bitter end.'

'Aye, we would,' said Tullus, sighing. Arminius and his people were murdering bastards, but their resistance was understandable. The Romans were the invaders of their land, not the other way around.

'Talking to yourself again? It's a habit of the old, I suppose.'

'Who are you calling "old"?' retorted Tullus, but with no heat.

Fenestela rested his forearms on the crude-hewn timbers that formed the top of the fortifications. 'It seems like yesterday that we were in these parts with Drusus.'

'A quarter of a century, eh? Gods, but it went fast.'

'Now look at us. Greybeards, almost.'

'There's only going to be one greybeard between the two of us, and it's not me!'

'You've never understood its usefulness, have you?' Fenestela pulled his fingers through the wiry bush that decorated his chin. 'Warm in the winter, an attraction for women year round. It gives me . . . *gravitas*.'

'You're full of shit, Fenestela,' said Tullus, yet he was laughing too.

They stood for a time in companionable silence, passing Fenestela's wine skin to and fro.

Fenestela spoke first. 'Up here because you couldn't sleep?'

'Aye.'

'Thinking about the eagle?'

Tullus snorted. 'Is it that obvious?'

'To me.' Fenestela's eyes glittered as he turned to Tullus. 'Because I'm the same.'

Neither had to explain further. Arminius had been beaten and his followers scattered to the four winds. Some tribes continued to resist – first it had been the Angrivarii, returned from their campaign with Arminius, and now the Chatti and Marsi had risen up in rebellion – but Germanicus' huge army would see them beaten into submission one by one. For most soldiers this was enough, yet a festering sore lingered in the soul of every veteran of the Seventeenth and Eighteenth Legions. Their lost eagles remained unfound. Time was running out: another month and a half at the most and the legions would have returned to their forts, the year's campaign over. Yes, they would cross the Rhenus to renew hostilities come the spring, thought Tullus, but that guaranteed nothing.

'We have to face it: our eagle may never be recovered. Arminius may never be caught, or slain.' Fenestela spat over the ramparts.

'Aye,' rumbled Tullus, who'd been thinking about little else since their victory at the Angrivarian wall. An important but tiny part of the vast machine that was Germanicus' army, he could do little other than his duty, and pray for the best outcome.

'What will you do if that proves to be the case?'

Tullus threw an arm around Fenestela's shoulders. 'I will thank the gods for you, and all the reprobates from the Eighteenth. You miserable lot are alive when so many aren't. That counts for a lot. A *lot*.'

'Wise words.' Fenestela's voice was huskier than usual.

Tullus raised the skin high. 'To friends and comrades.' He drank and handed it to Fenestela.

'To friends and comrades.' Fenestela took two long swallows, then another.

Tullus breathed in and out. Out and in. In the long, bitter years since the ambush in the forest, anything less than vengeance on Arminius and the recovery of his old legion's eagle would have seemed unthinkable, a betrayal of the dead. Reality was forcing Tullus to be pragmatic. He'd given his utmost to this summer's campaign. Germanicus had done well – better than any Roman general since his father – yet every prize had not been won. That was sometimes how life was, thought Tullus. A man might not like his fate, but he dealt with it. Accepted it. If he didn't, bitterness could eat him up from the inside, like maggots in a corpse's belly. Tullus didn't want to be a sour old wine sponge, the type that sat complaining into his drink, whom men avoided.

'I was thinking that when we get back, I'd promote Piso to *tesserarius*. What do you think?' The century's tesserarius had died at the Angrivarian wall.

'A fine idea. He's been a good soldier this past year or two. Foolish at times, but that will soon stop if he's given responsibility.'

'That's settled then,' said Tullus, pleased. 'I could even recommend you for centurion.'

Disbelief and then shock twisted Fenestela's features. 'Don't you fucking dare!'

'You wouldn't like it?' Tullus made his tone as innocent as possible.

'You know I wouldn't, *sir*. Too much responsibility.' He cursed as Tullus began to chortle. 'Very fucking funny!'

'It never fails,' said Tullus, wiping tears from his eyes.

'Screw you, *sir*.'

Tullus shoved the bag at Fenestela. 'I'm for my bed. You turning in?'

After a long pull, Fenestela lowered the skin. 'Aye. This is finished.'

Tullus was glad of a clear head the following morning. As primus pilus, there was no pressing need to supervise his men as they guarded the camp's main gate and a section of the defences, but long years of monitoring those under his command meant that he did it anyway. His presence meant that he witnessed the arrival near midday of an exhausted, mud-spattered messenger on a blown horse. Thirty auxiliaries, equally tired-looking, accompanied him. Tullus clattered down the ladder, meeting the rider as he urged his mount through the gateway.

'Greetings!' cried Tullus.

With a perfunctory salute, the messenger made to ride by. He scowled as Tullus took hold of the reins. 'I bear important news for the legates!'

'I'm the primus pilus of the Fifth, maggot.' Tullus' smile was icy. 'You can call me *sir*!'

'Your pardon, sir. Now, if I could get past?'

Tullus felt a prickle of unease. 'Nothing terrible has happened, I trust? Is Germanicus well?' The governor had taken ship with one army group some days since, his plan to skirt the southern edges of the German Sea before reaching the shelter of the Flevo Lacus.

'There was a storm, sir. Germanicus is safe, but many ships in the fleet foundered or were carried out into the open ocean. Hundreds of men have drowned.'

Tullus again felt grateful that his legion hadn't been chosen to return by ship. 'The gods be thanked that Germanicus is unharmed. Where is he now?'

'In the Chauci lands, but he's marching this way.'

'And we're to go and meet him.'

'I couldn't say, sir.'

'Of course not. On your way.' Tullus stepped back.

With a respectful salute, the messenger rode into the camp, his escort on his heels.

Tullus peered up at Fenestela, who was standing on the rampart. 'D'you hear that?'

'Aye, sir. It's a relief that Germanicus is alive.'

'Too bloody right,' said Tullus. The last thing the army needed was to lose such a charismatic leader.

'Another messenger approaching, sir!' roared Piso.

What now? wondered Tullus, taking his foot off the first rung of the ladder. He returned to his position. This messenger knew him, and reined in the instant Tullus stepped into his path.

'Sir!'

'Come far?' asked Tullus.

'From the south, sir. The Marsi have regrouped, and are attacking our patrols.' The messenger's eyes roved towards the centre of the camp and his destination, the headquarters.

'On you go,' said Tullus. 'Tubero and the other legates need to hear your news.' He watched the messenger and his escort ride off, before joining Fenestela on the walkway. They exchanged a grim look.

'We won't be going home just yet,' said Tullus.

Chapter XXXIII

A rminius dreamed of Maelo, blood and death every night. Maelo, alive, laughing, and then dying as an anonymous Roman stabbed him in the neck. Every time, Arminius screamed a warning and struggled to reach Maelo before the fatal blow. Always he failed, and woke drenched in sweat and sobbing for breath. Desperate to stay awake so that the nightmare might end, time and again Arminius was somehow drawn back into sleep, where the horror continued.

The blood he saw covered not just Maelo but thousands of corpses on the battlefield at the Angrivarian wall. It dripped from the feeding ravens' beaks. Smeared the wild pigs' snouts red. Great clotted pools of it filled ruts and indentations in the dusty ground. Blood caked Arminius' own arms and body. If he touched his cheeks, his fingers came away crimson. Whether it was his own gore or that of others was never clear, but he could not cleanse himself, try as he might.

Sometimes he saw Thusnelda and their baby son standing on the body-strewn ground. His heart would give a painful squeeze, and he'd reach out, but they were never close enough to touch; she never heard his shouted greetings either. Most painful of all was that Arminius never saw his son's face. It was always concealed by Thusnelda's body, or a throw of the swaddling clothes. Once he got so close that another step would have seen him touch his son's cheek, made him turn his head — only for a sentry to wake him about a late-arrived messenger. By the time Arminius had returned to bed, eager to resume his dream, the sky had been paling and the camp coming to life. Sleep had evaded him, and Arminius could have sworn he heard Donar laugh.

Gerulf also featured in his troubled night visions. Sour-faced, snide-voiced, he harangued Arminius, accusing him of pretensions towards kingship, poor leadership and overwhelming arrogance. 'You're dead,' Arminius said, only to have Gerulf laugh in his face.

'Murdered by Maelo, but my blood's on your hands too, Arminius, along with that of thousands of others. We should never have listened to you.'

'If you hadn't followed my lead, this entire land would be part of the Roman Empire,' Arminius would scream.

It was as if Gerulf couldn't hear.

During yet another repetition of the nightmare, Arminius' fury burst forth. He lunged at Gerulf, set on murder. Gerulf laughed and evaded him with ease. No matter how hard Arminius chased, his quarry could move faster. Arminius woke, clawing the air. Alone. Faint smears of light marked the tent seams – dawn was close. An inarticulate scream of rage, grief and frustration escaped Arminius, and he beat his fists against his skull, relishing the pain, wanting it to end *his* agony.

His eyes fell on his sword. Finish it now, he thought. Slide the blade in deep, the way Varus did. There'll be brief agony, but then it will ease. The guilt and shame will vanish. The fools who surround me will disappear. Despair overwhelming him, Arminius eased the sword half out of its scabbard. Dull silver, etched with myriad pits and scratches but lethally sharp, it would give him a swift end.

Coward, said a voice in his head. Kill yourself now, and Donar will see that you never enter the heroes' hall. Those who lie down after a beating, those who take the easy way out do not deserve to sit with heroes who died in battle, men who were brave to the end. Do it if you wish, weakling, but know that you will never see Maelo on the other side, or your family when the time comes for them to cross.

Jaw clenched tight, Arminius shoved the blade home again. Laid it down.

His pain would continue, and somehow he would find a way to live with it. Life is meant to be hard, he told himself. Brutal. The gods give sometimes, but they also take away. They humour us at times, but for the most part they smile at our antics, laugh at our misfortunes and watch as we stumble through this miserable existence. All we can do is keep living. Keep trying, while there is strength in our bodies.

Arminius flung back the tent flap. In the refreshing cool before dawn, the camp was yet silent. A fraction of its former size – now only his Cherusci kindred remained – it still filled him with pride. We are not beaten yet, he thought. My people think of me as leader, even my uncle Inguiomerus. We will continue the fight against Rome, do whatever it takes to remain free.

Instant frustration stung Arminius. It was well and good to have plans for the future, but in the short term there was little to be done. Seeking battle with the Romans again this summer was out of the question. Mauled and battered from the struggle thus far, his uninjured Cherusci warriors numbered little more than four thousand. Another fifteen hundred would live, but a greater number would never return home. Other tribes had fared worse – more than half the Angrivarii had been wiped out. Mallovendus' Marsi had lost a similar number of warriors.

It was hard to know what the chieftains thought of Arminius now. With Germanicus' legions out to harry the tribes, there had been no question of licking their wounds in one camp. A whipped dog seeks its kennel, thought Arminius, but whether each tribe's lands would offer any security against the vast enemy army was far from certain. Informers among the Roman auxiliaries – there were still some, for which he was grateful – had reported that a large part of Germanicus' host had already marched away to deal with the Chatti. Mallovendus, one of the few chieftains to seek out Arminius before he'd left, had been worried about this too. 'It's well for you, Arminius. Your people live far from the Rhenus, and the Romans can never linger such a distance from their forts. It's different for the Marsi. Different for the Usipetes,' he'd added, glancing at Gervas, who had given an unhappy nod of agreement.

A spark of hope flared in Arminius' heart. Gervas would support him when it came to rallying the tribes again. He had said as much before leaving. The Usipetes were not numerous, it was true, and their strength was diminished from the struggle against Rome, but winning allies was all about having one to start with. If only it was that simple, thought Arminius, rubbing tired eyes. By the summer's end, some of his recent supporters would have bent their necks to Roman rule. Such arrangements weren't set in stone, of course: his own Cherusci had been allied to the empire before his ambush seven years before. Yet it was probable that tribes which had suffered a recent, resounding defeat in battle would be reluctant to join a fresh campaign.

Arminius sucked on the bitter marrow of that, and his fresh-found resolve faltered. It wasn't surprising that two summers of indecisive clashes and heavy losses had sapped the tribes' will to fight. He worried that his personal charisma, so useful in the past, would not win the chieftains over again. I need help, Arminius thought. Gervas was willing, but his youth would count against him when he stood before men twice his age. Mallovendus would suit well, if only he would accept Arminius' leadership again.

Memories of the night he'd forged his alliance, when the chieftains had hung on his every word and his name had resounded to the rafters, spun in Arminius' mind. The eagle, glittering, imperious despite its captivity, had focused men's attention, a powerful reminder of Varus' legions' fate. Arminius laughed at the simplicity of it. With an eagle in his possession, men would be sure to listen. Germanicus' army had recovered the one he'd gifted to the Bructeri, but the Marsi and the Chauci had theirs yet. Arminius was wary of entering Chauci lands: too many of the tribe fought for Rome; they'd also rebuffed his attempts to woo them to his cause. The Marsi hated the empire, however, and Mallovendus was still well disposed towards him.

It was settled, thought Arminius with satisfaction. He would persuade Mallovendus to hand over the tribe's eagle. If the Marsi chieftain wouldn't listen to reason, other methods could be used.

Chapter XXXIV

◫◫◫

The legions were now too far from the coast and navigable rivers to receive grain brought from the Rhenus forts, so Piso was on patrol, scavenging for supplies. Since the return of Germanicus and his forces, the army had grown to its previous size, necessitating the most enormous quantities of food daily. Strong detachments of troops ranged through the countryside either side of the marching column, their task to locate stores of grain, livestock and anything else worth appropriating. The task fell to the auxiliaries for the most part, but the volume of supplies required had also seen regular legionaries pressed into service. As primus pilus, Tullus would have been excused such duty, and his men too, but in his mind it was time to blow out the cobwebs and get some fresh air. 'If I'd known how much fucking paperwork there was when I accepted the position, brothers, I'd never have said yes,' he'd revealed amid much laughter.

That had been several hours earlier. Perhaps eight miles from the army column, Tullus' century and a second one were scouring the landscape with a dozen mule-drawn wagons in tow. Midday was at hand, and the still-climbing temperature bordered on the uncomfortable. A heat haze shimmered in the air, and the hard-baked ground radiated an unpleasant warmth of its own. Piso's skin prickled, in particular at the points where his tunic, neck scarf and plate armour met. He ran a finger around the area, pulling at the fabric here and there where his flesh was being pinched. He was well used to wool garments, but the conditions made them hard to wear.

Better for it to be overcast, cold or even raining, he thought with a sour glance at the sun's burning orb. The humour of his opinion wasn't lost on him. If the weather had been poor, he would be complaining about that instead. Men grumbled to pass the time, to keep the sense of dread at bay. The proof of it was listening to Metilius drone on about the slim pickings they'd had.

'How many farms have we come across – ten?' Metilius looked around for a response.

'Nine,' said Piso.

'Ten,' countered Dulcius, smirking.

Metilius glowered. 'Who fucking cares? The wagons aren't even a quarter filled.'

'We're like a cloud of locusts to the savages,' said Piso. 'They don't want to starve this winter, so everything is being hidden.'

'You're not feeling sorry for them?' sneered a man in the rank behind.

'Who was at the Saltus Teutoburgiensis, maggot – you or me?'

'I meant no insult,' said the soldier, quailing a little before Piso's glare.

'Watch your mouth.' The comment had hit a raw nerve. If there had been warriors in the farmsteads and longhouses, Piso would have had no compunction in killing them, but the only people they'd met today had been old, lame or sick and those few who were unwilling to abandon their homes. Not all were dead now, but some were. Spitted on swords and javelins. Stamped to death. He'd even seen a greybeard battered into the next world with a length of timber. And as for the women, well, lack of teeth and wizened dugs hadn't stopped them being raped. Tullus and Fenestela didn't condone such behaviour, but they couldn't be everywhere at once.

'Starve in the winter, or die today on our blades – what's the difference?' asked Metilius.

Piso didn't have an answer. Maybe that was why Tullus hadn't punished anyone. Perhaps a swift death was better than slow starvation during the long, dark months to come. This *was* what many of the tribespeople would face, for Germanicus had ordered that the as-yet-unharvested wheat and barley should be fired whenever possible. 'If we can't take it, the savages aren't to have it either,' Tullus had said at the outset of the patrol.

Curse the lot of them, Piso decided. Why couldn't the Germans just bend their knees, accept Roman rule, and stop fighting? This patrol, this whole campaign wouldn't be necessary. Was it so hard to pay taxes and call the emperor a god? Millions of people throughout the empire did it and lived a peaceful existence. The tribes would learn the hard way in the end, he thought. Everyone did.

'Think the Marsi will fight us again?' asked Metilius. After a spate of attacks on Roman patrols, Germanicus was leading more than half his army to the tribe's territory. The Fifth, along with several other legions, was part of the force.

'They'd be fools if they did. We'll outnumber them six – seven to one? The filth will surrender once we get there.' This was Piso's heartfelt desire and, he suspected, that of his tent mates. The summer's campaign hadn't been that long but it had been brutal. They would fight if needs be, but far better they got to march back to their forts without losing more comrades.

'If they don't, the bastards will get what's coming to them.' Metilius' leer was unpleasant.

'Piso!'

Tullus' shout snapped Piso back to the present. 'Sir?'

'Farm, over there.' Tullus was pointing off to their left. A quarter of a mile distant, surrounded by small fields, a single longhouse with a few outbuildings was visible. 'Take twenty men and a wagon. See what you can find. Follow our trail after.'

Piso's chest puffed up with pride – public acknowledgement by Tullus was rare, and such duties tended to fall to Fenestela or one of the other junior officers. 'Yes, sir!' Falling out of line, Piso called Metilius, Dulcius and his two remaining tent mates to join him, as well as some of the men from three other contubernia. Piso sent one man to the end of the patrol with instructions for a wagon to come after them down the narrow, rutted track that led towards the farm. 'Form up, four wide, five deep,' he bellowed.

'After me.' Feeling more than a little self-conscious because of this new responsibility, he set off along the path.

Within a dozen steps, the comments began. 'Listen to him,' muttered Metilius. 'A proper optio!'

'Centurion, you mean,' said Dulcius.

'I thought he sounded like a tribune myself,' added another voice with a chuckle.

Piso held a brief debate with himself. Better to quench flames at once rather than watch them grow, he decided, not least because Tullus was watching.

'Enough!' Piso barked. 'Keep your eyes peeled and your javelins ready. There could be warriors hidden in the buildings.'

In the pasture adjoining the longhouse, a solitary calf bellowed for its mother, which was grazing nearby.

'Listen: that's their call to arms,' declared Metilius.

Snorts of suppressed laughter rose.

Piso wheeled, furious. 'Fucking shut up, Metilius!'

Metilius' lips thinned, but he didn't answer back. Piso raked the rest of his comrades with flint-hard eyes. Some were surly-faced and resentful, but they held their peace. Most avoided his gaze, which was gratifying. Tullus' voice echoed in Piso's head. *Discipline. It's all about discipline. They understand that.*

He studied the calf and cow, wondering why such valuable livestock hadn't been moved into hiding. Responding to the bellows, the cow began walking towards its calf. It had a pronounced limp and, looking closer, he could see that its left hock was swollen. The cow was too lame to reach the forest, Piso decided, and the calf had remained because it still needed its mother's milk to survive. His grip on his javelin tightened. 'Someone will have stayed behind to watch over those beasts – keep your eyes open!'

There were no smart comments this time. Splitting his men into three groups, he sent two to search the outbuildings while he led half a dozen towards the longhouse. Smaller than most, its mildewed roof, sagging door and crumbling walls were evidence of poor maintenance. Piso's nervousness eased a fraction – this was no farmstead run by a father with many sons. Like as not, its only inhabitants were old, as slow on their feet as the cow in the field.

His German wasn't good, but he could make himself understood. 'Is anyone home?' he called when they were twenty paces from the door. 'Come outside!' There was no answer, and Piso tramped closer. A quick glance at the other groups gave him no cause for concern. Ten steps from the threshold, and he repeated his command. 'Outside!'

Something, or someone, stirred inside, but the doorway remained empty.

Piso ran his tongue over dry lips. 'Form a line! Javelins ready.' As his men obeyed, he shouted, 'Come out! If you are unarmed, you have nothing to fear.'

Dragging footsteps within had him level his javelin. With tense faces, his comrades did the same. A half-incredulous, half-relieved laugh escaped Piso as a stoop-shouldered, white-haired old man shuffled into view. Dressed in threadbare tunic and patterned trousers, and using a walking stick, he was four score years in age if he was a day. He regarded Piso with rheumy eyes and croaked, 'Kill me, but spare my grandsons.'

Piso's belly tightened afresh. 'Grandsons – how many? Where are they?'

'Three.' Rheumy Eyes inclined his head. 'Inside.'

'Tell them to get out here!' Piso snapped, unhappy with the potential risk of entering the gloom of the longhouse. 'Now!'

'You won't kill them?'

'We're here for food and supplies,' said Piso. 'No one will be harmed.' His steady gaze met that of Rheumy Eyes. 'But if we have to go in there—'

Rheumy Eyes let out a long sigh. 'I know.' He turned his head towards the door. 'Come out, boys, slowly. You have nothing to fear.'

More noise inside. Piso's heart thumped, but he smiled as a tousle-headed boy of about seven years walked out, blinking in the bright sunshine. Darting to his grandfather's side, he stared at Piso and his companions with a terrified expression.

Second to emerge was a stockier version of the first child. A few years older, with a truculent set to his jaw, he stood on the threshold, clutching an old *framea*.

'Put that down!' squawked Rheumy Eyes.

'Drop the spear!' ordered Piso.

The boy didn't obey. 'You killed my father!' he cried.

'We've killed nobody,' answered Piso, keeping his tone jovial. 'Let go of the spear, and go to your grandfather.'

'Your kind slew Father! He was at the Long Bridges, and he never came home. Curse you all!' Fat tears rolled down the boy's cheeks, and he raised his spear.

'Stop,' Piso shouted. Too late, he heard his comrades' reactions. Too late he twisted around to order them to hold. Three javelins shot past, punching the boy to the dirt like a piece of skewered meat. 'You fucking idiots!' Piso screamed. 'He wasn't going to throw. He was too scared!'

Even as his companions' protests rose, feet pounded the earth. Piso spun. There was a blur of movement in the longhouse doorway. Face twisted with grief and rage, a burly youth came charging outside. He shot a look at his dead brother, then levelled the framea in his right fist and threw.

Piso was still lifting his shield when the spear took him in the throat. Stars burst across his vision, and blinding agony consumed his brain. Falling, he was falling. He didn't feel the dirt that struck his back but above him, he saw the bright blue bowl of the sky and the white-yellow disc of the sun. Gods, it was beautiful. Further thought escaped him as everything went dark. He tried to lift a hand to pull at the spear jutting from his flesh, but it was too much effort. 'Piso! Piso!' he heard a voice calling, as if down a long passageway.

Was it Metilius? Or Vitellius? Piso wasn't sure.

He let go.

Chapter XXXV

ᒪᒪᒪ

T he ground had been roasted over the previous month, rendering every track and path concrete-hard, so Tullus heard the pounding hobnails long before he saw the running soldiers. Assuming that it was one of the men with him, he turned. There were no shouts of alarm, no enemy war cries. One of the wagons had lost a wheel, he decided. Perhaps a messenger had come from the army column with fresh orders.

An unpleasant feeling crept over him, therefore, to recognise Metilius and Dulcius, purple-faced with effort, charging along the side of the patrol. 'Halt!' roared Tullus at the men. He strode in the pair's direction. 'What is it? What's happened?'

The pair came skidding to a halt. They exchanged a grim look.

Cold fear uncoiled in Tullus' belly. 'What in Hades is going on?'

'Piso, sir.' Metilius' face crumpled.

'It's Piso, sir,' said Dulcius, panting. 'He's—' Emotion overcame him too.

'Dead,' grated Tullus. 'He's dead?'

They both nodded.

They've gone mad, or I'm dreaming, thought Tullus. He clenched his jaw until it hurt. Metilius continued to cry. Dulcius looked as if he were about to vomit. Tullus wiped his brow and took a slow, deep breath. 'Patrol, about turn! The wagons are to remain here.' he yelled. 'Walk with me,' he ordered the two soldiers. 'Tell me everything.'

Tullus had fought so many battles that they tended to blur in his memory, but he would remember the simple yet stark scene at the longhouse for the rest of his days. The vivid blue sky and hot sun overhead. The still, heavy air. The narrow, ridged track. The beech trees surrounding the farm buildings. The lame cow, suckling its contented calf. His men, standing around, shocked-looking, grieving. The bodies of Piso, a sturdy-framed boy and a strapping youth laid out side by side. Bloodied spears scattered on the ground. An ancient, white-haired man on his knees, hugging a small, tousle-headed boy.

Tullus' heart wrenched as he stood over Piso. Another man of the Eighteenth gone, another body that will never be buried with his comrades, he thought. Bleakness swamped him. No one could have saved Piso, not the best surgeon in Rome. The gaping cut in his throat would have ended his life in the space of time it took a man to count to twenty.

Granite-faced, Tullus regarded the men who'd stayed as Metilius and Dulcius ran to find him. 'Find anything worth taking?'

'A small amount of grain, sir. A ham. Some vegetables. And the cow and calf, of course.'

Piso had died for fucking nothing, thought Tullus, but he let none of his turmoil show. 'See the goods loaded on the wagons and the beasts slaughtered for meat, then fire the buildings.'

'Aye, sir. What should we do with the prisoners?' Metilius' voice.

Tullus glared at the old man, who, like his grandson, was weeping. He was wholly unmoved. It was as if the pity he'd felt for the area's farmers during the previous days had never existed. There was a taste of ash in his mouth.

'Crucify them.' Cold-hearted, he repeated the words in German.

The old man cried out and, unnerved further, his grandson began to wail. Dulcius couldn't conceal his shock. 'Even the boy, sir?'

'You fucking heard!' screamed Tullus, spittle flying. 'These two cunts are no different to the filth who slew Piso. They would do the same given half a chance. Crucify both of them – the boy first, so his pederast of a grandfather can watch. Do it now!'

Chapter XXXVI

꒰꒰꒰

The last part of Arminius' journey had been the worst. Used to evading Roman forces, he and his hundred companions had had to use all their skill to avoid detection in the final five miles to Mallovendus' settlement. The landscape swarmed with the enemy. Auxiliaries, both infantry and cavalry, ranged far and wide in their search for hostile tribesmen. Regular legionaries scavenged the area for food and livestock, destroying farms as they went, and were more than capable of dealing with Arminius' small force. In the end, he split his men up and arranged to meet in the woods close to Mallovendus' village. Hidden from prying eyes, they passed the hours until dusk brooding, whetting their blades and batting away the biting flies.

Brimful of rage at the need for secrecy – this was tribal land, not the empire! – Arminius set out with Osbert and a score of warriors. The Marsi settlement appeared abandoned, or near as, but Arminius didn't want to risk his entire force. The Romans might have set a trap.

His concerns were soon set aside. Not a legionary was to be seen. Only a handful of longhouses had smoke spirals rising from their roofs. No bands of chattering children hurtled about, getting under adults' feet. Instead of the usual cacophony of challenging barks from the resident dogs, silence reigned. No youths loitered, no gaggles of greybeards sat about, reminiscing about the past.

Arminius and his companions were deep inside the settlement before anyone noticed, let alone questioned their presence.

'Hold!' Mail shinked as a tall warrior appeared from under the eaves of a longhouse. He levelled his spear. 'State your name and business!'

One sentry? Arminius' first thought was that Mallovendus' fortunes had sunk low, and his second that the lack of strength might prove useful if the Marsi leader proved uncooperative. 'I am Arminius of the Cherusci,' he said in a hearty tone, 'come to seek counsel with your chieftain.'

The sentry stepped closer, peering up at Arminius. He grinned. 'It *is* you.'

'As I said.' Arminius' tone was dry. 'Is Mallovendus here?'

'Aye. Come inside. I'll announce you.'

Taking only Osbert, Arminius followed the warrior. The aroma of roasting meat hit his nostrils crossing the threshold, and his belly twisted. It had been days since he'd eaten more than stale bread and cheese. The smell was all that remained of the welcoming scene that had greeted him upon his last visit. The longhouse was almost empty – half a dozen warriors lounged about on furs, talking in low voices. A bored-looking slave tended a haunch of beef that was roasting over the fire. Several women were preparing food in the kitchen area. Mallovendus sat alone at the table where the chieftains had discussed what to do, his head bowed over a beaker.

Arminius crossed the floor with silent steps. 'Mallovendus.'

The Marsi chieftain jerked around; his face twisted in surprise. 'Arminius?'

'Here I am.' There was pleasure in Mallovendus' eyes, thought Arminius, and something else. Wariness – or was it more than that?

'This is an unexpected pleasure. Welcome!' Mallovendus stood to embrace Arminius in a bear hug. He did the same to Osbert. 'Come. Sit!' Mallovendus clicked his fingers. 'Bring cups, and more beer.' To Arminius, he said, 'You're not alone, surely? Have you men outside?'

'Some, aye.'

'It would be too much to hope that you'd brought all of your strength.' Mallovendus waved a hand as Arminius began to speak. 'No need to explain. Even if we'd decided to fight on against the Romans, you'd be throwing your warriors' lives away to have them join us. My tribe is weaker than ever before.' He called to the sentry. 'Arminius' companions are to come in. Straitened times or no, guests must be made welcome.'

'My thanks.' Arminius watched as his warriors filed inside, outnumbering Mallovendus' more than three to one. If he noticed, the Marsi chieftain didn't seem perturbed, which was reassuring. One way or another, the eagle will be mine, thought Arminius. 'Your settlement is empty – have your people taken to the forests?'

'Aye. The Romans are close, and in great numbers. It's for the best.' Mallovendus' face was angry and sorrowful. 'Your journey must have been difficult. The legions are swarming like rats.'

Arminius made a dismissive gesture. 'My troubles are as nothing compared to yours at this moment. Has Germanicus sought meetings with you and the other chieftains?'

'Any neighbours of mine who haven't been slain have had to swear allegiance to the emperor. Those who refused were butchered, along with their people.' Mallovendus thumped the table. 'I am to be next. A Roman messenger came today, ordering me to present myself to Germanicus in the morning.'

'Will you obey?'

Mallovendus sighed. 'I have no choice, Arminius, unlike you. My people are staring death in the face. Were we to escape it this time, my lands are close enough to the Rhenus always to be in danger. I will bend the knee, and accept Germanicus' punishment. You would do the same.'

'I would,' admitted Arminius, gladder than ever for the hundreds of miles that lay between his home and the empire.

'Forgive my mood. I should be playing the host.' Mallovendus took the beakers brought by the widow who'd shared Arminius' bed the previous winter. Filling ones for Arminius and Osbert, he raised his own high. 'To better times.'

'To better times,' said Arminius, and drank. He caught the widow's eyes on him, and his groin stirred. There might be time later for a swift tumble in the straw. He put the appealing notion aside. Spilling his seed mattered as nothing compared to securing the eagle.

Mallovendus drained his cup. Wiping his mouth with the back of his hand, he belched and poured everyone another measure. His expression grew sombre. 'Welcome as you are, Arminius, what brings you to my door?'

Arminius was ready for this plain speech; he'd prepared his words. 'Our defeats this summer have been grievous, but they do not mean the end of our war with Rome. A fresh opportunity to destroy their legions will present itself.'

'Maybe.' Mallovendus sucked on his moustache. 'One day, maybe. But my people are done fighting for now. I can promise nothing—'

'I'm not asking for Marsi spears.' Arminius fixed his eyes on Mallovendus. 'I want the eagle I gifted to you after the ambush on Varus.'

'*This* is why you're here.' Mallovendus' expression grew crafty. 'Why not ask the Chauci?'

'Their lands are far off.'

'Safer to travel to, however.'

'Most of their chieftains are no longer well disposed towards me.'

'Why might that be?'

Arminius' shrug was careless. 'I asked several times for their support, yet their warriors preferred to fight with Rome. To ensure they understood the way things stood between us, I sent back their last messenger's head in a basket.'

Mallovendus let out a disbelieving hiss. 'You are a fool, Arminius!'

'My temper got the better of me.'

'Just a little! You'll live to regret it, mark my words.'

'Perhaps.' Arminius shrugged again.

'And so you come to me.'

'Aye.'

They stared at each other. Time passed, and neither spoke. At length, Arminius realised that Mallovendus wasn't going to comply. He tried a different angle. 'Men who've been beaten forget their past victories. I have to have visible proof that we crushed the Romans.'

Mallovendus shook his head with evident regret. 'I hear you, but I can't give you the eagle.'

Arminius fought to keep his tone calm. 'Why not?'

'Germanicus is a ruthless bastard, like all his kind. The terms he demands will be punishing. The eagle is a powerful bargaining chip, and he'll pay a high price for it.'

'No! I forbid you to make that trade.'

All trace of friendliness left Mallovendus' face. 'Do not tell me what I can and cannot do in my own home!'

Again they locked gazes, and Arminius thought: My dagger could be between his ribs before he's put down his cup. But the eagle's location might forever remain unknown if he did that, and so he nodded and sipped his beer. 'I meant no insult.'

'Of course you didn't.' Mallovendus' smile didn't reach his eyes.

'I'll take my leave. Gratitude for the drink.' Arminius got to his feet.

'Stay and eat with us.' The protest was weak.

'Thank you, but no.' Catching Osbert's eye, Arminius gave him the prearranged signal, a slow dip of the chin. His men, who had been waiting for this, moved, unobtrusive, calm, to stand over every Marsi warrior. Arminius, who was behind the still-seated Mallovendus, drew his dagger and pressed it to his host's neck.

Mallovendus went very still. 'You *dare* to draw a blade under my roof?'

'You leave me no option,' said Arminius. Mallovendus tensed, as if about to leap up, and Arminius pushed the dagger's tip in hard enough to draw a fat drop of blood. 'Think before you move. Your men will also die.'

'Filth,' hissed Mallovendus, but he relaxed back on to his stool. 'Do your worst. I will never reveal where the eagle is hidden.'

'No?' Arminius glanced at Osbert. 'Hold down the youngest warrior – that one, with blond hair. Gouge out his eyes.'

A great cry escaped Mallovendus. Swift as lightning, Arminius wrapped an arm around his throat and leaned even harder on the dagger. 'Go on,' Arminius whispered. 'I'll willingly send you to the other side.'

Quivering with rage, Mallovendus subsided. Arminius watched with satisfaction as the young warrior was manhandled, roaring and shouting, to the table and slammed down on to his back in front of Mallovendus. Knife in hand, Osbert looked to Arminius.

'Where is the eagle?' enquired Arminius again.

'Donar take you, whoreson!' bellowed Mallovendus.

Arminius nodded at Osbert, who leaned over his victim.

A soft shuffle of footsteps. Arminius sensed someone behind him. It couldn't be one of the Marsi warriors – they were all being guarded. Unable to relax his grip for fear of Mallovendus' reaction, he twisted his head. Before he could make out anyone, pain lanced through him. A knife pricked through his tunic, low down on his right side.

'My husband told me once that the liver lies in this area.' The widow's icy voice was a world away from the seductive tones she'd used when they had lain together. 'Stick the blade in deep enough, and the bleeding will never stop. A slow death, he said, and an unpleasant one.'

Arminius laughed. 'You wouldn't do it.' The words had only left his mouth when the widow shoved the knife tip into his flesh. He cried out. Several of his men raised their weapons.

'Don't tempt me,' advised the widow.

'Stay where you are!' Arminius barked. With reluctance, his warriors obeyed.

'The boy is to be released,' said the widow. 'Your men are to leave the settlement, without any fuss.'

'And me?'

'You will stay behind as surety,' said Mallovendus, his good humour returned.

'The instant my warriors have gone, you will cut my throat.'

'Not everyone is a treacherous dog like you.' Mallovendus twisted out of Arminius' grip, his face cold and set. 'Because of our previous friendship, you will be released unharmed. I swear this to you before Donar, bringer of thunder.'

Arminius' eyes searched Mallovendus' long and hard, but he could see no sign of deceit. He nodded, accepting defeat even as fury consumed him.

'Let the boy go, Osbert. Take the men to our camp. I'll find you there.' Osbert hesitated, and Arminius barked, 'Do it! The mad bitch will gut me.'

Glowering, Osbert did as he was told. When he and the others had departed, the widow moved away from Arminius with a scornful remark about his manhood. The chuckling Marsi warriors took her place but, true to Mallovendus' word, no one laid a finger on Arminius. Instead, he was offered a platter of bread and roasted meat.

The food tasted like ash. Despair was not an emotion familiar to Arminius, but it swamped him now. Without the iconic eagle, his chances of winning allies among the fresh-beaten tribes were small indeed.

Chapter XXXVII

▨▨▨

U nder a warm morning sun, astride his horse, Tullus was waiting with the senior officers of five legions: his own, and the four others selected by Germanicus to subdue the Marsi afresh. On an expanse of fields behind them, every soldier of the Fifth was massed, cohort by cohort. A short distance in front sprawled the largest Marsi settlement, and home of Mallovendus.

Three days had passed since Piso's death, and the army had reached its destination. The march hadn't been without incident. Angered by the Romans' new policy of destroying every farm in their path, Marsi war bands had mounted attacks on the column. All had been driven off with heavy losses, and one annihilated to the last man. Tullus and his soldiers had played their part. Grief-stricken by the loss of Piso, they hadn't needed the order to take no prisoners.

The countryside had emptied before their destructive swathe, and the final approach to Mallovendus' village, several miles of well-laid wooden road, had been eerie: not a living soul was to be found in or near any of the many longhouses. Only the scouting auxiliaries had had sight of people, fleeing into the nearby forests and woods. Rumour had been rife among the high-spirited legionaries that the main settlement would also be abandoned, but the approach of a solitary messenger an hour since had changed everything. Carrying a mistletoe branch to signify a truce, the warrior had borne word that Mallovendus would meet Germanicus or his appointed official to seek terms.

Wary of a trap, Germanicus had ordered the auxiliary cavalry to search the settlement. News that the place was empty apart from Mallovendus' longhouse, where about a hundred warriors had gathered, had been greeted with widespread exhilaration. Distrustful, averse to risk, Germanicus had taken no chances and deployed an entire legion to bear witness to an immediate meeting. The remaining legions were close by, and easy to summon if the need arose.

Tullus, still much affected by Piso's death, was disappointed at this lack of resistance. He longed to kill yet more of the enemy. Piso had been worth a thousand cocksucking, sister- and daughter-humping savages, he thought. More. Piso's value was greater than every last cursed tribesman to walk the earth.

Gritty-eyed, dry-mouthed and with a thumping head induced by the skin of wine he'd had the night before, he wondered with growing irritation when Germanicus would appear. It wasn't for him to say a word, any more than it was for the other *primi pili*, or the tribunes. Even Legate Tubero, sweating in his crested helmet twenty paces away, had to wait.

A short time later, trumpets announced Germanicus' arrival. Looking like the god of war Mars come down to earth, the governor was resplendent in burnished armour, red general's sash and a silver-embossed helmet. Measured nods acknowledged every officer present as he manoeuvred his horse into position. 'Any sign of Mallovendus?' he called to Tullus.

'No, sir. He must be waiting for your summons.'

Germanicus' answering smile was thin. 'Give the order, Tullus.'

He eyed the dozen musicians who stood nearby. 'Trumpeters, sound!'

The long and piercing call that followed delivered a message decipherable in any language: Present yourself. Mallovendus must have been watching from hiding, because he appeared not thirty heartbeats later, flanked by a small retinue of warriors. That's right, worm, thought Tullus, come when your master calls.

'He is to have no one by him when we speak,' said Germanicus. 'See to it, Tullus.'

'Sir.' In general, Tullus would have regarded it as suicide to ride alone towards a group of hostile Germans. Today, he took huge satisfaction from this show of confidence. If the warriors attacked, he would have a chance to lay in the mud Mallovendus, one of Arminius' main henchmen. If he himself were slain, he would join Piso, Vitellius and the rest of his slaughtered men in the afterlife. Given his recent dark mood, that was to be welcomed. With urging knees, he drove his horse into a trot, then a canter.

He rode right up to the defensive line the warriors had formed in front of their chieftain, enjoying their flinches and involuntary half-steps backward. 'Where is Mallovendus?' he demanded in German.

'Here I am,' replied a coarse-featured, red-haired brute clad in a rusted mail shirt and dark green trousers. 'Who are you?'

Tullus ignored his question. 'Germanicus will speak with you – alone. No honour guard. No warriors. No weapons.'

Mallovendus' face flushed at this disrespect, but he nodded his acquiescence.

'Follow,' ordered Tullus, turning his horse in such a tight circle that several warriors had to step out of his way. He rode off without looking back, revelling in the invisible hatred that floated after him. There might only be a hundred pairs of eyes watching from the settlement, but the humiliating image of their chieftain walking alone and unarmed towards Germanicus would sear itself into their memories, and the implied message would soon pass through the tribe and beyond. Resistance is futile. Rome is all-powerful. Bend your knee to the emperor, or suffer the consequences.

'Stay by me, primus pilus,' said Germanicus as Tullus reached him. 'I don't trust this savage Mallovendus, even if he is on his own.'

'Honoured, sir.'

Mallovendus came to a halt. He dipped his chin. 'Germanicus.'

'You are Mallovendus?' demanded Germanicus, gesturing at the interpreter, a Chauci auxiliary officer.

'I am.' It was bad Latin, but comprehensible.

'Not content with joining Arminius' rebellion, your people continue to attack my legions.' Germanicus was angry.

There was a short delay as the interpreter translated and Mallovendus responded. 'He begs your forgiveness,' said the interpreter. 'It was a mistake to take up arms against the empire. His people are also sorry.'

'*Sorry?*' Germanicus' face twisted with contempt. 'Tell that to my dead legionaries! Will "sorry" bring back the wagons destroyed, or the equipment burned?'

Mallovendus shook his shaggy head, no, when the interpreter relayed Germanicus' words. He was careful to keep his gaze directed at the ground, but his fists kept clenching and unclenching. Go on, Tullus thought, fingers on his sword hilt. Try something, maggot.

'Your people will pay Rome for their treachery,' said Germanicus. 'Coin. Cattle. Furs. Slaves. I care not how, but the total value will be a thousand thousand denarii.'

The interpreter did his work.

'Too much,' said Mallovendus in his heavy-accented, poor Latin. 'My people . . . not wealthy.'

Germanicus' laugh was harsh. 'Find the means, fool, or suffer my legions' full wrath.'

The two studied each other, Mallovendus bristling with impotent rage, Germanicus cold-faced and contemptuous.

'I have something you want,' said Mallovendus in German.

Curious, Tullus leaned forward, but Germanicus had to wait until the interpreter had translated the sentence.

'What could you possibly have that I desire?' sneered Germanicus.

'*Aquila,*' said Mallovendus. 'I have . . . eagle.'

The world stopped. Stunned, Tullus bit his cheek until he tasted blood. He fixed Mallovendus with an icy stare. '*You* have an eagle?'

Mallovendus nodded as the interpreter said in Latin, 'He has one of Varus' legions' eagles.'

A ripple of excitement swept the watching officers. Tullus' heart banged in his chest.

'Prove it,' Germanicus demanded.

The interpreter translated; Mallovendus shook his head and replied.

'He will prove it,' said the interpreter, 'but his people will only pay a quarter of the amount you demanded.'

Germanicus raised himself in the saddle. 'They will pay every last coin I order them to, or be butchered!'

But Mallovendus did not back down. 'Kill them all,' the interpreter relayed. 'That way, you will never get your eagle back.'

An impasse reached, both men glared at one another.

Tullus cleared his throat. 'May I speak, sir?'

A glance from Germanicus. 'Aye.'

'Which eagle is it?' Tullus barked at Mallovendus in German. 'Which legion did it belong to?'

'The Eighteenth.'

Tullus swayed in the saddle, lightheaded. From a long way off, he heard the interpreter repeating Mallovendus' reply in Latin. The Marsi had his old legion's eagle. It was close by – it had to be. After all these years—

'Tullus – are you well?' asked Germanicus.

He blinked, pulled a smile. 'I'm fine, sir.'

'This is your eagle, is it not?'

'Aye, sir.' Tullus' voice was thick. He wanted to plead with Germanicus, to beg him to accept Mallovendus' terms, but pride wouldn't allow it. He stitched his lip, praying that the governor felt the same way about the eagle.

Germanicus' eyes moved from Tullus to Mallovendus and back, and then away again, into the middle distance.

High above a buzzard called, its lonely screech deriding the unfolding drama.

As Tullus studied Mallovendus, a solution came to mind. Torture the bastard until he reveals the eagle's location. Appealing though it was, it would never happen. A pragmatist, Germanicus would want both the standard *and* as much tribute as the Marsi could afford.

'You will give us the eagle and five hundred thousand denarii,' said Germanicus, confirming Tullus' suspicions.

Mallovendus seemed about to speak, but Germanicus cut him off. 'You are in no position to bargain! Refuse my offer and my legions will reduce your settlements to ash. Your people will be enslaved or slain, down to the ancients and babes in arms. This I swear before Mars and Jupiter.'

Nerves jangling, Tullus looked on as the interpreter played his part.

Mallovendus' shoulders bowed. 'Very well.'

Germanicus' expression became triumphant. Tullus' heart sang. After all the horrors that he'd been through, the Eighteenth's eagle was to return where it belonged.

'The standard is hidden near here,' said Mallovendus.

'Is it guarded?' demanded Germanicus.

'Ten warriors, and a priest.'

Tullus wanted to shout with delight.

Germanicus' hawkish gaze moved to Tullus. 'I think you should take charge of this enterprise. Are you willing?'

Tullus came to attention. 'I've never wanted anything more in my life, sir.'

Chapter XXXVIII

⌐⌐⌐

Little more than two miles away, Arminius was still in his hiding place close to Mallovendus' settlement. He'd spent the night thinking of ways to force the Marsi chieftain to reveal the eagle's location, but had set them, one after another, aside. Storming Mallovendus' longhouse with his full force had been the most likely to succeed. His warriors would have won the fight, but plenty would have died, and Mallovendus might also have been slain, taking with him his secret.

There was nothing to do but return home, Arminius decided with bitterness. Perhaps bridges could be built with the Chauci during the autumn and winter. It was a faint hope – what had he been thinking to execute their messenger? – but there was nothing else to cling to. Blanket rolled up, tent taken down, weapons checked, Arminius glanced around the clearing. 'Ready?'

His warriors muttered their assent.

'We'll split up, as before. Mallovendus said Germanicus' forces are camped to the south of his settlement, so head north at first. Our meeting point this evening—' Arminius cocked his head. Someone was approaching their position, making plenty of noise. Romans? he wondered. Marsi warriors? There was no way of knowing. 'Spread out! Attack on my signal,' he ordered, easing himself into the bushes. In no time, his men had formed a deadly circle overlooking the clearing.

Tension laced the air as the interloper drew nearer. Arminius' mind spun with possibilities. Was this a trick to divert their attention as other enemies flanked them? Could Mallovendus have had a change of mind?

Arminius' confusion grew as an unarmed warrior he didn't recognise emerged, hands held up in the universal gesture of peace. In the prime of life, black-haired, stocky, the warrior wore a simple brown tunic and Marsi-patterned trousers. 'I seek Arminius of the Cherusci,' he called.

'Who are you?' shouted Arminius.

'My name is Degmar. I have urgent news.'

'Did Mallovendus send you?'

The warrior shook his head. 'He has no idea I am here.'

Arminius' doubts remained. 'Are you alone?'

'Aye.' Degmar turned towards his voice. 'Arminius?'

Arminius stepped into the clearing.

'Well met.' Degmar dipped his chin in respect.

'Why are you here?' demanded Arminius, still suspicious.

'Not all the Marsi agree that submitting to the Roman yoke is the best idea.' Degmar's eyes were full of anger. 'Some of us want to fight on, to wage a war from the forests. Mallovendus will have none of it. You are cut from different cloth.'

'You wish to join us?' asked Arminius, thinking: One warrior will make no difference to my lot.

'In part.'

Arminius' irritation flared. 'Stop wasting my time.'

'I know where the eagle is hidden.'

'*How?*'

A smile. 'I followed some of the warriors chosen to guard it one night.' He paused. 'They say you want the eagle to rally the tribes, to continue the struggle against Rome. That *is* what you plan to do?'

'Until my dying breath,' swore Arminius. 'Having an eagle proves to men that Rome's legions can be defeated – can be wiped out.'

Degmar nodded his satisfaction. 'We'd best move fast. The first opportunity I had to leave unnoticed was when Mallovendus rode out to meet Germanicus, almost an hour ago. Gods only know what he has agreed to since then.'

'Take us there!' cried Arminius. 'We have no time to lose.'

Chapter XXXIX

⊡⊡⊡

T ullus was deep in the forest, picking his way along a narrow, overgrown track. Brambles flourished in the gaps between trees,
restricting his view, but by his calculation, they had come at least
two of the three miles described by Mallovendus. Dappled sunlight filtered
through the thick canopy provided by the sessile oaks, beeches and horn-
beams. Mossy boulders lined the banks of a burbling stream.

It was a green world, and benign compared to the living hell Tullus had
endured as part of Varus' doomed army. The footing was firm beneath his new
boots; his clothing was dry. A clear sky precluded any chance of rain, let alone
thunder. Jupiter was in a good mood, thought Tullus, and no wonder. A lost
eagle was about to fall into Roman hands once more. That meant the thunder
god's protection was over him and his men. He grinned. This was Rome's hour.

In single file behind Tullus came two centuries of legionaries. His column
was mirrored by two others, each fifty paces apart, making their way on a
parallel path. Pairs of Chauci scouts ranged ahead of the legionaries, their
task to spot any Marsi sentries, and to report to Tullus at regular intervals.
Thus far, they had seen no one, which tallied with Mallovendus' information. The forest was sacred, he'd said, and it was bad luck to venture within
unless sanctioned by one of the tribe's priests. Tullus and his troops would
only encounter the priest assigned to watch over the eagle, and the ten
warriors who acted as guards. The outcome of the mission seemed certain.

Trusted by Germanicus, about to see his deepest longing fulfilled, Tullus
hadn't had such a spring in his step for years.

Krrruk.

Tullus came to an immediate halt. His skin crawled as the raven called again. *Krrruk. Krrruk.* There was nothing special about hearing a raven – they were common enough birds – but here in this place, sacred to the Marsi, there was a mystical, gods-given feel to the harsh, repetitive sound. Tullus set aside his unease. No wretched bird was going to stop him taking what was his. *Nothing* would get in his way now. He muttered encouragement to the soldier behind and started walking again.

Nerves taut despite his determination, Tullus trod light from then on. When one of the Chauci scouts emerged from the bushes, he had his blade out and levelled in a trice.

'Not enemy,' said the warrior, a gaunt-cheeked type with almost no teeth. 'Friend.'

'Don't creep up like that then,' snapped Tullus, annoyed that he hadn't heard the scout approach. 'What news?'

'We . . . close.' The warrior's Latin was bad. 'Holy place . . . near.'

Tullus' heart thumped. 'You've seen the eagle?'

A shake of the head. 'Is hidden. Saw . . . warriors, and priest.'

'How many?'

'Nine warriors. One priest.'

'Mallovendus said ten guards.'

A shrug. 'Perhaps tenth . . . sleeping. Or having shit . . . in trees. Or Mallovendus wrong.'

One warrior more or less would make no difference, thought Tullus. He nodded his approval and sent messengers to the other columns, which were to halt until he and the warrior had spoken to their centurions. There would be no half-baked plan: everyone would know their task, ensuring the mission's success.

Tullus stood in a circle of his fellow centurions. The gaunt-cheeked warrior was by his side, a rough sketch of the Marsi shrine – the best name for the place – drawn in the dirt at his feet. A trio of stone altars dominated the centre of the sacred area. Close by were a number of small wooden huts, with tents, lean-tos and firepits in between. Given that the eagle wasn't visible, it was probable, the warrior had said, that it would be in a building. Tullus had agreed. The other, temporary structures belonged to the guards and the priest.

'Tell us the warriors' locations again,' ordered Tullus.

The warrior poked with his stick at the junction of the open ground and the tree line. 'Path to settlement here. Two warriors.' He jabbed at the largest firepit. 'Five here, cooking, sitting.' In front of one tent: 'Two here, cleaning weapons.' By the altar: 'Priest here, praying.'

'The clearing is about ten score paces across, you say?' enquired Tullus.

'Aye.'

Quick and precise, Tullus ordered four centuries to approach from the north, west and south. He would close in from the east with his units. The signal to move would be a sharp blast from his whistle. 'None of the filth are to escape. Clear?' His eyes raked the others until he was satisfied they had understood.

'Back to your men. I'll see you there, with the eagle.' In a low voice, Tullus added, 'Roma Victrix!'

His companions' fierce replies couldn't quite drown out the pounding feet of another of the Chauci scouts. Chest heaving, face streaming with sweat, he pulled up in front of Tullus. 'Someone in forest!'

Tullus' stomach lurched. 'Explain yourself!'

'Noise in trees . . . to the south. Large group moving . . . towards sacred place.'

'Mallovendus, the treacherous dog.' Tullus glanced at the centurions. 'Back to your soldiers. Make for the clearing as fast as you can. When you reach it, secure the eagle at all costs! G O!'

And then he was sprinting for his own men.

Tullus could feel Piso's ghost hovering over his shoulders as he ran. Why had he given Piso command at that precise moment? Fenestela would have handled the situation better – *he* would have anticipated what had happened, and been ready for the last boy's spear. It was a useless wish, but Tullus couldn't keep it from his mind. I'm a fool, he thought. An old fool.

If he'd been able to see Piso's shade behind him, it would have been smiling. Fail to recover the eagle and you'll shame me and my fallen comrades forever, it whispered in his ear. Cursing, Tullus pushed his legs even harder, until the gaunt-cheeked warrior was within sight once more. Trailing lengths of bramble dragged across Tullus' face and tugged at his helmet crest. The thorns left beaded lines of blood on his cheek. He didn't notice.

What he would have given to be twenty-odd years younger. The legionaries pounding behind kept pace with ease, the dead weight of their armour and weapons seeming half the burden of Tullus' equipment. His protesting knees crunched with every step; the muscles in his legs ached almost as much as his hips; his neck and wrists hurt too, from the weight of his helmet and shield. Piso's ghost and the burning image of the eagle kept Tullus moving. Allowed him to ignore the tight band around his chest, the crone with her needle in his calf and the stabbing agony of his injured toe.

Eyes fixed on the uneven track, he collided with the gaunt-cheeked warrior. The legionary next in line did well not to slam into Tullus.

'Listen,' said the warrior.

Tullus obeyed. Cold dread tickled his guts as shouts and cries carried through the trees. It wasn't Latin. 'Who are they – Marsi?'

'Don't know.'

'How many?'

A shrug.

'Move.' Tullus shoved Gaunt Cheeks on.

'They could be . . . many. Too many.'

'I don't give a fuck. Lead on, or you'll feel the point of this.' Tullus indicated his sword.

Sullen-faced, the warrior obeyed.

The brief respite had given Tullus a new lease of life, as had the proximity of the eagle. Heart pumping with pride, he almost didn't care how many savages there were at the shrine. He had more than four hundred of the empire's finest soldiers, among them every veteran of the Eighteenth. They would fight like demigods to recover the lost standard.

They burst out of the trees into a scene of utter confusion. Of the two sentries mentioned by the gaunt-cheeked warrior there was no sign. A thin, bearded priest stood atop the largest altar, brandishing a staff and shouting orders. Mail-clad warriors were ranged from one side of the clearing to the other, in a line facing Tullus. Behind, men were hurrying between the tents and huts, and beyond that, trees loomed. Tullus saw the warriors' purpose. If the legionaries were held back until the eagle had been carried into the forest, it would be lost again, possibly forever.

'First Century, spread out! Form a line, twenty wide, three deep. MOVE!' He could see the Second Century's men emerging now. Tullus barked out the same orders again, and threw a desperate look at the huts. A metallic glitter – something carried by a bearded man exiting a hut – changed his mind. Time, he had no time. 'First Century, form wedge instead. Behind me! Second Century, form wedge and follow!' With no idea if his order had carried to the second unit, he blew his whistle to signal an all-out attack from the rest of the cohort.

Tullus seethed with impatience as his men hurried in behind him. Metilius and Dulcius were there. More of his veterans from the Eighteenth had formed a third row, but the other soldiers were taking an age to get in place. Tullus stared again. It was impossible to tell at this distance, but he could have sworn the man carrying the eagle resembled Arminius. Bastard! thought Tullus. It would be just like him to try and take the eagle for his own. Tullus checked again – there were five ranks in the wedge now, still too few to be sure of success, but if he waited any longer—

'With me!' he bellowed, and charged.

Chapter XL

▩▩▩

'Arminius!' roared Tullus. Close now to the line of warriors, he could see the Cherusci leader conferring with several of his men. The eagle, tarnished and missing its lightning bolts, glinted on his shoulder. 'I see you, whoreson!' Tullus cried.

Arminius gave no sign of having heard. He pointed here and there, giving orders, and then headed away from the battle lines. Stricken, Tullus whipped a glance over each shoulder: Metilius and Dulcius were there. There were more men behind, but Tullus had no idea how many. It would be enough, he decided. 'We do this for Piso, and for our brothers from the Eighteenth. Yes?'

'YES, SIR!'

Tullus was fifteen paces out from the enemy line. Steady, well armed, the warriors looked to be some of Arminius' best. It was madness to attack without being fully prepared, but every heartbeat mattered. *Jupiter, stay with me. Fortuna—* Tullus killed that thought. *Better not to tempt the old bitch.*

He fixed his eyes on the closest warrior, a solid-framed man with a bushy red beard not unlike Fenestela's. 'ROMA!' cried Tullus, louder than he'd ever done. The warrior flinched, just a little, exactly what Tullus had hoped for. Desperate to win any kind of advantage, he repeated his cry. Crash went their shields, and even though the warrior had braced against the impact, Tullus' momentum, with more than ten men behind, drove him back several steps. Tullus was already hooking his right arm around the warrior's shield, his blade searching for contact. All it found was the outside of his enemy's elbow, but that was sufficient. The warrior cried out, and Tullus shoved him back another three paces.

Rising up on tiptoe, Tullus headbutted the warrior, the brow of his helmet catching him on the nose, splitting skin, mashing flesh. Blood sprayed, and the man groaned and stumbled. Tullus angled his left shoulder further forward, into the curve of the shield. With a powerful push of his thigh muscles, he drove the warrior, mouth open, eyes filled with fear, down on to his back. Tullus stamped on the injured warrior's face in passing, but there was no time to finish him off.

'WITH ME!' Tullus ordered.

'Here, sir!' Metilius' voice. 'Yes, sir!' added Dulcius.

The rest of his men would follow through the gap in the enemy line, thought Tullus, driving his tired legs forward. They had to. He would push on regardless. Arminius was vanishing among the trees some fifty paces ahead, warriors on either side. A shout formed in Tullus' throat, but he saved his breath.

Screaming at the top of his voice, the priest leaped down from the altar right in front of Tullus. His only weapon a staff, he charged. A swingeing blow from it smashed the transverse crest on Tullus' helmet. Tullus' reply was to ram his blade into the man's chest. A choking cry, and the priest's eyes bulged. Sword wrenched free, Tullus didn't wait to see him fall. Somehow managing to grasp his whistle with his fingertips, he put it to his mouth and blew a series of short blasts: the charge. Let Fenestela hear, and give chase, he prayed.

On they ran, a hundred paces into the forest, and another hundred. Here the trees were older and bigger, mighty gnarled trunks from an earlier age, when the German gods had reigned supreme over the land. Many had horned cattle skulls nailed at eye level; there were also human ones. The light dimmed, and the ground underfoot turned soft. Somewhere above a raven called. *Krrruk.*

This is Rome's hour, thought Tullus, not the Germans', curse them. Nonetheless, he slowed. An ambush by Arminius' warriors could mean the difference between success and failure. 'How many are we?' he threw over his shoulder.

'Ten, sir,' came the shouted reply. 'More are coming, I think.'

Ten. Shit, thought Tullus. He hadn't been able to count the number of men with Arminius, but it was more than he had. His hesitation was momentary. They had to press on. 'Stay close,' he ordered.

His suspicions bore fruit inside fifty paces. Half a dozen warriors came screaming to the attack, three from each side. 'Metilius, Dulcius. Stay with me,' cried Tullus. 'Third and fourth ranks, follow when you can!' Gambling that the warriors wouldn't expect him to break away, he broke into a sprint. By the time the enemy had realised his ploy, the seven remaining legionaries had engaged them. A brief rictus of satisfaction twisted Tullus' face, but it vanished as the track split. Footprints led off in both directions. You clever bastard, Arminius, thought Tullus, lurching to a stop. Pick the wrong way, and he would never catch his adversary. Divide his forces further, and the lone man risked being outnumbered.

'Which way?' he asked of Metilius and Dulcius. 'Any ideas?'

Metilius dropped to a knee by the left path. He peered at the confusion of footprints, muttering under his breath and probing the earth here and there with a finger. Moving to the second track, he did the same.

'Well?'

'This one, sir.' Metilius was pointing to the right.

'You're sure?' Urgency oozed from Tullus' voice.

'One set of prints are much deeper, sir.' Metilius saw Tullus' confusion. 'The eagle, sir. It's made of gold.'

'Of course!' Tullus shoved past Metilius. 'Come on!'

They ran.

A quarter of a mile.

Half.

By the time they'd covered a mile, Tullus was losing hope, and struggling, thanks to his injured toe. They were still on Arminius' trail – the footprints were plain to see – but they hadn't had even a single glimpse of their quarry. It was time for drastic measures. 'Metilius. Dulcius. Press ahead. I'll follow.'

They needed no second telling, and took off like a pair of hunting hounds.

Tullus cursed his pride for not giving the order long before. Sucking in a lungful of muggy air, he dropped to a walk. Catch your breath, man, he thought, or you won't be able to fight. A score of paces, and his heart rate had slowed. He broke into a lumbering run. Fifty paces, then walk. Twenty steps to recover, then run. In this manner, ignoring the pulsating pain from his toe, he covered perhaps a quarter of a mile.

Loud shouts drew his attention like that of a hovering hawk to a mouse. Fresh energy flowed through Tullus' veins, and he charged along the track, soon emerging on to a gentle slope that ran down to a river. A cry of triumph left his lips. The watercourse, wide and deep, had come to their aid. Four warriors – Arminius one of them – were trying to ford it. The first man was chest-deep, and perhaps a quarter of the way across. Buffeted by the strong current, weighed down by his armour, he was struggling to stay on his feet, which explained why Arminius, mail shirt off and the eagle clutched in his grasp, hadn't yet joined him. The third and fourth warriors had been acting as sentinels, guarding Arminius' back. They were yelling an alarm now, even as Metilius and Dulcius hared down the incline.

With a roar, Tullus charged after.

Shrewd to the last, Arminius laid down the eagle and joined his men. Kill one of the legionaries before he arrived, thought Tullus, and the Germans would maintain their numerical superiority. Cursing, he pushed his tired limbs to new efforts. To his relief, Metilius and Dulcius remained unhurt as he skidded in alongside, to face Arminius.

The six men drove at each other with grim purpose. Young and fit, Metilius and Dulcius held their own. Tullus, weary and in great pain with his toe, soon began to flag. More than a decade Tullus' junior, Arminius pressed home his attack with malevolent purpose. He began to taunt Tullus. 'Ready to die close to your eagle? So near, and yet so far!'

Tullus' anger burst into flames, and he pounded Arminius' shield with his sword, cracking it. His respite was momentary; Arminius came powering back at him, shield boss and blade performing a deadly one-two dance that threatened injury or death with every blow.

'Degmar – it's fucking Degmar, sir,' cried Metilius.

Tullus' eyes flickered to the side. Astonishment seized him. It *was* Degmar, fighting with Arminius. His gaze shot back to his front, just as Arminius barrelled into him. The air was driven from Tullus' lungs with a loud oomph. Winded, he stumbled backwards to fall first on his arse, and then his back. He had the wit to clutch his shield tight, protection for his body, but his sword fell from his grip. Arminius crouched over him with a fierce grin, and Tullus knew death was at hand.

Arminius drew back his right arm.

Tullus' right hand scrabbled in the dirt for his blade, but it wasn't there. What a stupid way to die, he thought.

An inarticulate cry split the air. Arminius staggered as someone crashed into him, then fell.

'Up! Get up!' A hand appeared in his vision, beckoned.

Tullus took the grip and was heaved to his feet. To his astonishment, he found himself face-to-face with Degmar, who gave him a tight smile. 'Repaying my debt,' he said.

Before Tullus could speak, Degmar let out a quiet, surprised 'Ooh'. His lips twisted, and the strength left him. He slumped sideways, and Tullus saw that Arminius, recovering his footing, had stabbed Degmar in the groin, below his mail shirt. Still weaponless, unable to save Degmar, Tullus shuffled back on a desperate search for his sword. He retrieved it just in time to face a triumphant Arminius. A few steps behind, Degmar had dropped to one knee. From between his cupped hands, bright red blood gouted.

Driven now by anguish, Tullus advanced. 'Come on, you whoreson!'

'Old man!' sneered Arminius.

'Here I am, sir!' Crimson smears across his face, Metilius materialised by Tullus' right shoulder before Arminius could close in.

'Where's Dulcius?' hissed Tullus.

'Cutting apart the savage who was in the river, sir.'

Tullus' spirits soared. 'Fortune turns against you, Arminius.'

Disappointment filled Arminius' eyes. He tensed.

Tullus intuited his purpose – to try and seize the standard. 'Forward, Metilius, quickly!' They drove at Arminius, shoulder to shoulder, forcing him into the water, leaving the eagle behind. He floundered, fell and was taken by the current. His head appeared a short distance away, and went under again. Tullus hoped Arminius might drown, but wasn't surprised to see his enemy break the surface again and with powerful strokes swim to the opposite side. Arminius clambered out, threw Tullus a vengeful glance and vanished among the trees.

Too weary to contemplate pursuit, unprepared to risk his men's lives and overcome with emotion, Tullus bent to pick up the eagle. The legion number had been hacked off, but he knew the standard for the Eighteenth's because of a deep scratch on one of the eagle's wings, damage sustained once when the aquilifer had fallen, smacking it off the side of a building.

With a shock, Tullus remembered Degmar. The warrior lay unmoving amid a puddle of his own blood.

'Hold this.' Tullus pressed the standard into a delighted Metilius' hands.

Degmar stirred at Tullus' approach. 'You have the eagle?' he whispered.

'Aye.' Kneeling, Tullus gripped Degmar's hand. There was a weak response.

Tullus' joy at recovering the eagle was leavened by a jagged grief. Degmar had saved his life and those of fifteen of his men in the savage aftermath of Arminius' ambush. Now he was dying, and there was nothing to be done: the quantity of blood around and under him was too great. Tullus leaned closer. 'In different times, we could have been friends.'

'We still can be, on the other side.' A shallow cough. 'I'll wait for you.'

Tears blurred Tullus' vision. 'I would be honoured.'

'I'm cold. So cold.' Degmar's gaze had gone out of focus. 'Tullus?'

'I'm here.' Tullus squeezed Degmar's hand tight. 'I'm here with you, brother.'

Degmar's lips twitched. 'Broth—'

Like that, he was gone, and Tullus' heart wrenched. He knelt for a time in silence, wishing that things might have been different, and then, gentle as if he were moving a stray hair from Sirona's face, he closed Degmar's staring eyes.

Chapter XLI

﷽﷽﷽

T ullus speared the staff bearing the eagle into the earth, standing it upright. He, Metilius and Dulcius fell to their knees before the golden bird. No one spoke. Choked sobs escaped Tullus' throat, but he felt no shame. Metilius and Dulcius were also weeping. After so long, after so much suffering and so many deaths, the Eighteenth's eagle was theirs once more.

Thank you, great Jupiter. Gratitude, mighty Mars. Fortuna, you are the finest goddess of all, Tullus thought. Each of you will have a prize bull on my return to Vetera. He lifted his gaze to the eagle. Despite its years of captivity, the damage sustained, it had lost none of its majesty. The hairs on Tullus' arms prickled. The eagle seemed to be staring at him – it *was*. Imperious as ever, its gaze penetrated his soul. Soldier of Rome, he fancied it said. You have ended my captivity. For this I am grateful.

Old grief surged in Tullus, and his eyes closed. For the ten-thousandth time, he relived the ambush seven years before. Rain. Wind. Thunder. Marsh. Trees. Mud, mud everywhere. The Germans' chanting, coming unseen from the forest. Volleys of spears humming in. Naked berserkers. Hordes of screaming warriors. Men – *his* men – dying in droves, no matter how he tried to keep them alive.

Battered and bloodied, Tullus and those who yet lived struggled on, hoping against hope to survive. He hadn't been there when the Eighteenth's eagle had been taken. Senior centurion of the Second Cohort, it hadn't been his job to be with the iconic standard, but that hadn't stopped the pain and shame of its loss cutting like a blade. In those moments of black despair, Tullus had wanted to lie down and die. His soldiers' lives, which he'd held in the palm of his hand, had stopped him. Without him, as Fenestela had snarled, they would have perished. And yet I saved so few, thought Tullus, scourged by shame.

His eyes were drawn again to the eagle. He started. Around the golden bird, shadowy figures loomed. Afer and Vitellius. Piso, and scores of his men, too numerous to count. Convinced they had come to curse him, Tullus quailed. Nothing happened, and he gathered the courage to stare more closely. To his astonishment, the ghosts were smiling. Giving nods of approval. Some were saluting. You recovered the eagle, said a voice in his head. The Eighteenth's honour has been restored.

Tullus hung his head. Tears flowed down his cheeks. I did my best, he thought. It's all I have ever done. He heard no reply, but a sense of acceptance washed over him, as if his dead soldiers were giving their blessing. Unmanned, Tullus wept like a child. 'You were good boys,' he whispered. 'Good boys.'

It was some time before his tears stopped. Drained, spent, Tullus wasn't surprised that his men's shades had vanished. The eagle was again a carved piece of gold. Magnificent, but inanimate. He studied it for a long time, but it did not move. Its fierce gaze was fixed into the distance. Tullus wondered if the whole scenario had been a figment of his imagination.

The warm glow in his heart – a long-wished-for acceptance – meant that it didn't matter either way.

Tullus didn't care that they were deep in Germania rather than in Rome, or that he had only a cohort as escort – their return to the army felt like a triumph. He was the general, not carried in a chariot but pacing proudly before his cheering men with the eagle borne aloft. Beard bristling with delight, Fenestela strode beside him. These were moments to remember for the rest of their days, thought Tullus.

A cavalry patrol rode closer to see what was going on. Spotting the eagle, the riders shouted in appreciation. The legionaries of a scavenging party mobbed his men, promising to buy them wine. Even an official messenger paused to have an admiring look. It was he, Tullus decided later, who must have first spread the news among the main body of troops. The tumultuous welcome as they neared the marching column was heart-warming. In soldiers' minds, the recovery of an eagle lost in battle ranked higher than almost anything, but Tullus hadn't expected trumpets to sound, or for the men in their path to be ordered off the track.

'What's this?' he asked a grinning centurion.

'Everyone knows what you've done, primus pilus. You're a hero. Take the eagle to Germanicus – he'll be waiting.' With a flourish, the centurion swept his arm in the direction of the governor's position.

Tullus glanced at his men. They were beaming from ear to ear. Fenestela chuckled. Tullus smiled – and laughed out loud. They had done it. They had fucking *done* it! He squared his shoulders, gave a firm nod to the centurion, and called over his shoulder, 'Follow!'

The walk thereafter passed as if in a dream. Tullus' ears rang with cheers, with loud cries of 'Roma Victrix!' and 'Germanicus!' Soldiers chanted 'Eighteenth! Eighteenth!' which brought fresh tears to his eyes. When they reached the Fifth, the shouts became 'Tullus! Tullus!' His heart swelled by the unexpected acclaim, he nodded his thanks until his neck ached. He swigged from a wine skin offered by an optio he knew in the Twenty-First, and accepted claps on the back and praise from every centurion he came across. Tullus thought he would burst with pride. Small wonder triumphant generals had slaves to whisper in their ears that they were but mortal men, he thought.

His most public recognition came from Germanicus. Rather than wait for Tullus to approach, he slid from his horse and came striding to meet him, arms wide. 'This is a joyous moment! Well met, Tullus.'

Tullus planted the standard and came to attention. 'Sir!'

Germanicus came very close. His reverent fingers traced the outline of the eagle's head and its raised wings. 'You're sure this belonged to the Eighteenth?'

'Yes, sir.' Tullus explained about the scratch.

'I'm glad. The Seventeenth's eagle will come home one day, but this standard deserves to be yours. You have my congratulations.'

'If it weren't for you, sir, none of it would have happened.'

Germanicus acknowledged the praise with a dip of his chin. 'And without soldiers like you, I could do nothing.'

Tullus flushed like a beardless youth.

Germanicus clapped him on the shoulder. 'Shall we take your eagle back to Vetera?'

'Aye, sir!' This, thought Tullus, was the best suggestion he'd heard in his life.

Chapter XLII

▨▨▨

Ten days had passed since Arminius' abortive attempt to seize the Marsi tribe's eagle, and his mood was as dark as the lowering clouds. Dusk was falling as he stood by the edge of a large lake, deep in Cherusci territory. Close by, preparations for a long-awaited ceremony were well under way. Hammers rang as cauldrons were beaten flat. Armour was being cut up and spear shafts broken. Tethered horses grazed scrubby grass; the youths watching over them waited to be called forward. Six naked, ill-treated prisoners – five Chatti, one Roman – sat in miserable silence, guarded by a score of men. Those who had come to watch – hundreds of warriors, from various factions of the Cherusci tribe – had positioned themselves in a loose half-circle around the priests, who were chanting and praying to Donar.

Arminius saw none of the unfolding spectacle, did not feel the bites of the swarming midges. Eyes fixed on the blurred junction between sky and land, he stood, unmoving as a statue. Since the defeat at the Angrivarian wall, Maelo's death and the shattering of his alliance, things had gone from bad to worse. Thwarted by Mallovendus, then outmanoeuvred by Tullus, he had also lost most of the hundred warriors who'd been with him on his mission to capture the eagle. His humiliations seemed without end. Thunder crashed overhead, and Arminius stirred, throwing an angry glance at the blue-black sky. Everything I do, you turn against me, great Donar. Why?

The noise rumbled on. Light flashed deep in the clouds. One of the priests uttered a loud cry of 'Donar!' which was taken up with enthusiasm by his companions and the crowd. Unsettled by the chant, the horses flattened their ears and skittered to and fro. Aware that their time was approaching, the prisoners cowered.

Arminius' scowl hardened. His appeals, the priests' devotion and the sacrifices taking place would make no difference. The thunder god would remain silent, as he did so often. It was bitter to stand here in ignominious defeat, easy to think that Donar had never truly spoken to him. Perhaps the raven that had helped him to find the last eagle had been seeking fresh meat, and nothing more. Tudrus' offering of his own life had been an empty gesture, a pointless suicide aided by the priest.

Arminius' temper rose. Why bother with this contrived ritual? Gathering phlegm in his mouth, he made to spit but, despite his overwhelming cynicism, he could not do it. Maelo would have told him that testing the gods' patience was a bad idea, and even if none of the priests saw, omniscient Donar would. Grief lashed Arminius at the memory of his second-in-command, who was buried not far from this spot. His funeral had been magnificent, befitting a warrior of his stature. Arminius had stayed by the grave long after the other mourners had gone. Trapped in a black pit of despair, much of him had wished to exchange places with Maelo, but a white-hot desire for revenge – on Germanicus, on his legions, on Mallovendus – had held him back. That, and the fact that Maelo – bloody-minded as he was – would have laughed in Arminius' face for wanting to die rather than carry on.

Alone, this driving emotion could not grant success. Nor could his charisma. Like it or not, he still needed Donar's help. A sour expression twisted his face. The thunder god was listening to his thoughts this very moment, like as not, and laughing. All-powerful, all-seeing and -knowing, the deities pleased themselves. People served as mere playthings, their petty desires ignored. This is the way of things, Arminius told himself. The gods are what they are. Keep faith for long enough, offer them plenty of sacrifices, and they *can* make wishes come true.

'It is time,' called a voice.

Arminius turned. The oldest priest, a wrinkled creature with sparse white hair, was standing next to the altar, a large, flat slab of rock close to the water's edge. Pits and dark stains in its surface provided mute evidence of what was practised here. A timber platform had been erected close by, and a large bronze cauldron placed on the ground by one of its sides. Priests and acolytes clustered around, knives and ropes ready in their hands. Several of the prisoners began to wail. Arminius felt no pity. All that mattered was for Donar to be pleased by the offerings.

First to die were the horses. Led one by one to the altar, they had their throats opened. Wooden buckets were used to collect the blood, some of which was daubed on the prisoners' faces. Acolytes poured the rest over the stone altar and into the lake. A large red cloud spread outwards, staining the water. Arminius was minded of the Carthaginian general Hannibal's soldiers at Lake Trasimene, more than two centuries before. With Donar's help, he might do the same one day.

Gervas appeared by his side as the prisoners were urged to their feet. 'There should have been more.'

'You did well to take six men,' said Arminius with heart. After the clash with Tullus' soldiers, the last thing on his mind had been taking prisoners. Gervas, determined and stubborn, had insisted it was a good idea as they travelled east. Bone-weary, spirits low, Arminius had given him permission to go out at night with a few men. The half-dozen captives were the result: sentries over-powered and unfortunates who'd strayed from their patrols to answer a call of nature. 'Their lives will make a fine offering to the god.' I hope, he thought.

Gervas nodded.

The Chatti were driven to the base of the platform. Alone among his fellows to scorn death, a giant of a man offered himself to the waiting priest. Bundled up on to its flat surface, he lay down and peered into the bronze cauldron. Arminius felt a sneaking admiration – he couldn't imagine presenting his throat to the executioner's knife so easily, nor allowing an acolyte to grip him by the hair. A hush fell as the priest asked Donar in a sing-song voice to accept the prisoner's life.

Smooth as if he'd just been whetting the blade, the priest drew back his right arm. The man's body gave a violent jerk, and his feet drummed off the platform. Blood gushed in torrents, pattering into the cauldron. A reverent 'Ahhhhh' rose from the crowd. The acolyte held tight, keeping the corpse's head up and the blood vessels open. Time passed. Not until the flow had eased to mere drips did the priest move again. Dipping a crook-fingered hand into the cauldron, he swirled about in the blood.

How can he see anything but red liquid and froth? Arminius wondered, but superstition kept him quiet.

The corpse was rolled to the platform's edge, allowing the priest to open the belly. Soon glistening loops of grey-pink intestine had been laid out for inspection. The priest ran them though his hands like strings of sausage, mouth moving in a silent conversation. 'I see no signs of disease,' he announced at length.

'Ahhhhh,' went the crowd.

Fools. Arminius was unable to stop the thought.

'He was a brave man,' said the priest. 'His blood is clean, and pure. His bowels are healthy. The signs are good.'

'Nothing I couldn't have said myself,' muttered Arminius. He noticed Gervas' shocked expression. 'It's true. The warrior volunteered to die first. His blood is red, and it flowed fast. He was young and healthy, so his guts are normal.'

Gervas shook his head. 'You risk angering not just Donar, but the other gods.'

Arminius said nothing.

Blood-soaked, steeped in ritual, the ceremony continued. The four remaining Chatti warriors died one after another. Two cried like whipped children as they were manhandled to the platform's edge, and were quietened only by the priest's sharp blade. Their blood was pronounced sour, and their intestines unclean. Donar was asked to forgive their cowardice.

Cynicism aside, Arminius couldn't help but hope that the last pair of warriors went to their deaths well. Relief swelled in his chest as they did just that, silent, with clenched jaws and proud faces. In a loud voice, the priest pronounced the omens he saw in their blood and entrails to be propitious. 'Donar is pleased!' he said, eliciting fierce nods of approval from the crowd.

The Roman prisoner was the last to be dragged forward. Here was one of his people's bitterest enemies, thought Arminius, one of those who had butchered thousands of Donar's believers. The thunder god had to approve of his death.

Arminius looked on with satisfaction as the Roman showed his courage by walking up the steps to the platform and scorning the acolytes' helping hands. A moment later, however, the prisoner refused to lie down. The lead acolyte barked an order, but he appeared not to hear. Angry, the priest stared up at the Roman from his position by the cauldron. 'Down!' he ordered.

'Never,' came the reply in Latin. 'Cocksucker.'

Arminius sensed the looming danger, but he was too far away to stop what happened next.

Teeth bared, the Roman drew back his right leg and kicked the priest in the face. His hobnailed sandal smashed teeth, broke bone. The screaming priest flailed backwards, colliding with the altar. He fell and, with a solid clunk, the back of his head hit the stone. Limp as a greybeard's prick, he slid off the altar to lie in a tangle of limbs. Dead.

With Gervas on his heels, Arminius sprinted to the platform. 'Seize him!'

The shocked acolytes grabbed the laughing Roman, who did not resist.

Arminius checked the old man's neck for a pulse. 'He's gone,' he snarled at the first priest to approach, a younger, bearded version of his expired superior.

'This is a bad omen,' intoned the priest.

Arminius wanted to slit his scrawny throat. The situation *had* to be salvaged. Fear was spreading through those watching – he could see it. In a low voice, he said, 'Tell them that the ill fortune brought on by the old man's death will be washed away by the sacrifice of the Roman.'

A shocked look. 'It is not for me to predict the future. I can only speak of what I see in the prisoner's blood and entrails.'

'You can say what you fucking like,' hissed Arminius, thrusting his face into the priest's. 'Think I don't know that?'

The priest took a step back, his colour rising. 'Sacrilege!'

Arminius hesitated, but only for a moment. Something positive had to be said as the Roman was sent to the underworld, he thought. Good omens had to be predicted from his blood and organs. If they weren't, his warriors' morale would plummet. They might even refuse to fight the legions in the spring. He could not – would not – let that happen to his own people. Arminius abandoned caution. 'Listen, fool. The Roman is going to die, slowly and painfully. You will tell the warriors that Donar likes his agony. When his blood flows into the cauldron, it will steam with the god's fury at the empire's brutality. His organs will be healthy, and foretell Rome's defeat at our hands.'

The priest wasn't beaten yet. 'And if I won't say that?'

'You'll die in your bed. Maybe not tonight, but it *will* happen – and you'll lose your balls before your throat is cut.' Arminius' grey eyes bored into the priest's horrified ones. 'Understand?'

A jerky nod.

'Good.' Arminius flashed a broad grin at the acolytes restraining the Roman. 'We were deciding the best way for this filth to die. Open his belly first. Take his eyes second. Then you can break his arms and legs.'

Attention diverted, the acolytes shoved the prisoner down on to the platform. He kicked and struggled to no avail.

Arminius folded his arms. I did this for you, great Donar, he thought. Accept this Roman's suffering and death as but the start of what I will offer you. With your help, I will raise another army from among the tribes, and destroy Germanicus—

'What in all the gods' names was that about?' Gervas spoke in a whisper.

Arminius gave a little shrug. 'I was making sure the right omens were revealed.'

'You can't do that!'

Arminius bridled. 'I need my people confident in my leadership, not terrified because an idiot priest didn't see what was coming to him. With their spears at my back, I can forge another alliance to fight Rome.'

'You're not the only one who can unite the tribes!'

'No one else is capable.' Arminius gave Gervas a withering look. 'No one else has the ability to defeat the legions.' If he'd been paying attention, he would have seen again the odd expression that had skimmed over Gervas' face as they'd searched for Maelo's body, but Arminius had been carried away by his enthusiasm, his all-consuming desire for victory over the empire.

The omens for the future would be good, he thought, listening to the Roman's screams. Come the spring, the tribes would join with the Cherusci once more and when Germanicus' legions crossed the river, victory would be theirs.

Arminius could feel it in his bones.

Chapter XLIII

᭤᭤᭤

A month had passed since the army's return over the Rhenus, and autumn had the land full in its grip. Mornings were fine, but damp and chilly. Dew lingered in shady spots until after midday. Dusk fell early. The leaves on the trees had turned red-gold, and the bushes were heavy with blackberries and early sloes. Storms and rainy weather were common. Today was typical: cold, grey and overcast with frequent showers.

Tullus was at the heart of a little procession, leading the other mourners towards the fort's main gate. He'd been honoured when Piso's tent mates had asked him to take charge of the ceremony.

At the front strode two legionaries in plain tunics and metalled belts, the guards who would clear their path if needs be. They carried clubs, in place of the axes and rods borne by the bodyguards who marched at rich men's funerals. Next came a pair of musicians, trumpeters from Tullus' centuries. It was normal to have flute-players as well, but Metilius' opinion that they had no place at a soldier's burial had prevailed. The trumpets' harsh tones alone had accompanied them on their sad walk from their barrack building.

Fresh grief beat at Tullus. It wasn't a real funeral; Piso's body lay in a hidden grave deep in Germania. Unable to mark his death then in more than a simple fashion, he and Piso's comrades were putting things right with this act of remembrance. There were no hired mourners, women with white-painted faces to keen and tear their hair in make-believe sorrow at Piso's passing – that wasn't the tradition among soldiers – but Tullus had had three wax death masks made to represent Piso, his grandfather and great-grandfather. They weren't the best resemblance of Piso, let alone his long-dead ancestors, but they would do. The gods would understand, thought Tullus.

Behind the musicians, a soldier carried the Piso mask. He made constant lewd jokes and acted the fool, in the process keeping evil spirits at bay. Piso had had no slaves, no freedmen – these would have been next in the procession. After came the soldiers pretending to be his grandfather and great-grandfather, wax masks hiding their faces from view. Even though there was no corpse to bury, Tullus had paid for a carved stone casket, large enough to contain some of Piso's personal effects and the offerings made by his tent mates and friends. Borne on an ox cart and flanked by four more soldiers, it preceded Tullus, Fenestela, Metilius with Macula on a lead, Dulcius and the rest of Piso's comrades from the Eighteenth. Scores of soldiers from the Fifth brought up the rear.

Whether it brought bad luck to wear fine clothing or not, Tullus could not be sure, but the traditions around funerals were deep-rooted. He and the others were dressed in just their tunics, metalled belts and hobnailed sandals. Cloaks afforded them protection against rain and the chill wind; daggers were their only weapons. Deep in thought, remembering Piso, they walked with slow and measured pace, keeping up with those in front.

It didn't matter that the soldiers watching hadn't known Piso. Recognising the procession for what it was, they broke off from their tasks and stood with bowed heads. 'Swift passage to the other side, brother,' many called. 'Rest well, brother.' Officers also showed their respect, although Tullus suspected that was because of his presence. Piso would have basked in the acknowledgement, he thought.

'One of your men, primus pilus?' Tubero's voice.

His face blank, Tullus looked, found the legate watching him from astride his horse. A gaggle of staff officers and servants trailed in his wake. 'Yes, sir.'

'He fell in the summer campaign?'

'Aye, sir. Piso had been with me for years. He was in the Eighteenth.'

Tubero's eyebrows arched. 'A good soldier?'

'He was, sir. Just about to make tesserarius too.' He once left dog shit everywhere in your quarters, thought Tullus, and I wager he's laughing at you right now.

'He will be missed, I have no doubt.' With a stiff nod, Tubero rode past.

Tullus saluted. You won't be, he thought, revelling again in the news that Tubero was to return to Rome, where a life in politics beckoned. He could backstab to his heart's content there, and no soldiers would be harmed.

The mourners neared the main gate, where the sentries on duty were from the Fifth. Seeing the procession approach, the centurion in charge had his soldiers stand along the rampart as if on parade. Calling them to attention, he gave the casket a firm salute.

With a grateful look, Tullus passed into the gateway, but his despondency returned at once. Gods, Piso, if you had just killed the boy, you'd still be here, he thought. The screams of the child he'd had crucified after Piso's death rang in his ears, and Tullus grimaced. His sleep since that traumatic day hadn't been good, often broken by nightmares of the two piteous shapes on the crosses, and the burning longhouse behind. Whether it had been the right thing to do, he was no longer sure, but what was done couldn't be undone. The dead couldn't be brought back, and life went on.

He also had much to be thankful for. Fenestela was alive, as were the rest of his men. Sirona and Artio were safe and well. The eagle too was secure in the fort's shrine. There was talk that Germanicus would petition the emperor to rescind the ban on survivors of Varus' legions entering Italy. Arminius had survived, but his alliance was shattered, and rumours from over the river spoke of a swelling tide of resentment towards him. The next year's campaign into Germania would crush the last of the tribal resistance. After that, thought Tullus, he would consider retirement – maybe even marriage.

Under the great stone arch they went, out into the blustery autumnal air. Off to the right and past the downward slope of the gentle hill ran the wide, sinuous silver band of the Rhenus. Patrol vessels were visible on the water, tasked with ensuring there was no repeat of the night attack earlier that year. Scores of ships were moored at the wooden jetties, their crews repairing storm damage from the voyage home. The far bank, tree-bound and forbidding, was empty of human life. There'd be someone watching the fort, like as not, but Tullus wasn't concerned. They could scheme and connive to their hearts' content, but any attempt to cross the river would come at a heavy price.

'Sir.'

Metilius' voice brought Tullus back to the present. He was astonished to see Sirona, Artio and Scylax joining their party. They had been waiting a short distance from the front gate. Sirona was clad in a fine woven dress of dark red; Artio had her best clothes on. Scylax's coat had been brushed until it shone. Caught off guard, Tullus managed a surprised 'Sirona?'

She bustled in beside him. 'Piso was a good man. He didn't often get blind drunk, like some of your soldiers. I liked him. So did Artio, and Piso loved Scylax. We're here to pay our respects.'

Tullus' first thought had been to ask them to leave, but the set of Sirona's jaw and Artio's reddened eyes checked him. They had a right to be here, he decided. The women hadn't known Piso over well, but the young soldier had been like family to him, just as Sirona and Artio were. By extension, the two women were grieving his loss. 'Thank you,' he whispered.

Sirona answered by looping her arm into his. Artio took Sirona's other hand.

Fenestela gave Tullus a look of genuine pleasure. Metilius and the rest seemed pleased too, which increased Tullus' self-consciousness. He wasn't going to shame Sirona by shaking her off, though, so he raised his chin and walked on. Despite his embarrassment, it didn't take long before he began to feel good. A tiny smile creased Tullus' face. In all his career, he could never have seen himself like this.

Some hundred paces beyond the fort's defensive ditch, the first tombstones began to appear. Bodies could not be buried within a settlement's walls, and the road to the *vicus* was lined with the graves of soldiers who had served in the local legions. One day, Tullus himself would lie there. Not today, however, and not, he hoped, for many years.

His eyes wandered over the stone slabs with their painted carvings of legionaries, cavalrymen and officers. Some of the dead he'd known, more than he felt comfortable with, truth be told. This was the price of having served in Vetera for upwards of two decades. At least these men have graves, Tullus thought, not like his men in the forest. He pushed the dark memories away. Today was about honouring Piso's life, remembering him as he'd been. They would also celebrate the living, those who were here, who had survived the cauldron of blood, mud and death.

As if she were reading his mind, Sirona squeezed his arm. Tullus threw her a grateful glance.

Half a mile from the fort, the procession came to a halt. The trumpeters blew a final series of notes. The litter-bearers laid down their load. In silence, the mourners formed a part-circle around a new tombstone, its fresh colours vivid and eye-catching. Germanicus hadn't paid for this one – Piso's comrades had seen to that.

With Metilius and Dulcius, Tullus had chosen where it should be erected, a spot with a fine view of the fort, the vicus and the Rhenus. Most important, it was beside the memorial to Vitellius, Piso's friend who had died the previous year. Tullus had seen the stone several times in the mason's workshop during its commission, the last time only the day before, but he hadn't expected the emotional punch of standing in front of it: tangible, unrelenting proof that Piso was dead.

Between two carved columns, under an angled roof, Piso stared out at the world. He was in full armour, shield in one hand, javelin in the other. Every piece of his equipment had been carved with startling accuracy, and well painted. Tullus approved. You would have made a good tesserarius, he thought.

'We come to remember our brother, Piso,' he said. 'Some of you knew him better than others, but you all agree that he was a good soldier. Brave too, and not scared of risking his life for another. Piso would do anything for his friends. He loved a joke and, at times, his sense of humour took him into dangerous situations. I could say something about his dog Macula and a certain legate's tent, but discretion is advised, even here.' Tullus' gaze moved over his smiling men.

He let their affection for Piso swell for a moment before continuing, 'Piso's death was unfortunate. It needn't have happened, some might say. In the days following his passing, I was of that mind. I think differently now. It is not for we mortals to decide who lives and who dies. The gods give and they take away, whenever they please. Many say that the deities each of us favours in life are responsible for our deaths. Piso was fond of Fortuna. I see you nodding – most of you will have lost money to him at dice one time or another. I think that Fortuna, fickle as she is, decided to bring Piso home. Rather than grieve, fill your minds with an image of him on the other side, fleecing our comrades of their coin.'

Everyone smiled. Metilius managed a chuckle.

Tullus studied the words inscribed under the image of Piso, and slowly began to read them out loud. ' "To the gods of the underworld. Marcus Piso, of the Fabian voting tribe, from Mutina. Soldier of the Fifth and Eighteenth Legions, he lived for twenty-seven years. He fell in Germania." ' Tullus' voice caught. ' "His comrades had this stone completed." '

Quiet fell. Heads were bowed. The wind hissed through the short grass. Scylax whined, and was copied by Macula, as if they too were mourning. Tullus caught Metilius' eye, and nodded. Piso's remaining tent mates slid ropes under the casket and, together, moved to the edge of the deep, square hole that had been dug in front of the tombstone. The mourners arranged themselves around the grave. Hand over hand, Piso's comrades lowered the casket into the earth; then, with gentle tugs, they freed their lines. Sombre-faced, Metilius and Dulcius began to shovel dirt into the hole. A sob escaped Artio, and Tullus laid a comforting hand on her shoulder. He was thankful for the warmth of Sirona's touch on his other side.

'Rest in peace, brother,' said Metilius when the ground had been levelled. He bent his neck, a signal for everyone to do the same.

Eyes closed, Tullus remembered his men who had died, not just in Arminius' ambush and the campaigns since, but in the long years since he'd been promoted to the centurionate. There were so many that Tullus could not put a number to them. Good men, for the most part. Fine soldiers, who had followed his orders and stood shoulder to shoulder with their comrades to the end. Piso had been among the best. Tullus couldn't have asked for any more than that. You will never be forgotten, brother, he thought. Rest in peace.

The silence lasted a long while.

At last, feeling the chill, Tullus spoke. 'Time to toast Piso's shade. Who's with me?'

A loud chorus of approval rose.

'To the Ox and Plough,' said Tullus. 'There's an open bar — on me.'

'Piso would have loved that, sir,' said Metilius, grinning.

'He would.' How Tullus wished that Piso were standing there with the rest. The impossibility of the wish brought back his despondency as he led the mourners to the road. Doing his best not to show it, he smiled and pretended to listen to Artio's chatter.

Tullus had not gone far when the towering banks of grey cloud overhead parted. On a whim, he turned. Sunlight lanced down on to Piso's tombstone, illuminating his representation.

Tullus' heart warmed.

Piso was watching — he was sure of it.

Epilogue

Spring, AD 20

⌜⌐⌐

Deep in Germania

A massive fire blazed in the centre of the packed longhouse, sending waves of heat towards the rectangle of tables ranged around it. The pig suspended on a spit over the flames had been cooking since dawn; the room was filled with a rich, mouth-watering smell. Red-faced women served platters of steaming meat to the gathered warriors as fast as the flesh could be sliced off the bone. Hunting dogs skulked underfoot, seeking out fallen scraps. Boys moved in an endless procession from the barrels stacked against one side wall, carrying mugs of beer to the thirsty men. Drunken singing, laughter and shouted conversations competed in a deafening cacophony of sound.

Gervas had arrived in the Chatti settlement earlier in the day, one of a select band of followers chosen to accompany Arminius on his quest for allies. It had been a never-ending task since their defeat by Germanicus' legions at the Angrivarian wall. Futility coursed through Gervas' veins. They were no longer rallying the tribes against the Romans. As year after year passed without another invasion, it seemed that – for whatever reason – the legions might never cross the Rhenus again in force. Arminius' purpose now was to become king of the tribes. *Why then do I still serve him?* Gervas wondered. It was a question he had asked of himself more and more often of recent months.

And yet Arminius was dear to him now. Lacking purpose after the Romans' victory four years before, eager for a father figure since Gerulf's death, Gervas had been happy to stay with Arminius rather than return to his own tribe. The Cherusci chieftain was arrogant and mercurial, it was true, but he was also generous and warm-hearted, and quick to praise. During the springs and summers spent riding between the tribes' territories, seeking allies, Gervas had become Arminius' most trusted follower. Lavished with attention, he had buried his suspicion that his leader had been responsible for Gerulf's death. His misgivings returned now and then, but enjoying his new, exalted position, Gervas ignored them.

He shifted position on the hard bench, trying in vain to overhear Arminius' conversation with Adgandestrius, chieftain of a large faction of the Chatti tribe. Gervas' position – midway along one side of the rectangle – and the din made by at least four score drunken warriors made his task impossible. Arminius' stormy expression and jabbing forefinger marked him out as an unhappy man. He was never fully content, thought Gervas with bubbling resentment, unless people obeyed his wishes.

It was clear that Adgandestrius, a weasel-faced type with red hair, wasn't bending the knee – even now, he shouted something at Arminius and hammered a fist off the table, sending plates and cups flying.

How else do you expect him to react, Arminius? thought Gervas. The tribes do not need one leader. They do not want a king.

Sour-faced, Arminius rose from his seat and pushed his way through the gaggle of servants ranged behind his host and the other chieftains.

Assuming that Arminius was emptying a full bladder, Gervas returned his attention to his platter of meat. His cup of beer was almost untouched; he preferred to remain in control of his senses while those around him descended into drunkenness. Perhaps the disagreement was over something other than acknowledging Arminius' supremacy, he told himself.

'Enjoying the feast?' Arminius' breath, hot and beery, was in his ear.

Surprised, Gervas turned, pulling the expected smile. 'Aye, well enough. How goes it with Adgandestrius?'

'Fool. He's a fool.' Spittle flew from Arminius' lips. 'He won't listen to me. Says the Chatti are happy as they are.'

Gervas should have held his peace – Arminius was drunk – but could hold back no longer. 'Maybe he's right.'

'Eh?' Arminius' bloodshot eyes bored into Gervas'. 'Right?'

'The answer's the same from every chieftain. They'll follow you against the Romans, or if it will help their quarrel with another tribe, but they don't want you to lead them.' Gervas hesitated, then said, 'Our peoples bridle against the mere idea of kingship, Arminius.'

'You're wrong. Earlier on, three chieftains sought my counsel. They're unhappy with Adgandestrius. If I help to depose him, they'll support my claim to leadership of the Chatti tribe.'

Gervas didn't want to believe what he was hearing. 'Depose him?'

With a wolf's smile, Arminius drew a sly finger across his throat. 'You'll help, won't you?'

Despite the longhouse's heat, Gervas shivered. Then a white-hot rage filled him. Arminius had just indirectly admitted to murdering Gerulf. Gervas could see him, exasperated by Gerulf's combative nature, giving Maelo the order. I've been blind these four years, he thought. Blind and deaf.

'Later on tonight, we'll find the right moment.' Arminius leaned closer. 'With me?'

'Of course. I'll watch for your signal.'

'Good lad.' Arminius tousled his hair, and in a gruff voice said, 'You're like a son to me.'

Despite his fury, a lump formed in Gervas' throat, preventing an answer. He nodded.

'I'm off outside. Nature calls.' Arminius weaved off.

Gervas warred with himself for the briefest of moments. Arminius deserved no pity, he decided, memories of Gerulf bright in his mind. Being argumentative didn't merit being smothered in a snowdrift. Blood runs thicker than water, Gervas thought, always.

He waited until Arminius had gone outside. Then, fingertips brushing the handle of his dagger, he sauntered towards the nearest door.

Author's Note

❖❖❖

Writing an account of the ambush in the Teutoburg Forest – a story which I hope you have read, or will read, in *Eagles at War* – was something I had wanted to do for years. Cataclysmic though it was, the clash wasn't the end of the Roman Empire's involvement in Germany. After licking its wounds, Rome turned its mind to revenge. Leaving the massacre perpetrated by Arminius unanswered would have been unthinkable to those in power.

The empire's response took years to come to fruition, for a number of reasons. A bloody war in Pannonia (roughly speaking, parts of modern-day Austria, Hungary and former Yugoslavia) had only ended in AD 9. Replacement legions had to be moved to the Rhine, and a new governor – Germanicus – found. Not until AD 14 and 15 was Rome ready to strike: *Hunting the Eagles* covered this period; this book recounts the events of AD 16. While I have fictionalised some parts of the story, I've also recreated the real-life, tumultuous events, and stuck to most historical details that have survived. I apologise now for any errors in the three books.

Many of the characters in this novel were real people; these include Germanicus, Lucius Seius Tubero, Stertinius, Aemilius, Publius Quinctilius Varus, Drusus, Caedicius, Arminius, Mallovendus, Segestes, Thusnelda, Thumelicus, Flavus and Adgandestrius. Even lowly soldiers such as Marcus Crassus Fenestela existed. Scylax is the name of a dog in a Roman play; Macula means 'Spot' in Latin: my attempt at Roman humour! Centurion Tullus is my invention; so too are the men of Tullus' century; the Germans

Maelo, Degmar, Gerulf, Horsa and Tudrus; and Sirona and Artio. The last women's names belong to ancient Gaulish goddesses.

It's frustrating that few real German tribal names of the time survive. Gerulf and Horsa date slightly later than the first century AD. I had to invent Osbert and Degmar. To make them as authentic as possible, I used name stems from the Dark Age era. Arminius, Inguiomerus, Mallovendus and Adgandestrius are clearly Romanised versions of German names. Arminius may have been called 'Armin' or 'Ermin' – we are not sure. When writing *Eagles at War*, my editor persuaded me to use Arminius; I hope this doesn't make him sound too Roman.

It's not known how many men survived the ambush on Varus' army. My invented figure of about two hundred may be correct, but it's possible far fewer men made it. Some legionaries were captured by the Germans and later ransomed back to their families. It was they who were banned from returning to Italy, not the men who'd fought free of the slaughter. In my mind, there would have been a stigma attached to being a survivor, but it's my fiction to include Tullus and his men in the injunction – as it is to have Germanicus ask the emperor to part-rescind the ban. The attempted assassination of Germanicus and the burning of the boats is also made up – it's probably thinking in too modern a way to wonder why the tribes didn't attempt such things. Battles were formulaic for the most part, and commando-style attacks almost unheard of.

Few details about legions' eagles remain – most information comes from gravestones and suchlike. Having numerals to differentiate one standard from another makes sense, but I don't know if this is how it was done.

In the autumn of AD 15, Germanicus rewarded the officers who had distinguished themselves on the just-finished campaign. Centurions and ordinary soldiers would have been recognised then as well – this was a perfect opportunity for me to have Tullus reinstated at last.

The military offensive of AD 16 happened much as I've written it. Silius was sent east first, then the ships around the North Sea coast. The siege of Aliso was real. We don't know why Germanicus visited the site of his father

Drusus' altar, but it's likely to have had a powerful resonance for him. Ill omens were predicted at the time Drusus had it erected, and his fate was as I described. The annual soldiers' foot race to and from his monument in Mogontiacum was real — I featured it in *The Shrine*, the free digital short story that serves as a prequel to *Eagles at War*. Find it and two others at all online retailers, and for those of you outside the UK, also on the writing platform wattpad.com.

Building bridges over rivers with boats was standard practice for Roman armies. It isn't known if this was what Drusus had intended, but the legions of Julius Caesar and others did so. Spartacus did force Roman prisoners to fight as gladiators, but I made up Germanicus' recreation of this. The capture of Arminius' pregnant wife Thusnelda is recorded; so is his confrontation with his brother Flavus at the River Weser/Visurgis. This may well have been when Arminius first learned he had a son — but we can't be sure. Thusnelda's fate after AD 16 is unclear but, in my mind, her life will not have been happy. Arminius' torment at his own helplessness can only be imagined.

A German traitor did make his way to the legions' camp the night before the clash at Idistaviso with news of Arminius' intentions, and a disguised Germanicus wandered the tent lines, seeking proof that his men's morale was high enough to fight the next day. The Roman battle formation is recorded, down to the positions of the Raeti, Vindelici and Gauls. Hostilities were opened by the cavalry under the command of Stertinius and Aemilius. Next to cross the river were the Batavians, who fell for Arminius' ruse. Eagles were seen over the forest, but I had Tullus rather than Germanicus use them to encourage the legionaries into battle. Chains were found afterwards, and assumed to have been ready for use on Roman prisoners. German warriors hiding from the enemy were shot from trees by auxiliary archers. (As an aside: note my use of 'shooting' in the text rather than 'firing', which implies the use of gunpowder. I have also avoided using 'towel', because this word wasn't known two thousand years ago.)

The Angrivarian wall may have been a physical structure, to separate the tribe's territory from a neighbouring people, or it may just have been a border. I decided to have Arminius order its construction; the boggy ground to one side allowed the Romans to make a flanking attack, but the bodies used to block their path are my gruesome addition. After the Romans' initial attacks faltered, Germanicus had his troops withdraw and the artillery deployed. The humming slingshot bullets are not my invention but a very recent discovery from a Roman site in Scotland. Surely a type of psychological warfare!

The mention of a wounded legionary talking about 'four sausages for an as' comes from a description of an injured soldier in World War One repeating the price of cabbage over and over. We don't know how many tribes fought with Arminius that day – perhaps less than I have described. He was troubled during the fighting by an injury received at Idistaviso, an encounter he had survived thanks to a Chatti auxiliary, who had let Arminius flee rather than take him captive. I researched toe injuries. Tullus *would* have been able to march after the loss of part of a toe. Tubero played a prominent part in the battle. Sadly, he wasn't killed, but went on to a career in politics. The sources tell us that only one legion was ordered away from the battlefield to construct the day's camp, but due to the huge size of the army, I felt two was more probable – this allowed me to have Tullus withdraw without disgrace.

After rewarding his soldiers for their service during the campaign, Germanicus set out for home by sea. His fleet was hit by storms as it sailed back to the mouth of the River Rhine. Many ships were wrecked; others were carried to Britain where the soldiers were taken hostage by local tribes. Keen to show their loyalty to Rome after the summer's bloody events, German coastal-dwelling tribes paid the ransoms demanded. I was tempted to have a number of chapters with Tullus in Britain, but had to stay focused on his attempt to recover the eagle – thanks to my editor Selina Walker for this! Several tribes did rise up after the defeat at the Angrivarian wall, among them the Marsi. Mallovendus revealed the location of the eagle in his possession, and a light detail of Roman troops recovered it. Tullus had to be in charge of this operation, but we have no real idea who led the mission. The third and last eagle taken from the Teutoburg Forest may have been with the Chauci, or perhaps the Chatti – it's not entirely clear from Cassius Dio's description. In *Eagles at War*, I had part of the Chauci tribe fight with Arminius, but that has not been attested. It was my device to explain their having an eagle for this book.

The last standard was retrieved in AD 41, during the reign of the emperor Claudius. Readers may wonder why Germanicus' campaigns into Germany didn't continue in AD 17 and beyond. Soon after his last campaign had ended, he was ordered by the emperor not to renew them. Tiberius was following directives from Augustus' will, which decreed that the empire's borders were to be left as they were at his death. Thereafter, Rome's presence east of the Rhine ebbed away, although in recent years the discovery of the third-century-AD Harzhorn battlefield has opened up the discussion.

There are so many other things to mention. I want you, the reader, to know that the richness of archaeological finds means that many of the objects and details referenced in my books are real. German warriors sang a fearsome war chant named by the Romans as the *barritus*. Although their sacrificial practices were savage – hanging, throat-slitting and drowning in bogs – they were no different to other peoples from northern Europe. Their funerary offerings were as I described. They constructed sturdy timber roads across boggy land, plentiful evidence of which has been found. We know some details of how the Germans dressed, but it was my invention to have the tribes wear different-patterned trousers. The word berserker is Viking, but warriors sometimes fought naked.

Germanic tribes were ill-disposed to monarchs, preferring to select their chieftains on merit. Proof of this comes to us from Arminius' fate – four years after the campaign of AD 16, he was murdered by one of his own, because of his ideas towards kingship. In my mind, a man like Gervas (almost family in the novel) might have realised Arminius' true nature, and taken matters into his own hands. I had Adgandestrius appear in the final scene because he is recorded as having sent a letter to the Senate in AD 20, offering to kill Arminius if the Romans would provide the means. His offer was turned down by Tiberius, who said that enemies of the empire were to be dealt with openly, with 'spades and spears', not through deceit.

Legionaries based in Vetera were fond of eating many kinds of fish and bird, as well as other wildlife: deer, boar and beaver. Wooden tenement blocks in Rome often burned down. Altars were built in celebration on battlefields using armour and weapons on a manmade cross. It was common-place to publicise gladiator fights with murals daubed on house walls. Roman funerals followed strict protocol – if you want to see an excellent re-enactment of one, look up a video posted by the Ashmolean Museum on YouTube. Legionaries' gravestones tended to be rather stylised: the wording on Piso's emulates this.

Centurions are recorded as having called their soldiers 'boys' as well as 'brothers'. After an animal was sacrificed, it was butchered and the meat given to the poor. Despite what some people believe, Romans cursed a lot – a lot! The plentiful, lewd graffiti in Pompeii and the bawdy poetry that survives is proof of this. The 'C' word was one of the most common swear words used. So too was the word 'cocksucker'. 'Fuck' is less well attested, but there is a Latin verb *futuere*, which means 'to fuck'. My more frequent use of the 'F' word compared to the 'C' word is nothing more than an attempt to spare blushes. It's not certain if 'million' was used by the Romans, so I used the term 'a thousand thousand' instead.

In spite of its many glaring inaccuracies, I enjoyed the *Spartacus: Blood and Sand* TV series. I was taken with its archaic-sounding language, hence my use of 'Gratitude'. The phrase 'into the mud' is a nod to a great author of dark fantasy, Joe Abercrombie. Arimnestos is a tiny homage to the hero of Christian Cameron's stunning Long War novels, which are set in ancient Greece. (I cannot recommend Cameron enough – he's the best author of historical fiction out there.) I loved Gillian Bradshaw's Roman tale *Dark North*, set in Britain during Septimius Severus' reign. Its opening chapter served as the inspiration for Piso's mission in Tubero's tent. There are two homages to the film *Gladiator* in the book – see if you can spot them. Piso's internal grumbling in Chapter XXXIV was inspired by Russell Whitfield, a dear friend and author who walked the length of Hadrian's Wall with me and fellow scribe Anthony Riches in 2013. Russ's armour weighed much more than mine and Tony's, as he never stopped reminding us. He liked to complain about the weather, his armour, his back, his feet and – well, you get the idea!

The expression 'shoulder to shoulder' may well have been used by Roman soldiers, but my intent in this book was to honour the modern-day warriors who play rugby for Ireland. The hashtag #ShoulderToShoulder is used on social media when showing support for the Irish team. In *Eagles at War*, I also used the expression 'Stand up and fight', the Munster team's call to arms. Leinster – my province – got a mention in this book, with their more difficult to place 'Come on, you boys in blue'!

Although we know how legionaries were trained, and some of their fighting methods, much remains unknown. Wedge formations *were* used; so too was the 'saw'. By the early first century AD, soldiers were wearing two belts, one for their sword and the other for their dagger and 'apron'. The famous segmented armour was coming into use, but most legionaries still wore mail shirts. Many crimes were punishable with the death sentence, including theft from a comrade.

When trying to recreate how life might have been, it helps to travel to the places, or the general areas, where the historical events took place. I have been to northwest Germany three times now, researching this trilogy. There are lots of museums to visit, foremost among them the wonderful archaeological park at Xanten, historical Vetera and Colonia Ulpia Traiana. I highly recommend a visit, if only to see accurate reconstructions of a three-storey gate to the town, an amphitheatre, sizeable sections of wall, as well as workshops and a guesthouse. There's even a Roman tavern and restaurant where you can eat food prepared using ancient recipes. Not far to the east is one of the best Roman museums I have visited, in the town of Haltern-am-See. Some hundred kilometres further inland is the Kalkriese battlefield and museum; the location is thought by many to be the actual site of the battle of the Teutoburg Forest. In the summer of 2016, a find of gold coins dated between 2 BC and AD 5 lent further weight to the argument, but this may have been countered by another discovery of what may be the outline of a Roman camp. Cologne, Mainz, Bonn and Trier, cities with more great Roman museums, are only a short drive further down the Rhine. So too is the stunning cohort-sized fort at Saalburg.

The ancient texts are another route to the past. Without Tacitus, Florus, Velleius Paterculus, Cassius Dio and Pliny, my task of writing this trilogy would have been hard indeed. Their 'Rome-aggrandising' words must be taken with a pinch of salt, but they are vital when breathing life into two-thousand-year-old events. Bill Thayer, an American academic at the University of Chicago, has to be thanked here. His website, LacusCurtius, has English translations of almost every surviving Roman text. I would be lost without it. You can find them here: http://tinyurl.com/3utm5.

When writing historical fiction, textbooks are indispensable. A bibliography of those I used while writing *Eagles in the Storm* would run to pages, so I will reference only the most important, in alphabetical order by author: *Handbook to Roman Legionary Fortresses* by M. C. Bishop; *Roman Military Equipment* by M. C. Bishop and J. C. N. Coulston; *Greece and Rome at War* by Peter Connolly; *The Complete Roman Army* by Adrian Goldsworthy; *Rome's Greatest Defeat: Massacre in the Teutoburg Forest* by Adrian Murdoch; *Eager for Glory: The Untold Story of Drusus the Elder, Germanicus*, and *Roman Soldier versus Germanic Warrior*, all by Lindsay Powell; *The Varian Disaster* (multiple authors), a special edition of *Ancient Warfare* magazine. I have to mention the publishers Osprey and Karwansaray, whose publications are of frequent help, and the ever-useful *Oxford Classical Dictionary*.

Gratitude to the members of romanarmytalk.com for their rapid answers to my odd questions, and to Paul Harston and the legionaries of Roman Tours UK/Legion XX Deva Victrix for the same, and for providing men and materials for the covers of this and the other volumes in the trilogy. Adrian Murdoch and Lindsay Powell, named above, must be thanked for their patience, knowledge and generosity with their time.

They have also been kind enough to read both this book and the previous two, and to provide corrections and words of wisdom. You are both true gentlemen.

I am indebted to a legion of people at my publishers, Penguin Random House. Selina Walker, my wonderful editor, possesses an eagle eye quite like no other. She has also taught me much. Thanks again, Selina! Aslan Byrne, Lizzy Gaisford, Amelia Evans, Catherine Turner, David Parrish and Jasmine Rowe, thank you also! You work so hard to ensure that my books do well. I'm also grateful to my foreign publishers, in particular to the team at Ediciones B in Spain. Other people must be mentioned and thanked: Charlie Viney, my wonderful agent and friend. Richenda Todd, my copy-editor, a real star. Claire Wheller, my fabulous sports physio, who keeps my RSIs at bay; Jo Lott, my second amazing sports physio, who sorted out my right leg during the training for my Hannibal bike ride. I cannot express how grateful I am for that – the injury happened about seven weeks before I was due to depart. For a time, going on the trip looked doubtful.

Here I must make mention of the bike ride: you may know of my 'Romani walks' in 2013 and 2014, when I walked Hadrian's Wall and Capua to Rome for charity. I did these walks in the company of two great authors and friends, Tony Riches and Russell Whitfield. Watch the documentary of the Italian walk (narrated by Sir Ian McKellen) on YouTube: http://tinyurl. com/h4n8h6g – and please tell your friends about it!

Tony and Russ laughed in my face in 2015 when I mentioned cycling from Barcelona to Rome, following much of the Carthaginian general Hannibal's route. 'It's only sixteen hundred miles,' I said. 'The daily average climb is only five thousand feet.' Sensible chaps, they wouldn't listen, so I decided to go it alone. Well, not alone, but not with them. As I write this in early October 2016, I have just returned from the month-long amazing trip, still able to walk – in fact, fitter than I have been since I was twenty-two and playing rugby. I'm proud to say that

I have already raised over £17,000 for the charity Combat Stress, which helps veterans with PTSD, and Park in the Past, a community-interest company which plans to build a Roman marching fort near Chester, in northwest England.

Thanks to all of you who donated, supported and helped out with the fundraising. Here I must mention that Calvus, the unfortunate farmer turned legionary who died at Idistaviso, is based on Richard Hepple, the winner of a raffle I held during the drive to raise cash. Richard happens to be an old friend as well – picked by the random-number generator, I hasten to add. Sorry about how much abuse you got from the other soldiers, Richard! Big gratitude to the ever-generous Robin Carter, who always goes the extra mile with donations of books and money, and material help too. You are one of life's gentlemen, Robin. A massive thank you to Sam Wood and Dylan Reynolds of Ride and Seek Tours: two wonderful chaps, now good friends. Check out rideandseek.com for details of their amazing bike trips. Graeme Sutherland, Ben Weigl, Richie Mitchell and Jessica Shull, you were guides extraordinaire. Tony Kean, Patti and Steve Small, Jane Clifton and Tony Duckworth – you guys made the Hannibal trip so much more enjoyable – cheers. And Patti: 'TAXI!'

Heartfelt gratitude also to you, my wonderful readers. You keep me in a job, for which I am ever thankful. As I have said before, anything not to go back to veterinary medicine! Your emails and contacts on Facebook and Twitter brighten up my days: please keep them coming. I often give away signed books and Roman goodies via these media, so keep your eyes peeled. I'll also mention here that reviewing my books after you've read them, whether it be on Amazon, Goodreads, Waterstone's, iTunes or other websites, is *such* a help. The reviews don't have to be long or complicated.

Last of all, I must thank Sair, my lovely wife, and Ferdia and Pippa, my amazing, beautiful children, for the oceans of love and joy that they bring into my world, and for putting up with my slightly – should that be very? – eccentric life.

Ways to contact me:
Email: ben@benkane.net
Twitter: @BenKaneAuthor
Facebook: facebook.com/benkanebooks
Also, my website: benkane.net
YouTube (my short documentary-style videos): https://www.youtube.com/channel/UCoRPV-9BUCzfvRT-bVOSYYw

Glossary

⊡⊡⊡

Alara: the River Aller, a tributary of the Weser.

Albis: the River Elbe.

Aliso: a Roman fort on the River Lupia; possibly modern-day Haltern-am-See.

Amisia: the River Ems.

amphora (pl. *amphorae*): a two-handled clay vessel with a narrow neck and tapering base used to store wine, olive oil and other produce. Of many sizes, including those that are larger than a man, amphorae were heavily used in long-distance transport.

aquilifer (pl. *aquiliferi*): the standard-bearer for the *aquila*, or eagle, of a legion. The images surviving today show the aquilifer bare-headed, leading some to suppose that this was always the case. In combat, however, this would have been too dangerous; it's probable that the aquilifer *did* use a helmet. We do not know either if he wore an animal skin, as the *signifer* did, but it is a common interpretation. The armour was often scale, and the shield carried probably a small one, which could be carried without using the hands. During the early empire, the aquila was made of gold, and was mounted on a spiked wooden staff, allowing it to be shoved into the ground. Sometimes the staff had arms, which permitted it to be borne more easily. Even when damaged, the aquila was not destroyed, but repaired time and again. If lost in battle, the Romans would do almost anything to get the standard back, as you have read in this book. See also the entries for legion and signifer.

Ara Ubiorum: Cologne.

Arduenna Silva: the Ardennes Forest.

as (pl. *asses*): a small copper coin, worth a quarter of a *sestertius*, or a sixteenth of a *denarius*.

Asciburgium: Moers-Asberg.

Augusta Treverorum: Trier.

Augusta Vindelicorum: Augsberg.

aureus (pl. *aurei*): a small gold coin worth twenty-five *denarii*. Until the early empire, it had been minted infrequently.

auxiliaries (in Latin: *auxilia*): It was common for Rome to employ non-citizens in its armies, both as light infantry and as cavalry. By the time of Augustus, the auxilia had been turned into a regular, professional force. Roughly cohort- or double-cohort-sized units, they were of three types: infantry, cavalry or mixed. Auxiliary units were commanded by prefects, equestrian officers. It's possible that Arminius may once have been such a commander – and that's how I chose to portray him in *Eagles at War*.

Bacchus: the Roman god of wine and intoxication, ritual madness and mania. Dionysos to the Greeks.

barritus: the war chant sung by German warriors.

Bonna: Bonn.

camp prefect: see entry for legion.

centurion (in Latin, *centurio*): the disciplined career officers who formed the backbone of the Roman army. See also the entry for legion.

century: the main sub-unit of a Roman legion. Although its original strength had been one hundred men, it had numbered eighty for close to half a millennium by the first century AD. The unit was divided into ten sections of eight soldiers, called *contubernia*. See also the entries for *contubernium* and legion.

Civitas Nemetum: Speyer.

cohort: a unit comprising a tenth of a legion's strength. A cohort was made up of six centuries, each nominally of eighty legionaries. Each century was led by a centurion. The centurion leading the First Century was the most senior (this is Tullus' rank at the start of the book); the centurions were ranked after him, in order of their century: second, third and so on. The cohorts followed the same line of seniority, so that the centurions of the First Cohort, for example, outranked those of the Second Cohort, who were more senior than those of the Third etc. See also the entries for centurion, century, legion and legionary.

Confluentes: Koblenz.

contubernium (pl. *contubernia*): a group of eight legionaries who shared a tent or barracks room and who cooked and ate together. See also the entry for legion.

Danuvius: the River Danube.

denarius (pl. *denarii*): the staple coin of the Roman Empire. Made from silver, it was worth four *sestertii*, or sixteen *asses*. The less common gold *aureus* was worth twenty-five denarii.

Donar: the German thunder god, and one of the only tribal deities attested in the early first century AD.

Drusus: more correctly, Nero Claudius Drusus, brother of the later emperor Tiberius. Born in 38 BC, he began campaigning at the age of twenty-three. Three years later, Augustus entrusted the conquest of Germany to him. From 12 to 9 BC, he led consecutive and successful campaigns over the Rhine, dying after a fall from his horse during the final one.

equestrian: a Roman nobleman, ranked just below the class of senator. It was possible to move upwards, into the senatorial class, but the process was not easy.

Fates: Greek goddesses who determined man's destiny. The notion of a universal power of fate was less evident among the Romans, but some would have revered them.

Fectio: Vechten.

Flevo Lacus: the Zuiderzee, now the IJsselmeer.

Fortuna: the goddess of luck and good fortune. All deities were notorious for being fickle, but she was the worst.

framea (pl. *frameae*): the long spear used by most German tribesmen. It had a short, narrow iron blade and was a fearsome weapon. Used in conjunction with a shield, it was employed to stab, throw or swing at an opponent.

Gaul: modern-day France and Belgium. The region was divided into four provinces by Augustus: Gallia Belgica and Gallia Lugdunensis, Gallia Aquitania and Gallia Narbonensis. Three of the four were part of Tres Galliae – see relevant entry.

Germania: in the years AD 9–16, the Romans regarded the lands along the Rhine as two provinces, Germania Inferior and Superior. The territory east of the Rhine could have been known as Germania Libera, or 'free' Germany, or simply 'Germania'.

gladius (pl. *gladii*): by the time of the early principate, the Republican *gladius hispaniensis*, with its waisted blade, had been replaced by the so-called 'Mainz' gladius (named because of the many examples found there). The Mainz was a short steel sword, some 400–550 mm in length. Leaf-shaped, it varied in width from 54–75 mm to 48–60 mm. It ended with a 'V'-shaped point that measured between 96 and 200 mm. It was a well-balanced sword for both cutting and thrusting. The shaped hand-grip was made of ox bone; it was protected at the distal end by a pommel and nearest the blade by a hand guard, both made of wood. The scabbard was made from layered wood, sheathed by leather and encased at the edges by U-shaped copper alloy. The gladius was worn on the right, except by centurions and other senior officers, who wore it on the left. Contrary to what one might think, it is easy to draw with the right hand, and was probably positioned in this manner to avoid entanglement with the shield while being unsheathed.

Hades: the Roman underworld.

Hercules (in Greek, Herakles): the divine son of Jupiter/Zeus, famous for his strength and twelve labours.

Illyricum (or Illyria): the Roman name for the lands that lay across the Adriatic Sea from Italy: including parts of Slovenia, Serbia, Croatia, Bosnia and Montenegro. Illyricum included the area known as Pannonia, which became a Roman province sometime during the first half of the first century AD.

intervallum: the wide, flat area inside the walls of a Roman camp or fort. As well as serving to protect the barrack buildings or tents from enemy missiles, it allowed the massing of troops before patrols or battle.

javelin: the Roman *pilum* (pl. *pila*). It consisted of a wooden shaft some 1.2 m long, joined to a thin iron shank approximately 0.6 m long, and was topped by a small pyramidal point. The javelin was heavy and, when launched, its weight was concentrated behind the head, giving tremendous penetrative force. It could drive through a shield to injure the man carrying it, or lodge in the shield, rendering it unusable. The range of the pilum was about 30 m, although the effective range was about half this distance.

Jupiter: often referred to as 'Optimus Maximus' – 'Greatest and Best'. Most powerful of the Roman gods, he was responsible for weather, especially storms. Jupiter was the brother as well as the husband of Juno.

lararium: a household shrine where *lares* or guardian deities could be venerated.

latrunculi: a two-person strategic Roman board game. Little information about its rules survive, which makes playing it as the Romans did rather difficult.

Laugona: the River Lahn.

legate (in Latin, *legatus legionis*): the officer in command of a legion, and a man of senatorial rank, most often in his early thirties. The legate reported to the regional governor. See also the entry for legion.

legion (in Latin, *legio*): the largest independent unit of the Roman army. At full strength, it consisted of ten cohorts, each of which comprised 480 legionaries, divided into six centuries of eighty men. Every century was divided into ten sections, *contubernia*, of eight men. The centuries were each led by a centurion, each of whom had three junior officers to help run the unit: the *optio*, *signifer* and *tesserarius*. (See also the relevant entry for each.) Every century and cohort had their own standard; each legion possessed an eagle. The legion was commanded by a legate, whose second-in-command was the most senior of six tribunes, the *tribunus lati-clavius*. The camp prefect, a former *primus pilus*, was third-in-command; after him – we are not sure in what order – came the five junior tribunes and the primus pilus. One hundred and twenty cavalrymen were attached to each legion. (See entry for *turmae*.) Every legion also had fifty-five bolt-throwers, manned by specially trained legionaries. In practice, no legion was ever at full strength. Sickness and detachments on duty in other places and, in wartime, losses due to combat were some of the reasons for this.

legionary: the professional Roman foot soldier. A citizen, he joined the army in his late teens or early twenties, swearing direct allegiance to the emperor. In AD 15, his term of service was twenty years, with a further five years as a veteran. He was paid three times a year, after deductions for food and equipment had been made. Over a tunic, most often of white wool (and occasionally red), he probably wore a padded garment, the *subarmalis*, which served to dissipate the penetrative power of enemy weapons that struck his armour. Next came a mail shirt or the famous segmented iron armour, the so-called *lorica segmentata* (a modern name). The latter armour was just coming into use at this time – pieces of it have been found at Kalkriese. Neck scarves are depicted on Trajan's column and a few other friezes, but none have survived, so their frequency of use is unknown. Military belts were always worn, and for the most part covered by small tinned or silvered plates. It was common to suspend from the belt an 'apron' of four or more leather, metal-studded straps; these served as decoration and to protect the groin. Various types of helmet were in use during the early first century AD, made of iron, bronze or brass, sometimes with copper, tin and/or zinc alloy decorative pieces. The legionary carried a shield for defence, while his offensive weapons consisted of *gladius*, javelin and dagger (see entries for the first two). This equipment weighed well in excess of twenty kilos. When the legionary's other equipment: carrying 'yoke', blanket, cooking pot, grain supply and tools were added, his load came to more than forty kilos. The fact that legionaries were expected to march thirty-two kilometres/twenty miles in five hours, carrying this immense weight, shows their high level of fitness. It's not surprising either that they soon wore down the hobnails on their sandals.

'Long Bridges' or Pontes Longi: this was a Roman wooden road over an area of bogland in northwestern Germany, built more than ten years before the events of AD 15–16.

Lupia: the River Lippe.

Mare Germanicum or German Sea: the North Sea.

Mars: the god of war. All spoils of war were consecrated to him, and few Roman commanders would go on campaign without having visited Mars' temple to ask for the god's protection and blessing.

Mogontiacum: Mainz.

Novaesium: Neuss.

optio (pl. *optiones*): the officer who ranked immediately below a centurion; the second-in-command of a century. See also the entry for legion.

Padus: the River Po.

Parthia: an ancient empire encompassing much of Iran, Iraq, Syria, Afghanistan and southeastern Turkey.

phalera (pl. *phalerae*): a sculpted disc-like decoration for bravery which was worn on a chest harness over a Roman officer's armour. Phalerae were often made of bronze, but could also be made of silver or gold. I have even seen one made of glass. Torques, arm rings and bracelets were also awarded to soldiers.

Praetorians: historically the escort of an army commander during the Roman republic. Augustus established a permanent force in 27 BC. Some of the soldiers were stationed in Rome to protect him, but the majority were posted in nearby towns, perhaps because of the political sensitivity of having troops in the capital. Praetorian cohorts were recorded as part of both Drusus' and Germanicus' armies in Germania.

primus pilus: the senior centurion of the whole legion, and possibly – probably – the senior centurion of the First Cohort. A position of immense importance, it would have been held by a veteran soldier in his forties or fifties. On retiring, the primus pilus was entitled to admission to the equestrian class. See also the entry for legion.

Raeti: a confederation of Alpine tribes living in parts of modern day central Switzerland, the Austrian Tyrol and the Alpine regions of Italy and Germany.

Rhenus: the River Rhine.

Rura: the River Ruhr.

Sala: the River Saale.

Saltus Teutoburgiensis: the Latin term for the Teutoburg Forest. It's possible that the first word may mean other things, such as 'narrows'.

sestertius (pl. *sestertii*): a brass coin, it was worth four *asses*, or a quarter of a *denarius*, or one hundredth of an *aureus*. Its name, 'two units and a half third one', comes from its original value, two and a half asses.

shield: the Roman army shield or *scutum* was an elongated oval, about 1.2 m tall and 0.75 m wide. It was made from two layers of wood, the pieces laid at right angles to each other; it was then covered with linen or canvas, and leather. The shield was heavy, weighing between 6 and 10 kg. A large metal boss decorated its centre, with the horizontal grip placed behind this. Decorative designs were often painted on the front, and a leather cover was used to protect the shield when not in use, e.g. while marching.

signifer (pl. *signiferi*): a standard-bearer and junior officer. This was a position of high esteem, with one for every century in a legion. Often the signifer wore scale armour and an animal pelt over his helmet, which sometimes had a hinged decorative face piece, while he carried a small round shield rather than a *scutum*. His *signum*, or standard, consisted of a wooden pole bearing a raised hand, or a spear tip surrounded by palm leaves. Below this was a crossbar from which hung metal decorations, or a piece of coloured cloth. The standard's shaft was decorated with discs, half-moons, ships' prows and crowns, records of the unit's achievements and which may have distinguished one century from another. See also the entry for legion.

spatha (pl. *spathae*): the Roman cavalry sword, a much longer blade than the *gladius*.

subarmales (sing. *subarmalis*): see entry for legionary.

Suebi: a Roman 'cover all' term for a number of German tribes.

tesserarius: one of the junior officers in a century, whose duties included commanding the guard. The name originates from the *tessera* tablet on which was written the password for the day. See also the entry for legion.

Tres Galliae: three of the four Gaulish provinces were ruled by the imperial governor of Germania: Belgica, Lugdunensis and Aquitania.

tribune (in Latin, *tribunus*): a senior staff officer within a legion. During Augustus' rule, the number (six) of tribunes attached to each legion remained the same, but one was more senior than the rest. This tribune, the *tribunus laticlavius*, was of senatorial rank, and was second-in-command of the legion, after the legate. He was often in his late teens or early twenties, and probably served in the post for one year. The other tribunes, the *tribuni angusticlavii*, were a little older, and of equestrian stock. They tended to serve in their posts for longer, and to have more military experience. See also the entry for legion.

triumph: the procession at Rome of a general who had won a large-scale military victory. It travelled from the plain of Mars outside the city walls to the temple of Jupiter on the Capitoline Hill.

tropaeum: derived from the Greek word *tropaion*, this was a display of captured arms and weapons erected at the supposed point where an enemy army first broke. The manner of its assembly and construction was as I recounted in the novel. The description of Germanicus' tropaeum after the battle of Idistaviso is one of the surviving accounts of such displays.

turmae (sing. *turma*): thirty-man cavalry units. In the early principate, each legion had a mounted force of 120 riders. This was divided into four turmae, each commanded by a decurion. There were also 500-man-strong auxiliary cavalry units, called *alae*, which were commanded by prefects, equestrian officers. See also the entry for legion.

Vetera: Xanten.

vicus: the Roman term for a settlement without the status of a town.

Vindelici: a Celtic people living in parts of modern day northeastern Switzerland and southern/southeastern Germany.

Vindonissa: Windisch.

virtus: a desired characteristic in ancient Rome. It embodied bravery, excellence and manliness.

Visurgis: the River Weser.

vitis: the vine stick carried by centurions. It was used as a mark of rank and also to inflict punishment. A brutal centurion in first-century-AD Germany had the nickname of 'Cedo alteram', or 'Bring me another'.